Praise for
Angela Davis-Gardner's
Plum Wine
A Book Sense Pick

"A wonderfully romantic and well-composed novel . . . With such simple, stark and lovely prose, Davis-Gardner turns this trip back to Japan in the late 1960s into a believable excursion into the deep heart of a good young woman and her decent but damaged foreign friends, and into the minefield of questions that linger in American military strategy and foreign policy having to do with the use of nuclear weapons. Thus a novel that starts out in what appears to be a postmortem mood opens itself, and the sensitive reader, to life rather than death." —*Chicago Tribune*

"Powerful, affecting . . . After telling Barbara a sad story, Seiji introduces her to the concept of *awaré*—'graceful sorrow.' It's an apt description for the feeling that suffuses this elegant, moving novel." —*Kirkus Reviews*

"Davis-Gardner's exceptionally sensitive and enveloping novel illuminates with quiet intensity, psychological suspense, and narrative grace the obdurate divide between cultures, the collision between love and war, and, most piercingly, the horrific legacy of Hiroshima. But Davis-Gardner's ravishing tale also celebrates the solace of stories, and the transcendent bonds people form under the cruelest of circumstances."
—*Booklist* (starred review)

"Enthralling . . . Perfectly rendered . . . Davis-Gardner handles the Japanese mores of the time expertly, and the dialogue spoken by non-native English speakers is pitch perfect. She quietly wows with this third novel, which features a wonderfully inventive plot and a protagonist as self-possessed as she is sensitive."
—*Publishers Weekly* (starred review)

"*Plum Wine* moves gracefully from the personal to the political, from passion to guilt and betrayal. With simple, straightforward prose that belies the complexity of the characters and the mysteries of the story, *Plum Wine* pulls the reader into a culture that is foreign but recognizable, and into a past that touches our present." —*Charlotte Observer*

"Davis-Gardner is an excellent tour guide. . . . Visions of elaborate tea ceremonies, emerald evergreen branches and the golden plums that make Michi's wine make *Plum Wine* sensual, inviting, illuminating. The reader will pick up a few bits of vocabulary, and perhaps an appetite for eel, mochi cake, and most certainly the sweet drink that gives the book its name."
—Bookslut.com

"Davis-Gardner renders the lasting effects of the atomic bomb on individual lives in ways it is particularly important for us to remember when it seems it has become all too easy to forget." —Susan Neville, author of *Invention of Flight*

"A complex and lyrical story about love and betrayal, war and responsibility, humane and generous acts in an inhumane world, the contrast between the East and the West, and one woman coming to terms with the American role in destroying innocent lives after World War II and during the Vietnam War."
—Susan Richards Shreve, author of
Daughters of the New World

"What makes this book powerful is its commentary about the long-term effects of war, the inability of human beings to ever get over the past or to really understand each other's cultures, and the devastating consequences of American foreign policy."
—Rebecca Brown, author of
Excerpts from a Family Medical Dictionary

"*Plum Wine* is wayfaring in all the best ways, full of the exotic and the ordinary, and the exotic *in* the ordinary."
—Richard Bausch, author of *Crazies*

PLUM WINE

A NOVEL

ANGELA DAVIS-GARDNER

DIAL TRADE PAPERBACKS

PLUM WINE
A Dial Press Trade Paperback Book

PUBLISHING HISTORY
University of Wisconsin Press edition published 2006
Dial Press Trade Paperback edition / April 2007

Published by
The Dial Press
A Division of Random House, Inc.
New York, New York

Cover illustration: Utagawa Hiroshige, Japanese, 1769–1858. View from Massaki of Suijin
Shrine, Uchigawa Inlet, and Sekiya, No. 36 in One Hundred Famous Views of Edo. Edo
Period, Ansei Era, 8/1857.—Brooklyn Museum.30.1478.36. Gift of Anna Ferris.

Library of Congress Catalog Number: 2005021514

The Dial Press and Dial Press Trade Paperbacks are registered trademarks of
Random House, Inc., and the colophon is a trademark of Random House, Inc.

ISBN: 978-0-385-34083-0

Printed in the United States of America
Published simultaneously in Canada

www.dialpress.com

10 9 8 7 6 5 4 3 2 1
BVG

For Heath

To know the essence of plum blossoms . . .
Your own nose,
Your own heart.

Onitsura

ACKNOWLEDGMENTS

I am indebted to many people who read various versions of the manuscript of this book, particularly Laurel Goldman and the other members of my incomparable writing group: Linda Orr, Peggy Payne, Peter Filene, Dorothy Casey, Pete Hendricks, Christina Askounis, and Joe Burgo. Mikako Hoshino and Chizuko Kojima did thorough readings for cultural and historical accuracy, though any errors committed in this book are in no way their responsibility. My colleagues and friends Barbara Baines, Jon Thompson, John Balaban, Nell Joslin, Lou Rosser, Alexander Blackburn, and Mickey Pearlman also gave me generous readings.

The Japan Foundation awarded me a fellowship that allowed me to do final in-field research for this book in the summer of 1996. Keiko Suzuki helped me prepare for the trip with introductions and much sensible advice. While I was in Japan, the hospitality and wisdom of my former colleagues and friends at Tsuda College, Professors Fumiko Fujita, Mikako Hoshino, Ineko Kondo, Fumi Takano, Michi Nakamura, and Keiko Minemura, were invaluable. Mikako Hoshino's writings about nuclear weapons have been inspirational.

Among the many other people who helped me with research in Japan, I would particularly like to thank Professor Yoshiko Kuroda of Nagoya University; Tadatoshi Akiba, former mayor of Hiroshima; and Minoru Ohmuta, chairman, Hiroshima Peace Culture Foundation, where I was also assisted by Ikuno Sako, Mika Harland, Hidemi Hayashi, and Shinji Ohara. Painter Shikoku Goro spent an afternoon showing me his painting of prewar Hiroshima. Also in Hiroshima, my host Tomoe Yokohagi and her daughter Aya wrought miracles; interpreters Michiko Hase and Hiro Kamada not only translated conversations and documents but also entered into the spirit of my project with imagination and enthusiasm. Seiji Fukazawa, professor at Hiroshima University, guided me through the city; the generosity of Katsuko Nishi, Mayumi Takasu's parents, and Rie Kitano was extraordinary. In the Kansai area I am grateful to Shinobu Hirayama, Itsuko Fujita, Tomohisa Sato, Masao Tanaka, Kimie Sotobayashi, Shigenobu Sugito, and Kazuko Watanabe. In Hagi, artist Hamanaka Gesson gave me a tour of his pottery studio and his huge papier-mâché Daruma for good luck. My guides in Matsue were Kenji Tatano, Yuko Seii, and Hiromi Imamoto. In Tokyo, novelist Minako Oba, Professors Shigeo Hamano, Hideko Kitagaki, and Eiji Suzuki were encouraging and helpful in various ways, as were Yuko Hoshino and her mother, the efficient staff of the International House, and my assistants Yuko Itatsu and Towako Shibuya.

During my return to Japan I was reminded of life-altering

friendships with former students, including Kyoko Aburano (whose story "The Cross" first led me to understand the U.S. involvement in Vietnam), Shigeko Kobayashi, and Yoko Tajima, as well as my colleagues Teruko Kachi and her family, Tamura-san, and Taki Fujita.

Karen Smyers very generously allowed me to read the dissertation manuscript on which her book *The Fox and the Jewel: Shared and Private Meanings in Contemporary Japanese Inari Worship* (University of Hawai'i Press, 1999) was based; I have drawn heavily on her scholarly work about Inari religion and in particular the sacred and secular mythology about foxes in Japan.

Tony Moyer, director of North Carolina State's Japan Center, answered endless questions, loaned me many books, and helped arrange my return trip to Japan. North Carolina State University professor of Japanese John Mertz was also wonderfully helpful with research, as were Professors Neil Schmid, Richard Jaffe, and Kay Troost. Chris Troost, Frayda Bluestein, and Harold Hill also gave me invaluable assistance. The friendships of Kim Church, Anthony Ulinski, and Betty and Don Adcock were sustaining in many ways.

I am grateful to The Virginia Center for the Creative Arts, which afforded me time and peaceful space in which to work, and to North Carolina State University's College of Humanities and Social Sciences, which awarded me several research grants in the course of writing this book.

I referred to many books about Japan in the writing of this book. Of particular help were Richard Dorson's *Folk Legends of Japan;* Lafcadio Hearn's *Glimpses of Unfamiliar Japan;* Robert Jay Lifton's *Death in Life: Survivors of Hiroshima;* Betty Lifton's *A Place Called Hiroshima; A Call from Hibakusha of Hiroshima and Nagasaki: International Symposium on the Damage and After-Effects of the Atomic Bombing of Hiroshima and Nagasaki* (Japan National Preparatory Committee, ed.);

and *Unforgettable Fire: Pictures Drawn by Atomic Bomb Survivors* (Japanese Broadcasting Corporation, ed.).

Deepest thanks to my mother Evangeline Davis, my father Burke Davis, and Terry Vance, for their support and encouragement. This book would not have been written were it not for Ineko Kondo, who first invited me to Japan, and Fumiko Fujita, who did so much in helping me to return.

PART ONE

1

The chest arrived on a gray afternoon in late January, three weeks after Michi-san's death. Barbara sat huddled at the electric table in her six-mat room, eating peanut butter washed down with green tea and reading student quizzes on original sin. It had just begun to snow, white petals floating haphazardly up and down, as if the direction of the sky were somehow in question. She kept glancing out the window, thinking of Rie's refusal to turn in a paper. Michi-san would have consoled her about Rie, and advised her what to do. If only Michi were here: a thought that had lately become a mantra.

As she took another spoonful of peanut butter, there was a knock at the door. She extracted her legs from beneath the warm table and jumped up. Junko, Hiroko, and Sumi, the students who shared a room downstairs, had talked about dropping by. Barbara's apartment was a mess—she hadn't cleaned in days—but it was too late now.

On the kitchen radio, Mick Jagger was lamenting at low volume his lack of satisfaction. She left the radio on; the girls were "becoming groovy," as Sumi put it, about Western culture.

Outside the door, instead of the three bright student faces, was a small, formal delegation. Miss Fujizawa, president of Kodaira College, gazed at her beneath hooded eyelids. Beside her was Mrs. Nakano, the English department head who had hired her last year in Chapel Hill. Behind the women were two of the college workmen, Sato and Murai. They all bowed and said good afternoon, the women in English, the men in Japanese.

Clearly they intended to come in. Barbara mentally scanned her rooms; she could ask them to wait just a minute while she scooped up the dirty clothes.

"We are sorry to disturb you," Miss Fujizawa said. "Professor Nakamoto has made you a bequeathal."

"A bequeathal?" Barbara glanced at Michi-san's apartment, catercornered from hers across the hall; for the first time since Michi's death, the apartment door stood open.

"A sort of tansu chest. Not a particularly fine one, I'm afraid." Miss Fujizawa nodded toward the small chest that stood between the two workmen. "This note was appended to it," she said, handing Barbara a slender envelope. Inside, on a sheet of rice paper, was one sentence, in English, "This should be given to Miss Barbara Jefferson, Apartment #6 Sango-kan, with best wishes for your discovery of Japan. Sincerely, Michiko Nakamoto."

Barbara stared down at the precise, familiar handwriting. It was almost like hearing her speak.

"Apparently you were held in high favor," Miss Fujizawa said. "There were few individual recipients of her effects. May we enter?"

"Yes, of course. Please. Dozo." Barbara backed down the hall to the kitchen, where she turned off the radio. Miss Fujizawa, leaning on her cane, led the procession to the back of the apartment. Mrs. Nakano, ruddy-cheeked with a cap of shiny black hair, was next, followed by the two men who carried the tansu chest between them.

The chest was small, three-drawered, a third the size of Barbara's clothes tansu. She recognized the plum blossom designs on the tansu's hardware, the dark metal plates to which the drawer pulls were attached.

"It's the wine chest!" she called out, following them down the hall to the tatami sitting room. The workmen had placed the tansu between her kotatsu table and chest of drawers.

"Wine?" Miss Fujizawa and Mrs. Nakano said in unison. The women bent to pull open the top drawer. Miss Fujizawa began an intense consultation in Japanese with Mrs. Nakano. Barbara did not understand a word, but the tone of dismay was clear. Michi-san had told her that while Japanese men may drink a great deal, it was frowned upon for women of a certain class, and especially the women of Kodaira College. A little plum wine—umeshu—was acceptable, however, considered beneficial for ladies' digestion.

"It's just umeshu," Barbara said.

Over Mrs. Nakano's shoulder, she could see the row of bottles. Each one was wrapped in heavy rice paper that was tied with a cord and sealed with a large dot of red wax. On the front of each bottle was a date, written in ink with a brush, and below it, a vertical line of calligraphy, perhaps the date in Japanese. One night when she and Michi had been drinking umeshu, Michi had showed her the vintage wines, but Barbara hadn't noticed the dates. She leaned closer, looking at the numbers. A bottle of last year's wine, 1965, was in the right corner of the drawer; next to it was 1964.

Miss Fujizawa closed the top drawer and opened the next, still talking nonstop to Mrs. Nakano. Barbara wanted to reach past the women and touch the wines. She couldn't wait for them to leave.

Miss Fujizawa turned to her. "We are sorry, Miss Jefferson. We were under the impression that the chest contained pottery, or some such. Professor Nakamoto would not have meant to trouble you with these bottles. I will have them removed for you at once."

"But she meant . . ." She thrust Michi's note at Miss Fujizawa. "It says right here, this should be given . . ."

"The bequeathal letter refers to the tansu, not its contents," Miss Fujizawa said, with a dismissive wave at the note. "Doubtless she realized you needed another article of furniture into which to place your things." She glanced about the room, at the stacks of books and papers on the tatami matting, and on the low table, in the midst of student papers, the jar of peanut butter with the spoon handle rising from it like an exclamation point. Sweaters and underwear were heaped in the tokonoma— the alcove where objects of beauty were supposed to be displayed—obscuring the bottom half of the fox woman scroll that hung above it.

"Please," Barbara said. "I'd like to keep the wine, for sentimental reasons. It's only umeshu. Michi . . . Nakamoto-sensei . . . made it herself, from the plum trees on the campus and at her childhood home."

"You are mistaken, I believe. Umeshu is made in large jars, not in bottles of foreign manufacture. These must contain stronger spirits."

"But I saw these bottles—I'm sure this is umeshu. Please, it would be a comfort . . ."

Miss Fujizawa was silent, fixing upon her a basilisk gaze, her expression the same as the day she'd paid an unannounced visit to Barbara's conversation class and found her demonstrating American dances—the twist, the monkey, and the swim—for her giggling students. Barbara's predecessor, Carol Sutherland, would never have exhibited such behavior. There was a picture of her in the college catalogue, lecturing from her desk on the raised teaching platform.

"We can store the wine in the cellar of the hall," Miss Fujizawa was saying. "It will only be in your way, I think. A trouble to you." She laughed suddenly. "I do not think you are a drunkard."

Mrs. Nakano laughed politely, covering her mouth with one hand.

Sato and Murai bobbed up and down, grinning. Though they didn't understand English, they were used to humorous incidents at the gaijin's apartment.

"I believe she feels quite sad in consequence of Nakamoto-sensei's death," Mrs. Nakano said.

"Yes, exactly," Barbara said. She had a wrenchingly clear memory of Michi-san, wren-like in her brown skirt and sweater as she stood at Barbara's door, a plate of freshly cooked tempura in her hands. "I just wanted to see your face this evening—how are you doing?"

"We are all saddened by Professor Nakamoto's unfortunate demise," Miss Fujizawa said. "Miss Jefferson, if you would kindly wait in the Western-style room, we will see to the arrangement of the chest for you." She spoke in Japanese to the workmen, gesturing toward the open drawer of bottles. They came to attention and stepped forward. "Hai," they said, bowing energetically. "Hai, hai."

"I want the wine," Barbara shouted. "Michi-san gave it to me—you can't take it."

For a moment they studied her gravely. Then all but Miss Fujizawa tactfully lowered their eyes. "We are sorry we have upset you too much," Miss Fujizawa said. "We will leave you to your rest."

They turned and filed down the hall past the kitchen and Western-style parlor, Miss Fujizawa pausing at each room to take in its condition. The door closed.

Barbara listened to the footsteps going down the stairs, then sat beside the tansu, inhaling its dark, tangy odor. Michi had told her the chest was unusual in that it had been made entirely of camphor wood. The bottles of wine were stocky, the papers tight around them. She laid her hand on one of the wines, feeling the coolness of the glass beneath the paper. The coolness rose up her arm, and gooseflesh prickled her skin.

Michi-san had known she was going to die, otherwise she wouldn't have thought of leaving her the chest.

She looked at the note again. There was a date: 1.1.1966. New Year's Day, just a few weeks ago. She'd been in Michi's apartment that night. Had she written this before the New Year's dinner or afterward? She imagined Michi sitting at her table, the dishes cleared away, the pen moving across the page. Four days later, she had died.

Barbara leapt up and went across the hall to Michi's apartment. The door was closed, but not locked. She stepped inside and walked to the large sitting room. There was nothing but tatami matting and bare walls. Gone were the crowded bookshelves, the woodblock prints, the collection of bonsai, and the low table below the window. Michi had served the New Year's Day meal there, all the foods prepared just for Barbara: the chewy rice cakes called mochi and bream wrapped in bamboo leaves and served with carrots cut in the shape of turtles "for good luck and longevity." Had she said for *your* good luck and longevity? She thought of Michi's face, her sympathetic but penetrating gaze, her full lips; perhaps there had been a melancholy smile.

Miss Fujizawa had said Michi died of a "heartstroke." She must have had symptoms—angina—and sensed it coming.

Circling the room, Barbara touched the walls, which were cold and smooth except for one crooked nail.

The tatami still showed the imprint of the table legs. She and Michi had spent many evenings there, often with a cup of plum wine: "a night hat," Michi had called it.

"Why did you come to Japan, Barbara-san?" Michi had asked her.

"My mother," she'd said, going on to explain about her having been a foreign correspondent here in the 1930s, before the war, and how her mother had been talking about Japan for as long as Barbara could remember. That was why she'd taken Mrs. Nakano's graduate seminar, modern Japanese literature in translation, and one day impulsively asked if there might be an opening at her college. And she'd been at loose ends, she told her, a love affair over, her dissertation stalled.

Michi's Ph.D. had been in history—rare for a woman in Japan—but Barbara didn't know her area of specialization, or why she'd chosen history. She wished, as she had many times since Michi's death, that she'd asked her more questions. She looked around the empty room. It was too late now.

She closed Michi's door gently behind her. In her six-mat room, the tansu looked bereft, marooned sideways in the middle of the room. There wasn't space for another chest in here. She walked into the tiny tatami bedroom, just off the sitting room. The ugly metal bed filled most of the space. Not only was the bed too large, but lying in it she felt too large herself, like Alice in Wonderland at her tallest crammed inside the white rabbit's house. If she got rid of the bed she could sleep on a futon; Carol's was still in the closet. Then the tansu would fit here too.

The bed was on casters. She pushed it through the door, across the tatami six-mat room and into the Western-style room. She'd ask the workmen to come get it later. What a laugh they'd have; they had delivered a series of beds the first few weeks she was here, each one longer than the last, until one was found to accommodate her size.

Barbara settled the wine chest against the south wall of the bedroom so that it would be near her head when she slept. She had adopted the Japanese superstition that only the dead sleep facing north. She thought of Michi stretched out in her coffin, then quickly pushed back the image. Michi was ashes now, anyway. How could ashes face north? It was like one of those impossible Zen koan riddles.

Outside it was growing dark. The snow was coming down steadily now, a blur of white flakes.

Barbara drew the curtains and sat beside the tansu. The wines were arranged in reverse chronological order, right to left, like a Japanese text. There were no wines for the years 1943–1948; the gap was filled with crumpled paper. The oldest wine in the bottom drawer was dated 1930. Michi-san had been in her early forties when she died; she would have been quite a young girl in 1930, too young to make wine.

She slid open the top drawer again and took out the 1965 wine, made from last summer's plums. She untied the cord and broke the seal with her fingernail, then removed the heavy rice paper from the bottle.

She caught her breath. The inside of the page was covered with close vertical columns of Japanese characters. The calligraphy was meticulous but delicate, written with a brush rather than a pen. Most of the characters were intricate kanji, the literary ideograms that took Japanese schoolchildren years to learn. Barbara didn't know any kanji or either of the other alphabets; even the simplest character on this page—there was a backward C with a deep undercurl at the top—meant nothing to her. It was like looking at a page of unfamiliar music and not being able to hear the melody.

She lifted out the next bottle, 1964, and unwrapped it. This paper too was covered with writing. It was thrilling. "This is my history," Michi said with a bitter laugh the night she'd shown her the tansu. She'd told Barbara of her failure to publish in her academic field, which was almost exclusively the domain of male professors. Barbara had thought she'd been referring to the wines; making wine was a woman's work.

Barbara chose a bottle at random from the middle drawer. She fumbled with the knotted string, slipped it over the bottle; in her haste to undo the seal, she made a small tear in the paper. It could be blank. But as she unrolled it she saw more columns of Japanese characters and, at the bottom, an ink drawing of plum blossoms. Tears sprang to her eyes. She ran her hand slowly across the surface of the chest, her inheritance. Michi had left this to *her*.

Vivid with excitement, she walked through the apartment, to the kitchen where Michi had shown her how to "tame" her stove—twin burners that were difficult to light—through the Western-style room that now seemed eccentric rather than cold, with its funny, mismatched furniture, into the six-mat tatami room. The whole place seemed altered by Michi's gift, filled with her presence.

The fox woman scroll hanging in the shadowy alcove should go in the bedroom too. When Michi had first seen the painting—a woman in kimono with flowing hair and the head of a fox—she exclaimed, "Where have you found this?" Barbara explained that it was given to her mother by a Japanese man who said she must be a fox in human form, she was so bewitching with her long blond hair.

"This is an interesting coincidence," Michi said. "My mother claimed an ability to comprehend the language of foxes. There are many stories of fox women in Japan. I think this one illustrates the fox woman leaving her child."

Barbara took down the scroll and pulled out the nail; using her thick Japanese tourist guide as a hammer, she hung the fox woman in the bedroom beside the window.

It was still not quite dark, early for bed, but she wanted to be in the futon she'd made up, under the electric blanket.

She undressed and slid into the futon. The camphor fragrance of the chest filled the room, a subtle incense. Why would Michi have given the tansu to her, the one person on the campus who couldn't read Japanese?

Barbara glanced up at the fox woman. Her image was clearer than it had been in the recessed tokonoma. She seemed alive, glancing back over her shoulder for a last glimpse of her half-human, half-fox child, as she headed down a path lined with willow trees.

The fox's profile was delicately feminine, with just a suggestion of sharp incisors inside the slightly opened mouth. She could be speaking, saying good-bye. Maybe it was this angle and this light, but her face and figure had a pathos Barbara hadn't noticed before.

It was strange, she thought, how the placement of objects affected them. It was true for people too. She herself had never felt accurately placed, had never taken root anywhere. Being so alien here—blond, too tall, illiterate—had made her newly aware of how alien she'd felt for most of her life. Growing up, she'd been a Catholic in a town full of Baptists, a lanky girl in ballet slippers, always on the edge of things. She used to blame it on the South, with its elaborate manners and speech—not unlike Japan, in those ways.

She pulled the electric blanket up to her chin. In the dusk she could just make out the shapes of the window and the scroll beside it. She thought of the folktales Michi had told her, about figures leaving their paintings and scrolls going suddenly blank. A flock of sparrows was said to have flown from a screen once; a horse in a well-known painting regularly went out at night to eat grass. Her scroll was now a luminous rectangle in the dim light. It looked vacant, as though the fox woman had continued down the path and out of sight.

2

Snow continued falling during the night, sifting down
onto curved tile roofs and the groves of cryptomeria. By
the time Barbara walked from Sango-kan to the classroom
buildings, the snow had made a curving white river of the path
through the woods. The dark branches of trees against the
snow reminded her of ink brushstrokes on soft white paper.
Her mind lingered on Michi's calligraphy, the papers curled
from being wrapped around the wine. The calligraphy seemed
something she might have dreamed, and the snow an extension
of that dream. She paused at the courtyard between the classroom buildings. Snow melted as it fell into the pond; there
was a wrinkling of ice around the lotus pads. At the water's
edge stood a reproduction of the Venus de Milo—a gift from
Kodaira's sister college in America. The snow had remolded
her head and shoulders; with the marble-colored flakes swirling
around her, Venus looked as if she were still in the process of
being created.

Barbara's first class was nineteenth-century American literature, the last session before exams. She launched into her review, reading from notes she'd typed up earlier. Rie, the only
student not taking notes, stared at her with an expression of
amusement-tinged disdain. Wrapped around Rie's head was a
grimy protest bandage, a souvenir from last month's demonstration against the U.S. submarine at Yokosuka.

Barbara glanced out the window at the white roof of Sango-
kan, just visible above the snow-covered trees. There was time
to dash back between classes. She felt an almost physical crav-
ing to examine Michi's papers.

After class she escaped before Rie could corner her and ran to
her apartment, crunching through the snow. Her bedroom
floor was covered with papers she'd taken out of the chest this
morning, each one weighted down by its bottle. She sat down in
the midst of them and spread the 1965 paper flat on the tatami.
The page was alive with kanji that looked like tiny maps. The
brushwork was graceful and confident; the writing had an air of
significance. It was strange that Michi hadn't left the papers to a
family member or a colleague. She must have family somewhere; perhaps there had been an estrangement.

The section at the top of the page looked squeezed in, as if
an afterthought. It could be a note to her, an explanation. There
was one simple character—a graceful sort of T, with outward
flourishes at the bottom and a bar across the middle—that was
used twice. She went to the Western-style room for her Japanese kanji and kana book and looked through it. The character
had several different meanings, depending on its context—
weather, astronomy, heaven, paradise, the Milky Way.

Maybe she could catch Mrs. Nakano before the next class,
and ask her to read the urgent-looking section. She carefully
rolled up the paper and put it into an empty briefcase where it
wouldn't get crushed.

*   *   *

Mrs. Nakano was in the faculty lounge, drinking tea with Miss Yamaguchi, the linguist, and Mrs. Ueda, an elegant, middle-aged woman who always wore a turban-shaped hat in public to cover her thin hair. Barbara stood at the edge of the room, pretending interest in the notices posted on the bulletin board, all of them in Japanese except the exam schedule. She couldn't show Mrs. Nakano the paper with the other women there. Even if she showed it to her in private, she would likely tell her colleagues. Mrs. Ueda had been Michi's closest friend; she might be offended that Barbara had the papers. What would any of them think?

She was late for her conversation class. Sumi, Junko, Hiroko, Rie, and several other advanced students were seated around the oval table chattering in English. Barbara took her seat beside Junko and set the briefcase on the floor between her feet.

They began with a conjugation review: it is snowing, it has snowed, perhaps it will snow again.

Shigeko, an aristocratic-looking girl whose hobby was writing haiku and tanka, raised her hand. "Snow is finest at night, I think, when it may shine against the black heaven. But it gives me melancholy too, somewhat a ghostly feeling."

"I am the same," Rie said. "Snow is lyrical—very Japanese."

Barbara took a deep breath. "We have snow in America too," she said. "Even in the South. In fact, the weather in North Carolina is very much like Tokyo's."

"But is not the same," Rie insisted. "We have the beautiful tile roofs, the temples, the exquisite rocks in the garden where snow may gather. Poetry of snow you do not have, I think."

"Here on our campus the plum trees have blossomed early this year," Sumi said. "And now they are covered with snow.

This is a wonderful Japanese experience. We have poems describing this image."

"There's a poem like that in English too," Barbara said. "By A. E. Housman. Only it's about cherry blossoms, not plum."

"Jefferson-sensei can understand poetry of snow," Junko said. "She is Japanese in this way."

The others— all but Rie—murmured agreement.

Rie adjusted her protest bandage, then raised her hand. "Japanese poetry contains references a foreigner cannot easily grasp. In the haiku which says, 'The camellia falls, spilling yesterday's rain,' Buson had on his mind a beheaded samurai."

"This is often the case in Western poetry as well," Barbara said. "T. S. Eliot's *The Waste Land* is full of allusions many readers don't understand—yet they can still be moved by the poem. Thank you, Rie."

Rie's hand shot up again. "Here at Kodaira College, we have snow-viewing parties. This is very poetic." She folded her arms across her chest.

"It sounds lovely." Barbara paused, looked at her watch. Still half of the class to go. She'd left the papers strewn on the tatami. What if Miss Fujizawa sent the workmen while she was out? She felt a lurch in her stomach. "I'm going to dismiss you early today, so you can go practice at the language lab. The final tapes are due Friday—fifteen minutes, talking about anything."

As the students were leaving, Junko asked Barbara if she would join her, Hiroko, and Sumi for lunch in Kokubunji. Barbara hesitated, but the girls looked eager. They were her best friends here, closer in age than any of the faculty. They agreed on one o'clock; she could stop by her apartment on the way.

Rie was waiting for her outside the door. "Jefferson-sensei, I cannot write my final paper in American literature."

"Why not?" Barbara said, keeping her voice level.

"Original sin is a foreign concept to we Japanese. I cannot understand Mr. Hawthorne's *The Scarlet Letter*. I am in despair."

Barbara gazed at her silently, a stocky, broad-faced girl, with bangs that hung to her eyes; she seemed suddenly on the verge of tears.

"I have an idea," Barbara said. "Why don't you write about what you don't understand?"

"You want me to write what I do not know?"

"Yes, why original sin is strange to you. What is the Japanese idea of sin? Compare the Japanese and Western ideas of sin or evil. In Japanese thinking, what are the consequences of doing something really terrible—in this world, or in the afterlife?"

"Ah." Rie ducked a bow. "Perhaps I can do this."

Finally, Barbara thought. She walked briskly down the hall toward the door. Miss Fujizawa called to her from her office. "Miss Jefferson, could you please stop in?"

"Oh—Miss Fujizawa. I just sent the girls to the language lab—we're out early."

Miss Fujizawa waved her to a chair. "My apologies for having troubled you so greatly yesterday, Miss Jefferson. Please keep the wines for reasons of sentiment. However, perhaps you would like to store them in boxes, to free the tansu for your other uses."

"You're very kind," Barbara said. "Thank you so much, Miss Fujizawa." Relief surged through her. "I don't really need storage boxes, at least for now. I want to keep the tansu intact as a kind of ... memorial."

"I see." Miss Fujizawa frowned. Barbara shifted her gaze to the desk, to the incongruous sight of Whitman's chocolates there.

"Speaking of memorials," Miss Fujizawa said, "we are planning the memorial service for Professor Nakamoto on the forty-ninth day after her death. Normally, such a ceremony is held at the deceased person's home or temple. However, as she had no survivors to advise us . . ."

"I was wondering about that," Barbara said. "No survivors at all?"

"Not that I am aware. Therefore, we colleagues have decided to conduct the memorial on our campus." Miss Fujizawa's enormous bosom rose and fell with a noisy sigh; Barbara couldn't tell if she was feeling grieved or inconvenienced. "The end-of-the-year holiday will be postponed so that her colleagues will be present to speak their tributes. Would you care to offer some words about her?"

"I'd be honored. Maybe I could talk about her experience as a female professor of history? That's one thing she mentioned— though I'd have to ask Mrs. Ueda."

"I think it most appropriate that you make some personal statement about what she did for you. There will be others speaking about her larger contributions. Thank you for dropping in, Miss Jefferson," she said, rising. "I hope your students are progressing to your satisfaction."

"Oh yes, thank you, they are progressing wonderfully." She stood and bowed her way into the hall.

"Ah, Miss Jefferson!" Just emerging from his office was Mr. Doi, a bald, round-faced man who was Kodaira's Shakespeare scholar, and one of Miss Fujizawa's confederates. He liked to "tease" Barbara, as he put it, ever since she'd assured him that she felt qualified to take on the English Club's production of *A Midsummer Night's Dream* at the college festival. The event was to take place February 3, only a few days from now.

"You are not looking so cheerful," he said. "I hope this will not be the winter of your discontent."

Richard III. An easy one. "Indeed not. 'Twill be glorious summer by this sun of Japan."

"Very good, very good, Miss Jefferson," he said, laughing. "It seems I will never catch you."

"Maybe not." She headed for the outside door; he trotted along beside her.

"I hope you are polishing your lines," he said. She was to play Queen Titania to his King Oberon. "Shall we have some practice at lunch?"

"I'm afraid I have to meet someone."

"Oh, this is too bad. Always you are engaged."

She pushed open the door. "I'll see you anon, Mr. Doi."

The snow was slanting down, blowing against her face as she headed toward the back of the campus. She passed the buildings and the athletic field, a blank white rectangle bordered on three sides by snow-laden bamboo. From the distance floated the sound of someone playing the koto, dolorous strands of sound that usually made her homesick. Today, it seemed the essence of the mystery that she had entered.

The branches of the plum trees were layered with flowers and snow, just as Sumi had said. She held up one branch and shook loose the snow. Some flowers were frozen in the bud, and those that had opened were tattered and yellow. She ducked beneath the heavy branches and looked up at the matted whiteness. Michi-san had told her she liked to lie on the ground in the early spring looking at the blossoms against the blue sky. "Seeing the plum flowers always gives me hope," she had said.

To be speaking of hope implied a struggle with despair. She thought of the note Michi had written before she died, and the paper in her briefcase, the squeezed-in section with the character that could mean heaven. Was it a suicide note? She sucked in so hard the cold air burned her lungs. Standing absolutely still, she listened to the snow, aware for the first time of the faint noise it made as it fell, barely audible, as though something were concealed beneath the quiet surface.

*   *   *

The restaurant where Barbara met the students was a place she'd often gone with Michi-san, on the second floor of a building near Kokubunji Station. They sat at a Western-style table near the window. She and Michi had preferred the tatami section in the back of the restaurant. She put the briefcase beside her on the floor, touching her leg. There hadn't been time to stop by Sango-kan after all; the papers were still on the floor. She felt a flicker of anxiety. At least she'd locked the apartment this morning. They probably wouldn't go in. She always worried too much; you die a thousand deaths, her mother was fond of saying to her.

The waitress appeared; they all ordered miso soup and tempura. As they drank their soup, Barbara looked at the students, thinking of Michi-san introducing her to people the day after her arrival. "We all look alike to you, don't we?" she'd said with a sympathetic smile. Barbara had said no, but it had been true. Now she couldn't imagine confusing these girls. Junko, with her fine blue-black hair, elegant features, and daily practice of calligraphy, might have been a lady in the eleventh-century Heian court. Hiroko, an intense, bespectacled graduate student, was a self-proclaimed Marxist who kept trying to draw Barbara into conversations about communist China and Vietnam. Sumi, energetic and rosy-cheeked, with dimples at the corners of her mouth, was from the Japan Alps, the snow country Kawabata had written about in his most famous novel. She wanted to become a linguist, and was helping Miss Yamaguchi compile a lexicon of American slang.

The tempura came, fried prawns, sweet potato, lotus root. Once she had watched Michi make tempura, skillfully dipping battered chrysanthemum leaves into the sputtering oil. She had been wearing a white apron that fell to her ankles.

"Did Nakamoto-sensei ever cook tempura for you?" Barbara asked. She'd occasionally seen the girls going into Michi's apartment.

They nodded enthusiastically. "Very excellent cooker," Junko added.

"I've been thinking about her," Barbara said. "Her death was so sudden—do you know if she'd been feeling unwell, before she died?"

The girls looked at one another.

"The reason I'm asking is—she left me something—a tansu chest."

"Ah so desu ka?" they said, not quite in unison.

"There was a note with the chest saying it should be given to me—she must have had some premonition of her death. Do you know if she'd recently been to the doctor?"

The girls had a heated discussion in Japanese, then Sumi said, "I was the person to find her when I went in to tidy up as usual that morning of her death."

"How terrible," Barbara said. She thought how it might have been: Michi on her futon, her eyes open, staring at nothing.

"There was an empty bottle of sleeping medication at her side," Sumi said.

"You mean—you think . . ."

Sumi nodded.

Hiroko exploded something in Japanese, then said, "Every bottle has a last pill to be swallowed. We should not make so dramatic a speculation."

"But she left Jefferson-sensei the note before death," Junko said.

"Only about the tansu, ne?" Hiroko said, looking at Barbara.

Barbara nodded.

"I think she must have had pain in heart," Hiroko said. "This has happened to my grandfather, exactly."

Junko put down her chopsticks and leaned toward Barbara. "Let me tell you a thing Nakamoto-sensei spoke to me one time. I was consulting with her about a certain trouble, and she said how passions do not weaken as one grows older. She said this had been a surprising thing to her. It was surprising for me to hear her say, because Japanese sensei and student are at some distance. It is not like talking with you, or other American teacher. I was almost shocked, really, by her speaking this way. This remark of hers I think was personal, spoken from the heart. It is my feeling she had a secret grief."

Barbara felt a chill along her arms. The paper in her briefcase might answer that question. Maybe she should show it to them.

"I take a strong disagreement to my friend Junko," Hiroko said. "Passion does not always refer to romance. Nakamoto-sensei had passion for the cause of peace. Recently for example she has written an editorial letter regarding the Japan-Korea treaty. And several times we have spoken together about the Vietnam War."

"She never talked to me about the war," Barbara said.

There was a silence. In the air hung the unspoken response: Because you are an American.

"Hiroko is not correct, I think," Junko said. "I had confided to Nakamoto-sensei about my personal difficulty, and this erupted her own personal grief."

"This is romantic theory," Hiroko said, digging into her rice with chopsticks. "Heart illness is cause for Nakamoto-sensei's death, I am sure. She did not leave note of explanation. If it is suicide as Junko said, she would have left letter of apology or explanation. We Japanese never take our life without leaving such a letter."

"Never?" Barbara said.

"Usually never. This is our tradition."

Hiroko and Sumi began arguing in Japanese.

Barbara looked out the window at people streaming back and forth through the snow. Well-meaning as the girls were, they wouldn't make good confidantes. Any speculation she made about Michi's death, and certainly a revelation about the papers, would eventually become part of campus gossip. After final exams and the student festival, maybe she'd find a translator in Tokyo, though the thought of an anonymous person reading Michi's papers was somehow troubling. It was impossible to know what to do. The only person who could tell her was gone.

3

The day she learned of Michi-san's death, Barbara had been in downtown Tokyo, searching for a birthday present for her mother. She was back at Sango-kan, eating dinner, when the laundry man came to her door. He gave Barbara her laundry, then held out another brown paper package. "Nakamoto-sensei, no answer." He gestured with his head toward Michi-san's apartment.

Miss Ota came out of her apartment and spoke to the man in Japanese. "Ah so desu ka," he said with a great inhalation of breath. Miss Ota paid him, and he ran down the stairs.

When Miss Ota walked across the hall toward her, Barbara was surprised: she had expected her to slip back into her apartment in her slightly disheveled state. Usually so proper in a British sort of way—she'd done her graduate work on Henry James at Cambridge, where she'd adopted her habits of dressing in tweeds and drinking English tea—tonight Miss Ota wore a cotton kimono, which she held together at the waist

25

over a long flannel gown. Her white hair, normally worn in a neat bun at the back of her neck, hung limply to her shoulders.

"I'm afraid to say that Nakamoto-sensei is no longer living," Miss Ota said.

Barbara's first thought, along with a splinter of fear, was that there had been some lapse in communication.

"Nakamoto Michi-san is not here?" she said.

Miss Ota shook her head.

"Michi-san is not living here?"

"No, no." Miss Ota raised her hands.

"She is sick?"

"I regret to say . . . she has expired."

"Died?"

"I am afraid so, yes."

"Why? What happened?"

"She went last night, during her sleep," Miss Ota said. "The exact cause is unknown."

Miss Ota's face seemed to waver, and the whole hall went dim. "But—I just saw her. . . ." Barbara hugged the laundry and looked around her, at the dark hall.

"I am sorry for your sorrow," Miss Ota said. "She took good care of you, desu ne? Very sad, very very sad." Miss Ota pulled her kimono tightly around her and hurried back across the hall.

Barbara stared at the closed door of Michi's apartment. It seemed impossible. She had been with Michi-san yesterday afternoon, walking back from the main building with her.

She ran into her apartment and looked out the window in the direction of Michi's apartment, which protruded from the back of Sango-kan in an L. All the windows were dark.

Barbara got into bed without undressing and lay curled up, shivering, still holding the crinkling package of laundry. Michi had seemed fine yesterday. They'd had a normal conversation on the way back from the classroom building: Barbara's literature class, the rare January weather, the plum trees. Michi said the plums would blossom soon. At the place where the path narrowed, Barbara had walked behind her, Michi's small erect figure striding along in front, the muscular calves of her legs bisected by the seams of her old-fashioned stockings. They hadn't spoken again until they reached Sango-kan.

Michi had seemed a little distracted as they took off their shoes and put them in the cubbyholes. "Excuse me," she said, "I must speak to Mrs. Ueda." It was the last time Barbara would ever see her. "Thank you again for the New Year's dinner," she could have called after her. "You've always been so kind to me." But she had said nothing. There was only silence, and the whisk of Michi's slippers as she moved away from her down the hall.

Barbara sat up and turned on her light. She looked around at the bare walls, the sliding rice paper door of her closet half open. Her chest ached terribly. She looked at her watch: 10:30. It was early morning in North Carolina.

She tiptoed downstairs and dialed the long-distance operator from the telephone on the hall shelf. As she waited to be connected, Barbara imagined her mother at the kitchen table drinking coffee from her Limoges cup. She would be in her navy blue bathrobe and slippers and yawning over the newspaper. But when her mother came on the line, she sounded wide awake.

"Barbara! How are you, dear? I was just working on the lead for my column—did I tell you I'm doing a column for the *Raleigh Times*?"

"Yes you did, that's great."

"Jonathan says they want me to write some reminiscences about Asia, the kind of thing Flora Lewis used to do."

"Michi-san died," Barbara said.

"What? Who?"

"Michi-san. She's the one who's taken such good care of me."

"Oh, Bobbie, what a shame. What did she die of?"

"I have no idea, I just found out. It's a terrible shock—she seemed so healthy."

"You never can tell, I guess." There was a long pause. "That's too bad, dear. I'm really sorry."

"I hate it here," Barbara burst out. "I wish you could come visit."

"You're just upset about your friend. You'll be fine. What did you say her name was?"

"Michi . . . Michi Nakamoto."

"Do you have something to wear to the funeral?"

"Oh, Mother . . ."

"All I'm saying, Bobbie, is that sometimes it helps to get your mind on practical matters. That's what saw me through the divorce and all your father's shenanigans."

"I have to go now," Barbara said. She hung up the phone and walked slowly up the steps, her legs so heavy she could hardly lift them.

She got back into bed, lying on her stomach with the package of laundry wedged between her shoulder and the wall; it had a solid, comforting bulk. When she'd been homesick one of those first nights last fall, Michi had invited her to her apartment to watch a *Gunsmoke* rerun on television. She had sat beside Michi at the low table drinking plum wine as Matt Dillon and Chester conferred in Miss Kitty's saloon, the movements of their lips out of sync with the bursts of Japanese. Barbara could almost taste the strong, sweet wine. She'd drunk cup after cup, letting it ease the tightness in her chest.

One night Barbara showed Michi pictures of her mother when she was in Japan working as a foreign correspondent.

PLUM WINE 29

Michi had spread the pictures out on the table and they looked at the images of the tall blond woman in front of pagodas, temples, and a huge statue of the Buddha. Her mother's hair was arranged in a tight mound on the top of her head in a way that always made Barbara think of a hat. "You resemble her," Michi said.

"The same color hair," Barbara replied, with a hollow laugh. "That's about it."

Michi arranged the photographs in a stack, then laid them out on the table one at a time as she named the places: the Great Buddha at Kamakura, the Heian Shrine in Kyoto, the deer park at Nara. There was a picture of her mother looking back over her shoulder as she climbed toward a temple Michi thought might be at Hakone. And of the last, a photograph of Barbara's mother and a Japanese woman standing in front of a large building with a curved tile roof, she said, "This one you cannot see."

"Why not?"

"This was the Shintenza Kabuki Theatre in Hiroshima."

"Hiroshima!"

"Yes. It was never rebuilt. I wonder how your mother happened to be in Hiroshima. Americans were generally not allowed at that time, as it was the military center."

Barbara bent closer to the photograph. It had been taken from a distance, to include the whole building. The figures of her mother and the woman in kimono were tiny. "Couldn't this be some other Kabuki theatre?"

"No. The Shintenza was quite well known all over Japan. Has your mother written something about Hiroshima?"

"I don't know, I'll have to ask her. It's strange, she never talked about that, only Pearl Harbor. . . ."

Barbara's face went hot. "I'm sorry." She cleared her throat and looked back down at the table. "It's my first memory—

that day. I was only two. My mother was washing dishes by the kitchen window and heard someone yelling in the street." Barbara paused, censoring what her mother later told her she'd heard: We'll lick those yellow bellies in six months. "She started crying—I ran across the room and pulled on her dress, but she ignored me. It was one of those moments that seems stuck in time; do you know what I mean?" Barbara glanced up; Michi nodded. "When she finally looked at me, her face was blank, as if she couldn't remember who I was. She must have been thinking about people and places she knew in Japan—the time of her life, she always called it."

Michi was gazing at her intently. Her eyes seemed unfriendly, almost hard.

"All this must seem ridiculous," Barbara said.

"Not at all," Michi murmured, lowering her eyes. She began to reorder the photographs, lifting each one by its edges, aligning them exactly, one on top of the other, then tapping the edge of the stack lightly on the table. "You must forgive me," she said, placing the pictures before Barbara, "I am quite tired."

Barbara jumped up. "I'm sorry," she said again. She should never have mentioned Pearl Harbor.

At the door Michi smiled and patted her arm. "I would like to guide you to these sites of your mother someday."

Michi wouldn't be guiding her to any more sites. Barbara turned onto her back. Without Michi-san she couldn't make it here. She reached for the laundry and pulled it on top of her, crushing it against her chest.

At least they had gotten to Kamakura. She let the huge bronze statue of the Kamakura Buddha fill her mind: his calm face, his sleepy, hypnotic eyes. Michi had stood close beside her as they looked up at him. "He seems to be leaning toward us," Barbara said.

"Yes." Michi opened her guidebook to a picture of the Buddha taken from the hill behind. His back and shoulders were rounded, his head bent slightly forward. "I find this the most poignant view of him," Michi said, "humbly bearing all our troubles."

They bought tickets to go inside the statue, entering through a door set below the statue's left knee. The interior was cold and shadowy. An iron staircase angled up to a platform where, through hinged openings in the Buddha's back, they looked out at the view: a cloud of incense rising from a stone altar below, the hills of Kamakura beyond. Her mother had stood here, Barbara thought, gazing out at this same scene. She looked down at her hands wrapped around the railing. Her mother could have touched the same part of the cold iron bar. She felt a yearning so fierce it made her dizzy.

They left the temple and walked down a street lined with maple trees. The trees were in full autumn color, vibrant shades of red and orange.

"I think we have been in the Buddha's womb," Michi said.

"It's amazing, you should say that. I just realized I'm trying to make some connection with my mother that's almost physical—as though by putting myself in her place I'd *have* her in some way."

"Ah." Michi stopped walking and looked at her. "This is very interesting."

"My mother always wanted a daughter like her, someone adventurous but conventional. A suit-and-pearls kind of woman who takes flying lessons. Once she said if it hadn't been for this straw-colored hair"—she grabbed a handful of it—"she'd think there'd been some mix-up at the hospital."

"Your mother does not know you, I think."

"No, not at all."

"If she did she would appreciate you very much."

"Thank you." Barbara looked down into Michi's earnest face, her tired, intelligent eyes.

On the return train to Tokyo, Barbara and Michi sat side by side on a bench seat. Michi had looked tired by then, her face pale, her eyelids swollen. It was a long ride, and Michi fell asleep as the train swayed through the darkness. Barbara remembered their reflections in the window across the aisle, herself looking straight ahead, Michi with her eyes closed and her head drooping toward Barbara's shoulder.

The funeral was held at a Buddhist temple in the nearby village of Kokubunji. Barbara sat near the back of the incense-filled room with the students as the priest droned through the sutras. The casket was on a raised platform behind the altar; on the altar, between banners bearing Japanese characters she could not read, was a large framed picture of Michi-san.

The photograph must have been taken a few years ago; there was no trace of gray in her hair. She was wearing the same style glasses, however, cat-eyed frames upturned at the sides. Her face, too, was cat-shaped, broader at the forehead and cheekbones, narrowing at the chin. She had full lips and narrow, rather mischievous eyes. Her head was tilted to the side in that way she'd had when about to speak.

A sob rose into Barbara's throat. She thought of the night she'd arrived in Japan, like a nightmarish rebirth, dropped into a world where she understood nothing: the voices in the airport, the calligraphic neon signs blinking against the night sky. There was a greeting committee, cool-faced women whose names she could not fix on. The ride from the airport seemed endless; the woman beside her was silent as they drove through the dark. Finally they were at Sango-kan, and Michi was at the door, holding out her hand. "How tired you must be," she had said, and led her upstairs.

The priest's voice had stopped. People were rising from their seats. Barbara's head spun as she stood up. Was she supposed to go too? Maybe it was like the Catholic Church, where only initiates were allowed to approach the altar. If this were someone else's funeral, Michi-san would have whispered what to do.

Hiroko stepped into the aisle, then Junko. Barbara followed. Her legs were shaky but the dizziness had passed. At the altar, they sprinkled incense onto a smoldering burner, then climbed the steps of the platform to the casket. Michi-san's face was small and dark, a shocking contrast to the photograph. Her eyebrows were heavier than Barbara remembered and her forehead higher. She saw the cat-eyed glasses lying in the casket, carefully folded beside her shoulder.

Outside she stood with Sumi, Junko, and Hiroko. Rich McCann, the middle-aged Fulbright professor who taught a course on American foreign policy at the college, was headed toward a taxi. He motioned toward Barbara and pointed toward the opened door. Barbara shook her head, mouthed *No, thank you.*

"Will you go to the crematory, Sensei?" Junko whispered to her.

No one had mentioned a crematorium; she felt another wave of vertigo. "I'm not feeling well," she said.

The students whispered among themselves. "We will take you back to Sango-kan," Junko said.

"No, no, you go on."

Barbara noticed Miss Fujizawa beside her car talking to two elderly women and a younger man. The man stood slightly apart from the others, his features composed, almost stern. He had on a black turtleneck shirt and a loose jacket, instead of the usual businessman's suit. When he looked at Barbara, his eyes widened and he bowed, as though they had been introduced, then he turned away.

"Are those people relatives of Nakamoto-sensei's?" Barbara whispered to Sumi.

"The woman Miss Fujizawa is talking to owns a small restaurant at Takanodai. The blind woman is her sister-in-law. I think they and Nakamoto-sensei are old friends." Barbara glanced at the women; one of them was holding a cane. Her head was tilted upward and to one side; she couldn't see her eyes.

"Who's the man?" Barbara asked.

"The son of one of them," Sumi said. "I have heard that he was Nakamoto-sensei's student at one time."

As Barbara made her way through the crowd, she felt the man looking at her; she did not meet his gaze.

She set off down a street where she'd never been before, woods on one side, houses on the other. She had to get away, into the city.

Above walls she could see wooden houses, tiled roofs, windows glinting in the late afternoon light. There was the odor of smoke, fires being stoked for the bath, leaves burning. Michi's body would be on the way to the crematorium.

She walked more quickly, almost running, past a public bath, a small shop selling tofu. At the stationer's she stopped. Inside there were handmade blank books for sale, double sheets of rice paper stitched together and covered with crinkly paper. She chose one with a red cover, paid, and went on down the street. In the distance a train stopped, spilled out passengers, then glided on. As she got closer she saw the station sign: Musashi Koganei. She'd walked all the way to the next stop beyond Kokubunji going toward Tokyo.

She bought a ticket for Shinjuku, in downtown Tokyo. Michi had taken her to a sushi restaurant there. On the train, it was comforting to be packed in with all the other bodies. She hung on to the overhead strap and closed her eyes, swaying with the train, until she heard her stop called.

It was getting dark, the neon signs were already on. She headed toward the restaurant and entertainment district, and found it right away, the small sushi restaurant next to the Go Go Coffee Shop.

She and Michi had sat at the far end of the sushi bar. Barbara took a seat there and ordered the same thing they'd had that night: tuna, mackerel, octopus. She looked around—no one she knew—and asked for a beer.

She took the journal from her pocketbook. A man sat down beside her; she turned her back to him and put the journal on her lap.

"Dear Michi," she wrote, "there are so many things I wish I'd asked you. Were you married? People never called you Miss or Mrs., only Sensei or Michi-san.

"I don't know where you grew up, where you went to school, where you learned to speak English so well. What it was like for you, during the war. I knew your essence—or something of it—yet so few particulars. That is what I regret most of all."

4

The tansu was just as Barbara had left it that morning before class, one drawer open, several papers and bottles on the floor. Relieved, she wrapped the papers around the bottles and returned the wine to the drawers. She noticed that the dates on the outside of each paper—the only symbols in English—all looked recent. The brushstrokes were dark; not even the oldest dates were faded. Michi must have dated the wines for her, so she wouldn't get the years confused. She imagined Michi in the small room where she'd kept the tansu, dipping her brush into the flat ink container. What had she been thinking? Had she tried to predict Barbara's reaction, or considered the dilemma about translation? Michi had often urged her to study Japanese, but surely she didn't want her to wait the years it would take to learn all these kanji.

Perhaps she could locate a translator through a language school. She ran a hand lightly over a row of wines. She would figure out what to do.

Meanwhile, she would clean her apartment, make it a suitable place for the tansu.

She began in the kitchen, washing and drying stacks of dishes. The radio was tuned to the English-language channel. President Johnson had announced a resumption of the bombing of North Vietnam after a thirty-seven-day truce. She changed the dial to a Japanese station, the sounds of a plucked shamisen and a flute.

In the Western-style room, she swept and dusted around the albatross of a bed—still where she'd left it, angled across the floor—then sat down at her desk, piled high with papers and magazines. She unearthed several drafts of her incomplete dissertation: "Mausoleum of Hope and Desire: The Metaphysics of Time in Faulkner's *As I Lay Dying* and *The Sound and the Fury*." In another pile were pictures of herself and Michi at Kamakura.

There was the fleeting view they'd had of Mt. Fuji, a blurry snapshot taken through the train window. She flipped through several other photographs to the one of herself and Michi in front of the great Buddha.

Michi stood erect, her head turned slightly to one side. She was smiling, her eyes almost shut behind her glasses; the smile accented her pointed chin and high cheekbones. There was such a natural sweetness and wisdom in her face. Barbara, more than a head taller, stood with her hands in the pockets of her unbuttoned camel-hair coat, one strand of blond hair lifted by the breeze. In the background was the colossal Buddha, looking serenely down at them.

Barbara took the photograph to her bedroom and put it on the tansu; she'd get a frame for it tomorrow.

She picked up dirty clothes from the six-mat room and put a blue pottery bowl in the tokonoma. The floor of her bedroom closet was covered with clothes. When she started pulling them out, Michi's package of laundry, still in its brown paper wrapping, tumbled to the floor.

She untied the string and folded back the paper. On top of a stack of sheets and towels were two wide ribbons, one red, one yellow, their broad ends cut like swallowtails. She set the ribbons aside and unfolded a small cotton kimono, then a tiny nightgown embroidered with plum blossoms. These were child's things. There must be some mistake; the man had delivered the wrong package.

But beneath the clothes were some striped kitchen towels that she recognized, and an indigo and white cloth that had been on Michi's table.

Barbara slowly refolded the laundry, with the clothes and ribbons on top. She carried the bundle to Miss Ota's apartment.

Miss Ota was so long answering her knock, Barbara almost gave up.

"Excuse me," Miss Ota said when she opened the door. "I was attempting to secure a recalcitrant latch on my valise. Tomorrow I am journeying to my niece in Yonago for a brief visit."

"I'm sorry to disturb you...."

Miss Ota glanced down at the things in Barbara's arms.

"I just opened Nakamoto-sensei's laundry, and I was just wondering ... there are some child's clothes...."

"Yes, I see," Miss Ota said. "Please come in."

Barbara followed her into the apartment.

"Dozo," Miss Ota said, motioning her to sit at the kotatsu. The table was covered with handwritten pages, some in Japanese, some in English. "My magnum opus," Miss Ota said, gathering the sheets and putting them on a large rolltop desk in the corner of the room. "Now that I am retired, I attend to it exclusively."

"Is it on James?" Barbara slid her legs beneath the kotatsu.

"Oh yes, the influence of James on our twentieth-century Japanese writers. *The Figure in the Tatami* is its title."

"Like James's figure in the carpet?"

"Exactly," Miss Ota said, beaming down at her. "I will prepare some tea," she said, and bustled off to the kitchen.

The room was crowded with furniture and knickknacks. An English-style étagère stood near an ancestor altar. A row of glassed-in bookcases contained English novels in sets: Dickens, Thackery, Trollope. Henry James occupied two shelves. On top of one of the bookcases was a cluster of china figurines, English lords and ladies in periwigs.

Miss Ota returned carrying a rose-patterned tea service and china cups on a silver tray. She poured out the tea, offered cream, and opened the sugar bowl. "One lump or two?" she asked, picking up a cube of sugar with a pair of small silver tongs.

"Oh, no lumps, thank you." Miss Ota looked disappointed, so she said, "One, please."

Miss Ota dropped a cube of sugar into Barbara's cup, two into her own.

"How are you finding your students?"

"They're wonderful. So bright and interested."

"Kodaira girls are not like many Japanese collegians, who go to school for vacation. We have very serious scholars here."

"Yes, I can see that. Miss Ota, I'd ..."

"Now, you must have something to eat, so I will not be required to dine in the company of only Mr. James."

Miss Ota went off to the kitchen again, returning with a tray for Barbara, on it several covered bowls. "Please," she said, gesturing toward the tray.

"Chawanmushi!" Barbara exclaimed, opening the smallest bowl. It was her favorite Japanese dish; Michi had often made it for her. She picked up the spoon beside it and began eating the custard, delicately flavored with bits of shiitake mushrooms and spinach.

Miss Ota brought out a bowl of the custard for herself.

"I've taken your dinner!"

"This is all I am wanting. We say chawanmushi is the most beneficial food for old people and children, excellent for the digestion."

Barbara drank her miso soup, ate the baked eggplant and fish, and soon was scraping up the last grains of rice with her chopsticks.

"I am glad to see you eat so heartily," Miss Ota said with a smile. "When I return from Yonago, you must come join me often for dinner. The companionship is fine for me. Also, I think you must miss Nakamoto-sensei."

"Very much," Barbara said; she felt a tightening in her chest.

After a slight pause, Miss Ota said, "Naturally you are curious about things you have found in her laundry. Nakamoto-sensei had a daughter, yes?"

"She did? Are you saying she had a daughter?"

"She did have, yes." Miss Ota nodded.

Barbara stared down at the clothes. Michi-san had been too old to have a daughter who wore ribbons. "An adopted daughter?"

"Oh no." Miss Ota patted her belly. "Natural child, biological."

"But, then—she must have been young," Barbara said, meaning Michi-san, when the daughter was born.

"Yes—about your age, I should say, perhaps a bit younger. But she is no longer living."

"The daughter?"

Miss Ota nodded.

"She—expired?"

"She was never entirely well. It was some form of cancer which finally took her, last year, in early summer. She had been in hospital for quite some time."

"Michi-san never mentioned her," Barbara said.

There was a silence. Miss Ota put the lid back on her custard dish and carefully arranged her spoon beside it.

"Michi-san was married, then?"

"Of course," Miss Ota said primly.

"I mean of course ... but did he die too?"

"Yes, many years ago. They were only married the shortest possible time, I believe."

There was a knock at the door: Mrs. Ueda, come to announce that the bath was ready.

Miss Ota began talking to her in Japanese. "Ah so desu ka?" Mrs. Ueda said several times, then turned to Barbara. "I understand you have some clothing which may have belonged to Nakamoto-sensei's daughter. May I please have a look?"

Barbara reluctantly held out the package of laundry. Mrs. Ueda unfolded the paper and thumbed through the clothes. She carefully extracted the kimono and, holding it over one arm, ran her fingers lightly across the embroidery. "I well remember Nakamoto-sensei making such needlework as this for Ume. I can confirm that these items have belonged to her." She looked at Barbara. Her black eyes were fierce. "This package arrived at your apartment by coincidence, did it not?"

"Barbara-san was quite devoted to Nakamoto-sensei, however," Miss Ota said. "I think she will cherish these few personal items."

"Thank you, yes I will, very much. Excuse me." She took the kimono from Mrs. Ueda's arm. "I'll let you get to your bath, Miss Ota." With a nod to Mrs. Ueda, she slipped past the two women and went quickly across the hall.

She closed the apartment door behind her, then stood listening until she heard Mrs. Ueda leave. Her footsteps sounded wistful, going down the steps. It was selfish of her to hoard all these things.

In the bedroom, she took Ume's clothes out of the package. She picked up one of the ribbons—brilliant red with a deep cross-grain—and ran it through her fingers; she could imagine Michi gently brushing her daughter's hair. She put the ribbon back on the pile. There was nothing she could part with.

She held the nightgown against her. It came only to her waist. Ume must have been very young when it was made; maybe it was something like a christening gown. She traced the plum blossom embroidery with one finger. *Ume* meant plum. Michi-san must have named her for the trees she'd loved. Maybe Ume's death had caused her to lose all hope.

Barbara carefully refolded the gown. The silence was oppressive.

She poured a glass of wine from the most recent bottle and took a long swallow. From the wine chest she took an unopened bottle—1939, the year she'd been born—broke the seal on the bottle, and unrolled the paper. The page bristled with rows of characters. Michi had composed this just about the time Barbara's mother was pregnant with her—or perhaps she'd already given birth. An excruciating twenty-hour labor, her mother had often told her.

A couple of years later her mother had lost a baby, a stillborn boy. Her mother never talked about it but her father had told her, "Your mother was never the same after that. All the fun seemed to go out of her."

She unrolled the 1965 paper and studied it closely. Maybe Ume was mentioned on this page, since she had died during the year. Tears filled her eyes, bringing the calligraphy into sharper focus, for a moment creating the illusion that she could read it herself, if she tried hard enough.

She finished the cup of wine and poured another. If Michi and her mother had met, Michi would have told her how Barbara was adjusting here. "I know you must worry," Michi might have said. "I had a daughter myself."

5

The campus festival was held in early February instead of the traditional time, in mid-fall; Miss Fujizawa had been away in October, chairing a national conference on women's rights. In spite of the following week's exams, the students had transformed the campus. Banners and kites hung from the buildings and there were stalls in the courtyards where the girls offered roasted chestnuts, yakitori, and cups of tea.

Barbara and her advisees in the English Club were to perform their scene from *A Midsummer Night's Dream* in the auditorium. Although Barbara was directing the play, Mr. Doi had chosen it, ordering, without consulting her, paperback copies of the version he'd edited. They'd had a tense little conversation about it in the mailroom. "An unusual time of year for *A Midsummer Night's Dream*," she said. Her students had wanted to do Ibsen's *A Doll's House*. "Actually we have some disunity inside the play regarding time," Mr. Doi said. "Does it take place in May or midsummer?" She confessed she didn't know.

"You see! Moreover, we Japanese hang a winter scroll in summer and vice-versa. Contrast is part of our aesthetic."

In the dressing room Barbara changed into her Titania costume, a musty white wedding dress, then took her place on the stage, lying beneath a stylized Japanese pine the students had made of cardboard. Contrast was certainly going to be part of this performance, she thought. The set looked more Noh than Elizabethan.

The stagehands were having some trouble with the curtain. Mr. Doi, in his King Oberon getup of red bathrobe and glittery paper crown, worked frantically on the pulleys. The hum of voices beyond the curtain grew more pronounced. Barbara hoped Miss Fujizawa wasn't in the audience. She'd intimated that there were some prestigious guests expected for the student festival. Maybe—given her opinion of Barbara—she was touring them through the calligraphy and tea ceremony exhibits instead.

Rie stood beside Barbara, ready to rush forward for her opening monologue. She was an overweight but enthusiastic Puck in her turned-up shoes, green fringed tunic, and pointed cap. A bizarre metamorphosis, Barbara reflected, given Rie's animosity to Western culture. "Only Christians of the West are afflicted with original sin," she had written in her sketchy final paper. "In Japan we have no sin."

Finally the curtain groaned upward and shuddered to a stop. Rie skipped to the front of the stage. With a flourish of her arms and a deep bow, she said, "Welcome to this effort by the English Club. I, Puck, will do some summary of the midsummer mischief. Just recently our King Oberon has become angry at his Queen Titania because she was jealous of his flirting with other girls. To teach her a lesson, he has asked me, naughty Puck, to sprinkle confusion juice in her eyes."

Rie skipped heavily across the stage and bent over her,

breathing hard. She straightened and said in a loud stage whisper, "Now Titania will love the next creature she looks upon. By coincidence, the rustic man named Bottom has recently been turned into an ass."

There was laughter as Hiroko, in wooden geta clogs, a Japanese workman's outfit, and the donkey ears, came onto the stage and began to sing.

Barbara sat up and stretched. "What angel wakes me from my flowery bed?" She gasped and scrambled up when she saw Bottom; the audience howled as she pursued him around the stage.

"We will now skip some part," Rie said, "and the rustics will perform their play."

Barbara returned to her tree for an improvised second sleep. The rustics, with Hiroko/Bottom as Pyramus, Chieko as Thisbe, and Sumi as the wall, began to act out the play of the ill-fated lovers in comic pantomime—the actual lines being difficult to deliver, and comprehend, in English. Barbara shut her eyes, listening to the movements onstage and to the ripples of laughter from the audience as Sumi opened her fingers as a chink for the lovers to talk through, and the lion bounded on and off the stage. The suicides were to be performed as ritualistic disembowelment, with a cardboard dagger and exaggerated, Kabuki-like gestures. That had been Rie's idea; the audience would understand this form of suicide, she insisted. Barbara hadn't wanted to argue with Rie. But now as she lay with her eyes clamped shut, she thought of Michi's empty pill bottle, her small dark face in the coffin, the folded glasses.

There was a groan and a thud, then uneasy laughter. Another death was coming. She put her hands over her ears, and the laughter swelled. She must be contributing to the comic effect.

"You wake too soon, Queen," Mr. Doi shouted. "Where

is your cue?" He reached down to tap her forehead with his wand. "My Titania—think no more of this night's accidents than the vexation of a dream." He stared at her a moment. "Your ass," he whispered.

"What? Oh—" She turned to the audience. "Methought I was enamoured of an ass."

"There lies your love." Mr. Doi pointed at Bottom.

Hiroko stood, rubbing her eyes. "The eye of man," she began, "hath not heard, the ear of man hath not seen, man's hand is not able to taste, his tongue to conceive, nor his heart to report, what my dream was. This I will call Bottom's dream"— she held out her arms in a dramatic gesture—"because it has no bottom."

"There ends our play!" Mr. Doi shouted. The audience began to applaud.

"Not yet!" Barbara said. "Here comes Puck!" She waved Rie back on, but the curtain was already descending.

The stagehands, realizing their mistake, lifted the curtain partway. Barbara gestured for them to raise it farther and, laughing, took Rie's and Mr. Doi's hands to bow for the applause. "You never know what mischief will occur, Mr. Doi," she said, "on a midsummer night on a winter afternoon, which is actually the beginning of spring in Japan."

Before he could respond, Barbara hurried to the dressing room. It was over. And she hadn't seen Miss Fujizawa in the front row.

After changing out of the wedding gown, she went with Junko and Sumi to see the other clubs' demonstrations. They toured the display of flower arrangements, then went to stand outside the door of the debate room.

Rich McCann, Barbara's only American colleague at Kodaira, was leading a discussion on the Vietnam War. He had asked Barbara to stop by later because he might "need reinforcements."

Rie had already joined the Kodaira College debate club members seated on the platform, but she and the other girls sat silently while boys from their brother school, Keio University, squared off with Mr. McCann.

The boys were clustered in the front row. One of them challenged the United States's use of chemicals to destroy crops in North Vietnam. How could this be justified?

Mr. McCann glanced toward Barbara; she gave a little wave and backed away.

Junko and Sumi maintained a tactful silence as they continued down the hall. Once they'd asked her what she thought about the war; she had said she wasn't sure. Barbara thought of what Hiroko had said about Michi's opposition; she should ask Hiroko exactly what Michi's views were.

They went into the calligraphy room, lingering before each scroll. "Did Nakamoto-sensei make any of these?" Barbara asked.

"No, only students," Junko said.

"I wish I could read them."

"In shodo," Junko continued, "the characters may be changed according to the artist's intention, so a calligraphy scroll is not always easy to read, even for a Japanese person. You could make calligraphy too, Sensei."

"But I don't know the characters yet."

"You could learn, one at each time. In calligraphy, innocence and desire are most important."

There was a line outside the door of the tea ceremony room, but the students insisted that Barbara go in with the next group.

She was taken to the place of honor, on the right of the women performing the ceremony. One of them was stern and regal, with a prominent mole on one cheekbone. The other woman, white haired, was wiping the rim of a tea bowl with a cloth. Her head was cocked at a strange angle; she was blind, Barbara realized. These were the women she had seen at Michi-san's funeral. Beside her was a man wearing a short kimono jacket, loose workmen's pants, and a white cloth tied around his head. When he turned, she recognized him, the dark, steady eyes that looked right at her; he was the son of one of the women. She smiled self-consciously, picked up her tea bowl, and sipped from it. She did not look at him again during the ceremony. Afterward, he was waiting for her in the hall.

"Please forgive me to introduce myself," he said. "I am Seiji Okada. Your play was very fine."

"Oh … you saw it?" They were standing in the middle of the hall, people flowing by them in both directions. "There were so many errors—a comedy of errors."

"I enjoyed very much. You were very excellent." His face was composed, serious; he didn't seem anxious like most Japanese men, talking to her.

"My name is Barbara Jefferson. I saw you at Michi Naka-moto's funeral, with your , aren't they your mother and your aunt?"

"Yes." He nodded.

She wanted to ask which one was his mother, the blind or the sighted woman. "Nakamoto-sensei was my friend," she said. "I understand she was your teacher?"

"Yes, at one time. I have known her many years."

"I miss her so much. She was the only person here I could really talk to—in a personal way, I mean."

"I am helping some students with raku yaki. You know this form of pottery?"

"Yes, though I've never seen it made."

"Perhaps you will come see the demonstration."

"I'd love to—where is it?"

"You know athletic playing field? It is there." He bowed,

then walked quickly down the hall. His shaggy hair hung over the collar of his kimono jacket; he smoothed it back with both hands and glanced out the side window. She could tell he wanted to look back at her. She felt herself smiling.

Junko and Sumi were standing nearby, whispering and eyeing her.

"Which exhibit have you enjoyed most?" Junko said.

"They're all fascinating."

"Have you attended tea ceremony before?" Sumi asked, giving Junko a sideways, dimpled smile.

"No, but I've always wanted to—that was something my mother really enjoyed when she was in Japan in the 1930s."

"I think she must be very venturesome," Junko said. "I admire her."

The girls invited her to lunch, but Barbara told them she needed to go to her apartment. She combed her hair and put on fresh lipstick, then took the back path to the playing field, so the students would be less likely to see her.

The college workmen were tending a huge bonfire in the middle of the field; there was to be singing and folk dancing there tonight. Already a huge circle of snow had melted around the fire.

The pottery demonstration was going on at a small, low-burning fire near the edge of the field. Barbara joined the onlookers as Seiji took a fired piece from the ashes and set it on a bench beside a row of other irregularly shaped bowls.

"Would you like to try?" he asked, picking up a round lump of clay and holding it toward Barbara.

"I don't know how."

"I will make for you." He pounded the clay with one hand, then began to knead it. Barbara watched his hands as he worked, the strong fingers, the fingernails caked with tan clay.

He shaped the bowl quickly, picked it up with the tongs, and held it in the fire until it glowed. Then he set it to one side of the fire, in the ashes, and spoke in Japanese to a young man, who took his place.

Barbara moved to the edge of the circle and looked down at the finished bowls. He stood beside her. "Do you find these interesting?"

"I'm very interested in pottery, but I've never seen anything so beautiful as these bowls."

"Ah so? I am very glad." He bent over the bench and picked up a black bowl. "This is tea bowl like the one in today's ceremony. Please accept it as my gift."

"Thank you so much. Domo arigato gozaimasu." She bowed. They looked at each other and smiled. In this light she could see the reddish tint in his hair, and the lines in his face; he was older than she had thought at first. She looked back down at the bowl; it made a satisfying weight in her hands, light but substantial. "The bowl is wonderful. It was so kind of you to give it to me."

"I am happy for meeting you," he said.

"And I also—for meeting you." Suddenly nervous, Barbara looked across the field at the thick grove of bamboo. The tips were already green against the sky. "You said you have known Michi-san many years."

"Since my childhood," he said in a quiet voice.

"I'd like to talk to you about her sometime," she said.

"I would like this also," he said. There was silence. Then he said, "You have a special interest in ceramic?"

"Yes—in my home state there's a place called Seagrove where I used to go often. Their work is influenced by Asian design—that's how I first became interested in Japanese pottery."

"Ah. This is very good. Please come to visit my ceramic studio. It is on the way to Tachikawa, in Takanodai, next door to our small family restaurant. You may walk there, it is not far."

"I will do that." Her voice sounded too formal. "Thanks," she added, with a smile.

"If you come to the fire this evening, I can give you a map," he said. "Now I must return to raku."

Barbara took the tea bowl to Sango-kan, then went back to the classroom building and wandered through the exhibits, thinking of Seiji, his hands shaping the clay. She passed the tea ceremony room. The blind woman sat without moving, her head still cocked at that strange angle. The other woman, packing the tea things, gave Barbara a sharp glance. She bowed and retreated.

That night Seiji found her by the bonfire. He had changed into a black turtleneck sweater and jacket. "Please," he said, handing Barbara a small card with Japanese characters on it. "The way to my house is on the back. You will come soon?"

"Maybe next weekend?"

"I will wait for you." He bowed and turned abruptly, then hurried across the field.

6

It rained that week, washing away all traces of snow. On Saturday morning, when Barbara walked to Seiji's house, the Tamagawa Canal was swollen almost to its banks. The trees beside the canal were about to bud; in the distance their slender branches made a fine reddish mist.

Barbara picked her way carefully along the muddy path. The woods were empty, with no sign of life, not even a squirrel darting from tree to tree; the only sounds were her footsteps and breathing.

A boy in a black student's uniform sped past her on a bicycle, spraying her with muddy water. "Sumimasen," he called over his shoulder, then kept staring back at her. He looked forward just in time, turned sharply to miss a tree. Barbara looked down at her splattered stocking and the spots on the edge of her rose-colored silk dress. Even the tied cloth furoshiki in which she carried her gift of cookies for the Okadas had gotten splashed, brown speckles on the pink and gray silk.

She breathed in the crisp air, with its mixed odors of damp leaves and the subtle perfume of some winter-flowering shrub. Seiji wouldn't notice a few spots.

Far ahead she could see the retreating figure of the student, the fender of his bicycle flashing in the light. He passed a woman who was walking in the same direction, then the path curved and he rode on, out of sight. Barbara narrowed her eyes to look at the woman: short hair, and a small, sturdy figure. She was wearing a dark coat; at her side was a gray furoshiki. From this distance she looked remarkably like Michi-san. Michi must have walked here often, going to visit the Okadas. Barbara kept pace with the woman—she was striding along briskly, just as Michi had that last day she'd seen her on the path to Sango-kan. Barbara began to walk faster; she had to see her face. Soon she was almost running, slipping in the mud, keeping her eyes on the figure ahead as she moved along the path. Barbara had shortened the distance between them when the woman approached the busy street that led into Kokubunji and without pausing stepped into it. As Barbara ran to catch up, a bus stopped in front of her; when it pulled away the woman had vanished.

Barbara stood looking at the streams of cars and people flowing in both directions, a hollow feeling in her chest. Of course it hadn't been Michi.

The woods on the other side of the street were darker and deeply silent. She took Seiji's map out of her pocket and studied it. There was the path by the canal, continuing toward Takanodai and beyond to Tachikawa; this must be the way.

She walked past a small wooden shrine with an overhanging roof; marking the entrance was a red torii gate, two poles with upcurving crossbeams at the top. Before the shrine sat a pair of stone foxes, their ears alert, looking right at her. The foxes had weathered to a dull gray and were splotched with black lichen. The fox on the right had a patch of the lichen over one eye; the other fox had lost part of its snout, so that it appeared to be sneering.

She hurried on. It was just a shrine to Inari, with his guardian foxes. She'd seen one on top of a department store building in downtown Tokyo with Junko; there had been that same red torii gate. Junko had told her that the fox was believed by some to be the god Inari's messenger and by others to be the god himself. Those foxes had been charming and well tended, with red votive bibs around their necks and offerings of sake and fried tofu set before them in little cups and dishes.

A breeze stirred in the evergreens; winglike branches rose and fell. There was something unsettling about these foxes and this path. She thought of the fox woman scroll in her apartment, the sly backward glance over her shoulder. When she was a child that expression had frightened her, the way the fox seemed to be luring her on, into the distance. Now here she was, in that distance.

Just ahead was a clearing, a large field of winter wheat. Beyond the field she could see a road, and the thatched roofs of two farmhouses. There was a slight incline in the path; soon she saw open space at the end of the trees. Below her was a small settlement with several shops and a cluster of houses, their tiled roofs shining in the sun. Beyond the village a road bisected a patchwork of fields, wheat interspersed with rectangles of dark brown earth. On the distant horizon was a cluster of round metallic buildings glinting in the sun and some huge airplane hangars: it must be Tachikawa Air Force Base. A plane jutted up into the sky, leaving a plume of white smoke behind it.

Barbara followed the path downhill and took out her map again. There was the tofu shop and the public bath just beyond.

Several children were playing tag in the street. "Hello, Miss American!" one little boy yelled. "Hello," she called back, smiling and waving; the children scattered, laughing.

Barbara went past a grocery with displays of fruits and vegetables and a barrel of dried bonito fish out front. A housewife putting a leafy cabbage in her string bag looked up at her in surprise. There were a few more shops and a public phone where a young man in a cheap-looking suit was talking animatedly; his eyes followed her as she passed.

On the next corner was a small restaurant with a blue cloth noren curtain hanging over the entranceway. Labeled on the map as "Okada restaurant," it was marked with an arrow, an asterisk, and the words "Please come in."

In the window of the restaurant was a large plaster cat, one beckoning paw raised. Barbara parted the noren and stepped inside. It was a small place, only five or six tables. A cheerful young woman in kimono called out a welcome and gestured toward a table.

"Okada Seiji-san?" Barbara said.

The woman pointed to the rear of the building. "Outdoor," she said.

Barbara bowed her thanks, ducked between the flaps of the noren, and walked around the side of the restaurant. In the back were two long shed-like structures on either side of a dirt yard. Through the open door of the building on the left she could see a long table covered with clay pots. Outside the building were stacks of large wooden crates.

She looked from one shed to the other. The waitress was watching through the window. Was she supposed to call out, or go looking for him?

Seiji suddenly emerged from the building on the right; he was carrying a heavy bucket. In the instant before he realized she was there, Barbara saw his drawn, somber expression. Then his face lit up, and he made a sound of surprise. He carefully set down the bucket, pushed back his hair with one hand, and came toward her, smiling. He was wearing a heavy black sweater, loose trousers, and black rubber boots. On his forehead and one cheek were smears of dried clay. He stood before her and bowed. "You are here," he said.

"Yes." His steady gaze calmed her. "I brought this for your mother and aunt." She fumbled with the knot on the furoshiki and took out the tin of cookies.

"Thank you. My mother and aunt will enjoy." He paused. "I am glad you have come. Now the sun is shining in this place."

"Thank you," Barbara said, smiling. "I am glad also."

"Dozo," Seiji said, "may I show you my studio?"

She followed him to the open door of the pottery shed and stepped inside. The odor of damp earth was strong. The only light came from the open door and one cloudy window; it took a few moments for her eyes to adjust.

Near the door was a pottery wheel. There were tables arranged end to end the length of the room, all of them covered with glazed and unglazed ceramics.

"These are my finished ones," Seiji said, gesturing toward gleaming rows of tea bowls, larger bowls, and platters. Most of the glazes were dark, black with brown mottling, or dark brown with golden flecks. Barbara touched the rim of a black tea bowl, then laid her hand on a large black urn splashed with red. "Lovely," she said.

"You have good judgment," he said. "This one is by Hamada, number-one potter in Japan."

"Oh yes—at Mashiko. I've seen pictures of his work."

"You know Mashiko?"

"Just from books."

"I am fortunate I can study there, with Hamada-sensei."

She picked up a black tea bowl to admire, hoping it was Seiji's. "Are you going to move there, to study with him?" Maybe that was the reason for all the wooden boxes in the yard.

"To move there might be my dream. But I must stay home to take care of my mother. She is blind, and reliant on me."

"I'm sorry," she said.

He nodded his thanks. She wanted to ask more, but his face was closed.

He must be at least thirty, she thought. "Have you ever been married?" she asked. His mother's being blind shouldn't prevent that; a wife could help take care of her.

"No." He turned abruptly and began to rearrange the tea bowls at the edge of the table. "This has not been my fortune." He glanced back up at her. "I think you ask frank questions," he said, his eyes warming as he looked at her. "Beware, I may do the same."

"Please ask," Barbara said, smiling back at him. "Dozo. It's your turn."

"Do you have a boyfriend in America?"

"No," she said.

"Ah," he said, smiling broadly. "This is good."

"Yes," Barbara said. She cleared her throat, put down the black bowl, and picked up another, dark brown with a dusting of gold. It was smooth and heavy in her hands.

"You like this one? Please accept as my gift."

"But you already gave me a beautiful one."

"This is more considered than raku. May I make tea for you with this bowl?"

"Thank you," she said, "I'd love that."

She followed him to the next table, which was covered with fired but unglazed brown clay figures, torsos of warriors, horses, women with babies on their backs.

"These are haniwa," he said. "Do you know haniwa?"

She shook her head.

"It is from a custom in ancient time. I make them for Mashiko sales. Here is a pamphlet of information I have written. Please tell me your opinion."

Barbara held the paper up to the light. One side was in Japanese. She turned it over to read the other side, in English. " 'Guide of a haniwa, the history of clay idol. It is said that about 1700 years ago, when the Mikoto of Yamatohiko died, his people were buried alive in his grave. It must be beyond description, their miserable voices crying day and night. The custom of immolation with one's lord was popular from these times, until Noinosukune had idea of haniwa. When his empress died, he made men and horses from earth to lie with her instead of human being. Material of this haniwa is almost same as mud of old clay idol. We have been studying for many years and now we can make such a thing. The people who are interested in the classical art admire them. You may use them when you make a gift, or enjoy as a decoration of your room.' "

"I am afraid my English is very poor," Seiji said when she had finished.

"No, it's really quite impressive."

"Is there no way to improve?"

"Maybe just a few corrections. A little editing is all it needs."

"If you correct me, I will be grateful."

"I'd love to help you—if you would teach me some Japanese."

"Oh yes, this is fine exchange." He crossed his arms over his chest and smiled at her. "I think you will be excellent student."

"Actually," Barbara said slowly, "there's something I've wanted to have translated." She could imagine the two of them at the kotatsu in her six-mat room, sipping plum wine as they looked at Michi-san's writing. Seiji would be the ideal translator.

Not only had he known Michi-san well, but since he didn't live at the college, the writings wouldn't become common knowledge. "It's something Michi-san wrote."

His smile vanished. "Nakamoto-sensei?"

"Yes."

"What writing is this?"

"I think it might be a journal, or a personal history. Did you ever see the tansu where she kept her plum wine?"

He looked startled. "Wine tansu?" He glanced into the distance, then back at her. "Yes, I know this one. How have you seen it?"

"She left it to me after she died."

"She gave to you?"

"Yes. That's where I found the writing, wrapped around the wine bottles, on the inside of the paper. There seems to be a page of writing on every bottle."

She paused. Seiji was silent, frowning down at the ground. "Will you help me translate these writings? Since you knew her well . . ." Her voice trailed off.

"She left these writings to you to keep private," he said, looking up at her. "I think this because you do not read Japanese."

"But—don't you think she would have burned the pages, if she didn't want anyone to read them?"

His frown deepened; he was going to say no.

"It would be better for you to read what she wrote," Barbara said, "than someone who didn't know her as well. I'd thought of one of my students—or maybe someone at a language school."

"No language school," he said, slashing the air with one hand. "No student. I will read." He turned and walked out of the shed.

She followed him out into the yard. "I didn't mean to upset you. I'm sorry."

He turned suddenly, and they stood looking at each other. "Sumimasen," he said. "Please forgive my rudeness. I am glad to read these papers."

"Are you sure?"

"I am sure. Shall we have tea now?"

"Yes, thank you."

She followed him to a gate at the far end of the yard. They went past a high bamboo fence into a courtyard. To the right was a one-story house, its sliding doors open. Inside she could see a tatami floor gleaming in the sunlight, and one end of a table. At the other end of the courtyard was a smaller building with a thatched roof. In between was a garden, miniature evergreen plants set in raked gravel and a pond with shriveled black leaves on its surface.

"Please wait here while I take your gift, then we will go to tea house." He nodded in the direction of the smaller building, then turned and strode along the path to the house. At the entrance he quickly took off his boots and disappeared inside.

Maybe she'd committed a gaijin blunder by not introducing the subject of Michi's writing more gradually. There was no one she could ask; the only person who'd ever explained the rules to her was Michi herself. She thought of the time she'd taken her a huge bouquet of flowers and Michi had gently told her never to give so many; just three or five, she said, but never four, because the character for four, shi, is the same as for death. And now Michi was dead. The pure fact of it held her motionless for a moment.

She turned, startled, at the sound of feet on the stone path. Seiji was walking toward her, his head tilted back just slightly. She saw that he'd washed his face and combed his hair. He was carrying a dark blue jacket over his arm. When he came close he held it out to her. "I think you had better wear this," he said. "It may be chilly for you in the tea house."

It was a silk haori jacket with a blue-and-white-patterned lining. Seiji held the tea bowl while she slipped on the jacket. It was warm and soft. She hugged it around her. "That was so thoughtful," she said. "Thank you." She pulled her hair from beneath the collar and shook it out, conscious of him watching her.

"Now, please come." He led her along a path that wound through the garden and looped around to the other side of the tea house.

The ground in front of the tea house was covered with moss. There was a gnarled, lightning-shaped pine tree in front of the building and, at the base of it, a large version of one of the haniwa, the ceramic woman with the baby on her back. They walked on flat rocks set in the moss to the entrance of the tea house. As they stepped up onto the platform, their arms brushed together, almost imperceptibly, just the small whistling sound of his sleeve against her silk jacket. He moved quickly away and pointed out the small room to the left. "There is preparation area," he said. "This is tearoom, with low door to make us humble." He bent down to enter, and she followed, keeping a careful distance between them.

Inside the small tatami room were two cushions and a gourd-shaped charcoal brazier with an iron teakettle on its flat surface. In the left wall was a tokonoma, framed on one side by a tree limb that had been stripped of bark and rubbed smooth. An arrangement of three blue stones was on the tokonoma shelf. Above it hung a scroll, an ink painting of mountains shrouded in mist.

Seiji arranged a cushion for Barbara to sit on, facing the tokonoma. "Try not to be bored while I am preparing," he said with a little smile.

After Seiji went out to the kitchen, she sat gazing at the tokonoma, listening to the faint sounds of him moving about in the kitchen. She wondered if Michi had knelt here, looking at the same scroll, the same blue stones.

Seiji ducked inside, balancing the tea things on a tray. He knelt across from her and made tea with carefully measured green powder, hot water, and a bamboo whisk.

He placed the bowl before her. "Dozo," he said.

The tea was a frothy green, like puréed grass. She sipped, looking at him over the rim of the bowl. He gazed back at her solemnly. "It's delicious," she said.

"Now you must turn the bowl two times to the left and place it down regretfully, as though you loved it."

"I do love it," she said, setting the bowl on the tatami.

Seiji made tea for himself, and they drank in silence. After she had put the bowl down for the last time, she noticed that he was looking at her intently; she felt a warm tingling in her chest and arms. She looked at his mouth, wondering if it was true what she'd heard, that Japanese rarely kiss.

"You were well acquainted with Nakamoto-sensei?" he said.

"She was the only person I've met here who was honest with me," she said.

"Did she talk to you intimately of her own life?"

She hesitated. "Did you know Ume-chan?"

"Yes." He looked away from her and began to wipe his tea bowl with a white cloth. "When she was younger she liked to fly a kite. Always I will remember her bright figure in field, flying a kite."

He began to put the tea things back on the tray. "I am sorry I have no refreshment of cakes to offer. Please come again and I will make better tea for you. Today's is poor, I think."

"Oh no, this was wonderful—but I'd like to come back."

"Tomorrow afternoon, perhaps?"

"Yes," she said, surprised. "Tomorrow would be fine."

He bowed. "Please bring papers of Nakamoto-sensei at this time. I can write translations and return to you."

"You mean—leave them here?"

"I am afraid my English is lacking. It may take me some time."

"But—I can help you. We can do it together. I'll bring a dictionary. You read what it says and I'll write it down, okay?"

"Yes. But I think it may not be so simple." He went to the kitchen and returned with a wooden box and Barbara's furoshiki. She watched his hands—such long, graceful fingers—as he wrapped the bowl in the cloth, then put it inside the box and tied it with a brown ribbon.

She accepted it with a bow and thanked him; her knee cracked as she stood.

They walked to the front gate in silence. She was not sure what they'd agreed on about the translation, whether or not he understood she intended to bring one sheet at a time and take it home with her.

At the gate, she said, "Why don't you come to my apartment tomorrow? I could show you the tansu—you could see how many papers there are, each one wrapped around a bottle of wine. Do you drink plum wine?"

"Maybe if I come with my aunt or mother one day, this will be proper. Otherwise I cannot come to your room alone. Unless," he said with a smile, "I come on a ladder in the dark night like Romeo."

She laughed; she could feel herself blushing.

"In meantime," he said, his smile suddenly fading, "can you arrive tomorrow at three o'clock?"

"Yes," she said, "I will come at three."

Only after she'd left did she realize she was still wearing the haori jacket. She looked back at the closed gate; she would return it tomorrow. She walked down the street, past the vegetable stand, the phone booth, the soba shop. People seemed to be looking at her more curiously than before. As she turned from the street onto the path toward the woods, she imagined how she might appear to them, with her long light hair falling over the collar of the haori jacket, like the fox woman walking away, disappearing into the trees.

7

Barbara took a taxi to Seiji's house the next afternoon. After a day of nervous anticipation, last-minute indecision over everything—which of Michi's papers to bring, how to carry them, what to wear—had made her late.

He was waiting on the street, in front of the house. At the sight of him, the apology she'd worked out for forgetting the jacket yesterday and for being late vanished from her mind. "Hello," she said, slightly out of breath.

"Hello." His smile was radiant.

She handed him the jacket; he folded it over his arm and opened the gate.

"Dozo," he said with a bow, and led the way past the house. He had dressed up for her visit; his shoes were freshly shined and he was wearing dark pants, a white shirt, and a plaid sweater vest.

They followed the path through the courtyard, past the small pond and around the tea house. Walking on the flat stones across the lush green moss was like fording an artificial river. She stepped up onto the tea house platform more gracefully than the day before.

"Please enter," he said. "I will prepare tea."

She bent to go under the low door. The tearoom was humid, from the kettle steaming on the charcoal brazier, and fragrant with incense. In the middle of the room was a low table, on it a Japanese-English dictionary, two pads of paper, and two pens, all neatly arranged at one end. Barbara knelt beside the table on the cushion that faced the door. The other cushion was cater-cornered to hers rather than across the table; he had planned for them to sit side by side.

Seiji brought in two plates of bean cakes, then knelt beside the brazier to make tea. They ate and drank in silence, except for her occasional "Oishi—delicious" and his formal expressions of thanks. He seemed nervous, rarely meeting her eyes. She looked around the room, at the tokonoma with its scroll and careful arrangement of stones, at the way the low door framed the branch of pine like a painting. Everything had an understated elegance, shibumi, the Japanese aesthetic ideal Michi had explained to her.

While Seiji was washing the tea utensils and dishes in the kitchen, Barbara took from her furoshiki the single rice paper from the 1965 bottle. She had at first put in the 1964 and 1963 pages as well, but finally decided not to bring them. There was no point in continuing the argument about leaving the papers here, if they had time to translate only one. With a little flutter in her stomach, she put the paper—which she had rolled up and tied with string—on the table, then took out the blank book of rice paper she'd bought to record the translation. At last she would learn what Michi had written.

"I brought just one of the papers," she said when he returned. "The most recent. I thought that might be best to begin with."

"Yes," he said, but a slight look of displeasure crossed his face.

He picked up the scroll, gently untied the ribbon, and spread out the long paper on the table. From his pants pocket he took two small black stones and put one on the right and left sides of the sheet to weigh it down. He reached beneath his vest, took out glasses from his shirt pocket, and bent over the page.

He was silent so long that Barbara began to wonder if he was having trouble with some difficult kanji. Then she noticed that his eyes weren't moving; he was staring fixedly down at the paper.

She cleared her throat and shifted on the cushion.

"Nakamoto-sensei is writing about her daughter," he finally said. He took off his glasses and laid them on the table. "It is necessary for me to make some explanation first. Her daughter Ume-chan had a particular condition."

"Yes, I know," Barbara said. "Cancer. Miss Ota told me about it."

"Ah, but before that . . ." He consulted his dictionary, then held it out, indicating a word with one finger.

"Microcephaly? What does that mean?" She squinted to read the definition. "Small head."

"Yes. However, Ume-chan's head was actually of normal size. This condition causes retardation. Though nineteen years of age at her death, her mind was that of five- or six-year-old." He closed the dictionary and put it to one side.

"That's terrible."

"You are not aware of the cause for this?" Seiji said, looking at her directly.

"No."

"Nakamoto-sensei was living in Hiroshima on the day of the atomic bomb. At that time she was carrying the child Ume."

He touched his stomach. "As result of radiation exposure, she is born with this condition."

"I had no idea," she whispered. A silent television image of the huge, slowly unfolding cloud filled her mind. She thought of Michi looking at the picture of her mother in Hiroshima.

Seiji put on his glasses again. "I will translate for you now," he said. "January the first, 1966."

"But it's the 1965 bottle," Barbara said.

"Yes, wine must have been made in 1965 but she made her reflections in the past year at New Year's. You see, she goes on to say, 'Late and quiet in the house as I compose my first writing of the year.' First writing of the year is a tradition with we Japanese," Seiji said, then read on, " 'The air outside my window is black as ink. If I could dip my brush in the night, what a writing I would make.

" 'Had a living daughter been able to read the strokes of my brush, I would make such a writing for her. I would tell her, to be a mother is not so easy. Always, she will make her error.' "

Barbara felt prickles on the back of her neck. Michi-san was addressing her.

"Are you reading this section?" She pointed to the writing at the top of the page that looked as though it were an after-thought.

"No, this is only some weather condition. The day is mild, and so forth. As you shall see, this writing concerns Ume-chan, and family matter she would wish to tell her. Next she writes, 'This year of 1966 is Fiery Horse. My mother was born in last Fiery Horse year, sixty years ago. In superstition this is worst time for female to be born. Often I have thought this true of her. For she was tormented woman not well suited to be mother. Her chill toward me caused pain in my heart always. But I must also recall that on two occasions she gave me life.' "

Seiji paused for Barbara to catch up with the transcription. If Michi had lived, she thought, they would have discussed this directly. "Does she say what the second occasion was?"

He shook his head. "She goes on to write about her daughter. 'Ume-chan died with leukemia five months ago, on twelfth of July. Every day I am thinking of her. Often I see her face in my dreams.' "

There was silence as Barbara wrote. Her pen seemed loud on the thin paper. She glanced up at him; he had closed his eyes.

"Are you all right?"

"Ah—gomen nasai—excuse me." He found his place and continued reading. "Next Nakamoto-sensei is describing her shock, even though the doctor had made a warning to her. She says, 'All I can think as I looked down at her poor face on the pillow was, Where is the true life she should have lived?' "

Seiji looked down at the page, two fingers resting delicately on one of the smooth black rocks. She wanted to put her hand over his.

He looked up at her. "Please forgive me," he said. "But I cannot understand why Nakamoto-sensei has left this writing to you. I think there may be some mistake."

They stared at each other. "She did leave it to me," Barbara said. "She wrote me a note. It was taped to the tansu. There was no mistake—we had much in common."

"I would like to see this note," he said. "Also other papers in tansu—whole tansu with papers."

"I thought you were uneasy about coming to my apartment alone. Since this is so upsetting to you maybe I should get someone else to read the papers."

"No. Only I read these papers. I," he said, hitting his chest with one hand, "watakushi. You must vow this."

"All right." She looked at him, startled. "But would you

please translate that completely?" She pointed to the section at the top of the page.

"As I said, mostly weather condition. 'This day is mild one, with heavy mist. Today I have walked to see plum trees. They are making bud too early this year. Frost will cut off their fragrance. I am remembering the blind *anma* . . .' This means"— Seiji consulted his dictionary—"persons who give massage . . . 'blind *anma* drawn to our house in Hiroshima by the delicate odor of Mother's plum trees.' "

Barbara bent close to study the crowded characters. "Is that all?" she asked. The passage looked longer than that. "Are you sure?"

"Hai. That is all." He lit a cigarette, then returned to the main text. "Nakamoto-sensei is recalling the last day Ume was well enough to go out. It was on a Saturday one year ago last May. She writes, 'When I went to take Ume from hospital, I noticed that she has gathered more flesh. This seemed strangely hopeful to me, as I thought the illness would make her thin, but nurse said it was the result of medication. Ume's sweater and skirt are fitting too tightly and her hair has become quite sparse. It made my heart sore' "—he paused—" 'to see . . . kokoro . . . spirit . . . to see spirit of child caught in a stout womanly body which is now diseased.' " Barbara could see Ume's childlike face, a smaller version of Michi's cat-like one, set atop a fat body, swollen breasts and stomach.

" 'We went to Meiji Shrine and looked at iris flowers in bloom. Ume remembered that the iris are planted in a long curve line like a river. This pleased her very much. She ran awkwardly along the edge crying, Ayamegawa . . . Iris River!' "

Seiji waited for Barbara to finish writing, then went on. " 'For picnic was some makizushi and sugar-coated cherries, which were Ume's favorite treat. As I was setting out lunch, not attending, Ume broke off iris heads and brought them back to me in her skirt. I scolded her severely. Now I am feeling so badly to make last picnic a misery for her, chiding her for such a small thing. Ume dropped to her knees and cried. I put my arm around her and held her against my breast. At that moment I am thinking how she must have cried in my womb as I crouched by Motoyasu River on the day of nightmare.' "

There was a long silence. Seiji sat motionless, looking down at the page. Outside the tea house door, the light had changed, the cold light of afternoon; Barbara felt a sudden sharp longing for home.

Seiji put out his cigarette in one of the plates. " 'We were to go shopping,' " he continued, " 'but Ume had wet her skirt. I took her back to hospital. She was overexcited by the outing and my scolding. I did shopping and took things to her. I found her asleep with old kokeshi doll in her hand. The bow on her head seemed like butterfly had just rested there. In her sleep she looks like innocent whose life is just beginning.' " Seiji let out a long sigh and took off his glasses. "One more shorter section, then we will be finished." He pushed himself up from the table and stretched. His sweater vest rose above his belt; she looked at his waist, how thin it was.

"You must be tired," she said.

"Would you like tea," he asked, "or maybe beer?"

"Beer," she said. "Thank you."

He disappeared into the kitchen and soon returned with two bottles of Kirin beer. "No glasses, I am sorry," he said. "Can you drink?"

"Oh, yes." She held up her hand for the bottle.

He grinned down at her. "Lady professor drinking beer! Like Nakamoto-sensei," he added, his smile fading.

"Really?" Maybe Miss Fujizawa had worried about the plum wine because of Michi; maybe Michi had drunk too much. She could have washed down her sleeping pills with plum wine, or something stronger: an accidental overdose.

"Is it considered wrong for women professors to drink?" she asked.

"In public you should not drink a beer. Sensei has much respect and dignified position in Japan, especially the woman sensei."

Seiji resettled himself on the cushion and continued reading: " 'On this night along with Ume-chan I am thinking of Shoichi and little Haru, whose body was never found. I recall their faces most exactly from that day so long ago when we children went to gather chestnuts at Mt. Mitaki with father and mother.' "

"Haru was never found?"

He shook his head. There was a long silence; finally he cleared his throat and went on. " 'Yellow and wine-colored leaves covered the ground like a Turkish carpet. Shoichi gathered chestnuts with great diligence while Haru scampered about to pester him. I remember her teasing face peering around a tree, so charming and lively. I can see her heavy eyebrows and her fine, rather sharp Yamato nose. When I imagine Ume's true face, it is Haru's that I see.' "

Barbara wrote quickly, trying to picture Haru, Ume's true face.

"Here are final sentences," he said. " 'In recent years my memory of that day at Mt. Mitaki is clearer, as though I am moving closer to it rather than away. Perhaps if there is a land of rest as Mother believed it will be that place, and we will all be together there, Ume and I along with Father, Mother, Shoichi, little Haru, Grandmother Ko, Kenzaburo . . . and . . . others close to me in spirit.' "

Seiji took off his glasses and rubbed his eyes. "That is all."

"Who is Kenzaburo?"

"Nakamoto-sensei's husband. He died during war."

"Michi-san never mentioned him." She looked at Seiji as he leaned against the table, his face in his hands. "This must be unbearable for you," she said. "She was . . . your childhood teacher." He raised his head, not looking at her, and began slowly to roll up the paper. She saw that his fingers were trembling slightly.

"You were there too."

He went absolutely still. "Yes," he said.

She tried to picture the mushroom-shaped cloud, Seiji somewhere beneath it, just a child, but she could not; her imagination failed her.

She watched as he continued rolling up the paper. "I'm so sorry," she whispered.

He picked up the ribbon and slid it beneath the rolled-up paper, then tied it with great care, looping the ribbon over his index finger to make a small, perfect bow.

"Would you like to come see the wine chest?" she said.

"At this moment?" He looked up at her.

"Now, or whenever you want to."

"Thank you," he said. "I would like to go now. We can drive there together in my truck."

8

Seiji was an impatient driver, honking, weaving through traffic. But he seemed competent, his hands sure on the wheel of his truck. He obviously knew the way to the college.

"When was Michi-san your teacher?" Barbara asked.

"I was twelve or so. She was just beginning teacher."

"But you knew her later too, of course."

"Yes. Her family lived near to mine in Koi, a suburb of Hiroshima."

They stopped for a red light. Seiji took a cigarette from a pack on the dashboard and lit it.

"How old were you when ..." She paused.

"Thirteen years of age."

He peered up at the light, squinting a little through the smoke. She studied his profile; just a few years older and he'd have been a soldier.

The light turned, he stepped hard on the gas. She looked

away from him out her window. As a child she'd known nothing about the atomic bombings; she hadn't even been aware of
the war that she could recall. In college, she saw the film *Hiroshima Mon Amour:* the flashbacks of the flattened city, the
charred bodies, were still vivid in her mind, and in the fore-
ground, juxtaposed against the scenes of horror, the naked bodies
of two lovers, the shapes abstract at first, like a shifting landscape. "I know Hiroshima," the French woman said. "Tu ne
sais rien à Hiroshima," the Japanese man said, again and again.
"You know nothing."

When they reached the college he parked on the shoulder
of the road instead of driving in. The gate was open; there was
no one in the reception booth at the entrance. Still, she felt
tense as they walked past the library and the main building, following the gravel drive that wound through the trees to her
apartment. They met no one on the grounds of the campus. At
Sango-kan she was glad to see Mrs. Ueda's car gone; she was
going on a brief excursion, she had told her earlier in the day.
Miss Ota was still in Yonago.

Barbara and Seiji took off their shoes in the entranceway.
She set out the guest slippers for Seiji. The students' radio was
playing in their room but the door was closed. They walked
quietly down the hall and up the stairs. No one had seen them.
She felt as if they had entered through a seam in the world.

In her apartment Barbara ushered Seiji into the Western-
style room. "Please wait here," she said. "I'm afraid I've left a
bit of a mess in the room where the tansu is."

In the bedroom she picked up clothes—rejects from the
morning's indecision—and stuffed them into the closet. From
the floor she picked up hairspray, rollers, a mirror. The unwrapped bottles were also on the tatami, along with the two
papers she'd decided not to take to Seiji's house; she arranged
the papers beside the tansu.

She opened the top drawer of the wine chest, took out Michi's bequeathal letter, and laid it on the tansu beside the framed photograph of herself and Michi-san.

She walked through the sitting room—it was presentable enough—into the Western-style room. Seiji was by the window looking in the direction of Michi's apartment.

"I'm ready," she said. "Dozo."

He turned and smiled. "You have made the room tidy?"

He followed her into the small room and sat before the wine chest.

"Here's the note from Michi," she said, picking it up and unfolding it for him.

He studied the paper for several moments, then put it back on the tansu. "You have visited Kamakura together," he said, leaning forward to inspect the photograph.

"Yes—in October. These are the writings from 1964 and '63 bottles," she said, nodding toward the papers beside the chest. "Would you like to read them now?"

"Yes. But first, may I look inside?"

Together they pulled open the top drawer. He put his hand on the first wrapped wine and curled his fingers around it. After a few moments he touched the next bottle with his palm, then moved down the row of wines, laying his hand upon each one.

He closed the top drawer and pulled open the middle one. He gazed in at the bottles a long time. Very carefully he pushed the drawer shut and opened the bottom one. "Sah!" he exclaimed, looking in, then said something in Japanese.

"What?" she said.

His hand hovered above the oldest bottle—1930. She thought he was going to take it out, but he closed that drawer and pulled open the top one again. He took out the 1961 bottle, untied the string, and broke the seal. He read silently, making no offer to translate, then reached for the bottle and began to rewrap the paper around it.

"Could you read it for me now?" she asked.

"I think we shall take in order. We have read 1965, next one 1964."

Bossy, bossy, she thought, but held her tongue.

They took the 1964 and 1963 papers into the six-mat room and sat next to each other at the kotatsu. Barbara opened her notebook and waited as Seiji read through the most recent paper. "Now I can translate," he said. "Are you ready?"

"I believe I am ready, yes," she said, in a tone of exaggerated politeness.

He didn't seem to notice her sarcasm. "This is labeled first writing of the year as before, but she has recorded some notes made earlier. 'June 15. Plum ripening has surprised me. Being very busy with some things in absentminded way, I was late in finding the harvest. Most fruit had fallen from trees and made sour paste in the grass. Only those few on top were fine. Others I took from the trees in a careless manner. Tonight I am thinking of Mother in the garden of our house, many years ago, when Hiroshima meant nothing more than broad island.'"

He paused. Barbara looked at his erect back, his hands against the page, the fingertips white from pressing down so hard. This must be excruciating for him, suddenly forced to relive his memories of the bombing. She felt a little twist of guilt, thinking of her earlier impatience. "Can I get you something?" she said. "Tea? Wine?"

He shook his head.

"It's getting dark," Barbara said. She turned on the overhead light. "Is that better?"

"Yes, thank you. Nakamoto-sensei is recalling how her mother used to put cloth under the trees so plums could drop there without bruising." He cleared his throat. "She says, 'One day when I was tidying in the tea house she called to me from the garden, 'Michi, come see the golden jewels.' I can hear her commanding voice still, and see the plums on the cloth, a wealth of golden jewels, delicate skins shining in the sun. I knelt beside Mother and we gathered the plums. They were still damp from dew. Each one is feeling like a cool soft egg in my hand, an egg not hardened in its shell.

" 'When Mother was dying in hospital many years later she had some memory of those plums. For days she had been in a fever and since the bombing her only talk was of an evil fox trick—' "

"Michi-san told me her mother could understand fox language," Barbara broke in.

"This is not language she refers to," Seiji said. "It is what we call pikadon—flash and boom of atom bomb. Nakamoto-sensei's mother has attributed bombing to devil foxes. Also black rain after the bombs—this was fox weather of worst sort. Grandmother Ko had come to her mother from spirit world and told her this was so. Now I will translate Sensei exactly: 'The ghost of Grandmother Ko was in the room with Mother constantly, sometimes by the window, sometimes seated beside her in a chair. When Father brought the urn of Shoichi's ashes, Grandmother told Mother to put the ashes on her burns. Only this would heal her, she believed. Mother looked like a ghost herself with the ashes smeared on her face. Her only talking was to Grandmother, so I was startled when she turned to me quite suddenly and said in her old voice, 'Michi-chan, do you remember the golden jewels?' She laid her hand on my belly where the baby was growing and said 'Golden jewel.' So it was she who named her granddaughter Ume, golden jewel, fruit of plum tree. She did not live to see Ume born, but sometimes in the last years while Ume was in hospital I have felt Mother's presence with us in the room. I forgave her then for many things.' "

"Does she say what things?"

"This is the end," Seiji said, "nothing more."

He picked up the paper and slowly began to wrap it around the bottle. She watched as he replaced the string and painstakingly retied the knot.

"Maybe this is all we can read for one time," he said.

"Yes, I think so."

He stood in one easy motion and stretched.

"I wish I had something to give you to eat, but there's not much here."

"I'm afraid you are not a very good housekeeper," he said, grinning down at her. "What will your husband say?"

She stood, laughing with him, but felt tongue-tied.

"I think we had better go to some restaurant," he said.

They saw no one as they left the apartment building. The sky was dark, just a sliver of moon and a few stars. The only sounds were their feet on gravel and the movement of tree limbs in the slight breeze. Barbara glanced toward the path where she and Michi had walked that last day, a shadowy opening in the trees.

Seiji took her to a restaurant she had never noticed before, the Kamiya, on a small side street in Kokubunji. It was a loud, cheerful place, with waitresses in kimono calling out orders and clattering back and forth to the kitchen on their wooden geta clogs. There were prints of Kabuki actors on the walls; they sat at a table beneath a picture of a grimacing, cross-eyed warrior. Their waitress and several customers greeted Seiji and looked curiously at Barbara; he did not introduce her.

Barbara looked at the menu—in Japanese, she could make out none of it.

"Do you enjoy unagi—eel?" Seiji asked.

"I've never tried it." The thought of eel made her queasy.

"Another kind of eel—anago—is a specialty of my home, very delicious."

"Then I'll have some." She'd eaten jellyfish, like chewing a mouthful of rubber bands; eel would probably be no worse.

The waitress brought hot towels and tea. Seiji gave the order in Japanese.

Barbara wiped her hands with the hot towel; Seiji mopped his face and neck with his, then cleaned his hands.

"By *home*," she said, "do you mean Hiroshima?"

"Yes." He met her eyes. "Hiroshima."

"Do you go back there often?"

"Only two or three times. It is a new city now." There was a pause, then he said, "Where is your home in America?"

"North Carolina. It's on the East Coast, in the South." She drew a little map on a blank page of her address book: the East Coast, the ocean full of fish, Florida with orange and grapefruit trees, North Carolina with many trees and mountains in the west and in the middle of the state an asterisk at Raleigh, which she labeled "My house."

"This sounds like very wonderful place. I hope I can visit."

"I hope so too."

They sat smiling at each other, then she looked up at the samurai warrior.

"This print is made by Sharaku," Seiji said. "He was famous Japanese artist."

"Yes, I know. Michi-san had a Sharaku of a geisha."

Their food came, bowls of rice topped with dark, oily-looking pieces of eel. Seiji had also ordered sake, which was brought in a small ceramic bottle with two cups.

He poured sake into her cup. "Now you must do the same for me," he said.

She picked up the bottle—warm from the heated sake—and filled his cup.

He raised it. "Kampai.

"Do you like it?" he said, as she sipped the drink. "Yes," she said, though she had never cared for sake, like warm, overripe bananas. The eel was surprisingly good, with a rich smoky taste. She ate quickly, holding the bowl close to her face, Japanese style.

He bent forward and looked into her half-empty bowl in mock surprise. "I see you have a fine appetite."

She laughed, and lifted her cup for a refill. The sake was improving.

"Did you know about Grandmother Ko," Barbara said, "and the other things Michi-san wrote about?"

"Some particular details surprised me." She waited for him to go on, but he said nothing more.

"Was the 1961 paper interesting?"

He nodded, not looking at her.

"What was she writing about? Did she mention Ume?"

"She told about several things, a miscellany of the previous year's events." He concentrated on his rice, scraping the last grains from the bottom of the bowl.

"I've wondered so often about . . . Michi-san's death. Do you think it was really from a heart attack? Or do you think she could have . . . from despair . . ."

His head snapped up.

"Because of Ume?" she managed to choke out.

He laid the chopsticks across his bowl, lining them up until they were exactly even. His lips were tightly pressed together. "Perhaps it is not possible to know the soul of another."

"I'm sorry," she said. "Of course I have no idea. It was just . . ."

His face softened as he looked up at her. "You were friend to Nakamoto-sensei—this is natural thought."

There was another long silence.

"You don't ever call her Michi-san?" Barbara said.

"Maybe so, at times. But generally we refer even to friends by family name."

"Should I have called her that?"

"You are gaijin," he said with a shrug.

Gaijin. Outsider. She was reminded of that so often. At least gaijin were forgiven for most errors, since little was expected of them.

"When are you free to translate again?" she said. "I could come to your house some afternoon next week."

"Unfortunately I must to go Mashiko to make delivery."

"Oh." She could feel the disappointment showing in her face.

"The next week, perhaps," he said.

"I have to help with the freshman entrance exam—then I'll be traveling until graduation on March eighteenth."

"I see." She was glad to hear the regret in his voice.

"You won't be here for Nakamoto-sensei's forty-ninth-day memorial service, then?" she said. "It's on Friday."

"Yes, I will be returned then. We could meet afterwards."

"That would be great."

"Yes, very good," he said, nodding. "I will anticipate this."

He got up and went to the back; she saw he was paying the bill. They walked outside toward his truck.

"Are you going to speak about Nakamoto-sensei at the service?" Barbara asked him.

"No," he said.

"But you knew her so well." He said nothing.

When they got into the truck she said, "I've been asked to say something about her."

"Ah so desu ka?" he said, staring at her.

"It's strange, isn't it? I've only known her since last summer."

For several blocks they rode in silence, then he said, "What will you speak about her?"

"Her generosity, for one thing. One time she brought me a beautiful fish, a raw one with the head still on. She could tell I didn't know what to do with it, so she stayed and cooked it.

Then she wrote out a whole little recipe book for me, with 'How to Cook a Fish' on the first page."

"You did not know cooking?" He sounded shocked.

"Not Japanese style." The truth was, she could cook very few things; her mother couldn't stand to have anyone underfoot in the kitchen.

"You were intimately acquainted with Nakamoto-sensei?" He glanced at her.

She had an image of the two of them at Michi's table, the round paper lamp a moon of light. Between the conversations—while they ate or simply sat together—there had been, even from the first, a warm silence. "There was a connection between us that's hard to explain."

"Human feelings are mysterious, ne?"

They slowed in front of the college. "Shall I drive you to inside?" Seiji asked.

"This is fine, right here."

He pulled to the side of the road beyond the gate. The gate light behind them shone faintly into the truck; she could just make out his face.

"Thank you for the dinner," she said. "I enjoyed it very much. I look forward to reading more of the papers together."

He bowed, then held out his hand. "Good-bye American style," he said. They shook hands with an exaggerated flourish and laughed.

"It is strange how fate has brought us together … like arranged marriage," Seiji said with a smile. "I hope we will get along."

9

That night Barbara awoke suddenly, her heart pounding. A fox had been speaking to her in a language she'd understood in her dream, but the content was gone. All that remained was a sense of danger.

She turned on the light and looked at her scroll. The fox woman's face was enigmatic but benign. Her translation notebook lay beside the chest. She picked it up and thumbed through the pages. Seiji hadn't wanted to read that one paper. She'd had to prod him to translate the most important-looking section in the 1965 entry. She pulled open the top drawer of the tansu, releasing the pungent odor of camphor into the cold air, and took out the 1965 bottle. The loosely wrapped paper slid off easily. She studied the squeezed-in lines, then looked at her notes. Why would he have been reluctant to read about the weather on New Year's? Only I read these papers, he'd said, hitting his chest: I, Okada Seiji. Maybe she should have someone else have a look at that section.

She poured some wine into a cup already beside the tansu and arranged the electric blanket around her shoulders. She could take the paper to the International House—Michi-san had introduced her to the librarian, who would probably know of some translators. Though it would be much quicker if she found someone on campus. She went through the possibilities she'd considered before . . . one of the students, Miss Ota, Mrs. Nakano. Mrs. Nakano's office was just across the hall from Mr. McCann's.

Mr. McCann. Of course. He was fluent in Japanese. Several times he'd urged her to call on him whenever she had any difficulty. "Anything I can do for you, dear."

After drinking the wine she straightened the blanket and lay beneath it, turning from one side to another. Seiji would be furious if he knew she was going behind his back.

The next morning she went to Mr. McCann's office. The door was open. She looked in at him bent over his desk, reading a student paper. "Ah, Barbara." He looked up at her, then stood, brushing back his unkempt gray hair with both hands. "Come in, come in—I was just about to make some coffee."

She took a seat across from his desk. He made instant coffee, smiling at her several times, as if to hold her in place; there was always a slightly desperate edge to his friendliness. Mrs. Nakano had told her that Mr. McCann's wife had returned quite suddenly to the States last summer, unable to make the adjustment to Japan.

He arranged the coffees, then set a box of Whitman's chocolates in front of her. "Dozo," he said, "a little indulgence from home."

"Ah. Miss Fujizawa's source." She bit into a chocolate-covered cherry.

He rustled through the candies, chose two, and sank back into his chair. "So tell me, Barbara-san, how goes it?"

"I'd like to ask you a favor." She eased the rolled-up paper out of her briefcase. She noticed that her hand was shaking.

"Fire away."

"I wonder if you could translate a little piece of something."

"It would be a pleasure."

She unrolled the paper, took a deep breath. "This is confidential."

"Aren't you the mystery woman?" When she hesitated, he said, "Of course, I understand."

She put a blank sheet of paper over the manuscript so that only the squeezed-in section showed, and carefully laid both on the desk between them.

"Would you read—just that little part?"

"Only this?" He tapped the edge of the paper with his middle finger, then lifted the notebook paper with a fingernail.

"Only that," she said.

"A billet-doux?" He waggled his eyebrows.

She said nothing. Maybe this had been a mistake.

He leaned closer to the paper and followed the calligraphy with one finger. She could smell the coffee on his breath.

"Composed recently, I see. January 1 of this year—only instead of 1966 it reads Showa 41. This is the Japanese form of dating—using the name of the Emperor's reign—in this case for Hirohito, Enlightened Peace. Some irony there, eh?"

"What else does it say?" she asked, trying to keep the impatience out of her voice.

"The language seems feminine, I'd say, quite a poetic little description of walking after writing—I assume she means this." He laid a hand on one of the papers. Barbara resisted an urge to push it off.

"Yes," she said, "she is referring to some other writing on the page—which is in rather delicate condition," she added.

"There is unseasonable warmth, there is a mist. And the plum tree buds are quite large—plumped out, we might say— much too soon. She wants to close the plum buds shut with her hand. She is recalling Hiroshima. Hiroshima?"

Barbara kept her fingers tight on the papers. "Please go on."

"Hiroshima, where the blind masseur would be drawn to her home by the most delicate odor of plum blossoms. See what I mean? Rather poetic. She fears..." He hesitated; she nodded him on. "She fears that the plums may be blasted by the frost this year, and never bear fragrance."

He straightened.

"And—that's really all?"

"That's all. Unless you'd like me to read on."

"No, that was perfect ... thank you so much." She slid the papers away from him, almost giddy with relief. "Please don't mention this," she said.

"My lips are sealed."

At Michi's forty-ninth-day memorial service, Barbara sat in the front of the temple with other members of the faculty who were going to speak. Coming in, she'd seen Seiji seated alone near the back of the dark room.

The temple looked much the same as it had for the funeral, with the large photograph of Michi on the altar along with an arrangement of flowers and the urn of smoking incense. But instead of the coffin, there was, in the center of a table, a small box covered in white brocade; this must contain Michi's ashes. The box was shaped like a coffin, as though it were the result of some bizarre process of reduction. Barbara thought of what Michi had written in her journal about her brother's ashes,

their mother putting them on her face to soothe the radiation
burns. Now she was nothing but ash and bits of bone. Junko
had told her that one particular bone, called the throat Buddha,
was usually picked from the cremation ashes with chopsticks
and put into the ceremonial box along with the ashes.

What was the throat Buddha? She'd been too upset to ask.

She forced her gaze from Michi's wistful face and concentrated on the priest chanting sutras at the altar. He had a bald
head, wrinkled as a bloodhound's, and an austere, ancient face;
he looked wise, but who knew? She was tired of not understanding anything. Even the simplest utterances—a customer
discussing prices with a store clerk, the announcements that
came booming out over the loudspeakers in train stations—
seemed mysterious and profound.

The priest bowed, turned, bowed again, then murmured
something to the audience, evidently an introduction of Miss
Fujizawa. She pushed herself up from her chair with her cane
and strode to the front. Imposing in her black dress and pearls,
Miss Fujizawa spoke in rapid Japanese, from time to time
frowning at the audience over her glasses. Platitudes, Barbara
guessed: what a fine teacher Nakamoto-sensei had been, an es-
teemed colleague, a great loss for Kodaira College and the com-
munity. Barbara stared at Miss Fujizawa's broad face, the roll
of flesh beneath her chin. She'd probably known about that
empty pill bottle; what would she have concluded?

Miss Fujizawa sat down, slightly out of breath, and Miss
Ota rose to take her place. Barbara glanced down the row—after
Miss Ota, only two more speakers before her, Mrs. Nakano
and Mrs. Ueda. Her stomach tightened.

Miss Ota was speaking in English. Barbara looked up, surprised, listening closely to Miss Ota's soft voice. "... not in the
least of doubt," Miss Ota was saying, "that Nakamoto-sensei
was becoming a leading authority in the notably complex field

of Japanese and Western relationships. Alas, this was never recognized in the world at large, since she was of the female gen-
der. But we had many a discussion on these topics. One of the
prominent opportunities for this was two days we passed together when she was a doctoral student at the University of
California in the city of Berkeley, and I was en route from Lon-
don." Barbara leaned forward; she hadn't known Michi-san
lived in California. "We spent several hours exploring historical archives in Berkeley," Miss Ota continued, "in regard to a
research Nakamoto-sensei was pursuing." She lifted the page
she'd been reading and placed it beneath the others. "As well,
we visited collections of Asian art and on one particular afternoon enjoyed a lunch in that sector of San Francisco which is
inhabited primarily by persons of Japanese descent.

"It was Professor Nakamoto's great regret," Miss Ota said
with a glance toward Barbara, "and our considerable loss, that
she was not able in her brief lifetime to complete her written
study of Commodore Perry and the Western incursions into
Japan. Be that as it may, her students and those other of us
who knew her well were much improved by the breadth and
depth of her knowledge, not to mention her selfless generosity."
Miss Ota gave Barbara a little bow as she sat down; Barbara returned a bow of thanks. The English had been for her benefit.

Barbara was disappointed that Mrs. Nakano did not also
speak in English. She read from notes written on thin sheets of
paper: a carefully constructed biography, perhaps, like those
Mrs. Nakano had written out for each of the writers they'd
studied in her class.

Mrs. Nakano's talk was over too quickly. Mrs. Ueda rose,
leaving an empty space beside Barbara. She rubbed her damp
palms on the sides of her skirt. Mrs. Ueda began speaking with
evident emotion. Her eyes were swollen and she held a balled-
up handkerchief to her chest. Barbara watched her face, ashen

beneath the black turban, and tried to remember what Michi had said about her: a tragic life, a difficult marriage. She'd like to talk to Mrs. Ueda about Michi-san, though Mrs. Ueda had always seemed cool, almost unapproachable. They had exchanged only a few polite sentences.

Mrs. Ueda bowed; her speech was finished. Barbara's heart thumped wildly as Mrs. Ueda made her way back to her seat.

She stood unsteadily and walked to the front.

"Gomen nasai," she began, "for not speaking in Japanese." She looked down at the paper in her hand. It was trembling quite obviously. "Nakamoto Michiko-sensei," she began, "was like a mother to me. When I first arrived here, she greeted me at the door of Sango-kan so warmly. I found later that it was she who had prepared my apartment, filling the cabinets with food. She had given me her window seat cushions, her clock radio, even the pillow from her own bed."

Barbara glanced down at the page; she had already covered everything, much too quickly. "To tell the truth, I know little about Michi—excuse me, Nakamoto-sensei—in comparison with the rest of you. As a child knows almost nothing about her parents' real life when she is young, so it was with me regarding Nakamoto-sensei." She looked out at the audience and plunged on. "I was recently very surprised to learn that she was from Hiroshima, a survivor of the atomic bombing...." Her words hung in the air; the shocked silence came toward her in waves. In the front row everyone but Miss Fujizawa—who scowled up at her—lowered their eyes. A few rows back, Junko and Sumi were staring; Sumi's mouth was half open. She looked toward the back of the room, at Seiji; he was gazing at her steadily. "And—I—gomen nasai—all I can really say is— as you all know—that she was extremely kind and generous. Thank you." She walked to her chair, her face burning.

The priest returned, said a few more words, then everyone

stood. There was little talking. Barbara could hear a low-pitched murmur and the scraping back of chairs.

Miss Ota waited for her at the end of the aisle. "Your emotion was most touching," she said. She patted her hand, in consolation, Barbara felt. Miss Fujizawa gave her a chilly "Thank you, Miss Jefferson." Barbara turned to look for Mrs. Nakano, but she was gone, lost in the flow of people moving toward the exit.

Seiji had remained in his seat. On her way out, Barbara stopped and whispered to him, "Is it still possible to meet? I really would like to talk to you."

"I have some business with the priest," he said in a low voice, "but I will see you after in the Kamiya restaurant." He did not meet her eyes.

Outside, Junko, Hiroko, and Sumi were whispering among themselves. As Barbara walked toward them, they fell silent.

"You think I said more than I should have."

"We are surprised, Sensei," Sumi said. "We did not know Nakamoto-sensei was hibakusha."

Oh God, it was worse than she thought. "It was a secret, then," she said.

"Some hibakusha are in the public eye, speaking for peace," Hiroko said. "Others prefer to remain anonymous. She must have trusted you much, to confide this to you."

"Excuse me," Barbara said, "I must go do some errands—I'll see you later."

She walked quickly through the crowd; she had betrayed Michi and disgraced herself. Mr. McCann gave her a knowing smile; he'd made the connection between Michi-san and the paper. A sick feeling edged into her stomach.

In town, the Kamiya was empty of customers except for a workman at the bar. Even in midafternoon the restaurant smelled strongly of eel. She sat down beneath the print of the cross-eyed samurai. The waitress looked out from behind the back curtain, then appeared with a hot towel and tea. Barbara managed to convey in Japanese that she was expecting someone. The waitress discussed this piece of information with the man at the bar, and they both turned to look at her.

In the light of afternoon the restaurant was shabby; there were cheap vinyl covers on the tables and plastic flowers. Barbara drank her tea slowly. Seiji was taking a long time with the priest.

When Seiji finally arrived, he was carrying a package tied in a white furoshiki. She felt a moment of irritation; he'd stopped to do some shopping on the way.

"Hello," she said.

"Hello." He put the package on the chair beside him.

The waitress returned; he ordered a Kirin beer.

After the waitress had disappeared behind the curtain, Barbara blurted out, "I feel terrible. I shouldn't have said that about Michi-san—the students didn't even know."

"Although you are ignorant about hibakusha's reasons for silence, you have meant no harm."

"Thank you. It's true I *meant* no harm."

A waitress brought Seiji's beer. Barbara watched him drink, tipping back his head, his eyes half closed.

"I'd appreciate it so much if you could explain it to me—the hibakusha's reasons for silence," she said.

"Maybe one day I can explain." He set down the bottle and glanced toward the chair beside him. "I have brought the ashes of Nakamoto-sensei."

"What?"

He touched the furoshiki; she leaned forward to look. The rectangular shape of the box was visible beneath the cloth.

"Michi." Tears stung her eyes. "Where—what will you do with the ashes?"

"I will place in her butsudan—ancestor altar—for now. At some later time I will take to Hiroshima."

The butsudan had been in Michi's small tatami room. Barbara had seen it once, the night Michi showed her the wine tansu. A large dark piece of furniture, she'd hardly glanced at it.

"Where is the butsudan now?"

"At the house of my aunt."

"At your house? She left it—bequeathed it—to you?"

He looked down at his beer, swirling it in the glass. "Nakamoto-sensei lived at our house for several years, when she first came to Tokyo. And Ume-chan."

"So—you knew her very well."

"Yes." His hand went still; he continued to stare at the beer. His face was tight, his jaw working. She felt a twinge of guilt for having mistrusted him.

"I'm sorry," she said.

He nodded. "Thank you."

"I can understand why you feel—about the papers—that it's surprising she didn't leave them to you."

He looked up at her. "I am glad you can understand me now."

"My mother was a foreign correspondent in Japan before the war—even in Hiroshima. Maybe that's one reason she chose me."

"You have not mentioned this. What did your mother write about Hiroshima?"

"I don't know. At my apartment I have the only writing salvaged from my mother's correspondence days, a visit to Hakone. Everything else is lost."

Sipping her tea, cold now and slightly bitter, Barbara glanced at the chair where the wrapped box sat, just out of sight.

"Do you think Michi would forgive me for my outburst?"

When Seiji looked puzzled she added, "For speaking impulsively about her."

He smiled for the first time. "Yes. This is your nature."

They arranged to continue translating the next Monday at Sango-kan; everyone else would be gone on their vacation travels. They stood to leave. As Seiji carefully lifted the furoshiki, she could see the sharp corners of the box.

She walked home, taking the long way, up a side street and through the woods. It was almost sunset, with washes of dark beneath the trees. As she paused, looking down at the river, she imagined the white box floating slowly along the thin black ribbon of water.

10

Early the next morning there was a tap at the door.

"Rie!" Barbara stared. Rie's protest bandage was gone; her hair was freshly washed.

"May I speak to you, Sensei?"

"Of course. Would you like some tea? Or Coca-Cola?"

Rie declined. They went into the Western-style room, where Rie stood looking at the books on the shelf. "You have many volumes of Japanese writing."

"I studied contemporary Japanese literature with Nakano-sensei at my university last year, and since I've come to Japan I've bought everything I could find. In translation of course. I know it's not the same."

Rie turned to look at her. "I heard you speak at Nakamoto-sensei's service. Thank you for your sincere effort."

"I thought I'd disgraced myself, and Nakamoto-sensei too."

Rie shook her head. "In Japan we have two important

words, *tatemae* and *honne*. *Tatemae* means appearance and *honne,* true feeling. Many Japanese are more concerned with tatemae, but you spoke your feeling. I admire this."

"Thank you, Rie. Thank you very much."

"I am thinking further on original sin and wish to do another writing on this subject. Can you agree to read it?"

"Yes," Barbara said with a smile. "I can."

"Some say I also express my opinion too freely, ne?" Rie said. She laughed suddenly, showing dimples high in her cheeks. "I think we are in some way similiar after all."

"I guess we are," Barbara said. She followed Rie into the hall and watched as she ran down the stairs. Wonders will never cease, she could hear her father saying, and then her mother's inevitable rejoinder: Oh, but they will cease. Wonders will almost certainly always cease.

That afternoon, as Barbara was returning from the classroom building, where she'd recorded her grades, Mrs. Ueda asked her if she would please come in for tea.

Barbara had never been inside Mrs. Ueda's apartment before. It was laid out like Michi-san's with windows facing east and south. There was a pleasant clutter in the room, overflowing bookshelves and stacks of recordings.

Above one of the bookshelves was a print of a Japanese woman in a kimono with a salmon-colored obi. Michi-san's Sharaku print.

"Dozo," Mrs. Ueda said, gesturing toward the table. Barbara sat down and Mrs. Ueda went to the kitchen to make tea. The table was by the back window, where Michi's had been.

Mrs. Ueda returned with tea and bean cakes and settled herself opposite Barbara. She wasn't wearing the turban today.

Her hair was pulled back into a tiny bun; when she turned her head to the side, Barbara could see scalp beneath the graying strands. There were pouches beneath her eyes but her ivory skin glowed in the light from the window. From her fine, delicate features, it was evident that she had once been beautiful. "I noticed that you have one of Nakamoto-sensei's prints," Barbara said.

"Yes. She has given me her entire collection."

"I'm glad—Miss Fujizawa said there were few individual recipients."

"Most of her possessions were sold to benefit a certain hospital. But she has made her bequeathals first, has she not?"

"Yes." Barbara shifted uneasily. "I was very grateful to receive her wine tansu."

"I have never cared for umeshu, myself. I make it a habit to avoid all spirits."

Barbara nodded, smiling. Mrs. Ueda knew nothing of the writing, then.

"I have been thinking of your talk about Nakamoto-sensei," Mrs. Ueda said. "Has she spoken to you of her experience in Hiroshima?"

Barbara paused. "I was aware of it," she said.

"I am surprised by this."

"My mother was in Hiroshima in the late thirties. Michi—Nakamoto-sensei—and I talked about that. Maybe that's one reason she didn't mind my knowing."

"Perhaps that and the fact that you are non-Japanese." She poured more tea into Barbara's cup.

"Thank you. Mrs. Ueda, I realize now that I shouldn't have mentioned that Michi-san was an hibakusha—but could you please tell me why? I don't understand."

"The bomb survivors are associated with bad luck and death. Indeed, with their exposure to radiation, the victims themselves are considered a pollution. Hibakusha have become almost a pariah caste in Japan."

"It's hard to comprehend how victims of bombing could be considered outcasts."

"This has its beginning long ago in Japanese thinking. Any group which is different or in some way shamed may be regarded as outcast. Survivors of the nuclear bombings have trouble in marriage for fear their offspring may be affected. Though there are less rational fears too ... the sense of some taint. Defeated Japanese soldiers were looked upon in this light, especially after war atrocities were learned. All Japanese soldiers carried this burden, even if they were innocent of anything but defeat. My own husband suffered in this way when he returned from the war. He became a changed man."

"I'm so sorry," Barbara said. She tried to think of something appropriate to say. "You weren't from Hiroshima, were you?"

"No, I was in my home city of Gifu at the end of the war." Mrs. Ueda looked down at her cup, swirling the tea.

Barbara glanced back at the print. "The Sharaku is lovely, isn't it? It reminds me so much of Michi-san."

Mrs. Ueda looked up, studying her for a moment. "I have some other things you may like to see, belonging to Ume-chan."

"I would like to, very much."

Mrs. Ueda went into the adjoining room and returned with a rice paper box, which she set on the table. She opened the box and took out a framed photograph; Michi was squatting beside a young girl who looked toward the sky, her mouth wide open. Ume. In the background were white birds perched in trees.

"Did she show you this one?" Mrs. Ueda asked.

"No, I never saw a picture of her. When was it taken?"

"Ume had just turned seven years old. We made a visit to an egret rookery, the first year Nakamoto-sensei taught at Kodaira." She lifted a flowered red silk kimono from the box.

"Ume wore this one for Shichi-Go-San festival; that is day when parents take their children aged three, five, and seven to the local shrine. I also accompanied them there during the first year. Unfortunately I have no photograph of that occasion." She stroked the kimono, picking at a stray thread on one edge. "It was a bittersweet day. Even at her young age it was clear Ume-chan was not developing normally. Nakamoto-sensei made every effort to help her but could do little. At that time there was no assistance for hibakusha living away from Hiroshima."

"That must have been agonizing. But she was an extraordinary mother, wasn't she?"

"She was indeed, although she never felt herself adequate. I have never known anyone so devoted to her child. Or to her friend. I had a loss of a daughter some years earlier; Nakamoto-sensei always consoled me in my grief."

Mrs. Ueda looked back down into her tea.

"That's very sad about your daughter. How old was she?"

"Two years of age. Cholera took her, during early years of the war." Mrs. Ueda smoothed the kimono and gently returned it to the box. "There are a few other things here as well. Please have a look."

Barbara leaned forward and looked inside. There were some carefully folded kimonos and a wooden doll.

She picked up the doll. It had a round head with a girl's features painted on it; the body was a simple wooden cylinder with some faded red stripes painted around the bottom. "Is this a kokeshi doll?"

"Yes, quite an old one. Perhaps it belonged to Nakamoto-sensei originally."

Barbara held the doll to her face, thinking of Michi's description of Ume in the hospital after their picnic, the kokeshi doll in her hand: "In her sleep she looks like an innocent whose life is just beginning."

11

Monday morning, Barbara went into Kokubunji to buy food for Seiji's visit that afternoon: bean cakes and fine green tea, and for dinner—in case he should stay that long—salmon and snow peas. In the pharmacy, she tried to buy deodorant, using her pocket-sized Japanese-English dictionary. There was no word for *deodorant*, only *deodorize*. The young female clerk showed her air freshener, cleansing powder, toilet bowl cleaner. Finally Barbara demonstrated, raising her arm and rubbing beneath it; the girl stared at her and shook her head. Barbara looked at her watch; she'd have to make do with powder. On the way home she stopped to buy flowers: three yellow chrysanthemums for the tokonoma, a single stalk of iris—one blossom half open, the other about to bud—for the tansu.

When she got back to the campus it was almost deserted, just one or two people walking in the distance. The end-of-the-year holiday, delayed by Michi's memorial service, had begun.

Although students and faculty would return for graduation in mid-March, classes would not resume until April. As Barbara walked up the main drive, Miss Fujizawa came by in her chauffeured car. The car stopped, and Miss Fujizawa lowered the back window. "Hello, Miss Jefferson," she said, eyeing the flowers and groceries. "Aren't you going to explore Japan?"

Barbara explained that she was meeting a student in Kyoto on Saturday, after she caught up on some work, then went on—before Miss Fujizawa could inquire about the work—that she might visit Hakone for a few days. "My mother was there before the war."

"Indeed? Well, please take care of yourself, Miss Jefferson. We are responsible for your welfare. If we had known of your plans, my secretary could have made arrangements at the Hakone Hotel."

"Oh, it's fine," Barbara said, but Miss Fujizawa was already rolling up her window.

At Sango-kan Barbara was relieved to see Mrs. Ueda's car gone; she must be traveling too. Miss Ota had left for Yonago again and Miss Yamaguchi for Kyushu, to visit family there. She had the building to herself.

In her apartment she opened all the windows and sliding doors. It was an unusually mild day. She arranged the flowers in vases, then placed them on the tansu and on the tokonoma beside Seiji's tea bowls, which she'd already set out on top of wooden boxes. In the six-mat room, she put paper, pens, and her large Japanese-English dictionary on the kotatsu. The zabuton cushions were already arranged beside the table.

Exactly at two, there was a light knock on the door. She walked slowly down the hall, not wanting to seem too eager.

Seiji bowed solemnly. "I hope I am in good time." He held out three pale green lilies and a package of cookies. "The flowers express Japanese sentiment," he said. "The sweets are in memory of your home." On the package of cookies were Japanese characters, and in English, *Carolina Beauty Bourbon Snaps*. In smaller letters the label read, *Beautiful things are beyond time. Women's history never cease to yearn for beauty.*

"I think these suit you," he said.

"Oh yes—I mean thank you. Dozo." She gave two quick bows, then led the way down the hall to the sitting room. "I thought we could work in here. Please make yourself comfortable," she said, gesturing toward the kotatsu.

He gazed around the room as though for the first time. "Very fresh," he said, nodding his approval. "Ah." He looked at his tea bowls on the tokonoma. "I see I am in place of honor." He turned, grinning at her.

"Well, of course." She could feel herself blushing. "I'll go put these flowers in water," she said, then added with a smile, "Try not to be bored while I am gone."

When she came back to put the lilies on the kotatsu, Seiji was no longer there. She found him in the smaller room kneeling beside the tansu. The bottom drawer was open. He pulled out a tiny package wrapped in white paper.

"What's that?" she said. "Where did you find it?"

"In some paper behind the bottles."

He undid the package. Inside was another wrapping, worn red silk tied with a cord. Barbara reached out for it but he nimbly undid the cord. The silk fell away.

"Wah!" he said. "Kitsune!"

He held it between two fingers: a white fox, about three inches tall.

"Let me have it, please," she said, holding out her hand.

He carefully placed the fox on her palm. "I think there may be another," he said, and began to feel around in the wadded paper in the back of the drawer.

Carved from wood and coated with white lacquer, the small

fox had darkened and chipped over time; the figure was simple but expressive. There was a suggestion of legs, haunches, and a tail, which was raised and flat against the back. The ears were small pointed triangles. On the protruding snout were painted whiskers and the mouth, a simple line that curved slightly down. There was just a single slanting brushstroke for each eye, but the face conveyed an uncanny wisdom. She remembered what Michi had said about the language of foxes. This one looked capable of speech.

Seiji had pulled out another little package.

"Let me unwrap that one," she said, taking it from him. She put the fox on the tansu and ripped the paper off the second package. Inside was a layer of purple silk. She slid off the cord and shook loose the silk to reveal another small fox.

"This is mate, just as I thought." Seiji leaned close to her, his shoulder touching hers.

She picked up the other fox, holding one in each hand. They were identical except that one had a painted triangle for a mouth, as if it were speaking; the other mouth looked closed. "Do they have anything to do with fox language?" she said. "Or fox tricks?"

"Not the same. Do you know the Inari shrine with fox guardian?"

She nodded. "Like the one on the path to your house."

"Yes, but larger one too—there are many such big shrines all over Japan. Inari is god of agriculture and fox is considered his messenger. Some people who go to shrine make a prayer for something and then ask priest to bless two foxes such as these. When their wish is come true, then they return foxes to shrine. So we call them wishing foxes."

"Maybe Michi-san had some unanswered wish."

"These may be ancient foxes, much older than Nakamoto-sensei."

He glanced up at the fox woman scroll. "Has she given you this painting also?"

"Someone gave it to my mother when she was here—a man who said she was as beautiful as a fox woman."

He smiled at her. "I think you must resemble your mother, then."

"Thank you." She could feel her face reddening again. "Michi thought this picture illustrates the fox woman leaving her child. I don't know the story, do you?"

"We have many fox stories in Japan. Usually fox changes into lovely woman to trick man. Most popular one is fox wife. In the tale most schoolchildren know, a hunter spares the life of a fox. Next day a woman comes to his house and offers to be his wife. He agrees and they spend some happy years together with their child. But eventually the true shape of wife is revealed—perhaps as they pass by water. Always reflection in water will show true thing, fox figure instead of woman. So she must leave him and also their child."

"What a sad ending."

"This is very Japanese ending—we call it aware, graceful sorrow. There are other fox stories I can tell you like this, perhaps some with happier ending."

"I'd like to hear them," she said.

"We have many things to tell. It will take us long time, I believe."

"Yes," she said. "I think so too." She began to feel awkward, looking at him. She closed the bottom drawer of the tansu and opened the top one. "Shall we choose something else to translate? Maybe the 1961 paper that you read to yourself last time?"

"We should take them as we were going, I think," Seiji said, reaching in for the 1963 bottle.

She shrugged; it wasn't worth an argument. She picked up

the foxes from the tansu and followed him into the sitting room.

They sat together at the kotatsu. She put the small foxes in front of her and opened her notebook; he unwrapped the bottle and spread out the paper on the table. They moved closer together so she could hold down the left side of the paper, and he the right.

He put on his glasses and bent over the page.

"This is first writing of the year, as before." He ran his finger down the line of characters, then reached for the dictionary. As he turned the thin pages, Barbara looked at his hands, the fingers long, rather delicate, the nails scrubbed clean. "Will you please pronounce?" he said, pointing to the English word.

"Psychological."

"Ah yes." He leaned back over Michi's writing. "Now I can say for you." Barbara picked up her pen. " 'Emperor's daughter-in-law, Princess Michiko, has recovered her voice after several months of being unable to speak. It seems she did not have some stroke or hidden cancer as some had earlier thought. She was suffering from psychological condition, as result of unkind treatment from Emperor and her mother-in-law following the wedding to Prince Akihito.' " He read ahead silently, then continued.

" 'The experience of the Princess has reminded me of Grandmother Ko, who suffered harsh treatment from her mother-in-law. Also I am thinking of Mother, who was only a few months old when Ko has disappeared. This is a cruel thing for child to suffer, to grow up with empty space where mother should have been. It has shaped mother in her turn. I must be forgiving, and always be mindful of this regarding Ume-chan.' "

"Does she say why Ko disappeared?"

"This is not explained." He was running his finger down the

lines of text. "But next part will be very interesting to you, especially regarding tansu chest."

"My tansu?"

"Please listen. Nakamoto-sensei writes, 'All this day and night, when I should have been finishing up my New Year's cards, I have been in some other world, thinking of Mother and Grandmother. I have just read again Mother's stories about Grandmother Ko. Nothing else was so great treasure to her as papers containing glimpses of her mother.

" 'On day of her death Mother beckoned Father and myself to her and whispered we must take care of her papers, first writings of the year. She told us to look beneath a stone in tea house garden where she had buried them to protect from bombing raids. Some few days after Mother's death, Father and I found these papers in a wooden box, tied together in one roll.' "

"Her mother's stories!"

Seiji nodded. "First paper was made January 2, of Shōwa 5, when Nakamoto-sensei was eight years old. She says, 'Father and I read Mother's writing with great excitement, sitting together at her desk. That day in tea house we also discovered, standing in a dusty crate, bottles of wine Mother had made from plum fruit. Each wine had pasted on it the year of its harvest. As writing and making wine were begun in same year, I had idea to wrap papers around the bottles. Father said yes, and he must make a special tansu to hold these wines and papers.

" 'There were in Koi many trees knocked down by atomic blast but not burned. One was ancient camphor tree that was in shrine Mother liked to visit. With his own hands, Father made tansu from camphor wood. It was many weeks of work and exhausted him greatly but also gave him heart to live. He must make this tansu. Although after finishing he said it was only crude work, I can see he is proud. When we laid Mother's wine and writing into tansu I was very glad. Mother and Grandmother Ko will have some voice remaining in this mortal world. Then Father said to me, "You see, Michi-chan, I have made tansu large enough to contain more years of wine and first writings of the year. Please continue your mother's tradition. This would please her very well," he said. And so I have done.' "

Barbara and Seiji rose and went into the small room to look at the tansu, glowing in the light of late afternoon. "Beautiful, isn't it?" Barbara said. "It must have been very difficult to make."

"Yes. Mr. Takasu was not a craftsman of wood, yet this is quite fine." They knelt beside the chest. Seiji ran his fingers along the edges of one drawer and Barbara laid a palm against the side of the chest; it felt solid and full. "It is very unusual to make whole chest of camphor wood," Seiji said. "This is unique one, I think."

"Were you familiar with that camphor tree?" she said.

"I knew it very well."

They pulled open the bottom drawer again and looked at the oldest wines. Barbara touched the 1930 bottle with a shiver of excitement. There was so much waiting for her. "Shall we read this next?"

"Perhaps so." He looked thoughtful, distracted.

"Did you know about her mother's papers?"

He shook his head.

"I guess you knew about Michi-san's writing, though, since she lived at your house."

"No," he said curtly, "I did not."

"But the wine ... did you ..."

"Hai." He stood abruptly and left the room.

"Seiji?" She must have offended him.

She found him in the Western-style room. "Is something wrong?"

There was a long silence. "Please excuse me. The tansu has stirred difficult memories."

"Of course," she said. "I understand." He'd been close to her, her student. Then they had the tragic experience in common, hibakusha together.

She touched his arm. "Would you like some tea?" she said.

"Yes, thank you."

She went to the kitchen, put water on to boil, and arranged cups and the Carolina Bourbon Biscuits on a tray.

In a few minutes, Seiji pushed through the bead curtain. He looked around the kitchen, openly studying everything. He took a jar of peanut butter out of the cabinet, unscrewed the lid, and sniffed it.

"Would you like to try some?" Barbara spread some peanut butter on a cracker and handed it to him; their fingers grazed. His face was humorous as he chewed. His mood had changed so quickly.

She carried the tray back to the sitting room. They took their places at the table again and poured tea for each other. The biscuits had no bourbon taste that she could discern; they certainly weren't southern, but they weren't Japanese either. When she finished her tea, she held up the bottle of plum wine. "Would you like some?"

"Hai." They poured wine for each other. She sipped hers, savoring the rich flavor.

He downed his and held out the cup for more. "Very nice," he said, smiling at her. He touched the foxes arranged side by side on the kotatsu. "I hope you have some wish."

"Of course," she said, smiling back at him. "Doesn't everyone?"

"I think so." He turned and looked around the room. "Is this where you sleep?"

"No," she said, taken aback. "In the three-mat room."

"You don't like a bed?"

"I had one, but now I use a futon."

"Ah, very Japanese."

There was a knock on the door. Both of them froze. Maybe she wouldn't answer, Barbara thought. But that would look worse; whoever was there must have heard their voices.

She jumped up and hurried to the door. It was Mrs. Ueda, wearing a long-sleeved white apron; a scarf was tied around her head. "Hello," Barbara said, "I thought you were traveling."

"No, I was only out doing my shopping. I happened to find a nice bit of meat at Takashimaya. Would you care to join me for dinner?"

"That's so kind of you ... but I'm doing some work just now."

"But I think you must stop to have your meal." Mrs. Ueda lifted her head slightly, peering down the hall.

Barbara glanced behind her. Seiji was still at the kotatsu, out of sight. "A friend is here helping me with some translations," she said, "but thank you. Maybe another time?"

"Ah, yes, another time." Mrs. Ueda turned and quickly walked toward the stairs.

In the sitting room, Seiji was putting on his jacket. "I think I must go now. Perhaps you had better bring papers to my house next time. When can we meet again?"

"I was thinking of going to Hakone."

"Oh? This is wonderful place. How long will you stay?"

"Two or three days, I think, maybe until the end of the week. I'm supposed to meet a student in Kyoto on Saturday."

"Ah." He paused, then said, "I like Hakone very much."

"Do you? Maybe that would be a good place for us to continue our translation."

"Yes, yes," he said, nodding. "I think this would be excellent. Where will you stay?"

"At the Hakone Hotel," she said, remembering Miss Fujizawa's recommendation.

"I could stay at ryokan nearby," he said.

"I'm going on Wednesday morning," she said; that should give her time to make arrangements.

"Good. I will call for you at Hakone Hotel lobby at two o'clock in afternoon." He bowed and walked quickly down the hall.

Barbara stood listening to his feet on the steps. When there was no sound of voices in the vestibule, she let out a deep breath. Mrs. Ueda hadn't come out of her apartment.

She ran to the window of the bedroom just in time to catch a glimpse of Seiji, his hands in his pockets, his head held high, as he hurried down the gravel path; how familiar he seemed to her now.

12

The Hakone Hotel, a large stucco building perched on a steep hillside, faced Lake Ashi. In her article about Hakone, Barbara's mother had written about the famous inverted view of Mt. Fuji reflected in the lake, but today Fuji was hidden behind clouds. Surrounding the water were large hills, their peaks sheared off by the mist.

The hotel lobby was packed with an Australian tour group. Barbara was quickly registered and shown to her room, which was large, Western, and antiseptic looking. There was no view of the lake, only the back side of a hill.

She was early. She unpacked and looked through the bag she'd bought for carrying Michi's papers. Made of stiff leather and shaped like a doctor's bag, it had kept the fragile rolls of paper from being crushed. In the main part of the bag were the six papers she'd brought, three written by Michi's mother and three of Michi's; beneath the papers was a bottle of Michi's plum wine wrapped in a towel. In one side pocket of the bag were Barbara's journal, with her mother's article on Hakone tucked inside, and her translation book; in the other side pocket were Michi's foxes, in their silks and papers, nested in a cashmere sweater, and—added at the last minute—her diaphragm.

It was bold of her to have made this arrangement, what amounted to a rendezvous. Though she did have the excuse of visiting one of her mother's "sites." She sat on the bed and unfolded the brittle article her mother had written in 1938.

DISPATCH FROM HAKONE, JAPAN'S FAMOUS BEAUTY SPOT
by Miss Janet Girard

My hosts were determined that I should not miss Hakone, considered one of the seven beauty spots of Japan. Located in the Mt. Fuji area, Hakone is known for its salubrious climate, its mineral spas said to cure everything from dyspepsia to impotence, and its spectacular views of Fuji-san.

We were just in time for luncheon at the sumptuous Hotel Fujiya—and what a feast it was! Squab, bass from nearby Lake Ashi, roasted quail eggs served on dainty ivory skewers. There was a platter of what I took to be some form of pickled eggs but which, one luncheon companion informed me, had been preserved in the ground for 100 years, and excavated in honor of my visit. (Oh you shouldn't have, I said, and devoutly meant it!)

Barbara skimmed the rest of the article, which ended with a description of the Hakone Shrine, a haven in battle for hundreds of years. There was an allusion to Japan's military activities in China, with one "mama-san" unable to hold back her tears at the thought of her son in battle.

Not a frisson of nostalgia or regret. She refolded the article.

If Michi were here, she'd probably be sharing this room with her; they'd have talked about her mother. But then she wouldn't be meeting Seiji. She felt a stab of guilt mixed with excitement. What would Michi think about this meeting?

She took the journal out of the bag. "Dear Michi," she wrote, "here in Hakone to translate your writing with Seiji Okada. I feel so drawn to him. If I saw him on the street I'd turn around and follow him. It's frightening...."

The telephone shrilled. She jumped. A gentleman had arrived for her, the desk clerk said in a neutral voice.

He was seated in the lobby, but rose, bowing, as she entered. He looked as nervous as she, his face solemn, his clothes carefully considered—the sweater vest, the good brown pants, shined shoes.

"Shall we go sightseeing?" she said.

"Yes. Many fine sights here."

"I'd like to visit the Hakone Shrine where my mother was— it's across the lake."

They walked outside. The large tourist boat was just departing, a large sluggish wake fanned out behind it. A row of people were leaning against the rail.

"I think we may hire a private boat," he said.

They walked down the hill to the boat dock. There were low clouds and patches of mist on the water.

Inside the boathouse was a young man smoking and listening to a song on the radio. Seiji spoke to him in Japanese, then said to Barbara, "He can take us across to the shrine."

They stepped into a small boat, an inboard with plank seats. The young man flicked his cigarette into the water and started the motor; they roared out into the lake. The water was choppy; spray flew up into Barbara's face. She and Seiji bounced up and down on the middle seat.

The clouds had slid farther down the mountains.

She looked at Seiji, his fine profile, smooth skin. "I hope it won't rain," she said.

"Very changeable weather here. It may clear."

Around them were long drifts of mist on the water's surface, like sheer white fabric. They began to move through patches of fog. Barbara looked behind them; the shoreline was no longer visible. The landscape had become an intimate room.

He turned and smiled at her. She looked down at their hands, almost touching on the seat.

The boat nosed up against the dock. The boat was rocking; Seiji held her hand to help her out. The walked up the path lined with ancient cryptomerias toward the shrine. There were the long steps Barbara recognized from the photograph of her mother. "Michi was right," she said. "It is the place my mother visited."

They climbed the steps and walked around the shrine, which was made of ancient dark wood. It was open on all sides, except for one locked building. That must be the treasure house her mother had written about. There were no other visitors, no priest about. Seiji rang the gong and clapped his hands, a perfunctory prayer. She walked around the platform of the shrine, inhaling the odors of damp wood and age. The shrine had been here seven hundred years. She and her mother were tiny motes in all that time. Sacred space, layers of time—but she was aware only of Seiji's closeness.

They walked back down the steps. There was no railing. When she hesitated, he took her arm.

They returned on the cruise boat, standing close together at the railing. The fog had thinned; the lake and parts of the distant hills were visible now, though Mt. Fuji was still shrouded. Barbara looked at Seiji, the reddish tint of his black hair, the crease lines in his neck above his jacket collar. He turned and gazed at her, a steady expression.

After the boat docked they walked toward her hotel. "Where shall we do our translating?" she said. She looked behind them at the group of Australians moving up the path.

"Perhaps the inn where I am staying would be most convenient."

At the hotel she ran upstairs for the bag containing Michi's papers. When she went back outside, Seiji was smoking, looking out at the lake, where the fog had closed in again. He took the bag. "It's up the hill," he said, "only ten minutes."

He began to whistle softly, a little tune that sounded familiar. It was the song that had been playing on the radio at the boat dock. They did not speak as they climbed higher. The pine trees at the edge of the road were draped with mist.

The inn was small and quiet. There was no lobby or reception area. They took off their shoes at the entrance, and walked down the corridor to his room. In the center of the tatami floor was an old-fashioned coal pit kotatsu and above it a table covered with a heavy quilt. Seiji opened a sliding door that looked out into a garden. There were a few trees, a stone lantern, and beyond the trees a densely green hillside.

"Please sit at kotatsu," Seiji said. "I will request some warm drink."

She got beneath the quilt at the table, her legs dangling over the coals. The heat began to spread up through her body.

Fog moved through the garden like smoke, reshaping the plants and the view of the hill. There was an occasional clacking sound from a bamboo pipe at the end of a water spout, designed to make a pleasant cadenced noise.

Seiji returned and sat next to her beneath the quilt. A maid soon followed carrying sake and a plate of sembei crackers.

They drank the warm sake, looking out into the garden. "This is so peaceful," she said, though the silence was making her increasingly nervous. "Maybe we should begin our translating now?"

Seiji brought the bag to the table. "What do you have for us?" he said.

"Shall we start with Michi's mother's writing? I want to find out about Grandmother Ko." She handed him the 1930s papers and took out her notebook and pen.

He made a low whistling sound as he unrolled the 1930 paper. "These kanji are old-fashioned ones." He scanned it, running a finger down the lines of calligraphy.

"This is Nakamoto-sensei's mother writing, as we had thought," he finally said. "She has put her name here, Takasu Chie—Takasu being family name. It is done on January 2, her first writing of the year. She says that the last year was her first time to make umeshu. She has hesitated to start in making umeshu as mother-in-law has told her it is bad luck to stop once beginning. Now she must make every year."

"What would happen if you stopped?" Barbara asked.

"Plum tree will be unhappy," he said with a smile. "Or maybe Chie will make a poor wife. In Japan, plum tree is associated with woman." He bent over the page. "Chie writes, 'Michi is eight years old this year. Very lively girl like monkey, more like boy than girl. I say to Fumio, You must be sorry to have girl rather than boy. He says no, but I think it must be the case. Michi has unusual gift for learning at the English school. She prattles in English to the foreigners at Nakajima Inn and they make a pet of her.' "

Barbara looked up from her translation book. "My mother would rather have had a son too."

"Really? I am very glad she did not."

"Thank you." She could feel herself flush. "Is the Nakajima Inn in Hiroshima?"

"Oh yes, Hiroshima."

"Do you—did you—know that place?"

"I think it was in mountains, near Koi."

"It is gone now, though?"

"Perhaps. Though some places near Koi are still standing."

"I would like to see them—see all of Hiroshima."

He looked at her in silence, then said quietly, "You can go there. But it will be impossible for you to understand without native guide."

"Maybe you can guide me."

"Yes," he said. "I will."

"Thank you," she said, looking down at her notebook.

He cleared his throat. "There is one more part," he said. "It is about Nakamoto-sensei. 'Not long ago,' Chie writes, 'Michi is late coming home for dinner again. I said, What if you had no mother, Michi-chan, what if I were to go away and never return? She looked at me and laughed. Papa would take care of me, she said. Unnatural child.' "

He put down the paper and lit a cigarette. "That is all of our oldest paper."

The next paper was much longer; it made several thicknesses around the 1931 bottle. After studying it Seiji said the paper contained some difficult kanji called kanbun that would take him some time to translate.

They sat quietly, looking into the darkening garden.

"Maybe I should be getting back to the hotel," she said.

He poured more sake, and moved a little closer, so that their arms were touching. She was hypnotized by the light pressure of his arm against hers and the rhythmic click of the water spout. In the distance there was a bird call, a mournful but lovely sound.

"What is that?" she said.

"Some lovebird, I think."

She laughed. He put his arm around her, kissed the side of her face, then put his face against her hair, murmuring something in Japanese.

"What?" she said, reaching to touch his face. "What are you saying?"

"I am sorry for you to go."

"Me too. I don't have to right this minute." But he was already pulling back, standing up. She stood unsteadily. He held her arm, then released it.

They walked out of the inn and down the dark hill. Their hands brushed together, then caught. When they were in sight of her hotel lit up below they stopped. He put his arms around her gingerly and kissed her lightly on the lips. She slid her arms around him; she could feel his heart thumping against hers. He said good night and began walking back up to the ryokan. She looked after him until his figure blurred into the darkness.

Only in the middle of the night, when she awoke with a start, did she remember the black bag. Michi's papers—and her journal with those lines about Seiji—and her diaphragm: she had left it all behind, in his room.

13

In the morning it was raining, a cold, steady drizzle. Barbara woke at first light, but waited until nine before walking up the hill to Seiji's inn. Surely he wouldn't look in the bag before she came.

The front door was open but the hallway was dark and silent. She'd come too early. Though there was a light on down the hall, and she could smell something cooking. "Ohayo gozaimasu," she called out softly. As she approached Seiji's room she was surprised to hear the faint sound of conversation inside, men's voices.

She slid the door open an inch. "Good morning," she said. "I hope it's not too soon to begin our work."

"Ah, Barbara-san." Seiji walked toward her across the tatami. He wore a brown robe over his blue and white sleeping kimono; his feet were bare. "Please meet my friend, Mr. Kawabata," Seiji said. "He is our innkeeper and also a poet."

An elderly man with bright eyes and a long white goatee sat

cross-legged beside the kotatsu. He bowed from the waist, gazing at Barbara over reading glasses perched low on his nose; in his hands was one of Michi's papers.

"You've opened the bag!" she said.

"Yes," Seiji said. "I am fortunate to find Mr. Kawabata kindly willing to help with difficult kanbun in Chie-san's writing."

Mr. Kawabata said something in Japanese to Seiji.

"Kawabata-sensei thinks you are like apparition," Seiji said, "golden-haired woman coming into inn on a rainy morning."

"Domo arigato gozaimasu," Barbara said with a little bow, though she couldn't tell from the man's expression whether this was a compliment or not. "Please tell him I thought he was an apparition too." She knelt beside the kotatsu and reached for Michi's bag while Seiji translated what she'd said. The man burst into laughter.

"He thinks you are funny," Seiji said.

"Yes, I see he does." The man was now peering mischievously at her from the end of the table. He said something else in Japanese she didn't understand.

"Mr. Kawabata wants to know if you would please take some breakfast," Seiji said.

"I've already eaten, thank you," she said, bowing toward Mr. Kawabata.

"Please enjoy yourself at my inn." Mr. Kawabata bowed and waved her toward the kotatsu. He scrambled up, gave Barbara another of his impish smiles, and rattled off a few sentences in Japanese.

"He says please warm yourself at the fresh coals," Seiji said as Mr. Kawabata left, still talking. "His wife will bring tea right away. Meanwhile I will go to dress myself. I did not imagine you would be such early waker," he added with a smile.

"Really?" She smiled back at him as she sat at the kotatsu

and slipped her legs beneath the quilt. "Did you think I was lazy?"

"No, just enjoying sleep, like a cat."

Her face flushed. She watched as he took his clothes from a small suitcase. "Did you read anything else?" she asked. "Any of Michi's other papers?"

"Just one, from the 1931 wine, but it is quite long as you know. I could not have managed without Mr. Kawabata's assistance."

After Seiji left, she unsnapped a side pocket of the black bag and saw with relief that her journal and translation book seemed to be just as she had left them. And the diaphragm in its case, swaddled in the furoshiki. Of course he wouldn't go rifling through her things. She took out the translation notebook, then unfurled the 1931 scroll. Even she could tell that some of the characters were more ornate than Michi's. And the brushstrokes were more intense, clotted-looking in places. It was exciting not to know what Chie had written, yet to have the expectation that she would know. The process of translation—with Seiji as guide—had the quality of sexual anticipation.

In the garden, rain was splashing on a large stone beside the pine tree and soaking into the green moss. There were odors of wet earth and damp tatami matting and, from somewhere in the building, a hint of incense.

Mrs. Kawabata, a sweet-faced woman with white hair, brought tea and bean cakes. Just as she left, Seiji returned, wearing the same clothes he'd had on the day before. He was still barefooted, but his hair was carefully combed. He sat down beside her.

"You are reading?" he said with a smile.

"I wish I could."

"But then you would not have my company," he said. "I am very glad you need my assistance."

She could feel herself smiling. "I am too," she said.

Seiji took the scroll from her and cleared his throat. "Chie is here relating the life of Grandmother Ko," he said. "I think you may recall Nakamoto-sensei's references to her grandmother."

"Yes, of course." This was Michi's history. She flipped through her notebook to a blank page.

"It was written on January second of Showa seven—your 1932. Here at first is Chie describing Nakamoto-sensei as a young girl. 'Michi, your name means wisdom yet you are disobedient and wild. You do not listen to your mother. I will write this for you, for the day when you can understand. This is the story of your grandmother Ko.

" 'Ko came from Matsue in Izumo, the province of the gods.' This is now called Shimane province," Seiji explained to Barbara, "rural area on western coast beside the Sea of Japan." He sketched a little map at the top of the page she was writing on. " 'Ko was eldest daughter of Matsudaira, a wealthy samurai,' " he continued. " 'In appearance she was elegant as goddess. It was said that her hair was a long black river that flowed to her knees and shone like the night. Her skin was the hue of fine pearl.

" 'Ko was skilled in tea ceremony and flower arranging, also classical dance. Her father had allowed her to study at home with a tutor so she knew how to read and write many kanji.' This was unusual even for daughter of a samurai in those days of the last century," Seiji said. "Chie writes next that Ko also knew some of the English language and Greek as well from a foreigner who was intimate friend of the family. Ko was almost twenty—quite old for girl in those days—'and had received no

offer of marriage. All attempts with go-between were unfruit-
ful. The problem was her family was believed to be kitsune
mochi,' which Mr. Kawabata translates as fox possessed."

"What does that mean?"

"According to rumor, the family had seventy-five small foxes
in their house who were responsible for the Matsudaira family's
great wealth. Mr. Kawabata has explained that their methods
are very cunning, going out at the master's request and bringing back the treasures of others. The foxes were considered a
danger to any family Ko might marry with, for they would follow her and do mischief to in-laws. They would become rob-
bers for Matsudaira clan."

"Did people really believe this?"

"Oh yes, especially along the Japan Sea coast. If a girl is from
fox-owning family, she cannot find a husband."

"Even now?"

"Mr. Kawabata has heard of some instances even in these
days. However, Ko's father found a go-between from Hiroshima who knew nothing of fox rumors. The go-between
made introduction to a samurai family with young son. The
name of this family is Takasu." Seiji wrote the name in
Barbara's notebook. " 'Takasus lived in castle town area of Hiroshima and were proud family. They think Ko being from
wealthy family and a beautiful, refined girl sounds like good
bride for their frail and scholarly son Hiroshi. They do not
know Ko's true age—go-between tells she is fifteen years of
age—and of course they do not know of foxes. So the match
was agreed and Ko made long journey over the mountains and
south to Hiroshima so far from her family.' "

Seiji continued the map he'd started in Barbara's notebook
and drew a dotted line showing Ko's path from the Japan Sea
over the mountains to Hiroshima.

"Now Chie says"—he paused to look at a small page of

notes—" 'Young Takasu maid Roku who later took care of me told me story of my mother Ko arriving at family house in Hiroshima. She was wearing white bridal kimono with red kimono underneath and her dark eyes shone in white face of Shinto bride. Roku said young Hiroshi was struck dumb at first sight of her. Later, mother-in-law says Ko bewitched Hiroshi from the start, that she had suspicion from moment she saw her new daughter-in-law's prideful, cunning face.' "

Seiji looked at Barbara. "Next part is rather intimate. I hope you will not mind."

" 'From first night of marriage the union seemed unnatural to mother-in-law. The new couple spent many hours in their room both night and day.' This is unusual behavior for Japanese married couple," Seiji said with a quick glance at Barbara. " 'Hiroshi cared nothing for family business from that day on. He liked more than ever to write haiku and he learned to play a strange song on his shamisen, an Izumo melody Ko taught to him. They took bath together and could be heard laughing and making noises that mother-in-law thought unseemly. One late night in rain mother-in-law saw them unclothed in garden. Ko was riding his back and laughing like madwoman, her hair loose and wild down her back. Roku said mother-in-law saw sparks in the air around them.' "

Barbara could sense Seiji looking at her, but she kept her eyes on the page.

" 'Takasu son was much changed in way he behaved to his mother. Mother-in-law's husband took Ko's side at first, even though Ko was haughty and knew nothing of the household matters and showed no concern for learning how to keep the accounts of household or of the family rice business. She cared only for her vain pleasures. Roku told Chie how Ko could take all day at her toilette, with two maids to wash her hair in special infusion of herbs she insisted to have. When rumor floated down the mountains from Izumo about the fox-owning family and association with meat-smelling foreigner who taught Ko English, mother-in-law is not surprised.' "

" 'Meat-smelling'?"

"This was an old way of describing foreigner. Especially in days before Japanese people ate meat, they thought Westerners had peculiar odor. But this is only small point in story. Mother-in-law said Ko had face of fox with broad cheeks and pointed chin and her eyes were pointed like a fox. Takasu family had been tricked. This was fox trick and Ko herself was fox, mother-in-law believed."

"Do you think she was jealous, or she really thought that?"

"Maybe she persuaded herself to believe, desho? Nakamoto-sensei's mother writes in exact detail how mother-in-law set out fried tofu, known to be fox's favorite food, at every meal and everyone witnessed how much Ko enjoyed it. She ate a great deal of food, more than natural for human woman. Mother-in-law told Roku how once she followed Ko when she wanted to go to Inari shrine in secret. Mother-in-law watched from behind tree as Ko prayed at shrine before fox statues. She saw stone foxes wag their tails and snow fall in a circle around Ko, even though this was in summer. Very strange, ne?"

Barbara reached for the black bag, took out the foxes, and began to unwrap them.

"You have brought foxes!" Seiji laughed.

She put the little figures on the kotatsu in front of her.

" 'Father-in-law, being of scientific mind, could not agree Ko was fox,' " Seiji went on. " 'But mother-in-law was insistent. She said one day she was walking down Hondori Street in center of Hiroshima and thought she was walking through desolate field, so she knew Ko was shape-changing fox, which has power to cause illusions.' "

The door opened. Mr. Kawabata came in with his wife, who set huge ceramic covered bowls on the kotasu. Mr. Kawabata touched one of the foxes, exclaiming, and picked it up.

Barbara looked at Seiji. "What is he saying?"

"He is humorously saying that his suspicion is confirmed you are fox woman."

She stared at Mr. Kawabata, seeing herself as he must: blond, foreign, not quite human.

"You may take this as his praise," Seiji said. "He also says the foxes are antique."

"Maybe they belonged to Ko."

She was relieved when the Kawabatas departed. They began to eat stew with homemade noodles and chopped vegetables and meat. Barbara glanced at her translation notes and at the foxes. She thought of Ko praying at an Inari shrine, her head bent, the long shining blanket of hair covering her face. Ko must have been frightened and lonely in an unfamiliar place: an outsider, almost a foreigner like herself.

"The next part of the story is very harsh," Seiji said. "I am afraid you may be disturbed."

"I want to hear it."

Seiji took up the scroll again. " 'Two things occurred which settled dispute,' " he continued. " 'Large family rice warehouse burned down. Mother-in-law decided this was work of Ko. Then after Hiroshi went to fight in Russo-Japanese War, Ko gave birth to child, not boy but girl, and in 1906, Fiery Horse year.' As you recall," he said, looking up at Barbara, "this occurs once in sixty years and in those days many people believe was worst birth year for a girl. She is very bad luck because she will grow up to devour her husband. So often they will kill her."

"Did they?"

"Please hear the story. Chie writes that birth of girl is final proof to mother-in-law of Ko's fox nature, and Hiroshi is not there to take the side of his wife. A sorcerer is brought to do exorcism, to drive fox out from Ko. If she dies from this, it will mean she was a fox entirely. Some years later, Chie writes, Roku told her about the exorcism. Roku heard what was done from another housemaid who attended Ko.''

Barbara laid down her pen as Seiji continued reading. " 'Ko was put in room alone for many days without food so fox would be hungry and more willing to leave her body. On day of exorcism, pepper was put on her nose and in her eyes and mouth to drive out fox. Ko's bare skin was rubbed with red-hot sticks used to handle charcoal in brazier. Still fox would not come out, though he could be heard wailing inside. Sorcerer had to use small sharp tool like awl to drill holes in her breast and abdomen to let him out.' ''

Barbara put her hand on her chest. "No, go on, go on," she said when Seiji looked at her.

"That was worst part," he said. "This section is almost finished. Chie says that Roku said, 'No one ever saw Ko again in human form. Some thought she had died and was buried without proper funeral. Some say mother-in-law had priest bind wounds and sent her back to Izumo, but on the way over the mountains one of the servants saw a red fox run off into the trees, and when he looked into the old-fashioned palanquin, it was empty. Roku and other servants in family believed that Ko's spirit took form of fox whether had been fox before or not, and that she took human guise of a geisha staying in Hiroshima where she could watch over her child.' ''

"They murdered her!" she said. "And then made up these stories to ease their guilt."

"It is not entirely clear," Seiji said. "Chie writes, 'when I was an older girl I asked my grandfather Takasu about the fate of Ko. This took much courage, as Grandfather could be needle-tongued. I went into his room where he was smoking his pipe and reading his magazine of physics. I had rehearsed my question to be discreet, but I was so frightened that I spilled out, "What happened to my mother? Did she die in exorcism ritual?" "Where have you heard this?" he said. I told him, from Roku. "You should not listen to gossip of servant girls," he said. "Your mother and grandmother did not enjoy harmony. A place was found where your mother could live unharmed." When I asked which place, Grandfather shook his head. "You must put her from your thoughts," he said.

" 'Truly Grandfather has a tender heart. For when I was born in unlucky year of Fiery Horse, Grandmother thought I should be killed—a one-day visitor, as such baby was called—not to bring worse misfortune to family and to rid family of fox taint. However, Grandfather gave me to Roku, who had her own baby at the time—and both Roku and I know this to be fact. For many years I thought she was my mother. But later when I knew the truth I realized it was Ko's breast that I remembered and I could recall too her fragrant hair that wrapped me like a satin blanket. This explains why sometimes as a very young child I would wake suddenly in the night with sensation of hair or cloth having brushed lightly across my face and I felt a presence in the room at times, watching over me.' "

Barbara and Seiji sat in silence. She felt steeped in Ko's history, she and Seiji and Michi, Ko and Hiroshi, all part of it, figures in a tapestry.

"Maybe the geisha house is still there," she said. She could go look for it, she thought; she could visit one of Michi's sites.

Seiji shook his head. "This was in Hiroshima."

"Oh. Of course. But there could be records."

"No one recorded names of geisha." He began to roll up the paper. "And this is only fanciful idea of Roku and Chie that she is geisha. Takasu-san may have sent her elsewhere."

"Back to Izumo?"

"It could be. Though this might be too great disgrace. Perhaps she became servant girl in some other part of Japan. Or possibly she was killed after all. We can never know."

Seiji stood and stretched, then walked to the door and opened it. "Look, the sun is shining while it rains. This means fox wedding." He turned and smiled at her. "Shall we go out?" he said. "When the rain stops, we may have a fine view of Fuji-san."

14

Mr. Kawabata decided Barbara should see "the bird's picture" of Mt. Fuji, from the site of a volcano. He drove, talking and gesticulating as they went flying up the hill. Seiji and Barbara, in the rear seat, were thrown against each other on the curves. Barbara tried not to look at the sheer drop at the edge of the road. She thought of Ko, jostled along in the palanquin, crossing the mountains to be married.

"I think we will part from him soon," Seiji said in a low voice.

Mr. Kawabata began to sing in a high-pitched monotone.

Barbara glanced at Seiji, her eyebrows raised.

"He is reciting a poem," Seiji said, "inspired by the day and by the presence of a lovely fox woman. I am inspired also."

"By a fox woman?"

He smiled. "If you are fox woman, then I am fox man."

She laughed nervously. "Are there any fox men in Japanese stories?"

"More women in fox stories, I think. But fox woman usually does very little harm, only deceives."

"Deceit can cause harm."

The car lurched around a sharp curve. They turned onto a gravel road and stopped beside a rickety-looking ski lift. Barbara looked up at the mountainside: sheer rock above a rim of trees and for as high as she could see, the flimsy seats bucking their way along between pairs of spindly steel legs.

They bowed to Mr. Kawabata and waved good-bye. Seiji bought tickets and they waited on the platform. He held her arm as a seat came along from behind and lifted them off their feet.

They started off into the trees and soon were skimming high above them. Barbara looked down, her heart thudding. Seiji took her hand. "There is fine sight behind us," he said. She turned with him and saw the lake shining below in the bowl of green mountains; beyond the lake, Fuji-san glistened in the light. The cable car wobbled slightly. She closed her eyes and gripped Seiji's hand. "Are you faint?" he said.

"No," she said, with a little laugh. She looked at him, his face close to hers. His eyes were dark brown, almost black. She'd never noticed before the delicate eyelashes partly hidden by the folds of eyelid.

"I am happy for meeting you," he said.

He put his arm on the seat behind her, his hand just touching her shoulder. Something gave inside her, like a latch undone, and she let go, letting herself rise with the motion of the lift. She took a deep breath and looked around her. Everything—the vista of mountains, the filmy clouds—was brilliantly clear.

Several chairs beyond them was another couple. The woman was wearing a mustard-yellow coat and her hair shone blue-black in the sun. The man was smoking a cigarette; suddenly he flicked it into midair.

Barbara watched it fall, a white speck twirling down; it could cause a fire. But then she saw they were going over barren rock; here and there were clouds of rising steam.

"This is volcano's edge," Seiji said.

"When do you think it last erupted?"

"Many hundred years ago, I think. Yet still we can see the desolate effect."

He was staring fixedly down, his profile solemn. Maybe the barren landscape reminded him of Hiroshima, she thought.

They were silent as the lift began climbing at a sharper angle. Soon the jagged face of the mountain was before them, yellowish plumes billowing from fissures in the rock.

There was a jolt like a boat docking, then the cable car moved across the exit platform. Seiji took her arm as they hopped off. Her legs felt wobbly.

"We have survived," he said with a laugh.

They walked toward a row of small buildings. In one of them was a tourist center where they found a map of the area. A young female guide in uniform told them the way to the trail where they could see "the greater boiling."

The trail was on the other side of a parking lot, a raked path just wide enough for them to walk side by side. There was no vegetation, only rock. They went up a slight incline, past wet boulders hissing steam. The air smelled strongly of sulphur. There were patches of crusty-looking ground and gray mud bubbling up from crevices in the rock. A sign in English warned them to "Stay only on beaten track." Another sign directed them down a side path to "Viewing Spot."

They walked to the overlook where there was a wooden platform. The couple from the ski lift was already there. The man was smoking another cigarette and scratching at his leg as he looked down below him. The woman moved away, the collar of her yellow coat pulled across her nose and mouth. As Barbara and Seiji approached, the couple walked toward them. The woman seemed miserable, she thought, they both did. The man's eyes were bleary and he smelled of alcohol.

Barbara and Seiji leaned against the fence at the overlook. Below was a large area of bubbling mud. The sulphur smell of rotten eggs was stronger here, almost revolting. They headed back to the main path. Ahead of them the other couple walked single file, the man in front, the woman behind. The woman was wearing uncomfortable-looking high heels; her legs were slightly bowed.

"I saw those people on the train coming here," Barbara said. "I think they're on their honeymoon."

"But they are not like Ko and Hiroshi," Seiji said.

"No."

"What have you thought about the honeymoon of Ko and Hiroshi?"

"Very nice." She cleared her throat. "Wonderful."

"Passion is a good thing when it can be found, do you agree?"

"Yes," she said. He caught her hand, then let go. The after-effect of his touch altered everything around her: the water running over rocks, the yeasty mud, even the sulphuric mist, was sensual and surreal.

Through the steam she made out a small wooden stall at the end of the loop trail. The other couple was there, talking to a red-faced woman wearing a babushka-style scarf. She and Seiji stopped just before the stall and looked down at another bubbling mud pit where there was a man working, pulling a basket on a rope trolley. The basket was full of what looked like dirty rocks.

"These are eggs that have been cooked in hot volcano mud," Seiji said. "They are for sale." He nodded at the stall, where the couple was peeling eggs. Barbara watched the woman remove bits of shell; inside, the egg was black. The woman took a small bite, looking off into space. The man's mouth was full. His wife took another tiny bite, then wrapped the egg in her handkerchief.

Seiji led Barbara toward the booth. The woman behind the counter gestured toward the bowl of grayish eggs and said something in Japanese.

"Are they preserved eggs—some of those old ones?"

"She says they are fresh, just cooked today. We must try." Seiji took an egg and put one in her hand. It was still warm.

Barbara tapped her egg against the counter. The shell came off easily; the egg was glossy, the color of ink. Seiji was already eating his egg. Such a bizarre ritual, standing here in the rotten-egg odor. She took a bite, then another, almost like a normal egg except for the smell. But she finished it

The woman laughed in a way that sounded congratulatory.

"Did you find egg delicious?" Seiji said with an ironic smile.

"I guess it was one of the worst things I ever ate," she said.

"During wartime my mother made a kind of dumpling from grass in railroad track. That was worst thing I have eaten."

They walked on without speaking. She looked around at the ravaged landscape, wanting to say something, to ask the right question. She glanced at his face, stonelike now; it was unnerving how quickly he had changed.

As they neared the end of the trail she was relieved when he said, in a normal voice, "Shall we take some refreshment?" They went into the coffee shop and sat at a table beside a huge window that looked out on Mt. Fuji.

"Have you climbed Fuji-san?" she asked.

"One time I have climbed." He stared out the window.

"What's wrong?" she said.

He smiled with apparent effort. "Sumimasen. Sometimes I make a poor companion, I'm afraid."

They walked out to the parking lot to catch the bus that would take them downhill. They rode in silence, their arms touching. Mt. Fuji floated on the horizon. When the bus stopped in front of the Hakone Hotel, they got off and in silent agreement began to walk up the hill to his inn.

It was late afternoon, the edge of dusk, with a quality of light that gave nearby objects a pulsing intensity. The weeds by the side of the road loomed up at her, as if this were their last chance to be seen. The trees in the distance were already indistinct, a line of dark shapes.

Seiji's room had been straightened, the papers and her black bag moved from the kotatsu and arranged neatly beside it. Barbara looked through the papers; everything was there. The foxes were still on the kotatsu beside a small round lamp with a paper shade; the lamp gave out a soft glow. A maid came in with tea and asked about o-furo.

"Will you have a bath before eating?" Seiji said. "I think you will find relaxing."

"Is it a—large bath, or a private one?"

"There are separate pools for men and women," he said with a little smile. "Nice hot spring bath. She will show you." He nodded toward the maid.

Barbara followed her out of the room and down several corridors to the bath. The maid gave her a small towel, a basket for her clothes, and a clean folded yukata to put on afterward.

In the steamy room there was a small changing area and, beyond it, a bath the size of a wading pool. Around the edge of the tiled room were spigots, stools, and buckets for washing and rinsing off before getting into the bath.

When Barbara emerged from the changing area, she sat at

one of the stools and scrubbed herself. One of the women, her
skin red from the bath, came slapping across the room toward
her, held out her hand for Barbara's towel, and began soaping
her back. Barbara thanked her in Japanese and bent forward as
bucket after bucket of hot water poured over her. She stood
and followed the woman to the pool. The women laughed
when she put a foot into the scalding water, then drew it back.
Finally, holding her breath, she slid in.

"Atsui, desu ne?" one of the women said.

"Hai, atsui desu."

She leaned back against the edge, her eyes closed, and let
herself float.

When she got back to the room, he was already there in his
yukata. His hair was wet, and there were damp spots on the
front of his kimono.

"You were such long time," he said, "now I am thinking you
are a fish. Will you have wine?" The bottle of plum wine was
on the kotatsu, along with two small cups.

"Yes, please." She slid in beside him at the kotatsu. They
poured wine for each other and clinked cups.

The maid brought in dinner, miso soup, beautifully arranged slices of raw fish, bowls of rice, pickles. For several minutes, they ate and drank without speaking. The tuna was delicate,
with a rich, buttery consistency.

"Everything is delicious," she said in Japanese.

"Your pronunciation is very good. Also the way you hold
chopsticks. You are excellent student, as I predicted." He
touched her foot with his.

"Your skin is so warm," she murmured.

The maid returned, cleared away the dishes, then took two
futons from the closet and laid them side by side. She gave a
slight bow, not looking at them as she left. Seiji rose to open
the door into the garden, letting in the sounds of the waterspout

and the silky movements of the pine. He sat back down close to her.

"Shall I tell you a story of fox woman?"

"Please."

"This is ancient one, perhaps oldest fox story of Japan." He touched her hand, then turned it over and stroked her palm and fingers.

"A certain lonely man longed to have a bride. One day in woods he met a woman, very friendly and beautiful. He made her acquaintance and soon asked her to marriage. She readily agreed and they were married happily. Not long after, the woman gave birth to a son. The man's dog at about the same time gave birth to puppies and the dog became jealous of the woman at that time. Dog growled when she came near. Wife begged husband to kill dog but he had kind heart and could not do so. One day man found dog barking strongly at woman. To his amazement, wife jumped nimbly onto high fence and took her true shape, that of fox.

"But the husband was so fond of his wife he never could forget her. He begged her to always come back and sleep with him nightly, and she did. Her name is name of all foxes in Japan— kitsune. Some say this comes from double meaning in Japanese, another way same characters can be read, kitē neru, come and sleep."

"Kitē neru," she repeated, looking down at his hand covering hers.

He put an arm around her and she turned toward him. They embraced, her face against his cheek. His skin smelled like the soap in the bath, the faintest tinge of sulphur. He pulled back her hair, kissed her neck, then whispered in her ear, "Kitē neru. Kitsune. Come and sleep."

15

When Barbara awoke, the room was filled with light. She turned toward Seiji: he wasn't there. His futon was still beside hers but his clothes and suitcase were gone. Surely he wouldn't just leave. She got up and dressed quickly. A pot of tea was on the kotatsu, one cup beside it, no note anywhere. She opened the door to the garden. A lizard was sunning itself on a stone, a stripe of iridescent blue. The water pipe's loud *tock* made her jump.

"Ohayo gozaimasu." Seiji stepped inside the room.

"Where were you?"

"I was arranging with the innkeeper." He bowed slightly. "I hope you have rested well."

"Very well—it was wonderful."

"Yes," he said in a low voice, his eyes not quite meeting hers. "I regret that I must depart."

"Right now?"

"Hamada-sensei needs me to return to Mashiko to help with some oversea exhibit. This is day we agreed to return."

"What about our translating?"

"I have written one paper for you in your book." He nodded toward the black bag which stood beside the kotatsu. "Please have safe return journey."

She looked down at the kotatsu and the bag. He had packed up all of Michi's papers. "I may not return to Tokyo."

"Not return?" He looked shocked; she felt a sting of pleasure.

"Some friends have invited me to Kyoto for a week or two," she said, though she and Junko had not confirmed their plans. "I may decide to join them."

"Ah." He bowed. "Please have fine holiday."

"Oh, I will." She forced a smile. "And I hope you have a fine time with Hamada-sensei."

For a moment they stood looking at each other; she felt a wavering between them, almost like movement, then they bowed good-bye.

She listened to his feet go down the hall. There were voices, then the sound of his truck rattling down the hill. She picked up her pocketbook and the black bag and went out through the garden. There was no point in giving Kawabata and company the exquisite discomfort of witnessing the gaijin's departure. She half-ran, half-walked down the hill, the black bag banging against her thigh. It occurred to her that she hadn't looked carefully around the room; he could have forgotten the foxes. She stopped and felt in the side pocket of the bag; they were there, carefully wrapped. She looked up in the direction of the inn, no longer visible behind the trees, almost as if it had been a mirage.

In her room, she lay on the bed, thinking of Seiji, his face close to hers, the delicate lashes beneath the fold of eyelid. They'd slept wrapped together, his leg over hers; she'd never felt so close to anyone. Yet he'd left without a word about what had passed between them. Longing swept through her.

Get up, she told herself, move. She took her suitcase from the closet and started packing. There must be an early train. She couldn't stay here moping.

The front desk clerk told her the next bus left for the train station in an hour.

She walked down the hill. It was a clear day and the enormous snowcapped cone of Mt. Fuji towered above the lower mountains on the other side of the lake. It seemed startlingly close, the contours visible beneath the snow.

Barbara stood gazing at the reflection of Fuji-san on the water: the famous inverted view. It was shiny, too pretty, a postcard of Hakone. Wish you were here, she could write to Seiji.

On the bus going down the mountain she sat with Michi's bag on the seat beside her to discourage companionship and closed her eyes as if she were sleeping.

He had turned out the lamp and rolled toward her. "Seiji," she whispered. He traced her eyebrows, nose, and lips, then touched her breast lightly, a gesture that was a question. She pulled him to her. After, they lay holding each other without speaking. "Balabala," he murmured into her hair, "Balabala-san," making them both laugh. "Your name is too hard," he said.

"Give me a Japanese one, then."

"Ah—Kirekitsu. Kirekitsu-san. This will mean beautiful fox." She'd gone to sleep with his breath against her face.

Then, this morning, waking to find him gone. Perhaps there was some cultural subtlety she didn't understand. Maybe he didn't want the innkeeper to know. Though Mr. Kawabata hardly seemed prudish.

She would see Seiji again; he would call.

On the train, she had a car almost to herself. After the

conductor came through, she opened the black bag. Seiji had rolled all of Michi's papers into one sheaf and tied them together with paper string. In her notebook he had written out, in laborious, childlike script, Chie's 1933 entry.

"In raising my daughter," it began, "I have come to long for my mother Ko. I wish that she could be here to advise me about Michi-chan." Barbara skimmed the next couple of paragraphs, about the trials of raising a well-bred daughter. "This New Year's I have taken out my private box to look at possessions Ko brought with her from Izumo to Hiroshima in her dowry chest. Roku removed them from Ko's room on the day of her disappearance and, years later, gave them to my safe-keeping.

"There is a sheet of paper rolled and tied with an antique black silk ribbon. On it is a receipt, 'How to Make the Plum Wine.' It is this direction I have followed, in making wine from plum trees in our Hiroshima garden."

Michi had said she used her mother's recipe, but it had been passed down from Ko. She and Seiji were drinking Ko's wine. She thought of Ko and Hiroshi on their honeymoon nights, sparks in the air around them, and she closed her eyes. "Passion is a good thing when it can be found, do you agree?" The door had been open to the garden, letting in the cool air, the scents of earth. Seiji stroked her palm with his fingertips. "Kitē neru. Come and sleep."

He'd written out this translation while she slept nearby; from time to time he would have glanced at her. When she looked back down at the page and continued reading, she heard the words in Seiji's voice: "Most precious thing from Ko's dowry is ukiyoe print. Always as I look at the picture my heart is struck to see a small child reaching after woman figure who is leaving her home. The woman's head behind paper door reveals the profile of a fox. Fox woman leaving her child forever! Michi-chan, when you are reading this one day, please look at the print. In it is a portrait of your grandmother Ko, who comes from western Japan on the shore of Lake Shinji."

When Michi had seen the scroll in her apartment, she must have been thinking of this fox woman, and her own story.

"Some day this emblem of your grandmother Ko will belong to you, Michi-chan. Maybe in it you can understand me."

That print hadn't been on Michi's wall; she would have remembered it. Maybe it was in the tansu. It could be rolled up inside one of the papers.

She looked again at Chie's description of the fox woman: she could feel the longing of the little girl as she reached for her mother's hem. She remembered a moment she hadn't thought of for years: she and her mother walking across the living room in opposite directions and Barbara—she must have been nine or ten—blurting out, "Why can't you be more motherly?" Her mother had stopped in midstride. "I can't imagine what on earth you mean," she'd said with a laugh.

She leaned back against the seat. The rocking motion of the train lulled her. She closed her eyes again. Come and sleep, he had said. Kitē neru. A print of Kitē neru would be full of yearning too: morning light, dead cigarettes in an ashtray, and a futon, its covers thrown back, in the lovers' empty room.

16

When Barbara returned to Sango-kan, she was glad to find Mrs. Ueda there, with dinner prepared for her. She'd imagined a dark, deserted building. It was unsettling, however, that Mrs. Ueda had known exactly when she was returning—apparently Miss Fujizawa's secretary had called the hotel to inquire about her schedule. If she'd had a reservation with Seiji at the ryokan, it would be all over campus by now.

Mrs. Ueda had already set the table and put, beside Barbara's place, a letter bearing a Scots postmark. It was from her father, a few scrawled sentences and a photograph of him and Gina on a golf course. "I've wanted to golf here ever since I got my first chipping iron. How are you doing in the land of the geisha and the rising sun? Sure do miss you, Baby. Please write your old man." The picture had been taken from a distance, he and Gina tiny figures on an emerald green fairway. She could just make out his silver hair and dark eyes; he looked as far away as he was.

Mrs. Ueda was studying the picture through her reading glasses. "A distinguished-looking man. And your mother is quite youthful."

"She's my stepmother. My parents are divorced."

"Ah. And has your mother remarried?"

Barbara shook her head. "She's too bitter."

"It was his decision, then."

"Yes, though she was really just as unhappy. I think she wishes she'd been the one to break things off."

"I am sorry for her. After my husband returned from the war he took up with a pan-pan girl, a prostitute. I was bitter too, for quite some time."

"Did you get divorced?"

"No," she said with an abrupt laugh. "He drank himself to death with sake."

"I'm very sorry," Barbara said. "How about Michi-san? Did she have a happy marriage?"

Mrs. Ueda sighed and shook her head. "Poor Nakamoto-sensei's life was a hard one. Her husband was killed during the war."

"But—before that?"

"They had only a brief time together. It was happy enough, I suppose."

"Was it an arranged marriage?"

"I believe so, yes."

Barbara helped Mrs. Ueda bring dinner to the table, and they sat down to eat.

"I'm afraid the pork is altogether too dry," Mrs. Ueda said.

"No, it's delicious. And so kind of you to have it waiting for me."

"I'm afraid I haven't the knack for domesticity like Nakamoto-sensei."

"I wondered if you have a certain print of hers, by Yoshitoshi—the fox woman leaving her child."

"I do not have such a one by any artist. I would recall the subject." Mrs. Ueda filled her mouth with pork and, chewing, studied Barbara. "How have you heard of this print?"

"Michi-san and I had several conversations about foxes—she told me her mother claimed to understand their language. I happen to have a fox woman scroll with me that my mother got here years ago, and I'm interested in all those stories." She took a deep breath; she was babbling. "I know that Michi-san had this print at one time."

"Perhaps it was lost in wartime. So many things were lost in war."

When she went back upstairs, Barbara took the black bag to the three-mat room. She pulled open the bottom drawer of the tansu and began unwrapping Chie's bottles in order. There was nothing unusual inside the first few papers: no fox woman print, just the sheets of calligraphy she'd come to expect.

The writing on the 1939 paper was strange, more like random brushstrokes than calligraphy. The same was true of the sheets wrapped around the next few bottles.

There were no wines for the years 1943 or '44. The 1945 bottle had several thicknesses of paper around it. Maybe the print was here. She peeled off layer after layer of blank rice paper. There must be something important inside.

The final layer was soft white cloth; the bottle beneath it felt lumpy and strange. She laid it on the tatami to undo the cord and cloth. For a moment she stared, her mind moving slowly. The bottle was empty, its sides fused together. The glass looked squeezed, as though by a huge hand, and the neck was twisted back against itself. She stood, dizzy, and walked into the kitchen. She turned on the water and held her hands beneath it, then put her hands to her face. The bottle had been melted in the bombing. Maybe it was from Michi's house.

The newsreel image of the rising mushroom-shaped cloud came to her mind. Michi was down below it somewhere. Kneeling, screaming, her hands over her ears. Seiji was there too, just a young boy.

She went into the large tatami room. Everything had gone flat, as if she were walking around inside a picture. She picked up one of Seiji's bowls from the tokonoma, set it back down.

In the small room by the tansu the misshapen bottle lay on its cloth like a deformed fetus. She covered it quickly, returned it to the chest, and closed the drawer. She took a bottle of opened wine from the top drawer and drank from it, gulping it down. She should have waited until Seiji was with her before opening that bottle. Nineteen forty-five. She should have known.

Around her was a litter of papers and bottles. All the drawers of the chest sagged open. The air seemed heavy, pressing her down.

It was just growing dark. She pushed up the window as far as it would go. Nearby, a bird was singing, a liquid glide up and down. Some lovebird, I think, Seiji had said. The odor of woodsmoke began to drift up through the open door. Sato-san was making a fire for the bath.

She wrapped the rest of the 1930s bottles, the early 1940s. The sounds she made with the paper seemed magnified by the quiet, complete except for the sound of that bird, more distant now.

The fox print could be with one of Michi-san's own journal entries. She took out the 1949 bottle; it had to be Michi's, since her mother had died soon after the war. The 1949 bottle was also enclosed in several thicknesses of paper. She removed them carefully, four pages, the outer one blank, the other three filled with calligraphy. No print.

The 1951 wine had only one sheet of writing inside the outer paper, but she was astonished to find a photograph stuck to the bottle. She peeled the picture off carefully and held it in the palm of her hand: Michi and Ume. Michi was bending down to direct Ume's somber face toward the camera. Ume looked to be three or four, wearing a flowered dress and a big bow in her hair. Her head wasn't small—if anything her face seemed rather large. She had a sharp chin like Michi's. Barbara looked at the background, the bridge in the far distance. It was the Golden Gate Bridge. San Francisco. She felt a jolt of excitement, seeing them there. Michi had probably been in California that year; most likely she had written about it. She'd have this paper translated next.

There was nothing but calligraphy around the next few bottles. Then, beneath the 1955 paper, she found a photograph of Michi, Ume, and Seiji, kneeling together at a table. They seemed to be in the middle of lunch or dinner; Michi and Seiji had paused for the photograph but Ume was bending forward slightly, noodles dangling from her chopsticks. Michi was looking at Ume with a worried little smile—not unlike the way she'd looked at Barbara sometimes. Seiji was slightly apart from them and facing straight ahead. He looked uncomfortable, the outsider in this threesome.

She discovered one other photograph, beneath the paper of the last bottle to be unwrapped, 1959. It was of Seiji alone. He stood unsmiling, regal in a black kimono, before a glass case of tea bowls, probably an exhibition of his work. It looked as if it were a triumphant occasion, but his expression was solemn.

She thought of last night, how little he'd said. Perhaps it was characteristic. Perhaps he became more reserved when moved. The building was steeped in silence. A line from Lawrence Durrell came to her mind: "Does not everything depend upon our interpretation of the silence around us?"

She jumped up, hurried to the kitchen, and turned on the

radio. With the Mamas and the Papas singing in the background, she opened the black bag and removed the roll of papers she'd taken to Hakone. She began wrapping the Hakone papers around their bottles and putting them away. The 1961 paper seemed to be missing.

She felt inside the black bag and the side compartment—empty. Maybe she'd accidentally put the paper inside another one. She pulled open the bottom drawer of the tansu and took out the 1930s bottles again, unwrapping each one and looking at the dates on the back of the papers. She undid the 1960 bottle: only the one page. She felt beneath the tansu, then moved the tansu and searched behind it. She looked around the room. The paper was not here.

She hadn't taken out the papers on the train, just the notebook. The 1961 paper must still be at Hakone.

Barbara ran downstairs and picked up the phone. Speaking softly so Mrs. Ueda wouldn't hear, she managed to get through to the long-distance operator and then to the Akai Hana ryokan. Mr. Kawabata answered the phone.

"Kawabata-sensei—Jefferson Barbara desu."

"Ah!" he said, laughing. "Fox call to me on telephone."

I have lost something, she tried to say in Japanese—a paper—then repeated it in English. "A paper, I have lost a paper."

"You are lost?" he said.

"No—no. Sumimasen. Paper—do you have a writing I left behind? You were translating, with Okada Seiji. Do you have my paper?"

"No, no paper here."

The 1961 paper was the one Seiji had read to himself that day in the apartment and would not translate. Maybe he had taken it.

"Okada Seiji—Mashiko no denwa ..." She knew the words for telephone and have, but couldn't remember how to say telephone number. "Mashiko denwa arimasuka?"

"Mashiko denwa? Wakarimasen." He didn't understand.

"Mashiko denwa," she said again, almost shouting. "Denwa, please, onegai shimasu."

Mrs. Ueda's door opened. She was wearing her pink bathrobe and a towel wrapped around her head. "Is there some problem?" she said.

"A paper ... it's lost." She said good-bye to Mr. Kawabata and hung up.

"I am so sorry. Your paper was of great significance, I'm afraid."

"Maybe I left it on the train."

"If so, they will have saved it for you. Shall I telephone?"

"Yes—I'd appreciate that so much."

Mrs. Ueda made calls to several offices of the railway line and—just in case she'd lost the paper coming back from Tokyo—to the commuter train bureau for missing articles.

Mrs. Ueda hung up, shaking her head. "They have not been able to locate your document, I regret to say."

Barbara looked past Mrs. Ueda. Seiji must have taken it.

"You mentioned an Okada Seiji, I believe. Is this the Okada from Takanodai?"

"Yes."

"I see."

"I happened to run into him up there."

Mrs. Ueda stared at her.

"I met him at the college festival. We had a lot to talk about, since he was Michi-san's student."

"I see," Mrs. Ueda said again.

"Well, good night," Barbara said. "Thank you for your help."

"Do take care of yourself," Mrs. Ueda said.

"Please don't worry. I'll be all right."

In her apartment, she looked through the bag again, and once more went through the papers she'd taken to Hakone, all the while knowing it was futile. The 1961 paper was gone.

17

Barbara spent the next morning trying to reach Seiji, using the phone in the classroom building so Mrs. Ueda couldn't hear. There was no answer at his house until noon. She was sorry, his aunt said in a cool voice, a telephone number for him at Mashiko was not available.

"When you do speak to him," Barbara said, "would you please tell him I'm in Tokyo? He thinks I'm in Kyoto."

"Not in Kyoto," his aunt said. "Is there some further message?"

"No, no thank you."

After she hung up, Barbara went to her office and sat at her desk. Maybe she could write a note to him about the missing paper and take it to his house. She took out a sheet of paper, wrote "Dear Seiji," then crumpled it up. She'd find another translator, a professional with whom there would be no messy entanglements. Someone anonymous, discreet. Someone she could trust. That librarian Michi had introduced her to at the International House in downtown Tokyo should be able to recommend someone. She'd spend the night there; it would be good to get away, instead of waiting for a call.

In her apartment, she pulled open the top drawer of the tansu. The 1961 bottle looked naked, bare dark glass in the row of wrapped wines. She took the papers from the 1960 and 1962 bottles, rolled them together, and put them in the black bag with her overnight things. At the last minute she added the 1951 paper and headed for the train station.

The accommodations of the International House felt like home—twin beds, an armchair, a Western-style private bath with hot water. She lay down on one of the beds, exhausted; her body ached all over, as if she were coming down with something.

When she woke it was after five. The library would be closed. At least she could have a peaceful evening here. She took a long shower, washing her hair with the Prell shampoo she'd picked up at the American Pharmacy. The smell of the shampoo reminded her of Allen Haywood, her first kiss. They'd been standing on the front steps of her house, grinning at each other. Suddenly his mouth was on hers, and his hands in her hair. She'd been surprised by the way her whole body came alive. "I loved that," she'd said.

The news came on as she was getting dressed for dinner. The Senate had rejected an amendment repealing the Gulf of Tonkin Resolution. Defense Secretary Robert McNamara announced 20,000 additional troops would be called up, to join the 215,000 already in Vietnam. Allen hadn't gone to college; maybe he was in Vietnam. She snapped off the radio and went downstairs to the restaurant.

The dining room was crowded; there were no vacant tables. A Cambodian man sitting alone asked her to join him. He was handsome, in a rather fussy way, glossy hair, a brilliant smile, an ascot he kept straightening.

They exchanged names and occupations: he was in the diplomatic service, at the International House for a meeting that had just ended. "I'll be staying on awhile, however," he added. "May I ask you, are you entirely on your own?"

"I'm not married, if that's what you mean." There was no reason she shouldn't go out with him. He was probably intelligent; she'd learn some interesting things about Cambodia. She and Seiji had no commitment.

Their food came. He inquired after the quality of her meal in a seductive, mellifluous voice. After the waiter had cleared their plates, he edged closer. "Will you have some brandy, Miss Jefferson? I have a fine Courvoisier upstairs."

"No thank you," she said, picking up her pocketbook from the next chair. He must think an American woman was an easy mark.

He put his arms on the table and leaned forward. "In that case, shall we explore the Tokyo nightlife together?"

"I have an early meeting in the morning."

"Next evening, perhaps."

She shook her head and looked around for the waiter. "I'm very busy right now."

"This is regrettable." He leaned back in his chair, his arms across his chest. "If you have just one moment to spare, please tell me, if you would, Miss Jefferson, what is your opinion of American imperialist policy regarding Vietnam?"

She gave him her coldest look. "You practice a strange form of diplomacy."

"Legislators of the world, America," he spluttered, throwing up his hands. "America the all-knowing!"

She signed her check and fled upstairs.

What a horrible man. She got into bed with her *Time* magazine to blot him out of her mind, but the lead article was about the Senate hearings on Vietnam. She flipped a few pages. Cassius Clay was complaining about the draft. She threw the magazine on the floor and switched off the light.

More and more, people wanted to argue with her about the war; she needed to be better informed. She turned onto her other side. The bed wasn't as comfortable as a futon. The futon at the inn had been luxurious, thicker than the one at Sango-kan. She thought of Seiji beside her in the dark, his breath against her ear. Balabala-san. The missing paper could easily have rolled under the table, accidentally left behind. Or he might have borrowed it; he would feel he had the right. She thought back to their conversations about the tansu, how upset he'd been that she was the one to receive the papers. It was as if they were brother and sister, squabbling over an inheritance.

If only she knew what was on that 1961 page. The year, the weather: beyond that she could not imagine. She tried to remember what the writing had looked like, but she'd only seen it once, when packing for Hakone.

She dreamed she was sleeping with Seiji, their naked bodies covered with writing. The language seemed like English, but she could not quite make it out. When she bent forward to decipher the words, they began to fade, then sank into their flesh.

The librarian, a beautiful woman with a pale oval face and narrow eyes, remembered Michi's introducing Barbara to her in the fall. Yes, she had heard of Nakamoto-sensei's death, she said; it had greatly saddened her. When Barbara explained—without mentioning the author—her need to find a translator for an archaic text, she began making phone calls. "I have found the perfect one," she soon reported. "Mr. Natsume Wada, a scholar of Noh drama. He lives not far from your college, at Higashi Koganei. As it happens, he can meet you this afternoon."

Mr. Wada lived in an apartment above a sweet-shop called Golden Farce. He was a chain-smoker, a sallow, plump, and tired-looking little man. Barbara sat with him in a Western-style room in his apartment facing an open window. His wife brought tea and éclairs from the shop below. Barbara bit into the pastry—stale with a gluey yellow filling—and set it down again. "Not good," Mrs. Wada said, mournfully shaking her head.

"Oh no, it's good—excellent," Barbara said, and, with the tea, managed several more bites.

Mr. Wada invited Barbara into his study. They sat down, he behind his desk, she in an uncomfortable chair facing it. She looked through the papers—1960 and 1962, written before and after the missing page—and 1951, when Michi had apparently been in San Francisco. She handed him the 1960 page. "This isn't in kanbun," she said, "but I may bring others that are."

He unrolled the paper and smoothed it out on his desk, smoking as he began to read. Barbara watched the growing ash on his cigarette. When ash fell on the paper, she quickly leaned forward and brushed it away. "Please be careful," she said. "This is a very important paper."

He looked up at her. "How have you happened to possess this writing, may I ask?"

"A friend gave it to me."

"I understand," he said, nodding; he looked as if he understood something was not as it should be.

He put down the cigarette and spread his hands over the paper like a fortune-teller. "This woman has a troubled heart. She speaks of Ume, a retarded daughter. There are some touching bits of writing, and a haiku as well: that is to say, a Japanese poem written in a certain form."

"Yes, I know about haiku—and haikai and tanka."

"It is hard for a Westerner to understand the allusions," he said.

"I'm quite familiar with Japanese literature."

"But you don't read Japanese?"

"I'm afraid not. Only in translation."

"Ah," he said, lighting another cigarette. "Naturally this is not the same at all."

"No," she admitted, "it's not."

He smiled, covering his mouth. "I offer lessons in Japanese language, should you care to undertake a study in the future." When she did not respond, he looked back down at the paper. "I cannot promise to render haiku in precise form, syllable count and so on."

"Just the general meaning would be fine. What does it say?"

"I will type out for you."

"I have two others," she said, pulling out the 1962 and 1951 papers.

He unfurled the papers and scanned each one. "California!" he said, smiling at her when he looked at the second page.

"Actually, could you do that one first?" The photograph of Michi and Ume by the Golden Gate Bridge had been a clue, as she'd guessed.

"As you prefer. This will take some time, however, to make three translations. Shall you come back in, say, two hours or so?"

"I'll just wait if you don't mind."

While he typed, she took out her *Time* magazine but kept an eye on the cigarette, which he alternately held in his mouth and in his right hand, above the papers.

Finally he pulled a single-spaced sheet from his typewriter and handed it to her.

"January the second, 1951," she read. "This New Year I find myself in Berkeley, California, where Professor Ota, my kind teacher at Kodaira, has arranged for my graduate studies, a pursuit of which Mother always coldly disapproved. Mother would be pleased, however, that I plan to look for Grandmother Ko, sent to San Francisco as a picture bride many years ago."

"Wow," she said aloud. When Mr. Wada looked up at her she said, "This is wonderful. Thank you so much."

"I am sure is not so good," he said with a little bow. "However, I always try my best." He gave another bow to indicate he wished to return to work.

She bent back over the page. "Before Father died in past year he gave to me a letter written by Grandmother Ko from California in 1940. Although the letter was sent to Great-grandfather Takasu, he later passed it to Father.

"Largest mistake of his life, Father said, was to show this letter to Mother. Father had thought it would be some comfort to know Ko was still living. Instead it drove her to dementia and Father thinks hastened her death. She could not believe her living mother would so forget her, not even to inquire after her well-being. Ko has been in spirit world for long time, she insisted, and from there made her many visitations.

"I am determined that I in Mother's place must find some trace of Ko, and understand her life. I think it is possible that Ko is still alive, for she would be in about her sixties. According to letter, she had two sons and one young daughter, and she had gained some reputation as poet of tanka and haiku. It seems her husband died just before the year 1940, and left her in state of impoverishment. Father told me that Great-grandfather Takasu sent money to her until outbreak of war with America."

Great-grandfather Takasu must have been Ko's father-in-law. She thought of the early papers she and Seiji had read, the father-in-law opposing exorcism. He'd arranged the marriage to save her life.

"In spite of my resolve, I have made little progress in my search, only two phone calls to persons in San Francisco named Yokogawa."

Yokogawa. Ko Yokogawa, a melodic name; she sounded like a poet. With growing excitement, Barbara read on.

"Both persons say they do not know my relative but one suggests to visit the Japantown area in San Francisco to make inquiries.

"I find myself too busy, and torn in bits, trying to research my thesis and attend my class, while knowing how Ume suffers. I have found young Japanese girl, Tomoe, to stay with her. Though she is kind and cheerful she does not have experience to care for such a child. When I arrive home Ume clings to me for life. I tell her not to worry, in summer we will explore beautiful California together, and maybe find Great-grandmother."

Barbara read the page several times. She could picture Michi holding Ume, stroking her hair.

When Mr. Wada finished the other two papers, he folded them and put them in an envelope. In exchange she gave him the money envelope she had already prepared, with the amount of yen the librarian had suggested folded inside.

Outside she walked up and down the streets, not ready to read the other papers yet, or go home. She went into a noodle restaurant that reminded her of the one where she and Michi had gone in Kamakura. After ordering, she read the paper about California again. It was as if Michi were with her. She turned and looked through the window at people passing by, grateful to be present in this moment.

When she walked back to the station it was rush hour and the train going back to Kokubunji was crowded. She put the

1951 papers carefully in her pocketbook, then opened Mr. Wada's envelope and read his translation of the 1960 paper.

"This year I have helped Kondo-san make the mochi cakes." Who was Kondo-san? 1960. Michi was in Tokyo by then. Maybe Seiji's aunt. "She said perhaps I did not pound adequately, but my arms are tired. I suggested to her that we buy mochi from shop if these were not good ones and she was very sharp to me in her reply. As I felt unwell, I went to my room to rest on futon. I cannot help but cry. Ume lay down beside me, her face against mine. At moments such as these I cannot think of her as retarded. Understanding crosses between us like an electrical current."

"Then this haiku," Mr. Wada had written, "composed at the bottom of the page: 'White cloud of feathers / Captured by the trees . . . / Suddenly two birds break free into the air.' "

The train stopped. With a whoosh, the doors opened, and people pressed off and on.

As they started up again, Barbara looked at the poem, thinking of the photograph of Ume and Michi at the egret rookery; it must refer to that somehow.

"Hello, Miss."

She glanced up. Hanging onto the straps next to her were two American servicemen. They introduced themselves, Jim from Macon, Georgia; Coleman from Ames, Iowa, both on R & R from Vietnam. Barbara told them she was from North Carolina. "I just knew you was a southern girl," Jim said, grinning. "I bet you were Queen of the May at your high school too. What are you doing over here?" When she said she was an English teacher, Jim said, "Uh oh. I better watch what I say."

"How is it—what's it like in Vietnam?" Barbara asked.

They were silent, swaying in rhythm with the train. Coleman turned slightly away and looked out the opposite window.

Barbara stared at Jim's clean-shaven face, his thin neck, the Adam's apple that moved up and down as he swallowed. "There ain't no way to describe it." His small, marblelike blue eyes were fixed on the distance.

The train began to slow for the Kokubunji stop. "I'm sorry—I have to get off here," Barbara said.

"You know what I think about?" Jim said, his face suddenly alive. "Barbecue. When are you going back to the States?"

"I don't know—maybe this summer."

"When you get home, have a barbecue sandwich for me."

"I sure will—I'll do that." She shook hands with Coleman, then Jim.

Jim held onto her hand for a few moments, his palm growing damp. "Would you mind—" He swallowed hard, grinned at his buddy. "How about a kiss—for luck?"

Barbara glanced around the car: no one she recognized. "Sure," she said. "Okay." He put one arm around her, quickly pressed his lips against hers, and stepped back.

She squeezed his hand. "Good luck," she said, "to both of you."

The train had stopped. She went down the steps and turned to wave. The soldiers leaned forward, their hands raised. She had a glimpse of their smiling, anxious faces, then they were gone. The orange train clattered away, leaving behind an unnatural silence. Strange to kiss someone, then never see him again. The crowd streamed past her, a mass of black-haired people with closed, anonymous faces. She turned and let herself be carried along.

By the time the bus came, it was nearly dark. She took a seat near the rear, opened the envelope, and read the second sheet Mr. Wada had translated.

"Showa 37—1962

"A melancholy New Year, no calls or gifts. Outside my window, there is a steady drip of rain.

"Ume paces our room like an animal in confinement. A thorn grows in her heart. At night I hear her call out in her sleep, 'No, No.' When I wake her she begins to cry, but cannot speak. I am demon mother, to have caused her this.

"My own mother comes so often to my thoughts in these days it seems as if she wills it so. Absent though she was from me in life, with her face turned to the past, I cannot forget how she knew my gravest distress and succored me. I feel her attempt to do so once again."

"As before," Mr. Wada had written, "we have haiku in conclusion. 'Plum blossoms drift / White as bone / The rain drives silver needles through my heart.' "

Barbara refolded the paper. What could she mean, "demon mother"? Maybe bringing Ume into the world in such conditions. Not that she could help it: an atomic bomb falling on Hiroshima. She got off at the Kodaira College stop and walked slowly across the campus to Sango-kan, her body filled with sorrow.

18

The next morning Barbara found a telegram under her door: "Please come Mashiko. Ride Tohoku line from Ueno #13, then Mito line to Mashiko. There is Ryokan Shirakawa. Innkeeper will call to me. Come I am urgent. Miss Dear Jefferson. Truly, Okada Seiji."

Barbara read the message through once more. Miss Dear Jefferson. He urgently wanted her to come. She pushed back the kitchen curtains. He knew she was in Tokyo. Maybe his aunt had told him. Or he had guessed. It didn't matter. The day was beautiful, the sky cloudless. She could be out of here in thirty minutes, at the inn by tonight. He'd explain about the missing paper.

She packed her clothes—enough for a week—and headed downstairs. In the vestibule she wrote a note to Mrs. Ueda telling her that she was making a brief trip and put the note in Mrs. Ueda's cubby. Maybe she should run back upstairs and get some of Michi's papers. He'd be interested in Michi's search for Ko in California. She could ask him to explain the background of the 1960 and 1962 papers, though maybe that was clear from the 1961 writing. She'd have to keep a neutral face when he translated the papers that Mr. Wada had already typed out for her.

A door opened at the far end of the hall; she slipped outside. Seiji hadn't mentioned the papers. It was she he urgently wanted to see. She sprinted down the driveway toward the street.

Mashiko was a couple of hours northwest of Tokyo. In Mito she changed to a train pulled by a steam engine. It was like going back in time, with cinders blowing in through the open window and, in the fields, farmers in straw hats planting rice. The inn would be old-fashioned, discreet, two futons placed together. There would be a bathtub made of smooth hinoki wood, and a real kotatsu in their room. They would sit with their feet above the coals, the warmth traveling up their legs.

In Mashiko, the streets were full of pottery set out on tables and benches; inside the open doors of houses she could see potters working at wheels, glazing, pounding clay. On the hillsides were rows of low, rounded clay kilns. The inn was above the village, secluded in a grove of trees, as she'd imagined.

The innkeeper, a young woman in country-style pants, led Barbara to a large tatami room. Barbara sat at the table while the woman poured tea and set out some bean cakes. "Okada Seiji?" Barbara said. "He is expecting me," she added in Japanese.

"Hai, hai." The woman bowed and went to telephone him.

After about twenty minutes the door to her room slid open. Seiji bowed. "I am glad you have come," he said. "My feeling is unspeakable."

She jumped up, laughing. "I am glad too," she said.

They sat down on opposite sides of the table. "I have some gift for you," Seiji said, taking a small, ceremonially wrapped package from his furoshiki. She opened it, inhaling the delicate fragrance of sandalwood. Inside was a fan, an ink painting of mountains and clouds on heavy rice paper. "This is my impression of Mashiko," Seiji said. "I hope you will find Mashiko beautiful place. More beautiful than Hakone."

It seemed to be an apology. "Thank you," she said.

The innkeeper came in with more tea and a cup for Seiji; she left without speaking, sliding the door shut behind her.

Barbara poured out the tea. "What shall we do first?" she said. "Will you give me a tour of Mashiko?"

"Unfortunately this afternoon I must return to Hamada-sensei's studio—there is a kiln opening."

"But—" She set her tea down so hard it spilled onto the table. "You said it was so urgent that I come."

"Yes. I must see you."

"Well here I am."

"I did not know opening would be today. I am sorry. It is my fault you are angry."

She said nothing.

He took out a scroll of paper from his furoshiki and set it before her. "I have made some translation for you," he said.

"Michi's paper!" She reached for it. "I've been so worried."

"In my haste to return to Mashiko I forgot to mention. I am sorry you had cause for alarm."

"I'm just glad to have it now."

She unrolled the paper. Inside Michi's calligraphy was his translation written out on a sheet of lined paper. "Thank you," she said.

"Daijobu," he said. "It is nothing."

She read the translation through: The New Year was busy and the weather quite fine. The plums had been abundant that year. Michi had published an essay on Commodore Perry and had been invited to a conference in San Francisco, which she had been unable to attend. Ume was keeping well. There was no hint as to why Michi might have felt like a demon mother the next year, no expression of feeling at all.

"You were so interested in this one," she said, looking closely at the page. "When you first read it you seemed fascinated, but you didn't translate it."

"I don't recall," he said, frowning. "Of course I was very shocked and surprised by these papers. This has made me unable to speak at first."

"Yes, I can understand that." She put his translation inside the paper and slowly rolled it back up.

He came to kneel beside her. She pushed herself up to her knees and looked into his grave, dark eyes. He kissed her and they embraced, holding on so tight she could feel his heart against hers.

"I will return in evening," he whispered.

She had dinner looking out at the light fading from the sky. By the time the maid came to arrange her futon it was dark. She undressed, got into bed, and tried to read. It was after eleven when she turned off the lamp. She'd been a fool to come running up here, at his beck and call, her mother would say.

She was almost asleep when she heard the outside door open.

"Seiji?"

His dark shape moved across the tatami; he shed his clothes and slid into the futon beside her.

"Kirekitsu-san," he whispered, putting one arm around her.

"What if I'd gone," she said, "and someone else was here?"

He laughed. "This would be shock. Very sad shock," he added. "All day I am thinking of you."

"Then why didn't you come sooner?"

"I must wait until innkeeper is sleeping. Very long wait."

He whispered something in Japanese and began to untie her yukata.

"What did you say?"

"I think you are possessing me." He covered her mouth with his.

In the morning the shoji door glowed with soft light, the shadow of a pine tree just visible against it. He kissed the back of her neck. "Let us dress now," he said in a low voice. "I will go out and enter ryokan through front entrance. I can say I have come to have breakfast with you."

"They won't know you were here?"

"Perhaps. But they will not have to acknowledge."

They turned away from each other to dress. He opened the door, jumped down, and walked around to the front of the inn. Soon Barbara heard the cheerful voice of the innkeeper welcoming him. Seiji entered the room.

While the innkeeper went to get breakfast they sat in awkward silence.

"How was the kiln opening?" she finally said.

"Very good. There are many fine pieces. Today I must help further."

"Now?"

"I am sorry to say so, yes."

"I can't stand your coming and going like this. Why did you leave so suddenly from Hakone?"

"This is my flaw. It cannot be helped."

"What do you mean?"

"I am afraid I cannot love someone."

She opened and closed her fan, willing back tears. "But yesterday you said your feeling was ... and last night ... I don't understand."

"This is my flaw," he said again in a low voice.

The innkeeper came in with the breakfast, then went out again.

They ate in silence. He avoided her eyes. She could feel him drifting away from her.

"Why don't I help you today?" she said.

"In kilns?"

"Yes. Why not?"

"This is dirty work. You will spoil your dress."

"I don't mind."

They walked down a side road toward the studio. Hamada was sitting at an outdoor wheel, studying a bowl he had just made. A large man with a broad smiling face, he reminded Barbara of a jolly monk. Seiji was nervous, introducing her, but Hamada seemed delighted, looking her up and down. "We have new apprentice," he said.

Seiji and Barbara joined two other of Hamada's assistants at the kilns. It was difficult work, crawling into the low clay structures and bringing out the fired pieces one at a time. Each bowl and plate had to be cleaned and carried down the hill to the studio. She and Seiji fell into a rhythm, working together. By the end of the afternoon she was tired but content; he had let her enter his world. Before they left, Hamada presented her with one of his bowls, luminous black with touches of red.

That night Seiji again came into her room long after dark, through the shoji door. He was wearing a yukata and his hair was damp from the bath. There were traces of dried clay on his fingers, making them a little rough, like a loofah, as he stroked her face, her arms, her breasts. She felt as if she were clay being reshaped in his hands.

They were still, their arms around each other, then he sat up and lit a cigarette. He looked down at her, stroking her hair.

"When you said you cannot love someone," she said, "did

you mean you are afraid to love someone? I think that's been true for me."

He turned away to stub out the cigarette in the ashtray. "Maybe if I explain my life, you can understand me."

"I want to understand."

He lay beside her on his back. She could just make out his profile in the dark.

"As you know, I was born in the city of Hiroshima."

"Yes." She touched his hand.

"On the day of the bombing—there was something strange." He ran his hands through his hair and gave a nervous-sounding laugh. "I had toothache. Mother tied warm cloth against my jaw and said I must stay at home. Usually I would go with Father and young sister Itsuko to center of city where we were tearing down houses to make fire lane. This was because of bombing which was expected every day—Hiroshima had not suffered bombing like Tokyo and almost every other place. Father thinks I can work that day but Mother argues I cannot. I keep my long face when Father and Itsuko leave house but really I am happy not to work so hard that day." He sat up to light another cigarette, then lay back down.

"Of course you were happy not to work ..." She propped herself on her elbow to look down at him.

"Don!" She jumped as he hit the floor with one hand. "Suddenly, whole house was shaking. Maybe some terrible earthquake, I thought. I ran outdoor. Next to our house Nakamoto-sensei's house had tumbled partway down."

"Was Michi-san there?"

"No, she lived with in-law family, and her parents by lucky chance were away. Then I see huge black cloud rising high above city. Maybe ammunition plant has been bombed, but why no air raid noise? Soon whole sky is black. There is terrible silence. I ran down hill from Koi toward city. Everywhere was thick smoke, fallen houses. In city people in road dead or dying. Some people . . ." He paused. "I could not believe were human being—melted skin hanging from their arms. One of them spoke my name but I did not know him. He was burnt black as if fallen into hibachi."

Shivering, she lay down, her face against his arm. She imagined him running through the smoke, hand over his mouth, just a young boy. "Did you find your family?"

"I ran toward place of fire lane but everything is gone, buildings fallen down or burning. Maybe Father and Itsuko have run to river where many have jumped in to escape fires. I look in rivers and along streets. Finally I go to hospital. There I am happy to find Mother, but she is blinded by glass from streetcar and badly burned. She cries because she cannot see to help me search for Father and Itsuko.

"Outside hospital cremation pyre is burning. I think to throw myself there. If I had not complained of childish tooth ache Mother would not be blinded. It should have been myself, not sister, in fire lane. But I must take care of Mother and I must find Itsuko and Father. For weeks I walked through ruins of Hiroshima to find some sign of them but I cannot. Later we realized their bodies were incinerated in an instant."

They lay without speaking. Her chest felt painfully full.

He stubbed out his cigarette. "Itsuko-san should have remained at home, not her big brother." He put his hands over his face. "She has died in my place. Father must be ashamed of me." He pulled on his yukata and began to pace around the room.

"I thought I would find some remain of theirs, my sister's lunchbox or Father's watch. This was my obsession. There were many scavengers, orphans, and thieves from other towns.

I was sure one of them has taken my father's watch. I ask everyone I meet, even in black market, Who has seen a fine gold watch with sketch of Inland Sea engraved on its cover?"

"Did you find it?"

"No. I cannot." He came back to the futon and, squatting beside it, lit a fresh cigarette. He remained squatting, rocking slightly back and forth as he smoked. "One day I met a collector of shadows."

"What do you mean?"

"Some people—like Father and Itsuko—were vaporized in an instant by the bomb. Some left their shadows on the street or steps of buildings. Shadow collector chopped out some of these strange portraits and took them to his home. I began to help him with his work. I knew I would find shadow of at least my sister. I imagined how her silhouette would look, her head raised to see white parachute falling. I imagined she was looking at it closely so she could tell me later. Itsuko liked to tell her big brother things that she had seen," he said with a catch in his voice.

She moved closer and put her arms around him. They rocked back and forth together.

"Very long story," he said, pulling away from her. "I am afraid you may be tired."

"No," she said, "never." She touched his face. He took her hand and kissed it.

"How did you ... go on, after that?" she asked.

"Eventually my mother and I moved to aunt's house in Fukuyama, a small town on inland sea north of Hiroshima, where air was fresher.

"During this time I was away from Hiroshima I dreamed of it every night. I had little appetite even for the better food we had in Fukuyama. I became feverish and began to develop some boil on my skin. The family's doctor said I had atom bomb disease and my bones were melting. I might not live to see twenty years. Only hope for cure was rest in bed and cauterization with moxa—also drink what he called miracle green juice. This was from leaf of kale which aunt began to grow and ground up into juice for me. I spent five years as invalid."

"Five years—until you were eighteen." An entire adolescence spent in bed. "But you got well."

"The doctor was wrong. I was not so ill. Nakamoto-sensei persuaded aunt to take me to Red Cross Hospital in Hiroshima. There it was told by radiation doctor that my bones were not melting. Boils on skin had been only passing trouble. I was going to live."

"You must have been so happy—you and your family—and Nakamoto-sensei."

He shook his head. "I was ashamed. After years of lying in bed, I was ashamed. Also angry. I hate my thin body, now pale and weak. Such a weak man," he said, raising his voice, "alive only because of toothache. I did not explain my aunt and mother why I insist to walk home from Hiroshima, a distance of forty kilometers. At first I must sit down every hour, my legs feel like tofu. But I grow stronger. It takes me some weeks but I accomplish the walk home. My feet are so blistered I have to cut shoes away from them. After that time I walk each day, for months I walked until I was strong. I walked to chase away my anger too but it was to no effect."

They got back into the futon beneath the covers. "I am very selfish person as you now see. I could think of nothing but how angry I am. I had little education and no training for a job. I had a body of a man and yet was no man. I wished to be older and killed in war. One day I had dispute with aunt and I left Fukuyama. I walked north. I refused to take any transport. I determined to go to Tokyo to live; there I would find some job and not depend on aunt and mother and charity of neighbors."

"I think you were strong," she said. "Not selfish."

He did not seem to have heard. "On my way I tried to work wherever I can, but there are few jobs at that time, soon after war. I happened to stop in small village near base of Fuji-san where there was a potter at work. He let me try to throw pot." He gestured with his hands, as though holding a bowl. "I liked this and he said I had fine hand. This man had studied here at Mashiko. He suggest I may try this too. So when I walked north I went around edge of Tokyo and on to this place.

"It was spring when I arrived here, like now, green and peaceful place as you can see. It did not seem to ever heard of war. I walked through streets of Mashiko with tears on my face. Eventually I became apprentice to Hamada-sensei and remained three years working with him."

He looked at her. "So now you hear my life. I am surprised how much I say. No scar on outside. Some hibakusha has scar only on inside. I have not told this to anyone outside Hiroshima."

"I have no words to say how honored I am—" She fell silent. "Do all hibakusha ... find love impossible?" she asked.

He was quiet a moment. "Maybe you cannot understand."

She drew in a sharp breath. "But I'm *trying*..."

He took her hand. "Hai," he said. "You try very hard, I think."

The next afternoon Barbara helped Seiji package clay haniwa for shipping. They worked in a small studio, a windowless space with a dirt floor and the front side open to the road. There was a companionable silence between them as they lined boxes with stiff shredded papers and laid the haniwa figures inside. There were images of feudal soldiers, horses, and one Barbara remembered seeing at Seiji's studio, a woman carrying a baby on her back. Her mouth was open—for singing, Seiji said, though it looked to her as if the woman were wailing. She kept thinking of Michi in Hiroshima, holding her hands over her belly to protect Ume, and of Seiji, running through the black smoke.

It began to rain, large drops at first, pocking the dirt road in front of the studio. Seiji made tea and they sat down to drink it, looking out at the rain. Small birds were flitting about in the thicket of trees across the road.

"I wish to understand your life as well," he said.

"What has happened in my life is very ordinary in comparison to yours."

"My life would be ordinary if not for meeting with atom bomb." He looked at her. "Please tell me of your home."

She told him about growing up in Raleigh, the house on Stone Street, her mother's Japanese garden. "The real reason I came to Japan was to search for my mother—though I wasn't aware of that at first. And then I found Michi-san instead."

"I see." He studied her thoughtfully.

They fell silent, gazing out at the rain. She thought of Michi in California. Maybe looking for Ko had been a welcome distraction for her, after Hiroshima. She wished she'd brought the next paper about California for Seiji to translate. It was odd that he'd chosen the 1961 paper to read; at Hakone, they'd been working on Chie's papers. He could have translated the next one in sequence. "By the way," she said, "I didn't bring any more papers."

"We are not bored, I think."

She looked at him, his fine profile, the line of his jaw. The morning he lay in bed with his toothache he never could have predicted that in an instant his childhood would be shattered, his world gone. We are all so vulnerable, she thought, everyone; not just to bombs but to all kinds of calamity and change.

Tears gathered beneath her eyelids. It was a terrible waste, to live in fear of love.

That night as they lay on the futon with their arms around each other, she asked why his feeling for her was unspeakable.

"I do not know how to explain."

"Even in Japanese?"

"Even in Japanese."

"I feel unspeakable about you too," she said. "Very unspeakable."

He laughed, kissing her.

"Will you give me more lessons in pottery when we return to Tokyo?"

"Of course—now you are my apprentice, desho?"

"I hope you won't be so bossy," she said, keeping her voice light, "deciding which papers to read."

"Kirekitsu-san will decide," he said, pulling her toward him. "But I think we should continue as we were, with story of olden time."

PART TWO

19

CHIE'S JOURNAL, 1934

Michi is almost twelve years of age, but remains willful girl. She has blood of wild fox in her veins, from her grandmother Ko.

This New Year I have told Michi-chan the story of my long-ago surprise meeting with Ko. As a child, I enjoyed to jump off the bridge into the river in the hot summertime. One day I hit my head on a rock and was unconscious. A pretty lady pulled me out, a geisha, who took me to my house. That was when servant Roku told me about my mother Ko who was a fox and had taken up guise of geisha. Roku said when geisha left house that day she could see a white tip of fox tail beneath her kimono.

After the holiday was over and classes resumed in April, Barbara went to Seiji's house every weekend. In the early afternoon of Saturday or Sunday—and sometimes, both days—Barbara walked through the woods from the campus to Takanodai. During the first few weeks he would meet her at the front gate of his house and they walked through the courtyard to the tea house. Often he had a new piece of pottery to show her, and she brought him examples of calligraphy she was learning from Junko—fire, water, tree—each character practiced over and over with her brush until she was ready to execute it on a large piece of rice paper. *Bakeru*, for shape-shifting—she had a fox woman in mind—required only four strokes, but they were difficult ones that had to be exactly rendered. Junko told her that calligraphy when performed as an art may be interpreted by the individual—the important thing was to make each brushstroke using all her concentration of feeling. Barbara thought of Seiji, his breath against her ear, as she practiced *bakeru;* Junko had the final result mounted on a fine scroll bordered with handmade papers. Barbara gave it to Seiji with an awkward bow. "I don't know if you can read it, but it means bakeru—because you are transforming me too."

"This is very excellent," he said, looking suddenly shy; he hung the scroll in the tokonoma of the tea house.

CHIE'S JOURNAL, 1935

One day when Fumio supposed us going out to do New Year's errands, Michi and I made our way to the geisha quarters in Kamiya-cho. We went from house to house to find if anyone knows Ko, a beautiful woman from Izumo who may have become geisha. At each place I described her and told of the years-ago visit to my childhood home by a geisha who may have been a fox woman. Some laughed at my questions, I thought with some uneasiness. But at one house we met a geisha mother who invited us for refreshment. We looked to be weary, she said. We sat by the open shoji door looking out at the river. She seemed to draw me like magnet. Her face was that of an antique beauty, with a high brow and aristocratic nose. I asked if she was from Izumo or some other distant province. She replied that all geisha are from some other place than Hiroshima. As she was showing Michi to play the shamisen, an eerie mournful tune, I slipped out and left Michi to return on her own. When she returned crying some hours after, she said to me that she had become lost and very frightened. I instructed her that she must recover her fox instinct for finding the way. She is almost thirteen, too big to rely on me always.

During each visit Seiji prepared tea and Barbara took from her bag the paper she had brought. In April and early May these were all from Chie's journal. After arguing in favor of going back to Michi's papers—she was impatient to read the next California entry—she gave in to his wish to follow them in sequence. And then she was glad she had lost the debate, she was beginning to understand Michi's history, and why she'd left her the papers. Both she and Michi had a fox mother in their lineage, an inheritance of absence.

She and Seiji spent leisurely afternoons translating and drinking tea. When the light began to fade from the room, Seiji pulled their futon from the cupboard. "What if your mother or aunt should come out?" she asked one evening as they lay twined together after making love. "My aunt gives tea ceremony lessons in the mornings only, and lately she is not well. Don't be troubled," he murmured into her hair. "We can be private here."

One afternoon when they had just begun translating, they looked at each other and without speaking began to undress. She closed her eyes as he touched her. "Kirekitsu-san," he whispered into her mouth.

He lay on the tatami, she astride him. She kissed his eyelids, his mouth, his underarm, inhaling the musky scent.

There was a voice outside, high-pitched. "Shigeko-san!"

"Don't stop," he said. "It's only my mother. She will not come."

Her hair fell across his chest. He took a strand of it into his mouth.

A sound. Scritch-scritch.

"What's that?"

"She is raking gravel." He pulled her closer. "Never mind," he whispered, "never mind."

That night as they left the tea house he showed her a back entrance from the side street, a narrow grassy strip that ran behind the pottery. From then on Barbara took the narrow back path to and from the tea house; by the end of April the long grass had been flattened, as though by a fox moving along the edge of a field.

CHIE'S JOURNAL, 1936

Baby is to arrive in two months. Roku has brought small Inari shrine for my sitting room. She shows me how to rub belly of fox figure and then my own belly. The child will be a boy, Fumio is certain, but I think will be another girl. Roku says I must be correct, as child of fox woman and human union, as she believes me to be, has ability to foretell the future.

Between visits to the tea house, Barbara thought constantly of Seiji, holding in her mind each detail of their lovemaking, letting the moments unfold slowly like the fragrant dried flowers he sometimes put into her tea. As she walked about the campus, the spring air, like silk against her skin, became his touch. She began to imagine a life with him, perhaps part of the year in Mashiko, part in the U.S. He would be sought after as a teacher of ceramics; they could teach at the same college.

In conversation class she let the students choose their own topics for discussion. Arranged marriage was the favorite topic until U.S. planes began shelling communist targets in Cambodia. All the students who spoke up were opposed to the bombing and to America's intervention into what one girl called "a family dispute among the Vietnamese." Barbara withdrew from the debate, day after day listening to the conversation as through a filter.

In composition class, as the students worked on their short stories, she stared out the window and thought of Seiji. She had memorized every part of his body, the contours of his back and buttocks, his narrow chest, the soft hair around his navel. Their lovemaking had grown more passionate; she imagined sparks in the air around them, like the sparks around Hiroshi and Ko.

CHIE'S JOURNAL, 1937

Little daughter Haru is eight months old. When I am holding her to my breast my thoughts drift to mother Ko. One day I went to geisha district with Haru so she also can meet grandmother, but cannot find the house where she has been. No doubt it has vanished, a common fox trick. Michi had petulantly refused to come. She says she does not believe in fox grandmother. I tell her she is a foolish girl, and someday she will be grateful I have introduced her.

Fumio has been much melancholy. His friend Murayama the painter was stoned to death in a field after a rumor he has spoken against war. Fumio refuses to give up all metal objects for war effort and has buried his bronze image of god Ebisu behind the tea house. In a dream mother Ko spoke to me; she warns we must be circumspect.

*   *   *

The other inhabitants of Sango-kan began to comment indirectly on Barbara's absence during the weekends. Miss Yamaguchi stopped by to ask questions about American slang, but found she was "fleeting the coop." Mrs. Ueda gave her curious glances when they met in the hall.

It was in early May that Barbara first met Rie on the path to Takanodai. The hardwood trees, now in full leaf, and the thick evergreens made a twilight in the woods. She saw someone coming toward her on a bicycle. At first she thought it was a boy; the biker had short hair and was wearing long pants. She stepped to one side of the path.

"Jefferson-sensei."

"Rie!" The girl's stout legs were planted on both sides of the bike. Her face was ruddier than usual and sweat had dampened her bangs.

"Are you going to Takanodai or Tachikawa?" Rie asked.

"I'm just walking—for exercise. There's a restaurant in Takanodai—sometimes I like to eat there."

"I know this place," Rie said. "Owned by Okada, the potter."

"You know him?" Barbara could feel her voice giving her away.

"Yes," she said with a smile. "Sayonara, Sensei—have a fine lunch."

The next couple of times Barbara and Rie met on the path, Rie said, with that same smile, "Going to Okada place, Sensei?"

One day Barbara said, "What about you? I always see you here at about the same time."

"I have some work in Tachikawa."

"You have a job?" She didn't know any of the students had

jobs. It was her impression they were almost always on campus, studying in the library or in their dorms, except for occasional excursions into the city with groups of friends. "What do you do?"

"This is my secret—you may say my shadow life. Sensei, I have been thinking more closely about original sin. I would like to make my senior thesis on this topic. Can you help me?"

"Yes," Barbara said; before she could ask more questions, Rie nodded good-bye and rode away.

CHIE'S JOURNAL, 1938

Fumio will not say so but he is dispirited not to have son. Roku predicts I will give birth again before long. She confessed that she has been putting a drop of fox saliva in Fumio's sake each evening. This will make child come soon, strong baby boy.

One evening Miss Ota came to visit. "I do hope I'm not troubling you, my dear," she said when Barbara came to the door. "It's been quite some while since we have had one of our little chats."

They walked down the hall to the large tatami room. Miss Ota peered into the smaller, three-mat room.

"Oh, my!" she exclaimed, stepping inside. "You have foxes. I am astonished." She turned to Barbara. "In my home of rural Yonago there is much fox superstition even to this day, but I do not know how you have found such things in Tokyo. How did you become interested in Japanese fox?"

Barbara told her about the fox woman scroll, how it had been given to her mother and passed down to her.

"I think fox woman has brought you to Japan." Miss Ota touched the little foxes on the tansu. "We call these wish or prayer foxes, as you may know. These seem quite an old pair. Has your mother also brought these home to America?"

"No—a friend gave them to me."

"Ah so?" Miss Ota looked at her expectantly, but Barbara volunteered nothing more.

CHIE'S JOURNAL, 1939

Shoichi has been born. It is my shame that birth of boy did not give me pleasure I have expected. For some time I have found myself in state of melancholy. One day I said to Fumio, Do you consider life of male child more treasure than Michi or Haru? He looks at me in surprise. I confess that I have kept from him the true year of my birth, that I was born in unlucky year of Fiery Horse and might have been "a one-day visitor"— killed because a girl—except for Grandfather and Roku. He is shocked at first but must come to his senses as a modern man. I see he has some pride in himself for this. I tell him that I may in fact be something stranger at my birth than human girl; maybe I am fox child. I confide the history of my parentage. He turns to look out into garden for some time, then laughs and slaps his knee. Later I hear him say to Roku that he fears my worry over baby and the war has made me ill.

One Saturday morning Junko tapped on Barbara's door. "I have some problem, Sensei," she said. "Can you advise me?" Her eyes were swollen and red; her long hair was tangled.

"What's wrong? Please come in," she added, looking at her watch; she planned to arrive at Seiji's house early. She was going to surprise him by dressing in a kimono she had just bought at Takashimaya.

Junko shook her head. "You may know I have some special boyfriend."

Barbara nodded. Junko had mentioned him in conversation class, a student at Keio University.

"We want to marry in next year but my parents say I shall have arranged marriage. It is very hard for Japanese girl to defy her parents. But I cannot live in this way." She looked up. "Jefferson-sensei, what shall I do?" she said, her eyes filling with tears.

Barbara leaned forward to take Junko's hands. "Obey your feelings. How can you give up someone you love?"

"I cannot give up." She began to cry. "Sumimasen," she said, "sumimasen, I am sorry."

"Please ask someone else, Junko. Maybe I was wrong to say that—I can't know what it would be like."

"Nakamoto-sensei would say the same. She was like you in passionate nature," Junko said, then ran down the stairs.

Barbara took a taxi to Takanodai. She didn't see Seiji on her way to the tea house. Crouched in a corner, she took off her clothes and put on the green silk kimono. She smoothed out the material of the kimono, pale green silk scattered with delicate sprigs of plum blossom, pine, and bamboo.

She heard his light footsteps on the stone pathway, then on the platform. "Very lovely," he said in a low voice. "Kimono is becoming for you."

"Do I look Japanese?" she said with a smile.

"No," he said with a laugh. "Not at all," and went to make tea.

She looked down at the sleeves of the kimono, feeling foolish and sad—absurdly sad, she told herself.

They had tea in one bowl, as was their custom these days, then he unrolled the 1940 paper. He sat reading it, a peculiar expression on his face.

"What is it?" she said.

"You will be startled," he said. "Chie writes, 'In this year I had a shock. Woman claiming to be my mother Ko has written to Fumio asking for money. She does not ask about me, only speaks of a young daughter who is hungry. She says she lives in state of California, in America. Her husband has died and she must make her way on her own.' "

Barbara arranged her face in an expression of surprise.

" 'Fumio wants to help her but I say no. This is trick of evil fox at war with my own fox mother. My real mother must be dead or she would come to find me. I explain to Fumio that bad fox can do many things. Only last week there was tragic accident in Iwakuni caused by fox taking shape of a train. Fumio cannot understand me. He is angry I have read his letter.' "

"That's really interesting," Barbara said. "Ko in California." She could hear her voice, flat from guilt. She'd never been good at keeping secrets. "How do you suppose she happened to go there?"

"It does not say."

"Maybe that's why Michi went to California."

"Did she speak to you of this?"

"Don't you remember? Miss Ota mentioned her studying in California, at the memorial service. Maybe her real motive was to look for Ko."

"She has gone there to study," he said.

He looked so sure of himself that she felt like arguing. But she watched silently as he unrolled the next paper. "Chie writes that this is fox language as spoken by her mother Ko. Please have a look." Barbara bent over the page with him. "Most is a mishmash of something like hiragana," he said, pointing out several characters, "and the rest, all meaningless strokes."

"Poor Chie. She went mad, didn't she? Her obsession with foxes—and her mother's desertion."

They unrolled the 1942 paper.

"The same?" she said.

"Yes, the same."

"Other people lose their mothers but don't become insane," Barbara said. "It must have been the possibility of her existence— and all the fox stories Roku told her."

"I think she felt much guilt and shame," Seiji said. "It was because of her being born that her mother was banished."

It was growing dark. He poured wine into their tea bowl. A light wind had come up, moving in the grass and brushing a limb of the pine tree against the wall of the tea house.

"Next we'll be reading Michi-san's writing," Barbara said.

"Hai."

She took a sip of the wine and handed him the bowl. "One of my students said I remind her of Michi-san because of my passionate nature."

"Eh?" He looked startled.

"Passionate opinions, she meant," she added with a smile.

"Nakamoto-sensei had strong opinion," he said.

"You must have felt very close to her."

He was silent so long she thought he wasn't going to respond. "If not for her, perhaps I would not be living," he finally said.

"Getting you to the right doctor . . ."

"Yes, and before this as well. When I was invalid in Fukuyama she came many times to visit. One day I remember especially is time she has brought my schoolbooks. It was the first term of school after the war. American law was, there could be no mention of emperor as god or Japan's military victories in textbooks. So first day of schoolchildren took calligraphy brushes and marked over passages as teacher told them with their black ink. This was necessary for new democracy— but for many Japanese this was more shocking than defeat in war. Can you imagine?" He drew his hand through the air as though holding a brush. "In one stoke, all our history, blackened out."

He let his hand fall on the table. She took it. "I can imagine—almost." For a few moments they looked at each other. "Dear Seiji," she said.

He rose and came to sit closer beside her, then slipped one hand inside the kimono. "Ah," he said, touching her bare breast.

She untied her obi and let the kimono fall open. He kissed her, the taste of wine on both their mouths. She put her fingers in the tea bowl and put wine on her nipples. He bent to lick them, gently sucking at her breasts, cupping each one in both hands as though it were a bowl. As they lay down together he whispered, "Sometime I wonder which is dream—this time with you, or my former life."

20

Michi's garden, behind Sango-kan, had been untended all spring. Barbara noticed the tangle of plants and weeds one morning when she was taking out her trash. Along one edge of the garden, beside the stones, were hyacinths, pendulous stalks of blossom, blue and some white, dense with fragrance. A large patch of daisies occupied one corner. A leafy shrub was covered with round fat buds.

The garden was divided by a curving line of rocks. The other side was dominated by weeds, except for a row of feathery stalks—carrots, maybe—and another row of dark green plants she didn't recognize. Kneeling on the dirt, she worked a carrot loose from the soil. It was tiny, as long as her little finger. She laid it on one of the stones and began pulling weeds.

As she was tugging at a clump of grass she looked up, surprised to see Miss Ota standing beside her. "I am glad to find you caring for Nakamoto-san's garden," Miss Ota said. "She would be very pleased—and you look to be quite at home."

"I feel at home—in many ways." Barbara stood up. "I wish I could stay on at Kodaira," she said, with a rush of feeling that brought tears to her eyes.

"Is this so?" There was a pause, then Miss Ota said, "Perhaps I could speak to Miss Fujizawa on your behalf."

"Oh, could you? I would be so grateful."

"I suggest you speak to Mrs. Nakano; meanwhile, I will work behind the screen."

A few days later Barbara was summoned to Miss Fujizawa's office. She took a small, artfully arranged vase of hyacinths and daisies and set it on the president's desk. "From Nakamoto-sensei's garden," she said, with a little bow.

"Very pretty." Miss Fujizawa gave the flowers a brief glance. "Thank you. Miss Jefferson, I understand that you are getting on rather more agreeably now. As it happens, our foreign candidate for the next session has fallen through. Would you be willing to remain with us for another term?"

"I'd be thrilled, and honored. I love Japan and the students and the college—everything. Everyone has been so generous to me. Thank you so much, Miss Fujizawa."

"You're quite welcome, I'm sure." She allowed herself a little smile. "Your youthful enthusiasm is infectious. And how are you coming with your study of Japanese?"

"I've found an excellent teacher, Mr. Wada, in Higashi Koganei. I'll be going there several times a week," she added, though she had yet to make an appointment.

From her office she called Mr. Wada and scheduled a lesson. Eventually she would talk to Seiji in his language, no translations necessary. For now, though, she'd keep it as a surprise.

In the late afternoon, as she was leaving the library, Mr. Doi fell into step with her. "Mistress mine, where art thou roaming? Perhaps to some place in Takanodai?"

"What . . . ?"

"You have been spied with a certain gentleman."

"What's wrong with that?" she managed to say.

"I mention this only for your sake. As a female professor of Kodaira College you must be discreet." He bowed and walked away.

"I *am* discreet," she called after him. Two passing students glanced at her and ducked their heads.

He had a nerve. Mr. Doi would never warn a male member of the faculty to be discreet. She wouldn't let him spoil this. Seiji could find another place for them to meet. But while she was fixing supper she began to worry that Mr. Doi might speak to other faculty members, even Miss Fujizawa. Miss Fujizawa might change her mind about continuing her appointment.

The next day she dropped by the president's office to ask what courses she'd be teaching the next semester. As she was leaving, she added that her Japanese had progressed so well that she was helping someone translate some material into English, an article on haniwa. That should explain the Takanodai rumor, should Miss Fujizawa get wind of it.

During Barbara's American literature class, her gaze kept falling on Rie. Maybe she should talk to her, to make sure she wouldn't break her confidence. Rie looked steadily back at her, her expression unreadable. A conversation with her might only complicate things.

That night she went to the public bath with Junko, Sumi, and Hiroko, and said casually, as they were soaking in the hot water, how busy she'd been lately, working on a translation.

"Oh," Junko said, looking disappointed. "We thought perhaps you had some romance."

"Always Junko is thinking of romance," Hiroko said.

That night Mrs. Ueda came to see her. "There is something I have been intending to speak to you about. May I?"

"Yes, of course." A flutter started in her stomach. "May I offer you some tea?"

"No thank you."

Barbara led the way to the six-mat room. They sat at the table.

"Mr. Doi has said something to you, hasn't he?"

"He has done so. He and I agreed together that it would be best I speak with you woman to woman." Mrs. Ueda met her eyes. "Forgive my frankness, but I feel I must warn you, now that you are lengthening your stay—please take some care in your connection with Mr. Okada."

"What Mr. Doi doesn't know is that Mr. Okada and I have been translating some things—about ceramics."

"Must you go to Hakone to make your translation?"

Barbara's face went hot. Mrs. Ueda had overheard her distraught conversation with Mr. Kawabata, perhaps other conversations too. "We were staying in separate places—and no one saw us."

Mrs. Ueda said nothing.

"I'll be more discreet," Barbara said. "I'd appreciate it if you didn't mention this to anyone."

"You are a young woman alone here, without a mother to guide you. Therefore I feel it my responsibility to speak to you about Mr. Okada's reputation."

"What about it?"

"Perhaps he is not entirely loyal."

"You mean . . . ?"

Mrs. Ueda patted her hand awkwardly, as if it were a gesture she'd never tried before. "Maybe you had best wait to find romantic interest until you are returned home—it will be less complicating for you." She stood up.

"Wait—please tell me."

"I am sorry to cause you worry. I only wish you well," Mrs. Ueda said, and walked quickly down the hall.

Not loyal. It was Mrs. Ueda's tactful way of saying he was unfaithful.

She thought about the waitress in the Okada restaurant. Kimi, her name was. Kimi-san, Seiji called her. In the restaurant they spoke to each other in an easy, confidential way.

There could be women at Mashiko. His going to Mashiko so often might be an excuse, a cover. That's how it had been with her father, business trips, late nights at the office.

The memory of being with Seiji at Mashiko washed over her, that night he'd talked to her about his life, and the afternoon in the studio, their intimacy as they sat looking out at the rain.

By Saturday, when she was to go to Seiji's house, Barbara was ill with anxiety. She had trouble deciding what papers to take. They had finished Chie's writing and were to go on with Michi's but hadn't discussed where to begin. Chronologically the next writing was 1949 but she wanted to read 1952, when Michi was still in California. Finally she put all of Michi's papers in her bag. Maybe she ought to show him the deformed bottle; she'd never mentioned it. She put it in, then took it out; he might not want to be reminded.

As she walked down the street of Takanodai, a woman addressed her by name. "I am Mrs. Taki Kondo," the woman said with a bow. "Seiji Okada's aunt."

"Oh, how do you do." Barbara returned the bow. She recognized the woman now, regal looking, with heavy-lidded eyes and a mole on one cheek. "I was just going to visit your nephew."

"Yes," Mrs. Kondo said. Clearly this was no news to her.

"Miss Jefferson, would you be free to take supper with us this evening?"

"Oh—thank you," she stammered. "I'd be delighted."

They began walking toward the house. "This is our restaurant, of course," Mrs. Kondo said as they went past.

They went in the front gate and into the courtyard. "Sei-san is expecting you, I imagine," Mrs. Kondo said.

"Yes, I told him I'd be dropping by today."

She walked through the courtyard, trying not to hurry or look anxious.

He was in the kitchen getting the tea things ready. He turned and kissed her; she pulled back from him. "I just met your aunt in the street. I told her I'd love to come for dinner."

"To my house?"

"Isn't that all right?"

"Very nice," he said. "I am glad." But he was frowning slightly; he didn't look glad.

She followed him to the tearoom and watched as he made tea. Maybe this was what he always did, courting women.

He set the bowl before her.

"I have something to tell you." Her voice was more serious than she'd intended.

"Eh?"

"I'm going to be staying on through the fall—maybe even longer."

"Ah so?" His eyes widened. "This is wonderful." She waited for him to go on, but he said nothing more.

"You wouldn't be glad—to be free to go out with other women?"

"Go out?"

"Have romances with other women."

He laughed. "I do not want another woman. Why do you have such a thought?"

"I don't know." The knot inside her dissolved. "Some people at the college know I come here. We need to find another place to meet—an apartment or a room."

"This will be expensive."

"What will we do?" she said. "We have to be more careful."

"We will find some way," he said. He kissed her before taking the tea things into the kitchen. When he returned he looked at the black bag. "What have you brought for us?"

She took out the 1949 papers, three of them in one roll, and those from 1952 and '53.

"Wah. We will be busy," he said. "Too busy," he added, with a smile at her.

He picked up 1949 papers and read through them. It took him a long time to finish all three pages. Finally he said, "As you know, this is Nakamoto-sensei's first writing. It describes very difficult matter. I think it would be best for me to make this translation at leisure."

He wanted her to leave Michi's writing. "That will be all right, I guess," she said. "But please give them back to me soon."

"Yes, I will do." He rolled the pages together and stood up. "Would you be interested to see my new work?"

She followed him into the pottery. There were several pieces laid out on a table. All of them had a jagged, unfinished look, a primal quality. "I have made by hand instead of on wheel," he said as she touched the sharp edges.

"They're powerful," she said. "Strongly emotional."

"Perhaps because I think of you as I make them," he said. She took his hand and kissed it; he'd never expressed his feelings so openly before. He led her into a small room off the pottery. "No one can see us here," he whispered. There was a cot but no window. He closed the door; they were in total darkness. He kissed her. "Oh, Seiji," she said. They felt their way toward the cot and lay down. He reached beneath her dress and pulled down her underpants; she could hear the sound of his zipper. They kissed again, both of them trembling. She wrapped her legs around him. "Kirekitsu," he whispered. Afterward they lay still, his mouth against her ear, their hearts pounding. "I love being with you," she said. She wanted to hear him say he loved her. But he stood, pulled up his pants, and went to open the door. She lay there, looking at the rectangle of light for a few moments before she got up to compose herself for his family.

He gave her a cloth so she could wash off at the sink in the pottery. There was no mirror. "Do I look okay?" she asked, smoothing out her skirt.

"Of course," he said, smiling at her, "very okay."

At the entrance to the house, they stepped up onto the platform, took off their shoes, and walked into a large tatami room. The paper shoji doors were open all the way to the courtyard. Perpendicular to the door was a low table set for dinner.

"Tadaima," Seiji called out. "I am home."

Mrs. Kondo came out of the kitchen wearing an apron. "Please be welcome," she said to Barbara. "We will be eating shortly."

Barbara turned to Seiji. "Could you show me Michi-san's butsudan?"

Seiji and his aunt exchanged glances.

"I'm afraid that room is rather dusty," Mrs. Kondo said.

"I don't mind. I'd really love to see it."

He led her down a hall past several other rooms to a dark room in the corner of the house. There was only one small window; the only light came from it and from a bare bulb overhead. "This is where Nakamoto-sensei and Ume lived," he said.

Michi's butsudan stood in the middle of the room. It was a

tall wooden altar with shelves holding brass incense burners, oblong tablets inscribed with Japanese characters, and clusters of small framed photographs. The white box containing Michi's ashes wasn't in sight; it must be in some closed part of the butsudan.

On the top shelf of the altar was a picture of Michi as a young woman. She was standing before a flowering tree, a cherry tree heavy with blossoms. Without glasses, her smiling cat-shaped face seemed smaller and more delicate.

Barbara leaned forward to look at a sepia print of a family group: a woman in kimono with a baby in her lap and two little girls at her side. She studied the woman's severe face. "This must be Chie. And Michi," she added, looking at the mischievous girl in the sailor dress. "And Haru and Shoichi."

She looked at Seiji; he was staring down at the floor.

On the way out of the room Barbara noticed a recessed tokonoma, and a framed print hanging in the shadows. She stepped closer. A female figure in kimono was walking across a tatami room; her head, silhouetted behind a paper shoji door, was that of a fox. Crawling behind the fox woman was a small child, reaching out one hand to the departing woman. "This is the print described in Chie's journal—why didn't you mention that you had it?"

"I did not think to mention," he said.

They went back to the main room. Seiji's aunt showed Barbara where to sit, in the place of honor where she would have a view of the garden. Seiji's mother, Mrs. Okada, sat beside her. It was going to be impossible to talk to her, since her head was turned at that permanent angle in the other direction. Seiji sat across the table from her. Mrs. Kondo was beside him, in the place closest to the kitchen. No one spoke while she ran back and forth from the kitchen bringing food, miso soup

in covered lacquered bowls, pickles, cold spinach salad, and
sashimi, slivers of raw fish. Seiji looked miserable. Finally
Barbara broke the silence, speaking to his mother in halting
Japanese, asking after her health. Mrs. Okada turned to face
her and reached for her arm as she talked. "Hai, hai," Barbara
interjected several times, though she didn't understand what
was being said. Mrs. Okada's voice was touching, the way it
quavered. She thought of her going for Seiji's toothache medi-
cine, then the explosion, the glass in her eyes.

Mrs. Kondo returned to the table. She asked Barbara if she
wanted to say a prayer.

"Not really—I mean yes, if you do."

"I thought Americans liked to say some prayer before eating.
What we say as you may know is 'Itadakimasu,' Let us eat."
They all said itadakimasu and started eating in silence. Barbara
looked around the room; it seemed as though someone were
missing.

"Oishii," Barbara said, drinking her soup. "Delicious miso
shiru."

Mrs. Okada said something in her querulous voice.

"She is glad you like Japanese food," Seiji said. "Please excuse us for not inviting you sooner, she says."

"I'm just delighted to be here now." She gave her best
southern smile. "It's such a pleasure to become acquainted
with her and your aunt."

"My nephew tells me you are quite interested in the art of
ceramics," Mrs. Kondo said. "Tell me, what do you think of
his pottery?"

"It's gorgeous ... the shapes, the glazes ... everything is exquisite."

"Carol-san also admired his work," Mrs. Kondo said. "She
said it had strong force combined with refined air."

"Carol?" Barbara stared at Seiji. "Carol Sutherland, who taught at Kodaira College? You knew her?"

"I only knew her slightly. She came to study tea ceremony with my aunt."

They continued to eat in silence. Seiji avoided her eyes. Maybe Mrs. Ueda had been insinuating that Seiji liked to have flings with blond gaijin.

"Barbara-san is from the southern part of America," Seiji said.

"In Washington, your capital?" Mrs. Kondo said.

"No, in the state of North Carolina."

"Norse Carolina." Mrs. Kondo closed her eyes as though to summon it up. "I have not heard of it," she concluded.

"North Carolina is a little like Japan," she said. "The climate is similar, and the manners—I'm glad I'm going to be staying on another semester or maybe another year."

"I have heard this," Mrs. Kondo said.

"You have?" Barbara looked at Seiji. He was staring at his aunt. "Where did you hear it?" Barbara asked.

"From someone at your college, I cannot recall whom."

"Did you already know that, Seiji?" Barbara said.

He shook his head. "My aunt is always first with any gossip," he said.

There was a tense quiet as they finished the meal. Barbara kept her gaze on her plate. What a strange family. "I guess I should be going," she said.

"First we have special dessert," Mrs. Kondo went to the kitchen and brought back a carton of vanilla ice cream. "Happi Girl," she said.

"Happi Girl," Mrs. Okada repeated, clapping her hands together.

Mrs. Kondo held up the carton of ice cream for Barbara to

see: a smiling Japanese girl's face beneath what looked like an Eskimo hood; *Happi Girl* was written beneath the face in English. Mrs. Kondo dished the ice cream into bowls and passed a bowl to Barbara. "This was Carol-san's favorite. I hope you also will enjoy."

"It sounds as if Carol came here quite often," Barbara said.

Seiji's mouth was set in a thin line.

"We made quite a pet of her," Mrs. Kondo said. "Very nice, pretty, happy girl."

Seiji abruptly stood up and announced it was time to return Miss Jefferson to her college.

They walked out through the courtyard. He started to go through the gate toward his truck but she said, "Excuse me, I forgot my bag." She ran to the tea house, fumbled in the dark for Michi's papers, and put them all back in the bag. When she came out he was standing on the tea house platform. "I'm taking all the papers," she said. "Maybe we can read them later." She could feel his anger, but he made no comment.

They walked to his truck in silence. He didn't open the door for her as he usually did. Carol must have ridden in this truck. Their pet. She slammed the door hard.

They drove past the pottery buildings and bounced onto the street. "So," she said, "did you have a love affair with Carol?"

"I only knew her casually," he said.

They rode down the streets of Kokubunji, past the pachinko parlor and their eel restaurant. "Did you and Carol go to that restaurant?" she said.

"Perhaps one time, with my aunt. You are too jealous," he said.

"Am I?"

"Why have you taken back the papers of Nakamoto-sensei?" he said.

"Why shouldn't I? They're mine."

He said nothing.

"Why didn't you tell me about Michi-san's fox print?"

"I did not think to mention, as I said."

They didn't speak again until they reached the campus. He stopped the truck and sat staring straight ahead.

Her head was spinning. "Please tell me the truth about Carol."

He sighed. "There is nothing to tell. Only that my aunt likes to make mischief."

"What about you?" she said.

"What do you mean?"

She pushed open the door and jumped out. Without a glance at her, he pulled the truck back onto the road and drove away.

21

Barbara sat in the Western-style room drinking plum wine. Light from the full moon illuminated the back of the house and glinted in the windows of Michi-san's apartment. A blade of moonlight lay across the floor. Tomorrow she'd call Mr. Wada, have the papers translated right away. She tried to imagine what Michi would think: there was nothing but silence.

She went downstairs and around the back of the building to Michi's garden. Mrs. Ueda's windows were open, but no lights were on; she must have gone to bed.

Michi's cabbages were silvery in the moonlight, the patch of daisies a ghostly white. The other plants, robbed of color, were visible only as shapes that threw long shadows onto the ground.

She lay on her back in a bare spot, removed a stone that was poking her shoulder, then put her hands under her head and closed her eyes. Her body began to relax. It felt good to lie here on the solid earth, the moonlight against her eyelids.

She thought of the papers, the way Seiji had behaved. Michi would say have the papers translated by whomever you please. I left them to you, after all.

Early the next morning she called Mr. Wada, who said he was quite free to help. "My wife is doing some spring cleaning and will be glad to have me otherwise occupied."

He greeted her outside his apartment building and led the way upstairs. Mrs. Wada turned off the vacuum to say hello, and Mr. Wada led the way into his study.

Barbara took out the roll of 1949 papers and handed them to Mr. Wada. He frowned as he read. "This may take quite some time," he said.

"I don't mind waiting."

He invited her to have a look at his bookshelf. "There are some books in English, including the translations I have made of Noh drama. Please enjoy the balcony if you wish," he said, and took the papers to his desk.

Most of Mr. Wada's books were in Japanese, but there was a small shelf of works in English: *Ivanhoe, A Crock of Gold, The Complete Works of Lord Byron, Anne of Green Gables*—strange to see that here—and *Collected Poems* by Sir Thomas Wyatt. There were also six volumes of *The Japanese Noh Drama*, translated by Wada Masaru. She took down the Wyatt books and went out to the balcony.

She sat down in an uncomfortable metal chair. Across the street were a large pachinko parlor and a bar. Odors of restaurant food floated up to her from somewhere. Inside, Mr. Wada begin to type. She opened the book of Wyatt's poems; she'd liked them in college. "They flee from me that sometime did me seek," the first poem began. She snapped the book shut and went back inside.

Mr. Wada looked up, surprised. "I thought I'd just go for a short walk," she said. "I need some exercise."

"You may want to go for shopping," he said. "This will require an hour or so."

Mrs. Wada was struggling to take down some blinds in the living room.

"May I help?" Barbara asked.

"No, no," Mrs. Wada said, "please don't trouble yourself," but Barbara stood by while she removed the blinds and together they carried them downstairs to the back door. Mrs. Wada stepped into her wooden sandals. "Dozo," she said, gesturing toward another pair. "Please wear my husband's geta." They clattered down the outside steps to an asphalt area where there was a hose, washed the blinds, and hung them over a clothesline. Going back upstairs, Mrs. Wada told Barbara about her daughter now in Hokkaido and how much she missed her; she used to help with the spring cleaning. Mrs. Wada insisted there was no more to be done today and Barbara must stop as she must be tired.

Mr. Wada came in, looking somber, and gave Barbara a sealed envelope. "Please read when you return home," he said. Before she could ask Mr. Wada about the next language lesson or pay him, he bowed and retreated into his study.

Mrs. Wada went with Barbara down the flights of stairs. "Please excuse my husband. I am afraid he is not feeling so well. He suffers from lumbago and is easily tired. But thank you for being my daughter today."

Barbara walked dispiritedly along the street. Mr. Wada was so crotchety; maybe she should find someone else to help her. She looked at the envelope in her hand; she wasn't going to be able to wait until she got home to find out what he'd written.

She went into a coffee shop. The decor was garish silver and black. She sat by the window and ordered coffee. The only other customers were two young men playing Go; they glanced up and went back to their game. The heavily made-up waitress brought her coffee. She took a sip—it was awful, worse than the instant stuff in her apartment—and opened Mr. Wada's envelope.

JANUARY THE 2ND, NINETEEN HUNDRED AND FORTY-NINE, SHOWA 24.

Today I take up Mother's habit of making a first writing of the year. I remember my mother Chie kneeling at her desk, her stern expression. There was some beauty in her face, however, perhaps like her mother Ko, with her heavy eyebrows and long pale face. Now that I have been reading Mother's writings, I can deeply understand her longing for Grandmother Ko. I have been infected by it. Especially as a child, I have in my turn been yearning for Mother. Now I can at least realize the reason for her absence.

I remember, too, Mother's strength of will which led to my salvation. She would say this strength was from her fox mother. In some way this is accurate. She had at least animal instinct of love for her child.

Ume-chan, you are now three years of age. (Mr. Wada's note: "We Japanese mark age from moment of conception.") You are slow to speak, but doctors say not to have concern and recall for me that you were also late in your walking. I think you are like the slow growing ginkgo, a long time to make such a strong tree. Someday when you are grown, beyond my need of care and perhaps when I have died, you may find this writing, which I am making today in Mother's old tea ceremony house in Hiroshima. In case I have not told you full circumstance of miracle which saved you and I together, you may learn this part of your history in this my writing to you.

It was so sad, Barbara thought, Michi-san convincing herself that Ume would have a normal life. And here she was, in Ume's place. Prickles rose on her arms and along the back of her neck. She looked back down at the page.

Your father Kenzaburo was a good man of whom you may be proud. Though he had no taste for war, he bravely accepted his fate to be a soldier. Before war he had been a professor of botany at Hiroshima University. In the only letter I received from him he described foliage and seeds in jungle of Guam. His superior granted him permission to return home to Hiroshima some days in spring of 1945 and it was then you were conceived. In July of that year he died of dengue fever on Saipan, though it was some time after end of war before I learned this.

Barbara tried to visualize Kenzaburo—there had been no picture of him on Michi's butsudan that she could recall.

"My daughter, as you will know by the day you have found this writing . . ." Barbara reread the sentence again.

My daughter, as you will know . . . Hiroshima met its end on August 6, 1945, at 8:15 a.m. In one instant, the city I had known was changed to hell.

I was living with Kenzaburo's mother in the center of the city, an area called Castle Town. That morning I was in the kitchen preparing breakfast. Mrs. Nakamoto was outdoors in back of the house tending to some chores near the storehouse. I was unwell with nausea symptoms of early pregnancy and had tarried in preparation of rice and beans. Our maid Yuko once gave me a piece of lemon to suck when I had some nausea as a young girl. I remember closing my eyes to think of a slice of beautiful fresh lemon as I stood in the kitchen that morning. The memory of lemon was the last one of my normal life.

Barbara turned to the next page, the papers trembling in her hands.

Of bomb falling and house collapsing I have no clear memory. Perhaps some slight recollection though this may be from what Mother later told me.

Ume-chan, this is miracle story I wished to tell you. Mother—your grandmother Chie—had two weeks before the bombing gone to stay with her elder sister in Kaidahara. Father had insisted her to do this, as there was much uneasiness as to the fate of Hiroshima. Though it was the military capital, Hiroshima had not been bombed. There were many speculations about why this was so. Some thought some important American may live in the city, maybe even a relative of President Truman. Others believed that the Americans may be saving Hiroshima as place for their villas after the war since it is very beautiful place. But Father and Mother had dread of attack upon our city.

In Kaidahara Mother had strong visions each day of her mother, whom she believed was now a wise spirit fox. Though I think this was her own intuition, she was convinced that her fox mother was warning that her child Michi and unborn grandchild are in grave danger and she must go to them.

On the morning of August 6 she took early train from Kaidahara and then a streetcar from the station to house where we were. Mother had just stepped up onto porch of the house to call out "Good Morning" when the bomb fell. She had called out "Oha-," but before she can say "yo," there was a huge boom and flash of light and the house collapsed. The

porch shingles fell on her, but she was able to get free. If she
had been inside she would have been buried beneath the heavy
tiles and roof beams as were you and I. Though I do not recall
crying out, Mother said she could hear my weak "Mother,
Mother" and—with her fox mother providing her strength,
she said—she was able to free me from the rubble. She put me
across her shoulders and ran toward river. I was not conscious.
She has described that all around the houses were flat, as
though crushed by huge giant's foot, and many were in flames.
The sky was dark as night and there was thick greasy smoke.
People lay on the ground, dead, or softly moaning. Some were
scorched so black Mother could not recognize their faces.
Others stood in shock or moved like sleepwalkers. Many people leapt into the river to ease their burns. Mother's face and
hands were burned but she did not realize this for some days.

Barbara closed her eyes for a moment; the scene was as vivid
in her mind as if it had been etched there. She forced herself to
continue.

I can remember being at edge of river with Mother pouring
water over my face. She found a large branch and put me on it
and began to push downstream. There was an awful stench of
something like sulphur. All around in ghostly silence people
cried out, "Mother, Mother." I thought I was not awake but in
some terrible nightmare. Perhaps I did go to sleep then. I do
not remember the military officer who spoke to Mother. He
was standing at attention beside the bank, though his uniform
was in shreds. He had a hole in the side of his body and was
holding his intestines inside with his hands. Mother said he
looked directly at her and told her she would be wise not to
stay in river. Since I did not recall him and because his presence
was so commanding, Mother later decided that this was her fox

mother in the disguise of a soldier. Other evidence she said was
that after she took me up onto the bank he had disappeared.
Whatever the case, we have survived and did not drown in river
like many others. We then passed a night which I do not recall
and which Mother said was too terrible for words to describe.

It was perhaps the next day we made our way to our house.
I remember thick smoke from houses on fire and piled-up
corpses by side of road. Many persons walked like ghosts along
the roads staring straight before them. People lying on ground
called for water but we had none to give. By the side of the
road I saw a mother holding a dead baby to her breast. This
made me think of you, Ume-chan. I put my hands on my belly
and prayed for your safety.

"We ran up our street in Koi." Seiji had mentioned Koi.
Barbara read on more quickly. "Though many houses were destroyed a few were spared. We found our house badly damaged
but the tea house—I remember Mother's joy to see this—was
unharmed. All plum trees had lost their leaves, black on the
ground. We cannot find Father, sister Haru or brother Shoichi.
Mother ran next door to neighbor"—would that have been
Seiji? Barbara wondered—"and learnt that Father had gone to
search for Haru and Shoichi, who had been working in fire
lane, and for me.

There was the rumble of a truck outside—we went out to
see bodies, some live, some dead, being taken to Koi Elementary School grounds. We joined a flood of people heading up
the hills to Mitaki Temple. There we found water but no food
for many days. Eventually Father came, bearing Shoichi's
body; of Haru there was no trace. He was relieved to see me, as
he had found my in-laws' house on fire and Mrs. Nakamoto lying in the yard, her body skeleton and ash.

We cremated your young uncle Shoichi and put some ashes into one of Mother's tea bowls. Mother collapsed from grief and from that time on was in hospital. For weeks afterward we attended to Mother and continued to search for Haru-chan. Finally Father said we must accept that she has been incinerated in the blast. There were many months when my despair was very great. Sometimes I thought I would not continue to live, were it not for you growing inside me.

Barbara took a long breath as she turned to the final page.

Ume-chan, you were born the next February, not long after Mother's death. Father had by that time gone to stay in Kaidahara while our house was under repair. He had insisted me to come, but I refused. Still I was searching for some evidence of Haru-chan. I took my meals with the Okadas next door. Mrs. Okada had been blinded in blast and I was able to be some help to her. Okada father was missing, also young daughter Itsuko. Some days the Okadas' son Seiji and I roamed the city together, looking for some sign of our lost relatives.

At night I slept in the tea house. One morning I was too tired to rise. I thought I am too weak, perhaps I am dying. The possibility that I may not find Haru before I die caused me to begin crying. But then there were huge pains in my belly. Sei-san heard my cries and ran to tea house.

Sei-san must be Seiji; his aunt had called him that.

His mother was at Red Cross hospital, he said, but he will help me. He ran away and soon returned with a bucket of water, strips of cloth, and a blanket, which he laid over us.

I thought perhaps you would not come forth alive, Ume-chan. You had moved very little in my belly. When I heard your cry I was pierced with joy. Your birth was more a miracle than the blossoming of plum trees in our desolate landscape.

Seiji Okada was present at your birth, Ume-chan. He knelt beside us as I first held you to my breast. In that moment of assisting us, Sei-san has become a man.

Barbara stared down at the page, then at the black chairs, the streaked window, the two students playing Go. Everything seemed unreal, a thin surface that could be peeled away. The waitress came slowly toward her. She dropped money on the table and fled. Her feet carried her to the train.

In a daze she returned to the campus, walked into Sango-kan and up the stairs. The building echoed with her steps. In her apartment, she stood in the kitchen, holding the strands of bead curtain around her. It was unbearable to be alone. She turned and ran across the hall to knock on Miss Ota's door.

22

Dear child, what is it? Please come in."

"Michi-san," Barbara said. "The reason I knew she was a survivor of Hiroshima was from some writing she left to me."

"Ah."

"I just had part of it translated—what happened—on that day. How could she go on after that?"

Miss Ota led Barbara into her apartment; they sat at her kotatsu.

"Nakamoto-sensei would be most touched by your response to her writing," Miss Ota said. "Indeed, I am touched as well."

Barbara thought of Seiji, how he turned away from her as he read Michi's story. "Why didn't she leave it to a Japanese friend—someone who'd be closer to the experience?"

"Perhaps she hoped to enlighten you. As, it seems, she has done."

Barbara put her head in her hands. Miss Ota went to the kitchen and returned with two glasses of sherry.

"Thank you, Miss Ota. I don't know what I'd do without you."

"Your acquaintance is a comfort to me as well. A bright spot in my life." She sipped at her drink. "Not many people now living are aware that I was born in the state of Texas."

"Texas!" She couldn't imagine Miss Ota in Texas.

"My father was an agricultural specialist doing some work in plains of western Texas. We returned to Japan in my high school days. After I graduated from Kodaira College I went on to Cambridge, where I spent a number of years, though I never felt myself entirely at home. So you see I have always been a bit like the ugly duckling, not quite at ease in Western world or Japan."

Barbara nodded. "I see."

Miss Ota took her hand. "Now, will you kindly keep me company for the evening meal?"

Barbara lay awake much of the night, Michi-san's story running through her mind: Chie's premonition, the soldier by the edge of the river, holding his guts inside, the mother with a lifeless baby at her breast. Then Michi giving birth with Seiji's assistance. No wonder Seiji couldn't translate those pages on the spot. How petty her jealousy about Carol seemed now.

The next day after her morning classes Barbara walked through the woods to Takanodai, noticing for the first time that the trees were all fairly slender, none of the trunks of wider girth than the oak tree her father planted when they moved to Stone Street. This area had probably been heavily bombed in the Tokyo air raids. A devastated landscape lay beneath this tranquil green one, and beneath that, still another world.

She found Seiji in the restaurant eating lunch. Kimi was sitting across from him, the two of them talking and laughing. She stood by the door a moment, shifting the black bag from one hand to the other. When Seiji looked up at her his face changed, the smile suddenly gone. He said something to Kimi; she got up and scuttled off toward the kitchen.

Barbara sat down where Kimi had been. The plastic seat was still warm. They had been eating donburi, rice topped with vegetables and egg. "I'm sorry to interrupt," she said, "but I wanted to talk to you. In private," she added as Kimi re-emerged from the kitchen and began to busy herself behind the counter.

He stood, pushing back his chair.

"Don't you want to finish your lunch?"

He shook his head. She followed him out of the restaurant to the pottery. "Have you made some new pieces today?" she asked.

"Not today." He lit a cigarette and began rearranging some tea bowls on a shelf.

She glanced toward the little room where they had made love; the door was closed.

"I've brought back Michi-san's 1949 papers," she said. "I apologize for the other night. I was upset—about other things." She took the roll of papers out of the bag and handed them to him.

He accepted them with a bow. "Thank you," he said. "I think I caused the difficulty with my behavior. I have regret for this."

"Shall we—read them together?" She couldn't bring herself to confess about having had them translated; she could tell by his face that he'd never forgive her. "Whenever you have time," she added. He looked at her steadily. "Oh, Seiji, don't you want to see me anymore?"

He stepped forward and put his arms around her. She let the black bag fall and embraced him. He held her gingerly, the papers in one hand behind her back. "I want to see you," he whispered.

"When?"

He was silent a moment. "Boso Pennisula is beautiful place. We could read papers there, also have lovers' patch-up. Shall we make an excursion this weekend?"

"Yes." She kissed his cheek. "You keep the papers until then. Maybe it would be easier to write them out."

"If I have time I can do this." They walked back outdoors and into the street. "Please wait for me at the Kokubunji taxi stand on Saturday at nine," he said. "I will drive up for you then."

Saturday was a warm spring day. They rode with the truck windows open, talking very little, occasional comments that did not develop into conversation. At Barbara's feet was the black bag, which contained some of the papers from the 1950s, should they have time for them. She kept thinking about the papers Seiji had brought with him. When he read Michi-san's story, she'd have to act as though she knew nothing about it. He was driving intently, staring straight ahead. He was also likely to be thinking about the 1949 narrative, Michi's experience, and his own, not wanting to relive it in the translation. People always had secret thoughts; at this moment they probably were having the same ones, except that he was unaware of her duplicity.

They stopped for a traffic light. An old woman was walking on the side of the road, bent over by an enormous load of sticks on her back. "Seiji," she said. "The 1949 papers—did you write them out?"

He shook his head. "We can read together," he said.

The drive to the peninsula took only a couple of hours. They turned off the main highway onto a smaller road and were soon riding along a cliff beside the ocean. The water was a steely blue and flecked with whitecaps as far as she could see. Seiji pulled the car onto the shoulder of the road and they walked to the edge of the cliff. Huge waves buffeted the jagged rocks below them, throwing up spumes of white. The strong breeze blew her hair straight back and made her eyes water. She touched his hand; he wrapped his fingers around hers.

They stayed at an inn outside a small town. Across the road from the ocean, the inn had no view of water, as she'd imagined. Their room was tiny, with a dim overhead light and a flimsy table. She set her suitcase and the black bag in one corner of the room and followed the maid down the hall to a bath for one person. The water wasn't clean; there were a couple of hairs floating on the surface; she washed off and rinsed without immersing herself. When she went back to their room dressed in her yukata, he was not there. He reappeared a half hour later, flushed from his bath, and sat down across from her at the table with a newspaper.

Dinner was tempura that was too thickly battered and not very warm. He drank most of the bottle of sake and then called for more. His eyes were red by the time the maid brought the futon.

They undressed without speaking and lay side by side. She reached toward him, put one hand on his chest. He rolled over onto her. His breath smelled strongly of sake. She turned her face away as he moved above her; it was over quickly. "I am sorry," he said, "I am somewhat tired," then rolled away and went immediately to sleep, snoring slightly. She stared up into the dark, her eyes stinging.

Barbara awoke to the sound of Seiji sneezing. He got up and left the room. When he returned he was wearing a contagion mask. He looked pathetic, his mouth and nose covered with the mask, his eyes bloodshot. "I shall be poor companion, I am afraid," he said in a muffled voice.

"Don't worry," she said. "I'm just sorry that you're sick."

Breakfast came, miso soup and rice with fish and seaweed. He took off the mask to drink the soup, then put it back on and continued to read his newspaper while she finished eating.

"Would you rather go home?" she said. "Maybe you don't feel like translating today."

"No, I am able."

After the dishes were cleared away he unrolled the papers he had brought and she took out her notebook. She felt queasy, tasting the seaweed from breakfast.

He read haltingly, his voice so faint behind the mask that she had to lean forward to hear him. She wrote down everything, and tried to make appropriate responses as he narrated the story of Michi's mother stepping up onto the porch, the house falling, then her carrying Michi to the river. When he came to the part about the man at the side of the river, so formal in spite of pressing his intestines inside, she said, "Isn't that amazing?" Seiji did not look up. Following the calligraphy with one finger, he read more slowly about Michi and her mother making their way to Koi, finding their tea house still standing but the house destroyed. He started coughing, raised his mask and took a few swallows of tea, then blew his nose and lowered the mask. The next section was about his family, the lost sister and father, his mother blinded on the streetcar. "It's terribly sad," she whispered; there was a tangled pain in her chest.

He paused. She waited for him to go on reading the part about Ume's birth, the miracle of it, and the moment when he became a man. But he slowly put the three pages back together and began to roll them up.

"Was that everything?" she said.

"Yes."

She stared at him as he tied the papers together with a piece of string. He had deliberately left out that section.

He lifted his mask and lit a cigarette. As soon as he inhaled, he began to cough.

"You really shouldn't smoke," she said, but he waved one hand at her, jumped up, and went down the hall to the toilet.

When he returned he proposed going out to do some sight-seeing.

"Do you feel like it?"

"Of course. I am not so ill."

She took her camera out of her suitcase and they went out to the truck. There was a sharp wind from the ocean and the sky was a smudged-looking gray. "It's going to rain," she said. He shrugged and said nothing. She could feel sadness sinking into her.

They drove slowly along the coast looking out at the iron-colored water. The road curved away from the ocean and into a little settlement of houses and shops. Seiji went into a pharmacy to buy another mask, then they walked down the streets looking into windows: pans of shimmering white tofu in one shop, brushes and writing supplies in another, then a display of cheap Western-style clothes. There was a restaurant with plastic replicas in the window of food offered there.

As they walked, she glanced at him. He looked vulnerable from this angle, with the mask string looped around his ear. There was something poignant about his censoring that part of Michi's writing, the moment he'd become a man. A weak man, alive only because of a toothache, he'd said.

They found a restaurant at the edge of the ocean. The waitress seated them on the porch, so close to the water that they could feel the salt spray against their faces. He took off his mask to eat. The food was much better than the inn's, several kinds of raw and baked fish, which they washed down with beer.

"I wish to make apology for my aunt," Seiji said. "It is her bitter nature that makes her speak in such a way about Miss Sutherland. She only wished to cause you envy."

"So—you really didn't ... ?"

He turned to look at her. "Carol Sutherland is no one to me."

"I believe you." An enormous wave crashed against the rocks and receded. "Why would your aunt want me to be envious?"

He drained his beer. "Aunt is soured from her experience of life. During war with China she was married to a soldier and went with him to Manchuria. When husband was away fighting she must protect herself from Chinese men by dressing in trousers and cutting her hair. She wanted to stay on but eventually she must return." He turned the empty glass in his hand. "After war she learned her husband has married another."

"Without even divorcing her?"

"Hai. She has heard he lives in Tokyo. That is why she first moved to Tokyo, to find him, but she never has found."

"Why would she want to find him?"

"For divorce settlement. She had some little money from parents' family, enough to buy restaurant, but never any from her husband. This is a shame of behavior, ne? I have had severe difficulties with aunt but I cannot forget her hardship in life. Also she has been kind to my mother and myself, supporting us from after time of war until I could assist in restaurant."

She thought of Kimi, the two of them talking together yesterday.

"Is there anyone else—now? Some other woman?"

"Why do you suddenly ask these questions?"

"There was—a rumor."

He sat straight up, staring at her. "Who has spoken against me?"

"Mrs. Ueda said something."

"Ueda Setsu?"

"Yes, do you know her?"

"My aunt knows her, I believe."

"So—she doesn't really know you."

He shook his head.

"That's what I thought," she said. They sat gazing out at the water. When she looked at him again, she felt a rush of tenderness. "It's so nice to see you without the mask," she said, taking his hand beneath the table. "Why don't you just leave it off? If I'm going to catch your cold, I will anyway."

"This is our Japanese custom," he said. "We think it inconsiderate otherwise." When they stood up to leave he put the mask back on.

After they returned to the inn, Seiji took a nap, woke up for dinner, and then, as soon as the futons were brought out, changed into his yukata and got beneath the covers. "I am sorry to be so much fatigued," he said. She kissed his forehead and he turned onto his side. She lay with her hand on his back, feeling the gentle rise and fall of his breathing; she felt an impulse to tell him everything. "Seiji?" she whispered. He did not respond. "If you didn't feel like reading all of Michi's writing..." His breathing seemed to change. "It's all right," she said, "I understand."

23

Rie was absent from conversation class on Monday. When Barbara asked where she was—Rie had never missed a class before—there was some giggling but no one answered.

At lunch Junko told Barbara that Rie had an accident on Saturday, "a tumble into the Tamagawa Canal."

"Is she okay? Was she hurt?" Barbara asked. "She must have fallen off her bicycle," she added, thinking of all the dips and holes in the path along the canal.

"No, she had stopped to pick some flower too close beside the stream," Junko said. "She is in infirmary, but is hurt mostly in her pride, I think. Some students have unkindly said she tumbled in because she is too fat."

When Rie did not appear in class the next day, Barbara went to visit her in the infirmary, a dark room in the basement of one of the dormitories.

Rie was lying in a bed at the far end of the room, her eyes

closed. There were four other beds, all unoccupied. Barbara thought there might be a nurse, but there was no one in sight. She hesitated by the door. Maybe she would write a note and leave it on the little table beside the bed, along with dried squid, which Rie had once said was her favorite snack.

She tiptoed toward Rie's bed. The room seemed like a prison: windowless, with a cement floor. There was dim light from a globe in the ceiling. Barbara carefully set the squid on Rie's table, and felt in her pocketbook for a pen and some note paper.

"Sensei!" Rie sat up. One hand was wrapped in a bandage and there was a dark bruise on her forehead. Her eyes were puffy and red.

"I'm sorry—I woke you up."

"I was not sleeping. I am surprised you have come."

"I was worried about you."

"No one else has come to see me. I have no friend. And I am buffoon." Tears began to dribble down her face. She rubbed her head furiously with the knuckles of her good hand. "I think I shall kill myself but I am coward."

"All you did was fall in the river—it could happen to anyone."

Barbara touched Rie's shoulder. "Sometimes it takes more courage to live, doesn't it? I'm sure you have more friends than you realize. Junko is very worried."

Rie did not answer; her back had gone rigid, as if she were holding her breath.

"Does your hand hurt?" Barbara said. The bandage was grimy and unevenly bound, as if Rie had put it on herself. "Maybe we should have it X-rayed."

Rie shoved the hand beneath the covers. "I am ashamed to tell you this is my excuse not to attend class. If I cannot write I cannot do my lesson."

"But you'll fall behind—wouldn't that be worse?"

"Already I am behind. My class is graduated last March. I have been senior for over a year."

"In a few years that won't matter at all. Meanwhile, you could do your schoolwork here for a couple of days. What about your senior thesis—how is that coming along?"

"I have not begun. I am poor student, disgrace to my family." She started scrubbing her head with her knuckles again.

"Stop." Barbara caught her hand. "Write it now. Just a rough draft. You can pour out whatever you want to say—later it can be rewritten."

They were holding hands on top of Rie's head. Rie pulled her hand free and looked up at Barbara, a hint of a smile in her eyes. "I will write as you say."

"Good—and I can bring your other assignments to you, or Junko—would you mind if Junko came?"

"No," she said in a small voice, "I will not mind."

"I've brought you some squid." Barbara put the package on the bed beside her. "Well, I'll go now—do you have some paper and a pen?"

"Please ask Junko-san to bring me. Thank you, Sensei. I can never forget."

Two days later, when Barbara was going to her kitchen to fix breakfast, she saw a brown envelope that had been slipped beneath her apartment door. *Jefferson-sensei, In Confidence* was written on the outside. Barbara ripped open the envelope to find several sheets of paper covered with Rie's distinctive spiky handwriting. At the top of the first page Rie had written *Some Rough Idea for My Thesis,* then began,

First I will tell you Sensei what is my job in Tachikawa. I go there to repair dead bodies, faces of American soldiers killed in Vietnam. Are you shocked? I do this because it is job which pays very good wage. And if you do this job you can understand, for not many people would have strength to perform this work like mortician. But I can. Because of my inheritance I have strength to bear this work for my education and graduation from Kodaira College which my father is daily praying for. What you said about shame in not graduating pierced me. It is true. I must to do well for my family.

But let me tell you some guilty part of my job foremost. This repair of faces is attempted by American military so that bodies of soldiers may be sent to families in the U.S. looking less violent in their deaths. I believe this is dishonest and hypocrite. It would be best for family in America to see true face of war. But for my own selfish end I am making this job. Now it is my shameful secret but I have decided to have courage to some day write about this and about other things I have experienced for the world to learn. Not that I am so wise, but I know some things which world in general does not be aware of I believe.

Another surprise for you, Sensei, is that I was born in Hiroshima and was two years of age at time bomb was dropped. We were living on far side of Hijiyama hill in one small section of the city where rows of houses are left standing. My mother and I seemed to be unharmed though some time later my mother died from radiation illness.

My father was soldier on parade ground near ground zero. Through an undignified miracle his life was spared. Thinking of his fearless living in spite of indignity helps me find some courage.

I admire Father very much. After the bombing of Hiroshima he worked hard at many things and finally owned his own store selling needles. His mother, my grandmother, was a poor widow and seller of fish on the street without even

a shop. So you see I come from class of people unlike other
students at Kodaira. You know because of Nakamoto-sensei
there may be others on campus who have experienced the
suffering of Hiroshima or Nagasaki and also many bombing
raids in other cities, though most do not say, particularly
hibakusha which means atomic bomb victim. It is new breed
of untouchable class in Japan. But in strange way the
bombing of Hiroshima helped my family rise in fortune since
class boundary after war was not so important. Only living
and feeding oneself became of importance. Still we were not
rich but we had a house and I had for some years both mother
and father though I later grieved my mother very much. In
primary and high school I studied hard and my teachers
encouraged me to come to Kodaira. They raised money for
scholarship for me.

   Though I do not have personal memory of bombing my
family and city and fellow people are affected in most horrible
way to befall humans and other creatures since beginning of
time on our planet. Yes, Japan to her shame was aggressor in
war both in China and America and this ending was brought
upon us for this reason. But I think worst thing is use of split
atom, human discovery of nature's secret, to destroy. Perhaps
Japan would have dropped same type bomb on Washington
if possible. You asked me, what is Japanese idea of sin. For
Japanese there is no original sin. In Buddhism, belief is that
human in original state is pure and our effort should be to
return to the pure nature. Wrongdoings are committed
through ignorance and lack of compassion. We are all
brothers, ne? There is the saying, that dog could be your
mother. This suffering woman could be yourself.

   However there is some interesting point in your Adam and
Eve myth of human curiosity which I have been thinking of.
Maybe we can say that split of atom caused by human

curiosity is the original sin of mankind. Other things may be
done or learned from same curiosity for good or bad reason.
But Adam is like atom, do you agree? The tragic result of split
atom will affect all people from now until end of time.

Miss Jefferson, I heard you speak on day of Nakamoto-
sensei's memorial service. I have felt your sincere emotion.
You have learned about we hibakusha at closer hand than you
can do in America. Some time if you are willing I can tell you
more things and even show Hiroshima to you. Our once
Garden of Eden city is now only a memory beneath false face
of modern buildings.

I have told you my idea of original sin. I hope you will
accept me.

Sincerely,

Rie Yokohagi

Barbara sat stunned, holding the paper. Then she ran down
to Michi's garden, picked some red peonies that had just come
into blossom, and carried them in a vase to the infirmary. Rie
was not there; another girl who was in bed, sick with bron-
chitis, told her that she was in her dormitory getting ready for
class. Barbara went up to Rie's room and knocked on the door.

Rie pulled open the door. "Sensei!" The bandage was gone
from Rie's hand and the bruise on her forehead had faded to a
purplish yellow. She was dressed in a clean white blouse and
dark skirt and her black hair shone.

Barbara held out the flowers. "I am very moved by what
you've written."

Rie took the vase and bowed deeply. "Thank you, Sensei."

"Once I had a bad fall from my bike," Barbara said. "My
father made me get right back on—I hope you will too."

"I must do so, ne, to reach my job." Rie paused, then added
in a tentative voice, "One day maybe you can ride with me."

"I'd like to—but I don't have a bike."

"I can find for you."

The next afternoon Rie knocked on Barbara's apartment door. "Will you take ride now, Sensei? I have bicycle for you."

The bicycle was black, with rusted spokes and fat tires. Barbara swung her leg over the seat and tried the rubber horn; it made a tired, asthmatic sound.

"Will you fit?" Rie said.

"Perfectly. Thank you." They set off pedaling up the drive. Barbara's knees came almost to the handlebars as she pumped. It was difficult going up the slight grade of the driveway; there was only one speed, no gears to change. They crossed the street and rode down the path by the Tamagawa Canal, Rie leading the way.

It was a sunny afternoon, the air warm against Barbara's face. It was a relief to be away from the papers she'd been grading. She hadn't seen the wildflowers along the canal before—a profusion of miniature iris and some smaller pale blue flowers. The water was high, with a strong current. Rie must be a good swimmer. She imagined her clawing her way back up the bank.

"How did you get out of the river?" Barbara called ahead to her.

"I met with a large tree root," Rie said, glancing back over her shoulder. "I am very lucky, I think."

They passed the fox shrine, then rode through the wheat fields and began to climb the hill toward Takanodai. Rie leaned forward to pedal; Barbara had to stand, the bicycle wobbling back and forth. Finally she got off and pushed. At the top of the hill she got back on and glided behind Rie to the main street of Takanodai. Rie looked back at her with a strange little smile. For a moment Barbara was afraid Rie was going to head toward Seiji's house but she turned left and they rode away from the village.

They passed a farmhouse with a low thatched roof. The road

wound through the fields. Rie pointed out the crops, sweet potatoes, buckwheat, daikon radish. In the distance was the thunder
of an airplane taking off: Tachikawa Air Force Base.

"Is this the road you take to your work?" Barbara asked.

"Usually I go straight through Takanodai. I can go this way
but much longer. Shall we stop to refresh ourselves?" She nodded toward a grassy spot at the edge of a field.

They laid their bicycles beside the road and sat on the grass.
Tachikawa was behind them. They had a view of a farmhouse
on a hill, a woman in kimono hanging out clothes on a line.

"One more thing I will tell you about my job, Sensei," Rie
said. She pulled up a stalk of grass and studied it. "Maybe you
have heard of eta or burakumin, untouchable caste in Japan.
The reason for being 'untouchable' is that such people take care
of the dead bodies. This is perhaps one idea of sin for Japanese,
being unclean in this way." She glanced up at Barbara. "So I do
not tell others of my work."

"I understand. I won't mention it to anyone." She felt a
surge of affection for Rie, looking at her bent head, her thick
black hair glistening in the sun. "Your work must be ... I can't
imagine how hard."

"Yes, but I must do it. Buddhist priest may say this is my fate
because of poor karma in previous life. But I am glad to do. My
father is not well, so I may help in this way. Americans pay me
good salary. Sometime when I am working I think how ironi-
cal is this new meaning of saving face—saving face of American
soldier. To tell you the truth, Sensei, I am not always so angry
as I wrote. Sometimes I think of mother who will see her child.
This is human experience, ne, not American or Japanese?"

Barbara nodded, but could not speak.

"Shall I describe my work? Can you bear it?"

"Yes."

"There is cold room—body of soldier ..." With her hands

she described a table. "He is ready for burial, except for face. Maybe his ear is gone, or mouth." She touched her ear, then her mouth. "I can make new part ... any part I can make from wax, like a sculptor."

Barbara thought of the American soldiers she'd met on the train. Jim and Coleman. They might be dead by now.

"Even if part of face is missing, I can fix. First I sew with strong thread and curved needle to sew back and forth between flesh which is remaining." With one hand she made a sewing motion. "This makes foundation. Can you understand me?"

"Yes." She was shivering; she rubbed her arms. "Do you know their names?"

"No—I do not know his name. After foundation is complete, I fill hole in face with melted wax or Paris plaster. Then put on cosmetic to match color of flesh for white or black man. I must use very fine brush to make look like pore in skin. Americans say I am artist in repair of faces." She paused. "Can you guess, Sensei, where I first began to learn my art?"

"In some kind of special school?"

"Yes, but first from Okada-sensei. He was my teacher in ceramic."

"Do you mean ... Okada Seiji?"

"Hai. Okada Seiji."

"But he doesn't do—mortuary work, does he?"

"No, only bowl, plate, haniwa object, sometimes a piece of sculpture. Shaping clay is not so different from making a form in wax.... You are surprised, ne? I think you know Okada-sensei rather well."

"I've been studying with him too," she said.

"Ah so?"

"Yes—how to make bowls—and plates." Her face was burning. "I'm not very good at it," she added.

Rie looked away from her, down at her hands, then into the distance.

"Maybe we all have some secret life," Barbara said.

Rie met her eyes. "Don't worry, Sensei," she said. "We will be silent together, desho?"

24

The rainy season began in early June, days of gentle soaking rains. Barbara woke to the sound of it on the tile roof and to the odors of wet earth and leaves that blew in through the open window of the three-mat room. Remembering that Michi's mother had called these the plum rains, she went several times to the plum grove, where the golden fruits grew larger every week.

At the edge of Michi's garden, and elsewhere on the campus, there were hydrangeas in bloom, delicate masses of blue. Barbara picked armfuls of the flowers and buried her face in them, their heavy wetness luxuriant against her skin. She put vases of hydrangeas in every room of her apartment; their sensuous presence made her long for Seiji.

After their visit to Boso, she and Seiji had seen each other only a few times, and when they were together, he seemed nervous and remote. His aunt had reestablished her presence in the tea house, so most of their meetings were furtive encoun-

ters in the small room next to the pottery. One day Seiji said he
was looking for another place they could meet, "somewhere we
may be private together and continue to make our translation."

"I hope it will be soon," she said, putting her arms around him.

"Very soon," he promised.

The first couple of weeks in June, Seiji was busy working
on new pots and delivering them to Mashiko; this was fine,
she told herself, there were papers to grade and the end-of-
semester exams to prepare. They would be together during the
summer holiday, perhaps afterward as well. Meanwhile, she
had her Japanese to work on.

She was proud of how well the lessons were going, though
Mr. Wada said she needed to take more patience in learning
the written characters. He complimented her on her improved
speaking ability, but she was discouraged by conversations she
tried out on the train; often her comments to fellow passengers
set off a torrent of language she could not understand.

One night Barbara went to the main building to call her
mother.

"Bobbie?" came her sleepy voice.

"I'm sorry, I called too early."

"Usually I'd be up by now, you know me. But lately I've just
been so busy that I'm in a state of total exhaustion." Barbara
leaned against the wall while her mother talked about her writing, the bridge club luncheon she'd hosted, staying up until the
wee hours cutting the edges off watercress sandwiches.

"I'm in love," Barbara blurted out.

"What? Now *this* is something worth waking up for. Is it
someone at the consulate? Or that Fulbright man you mentioned?"

"Mr. McCann?" Barbara laughed. "No. He's Japanese. His name is Seiji Okada."

"A Japanese?"

"Yes. Why not?"

"Well—it never occurred to me, somehow. Japanese men are so—short," her mother said with a laugh.

"They've grown since the war."

"They have?"

"Better nutrition."

"Well, that's good." Both of them began to laugh. "Oh, me." Barbara could imagine her mother wiping her eyes. "What does this man do?"

"He's a potter, an artist, wonderfully talented. And he's just great—so sensitive and funny."

"Be careful, Bobbie, you don't want to get yourself into a mess."

"What kind of mess?"

"You know what I mean. Rushing into something you'll re- gret, like I did."

There was a long silence. "I've got to go, Mother," she said. "I'm late for dinner at Miss Ota's."

"Miss who's?"

"*Ota.*"

"Well, you don't need to snap my head off."

"I'm sorry, Mother. Good-bye."

She walked back to Sango-kan and went to her apartment to brush her teeth and comb her hair before going to Miss Ota's. Regret had always been her mother's theme. She'd heard the story many times, how her mother had gotten married too quickly, swept off her feet, she said, by her father's disarming ways. By the time she realized she'd made a mistake, it was too late, she was pregnant. She'd never added, Barbara realized,

234   Angela Davis-Gardner

that she had no regret about having her. Leaning close to the mirror, she thought of the Zen koan to "describe the face you had before you were born." She held to the edge of the sink, looking into her eyes until the face around them was gone.

Miss Ota served tinned corned beef, bok choy, rice, and, for dessert, some shortbread an acquaintance had recently sent from England. An East-West meal, she called it. "I had some hope it might make you feel at home. Though I am afraid I am not so skilled as Nakamoto-san was in putting our American guests at ease."

"But I do feel at ease. Especially with you. Thank you so much, Miss Ota."

"You are most certainly welcome, my dear."

For a few moments they concentrated on their food. Then Barbara said, "You mentioned in your talk that Nakamoto-sensei was doing some research in California. What was it about?"

"Commodore Perry and his opening of Japan to the West— the nineteenth-century American view of him."

"I was wondering—was she also looking for some relatives?"

Miss Ota raised her eyebrows. "How did you happen to know of this?"

"There was a reference . . . in that writing I told you about."

"I see." Miss Ota laid down her knife and fork. "It is true, she made some search for relatives. I tried to make some assistance at a particular archive where we hoped to find information about Japanese-Americans during the war. There was much displacement during that time."

"Did she find her relatives?"

"Not in the year that I was present. I must confess I did not make inquiry about these efforts when she returned. She was in state of distress over Ume and other matters and we talked only of those things."

*   *   *

The next time Barbara went to see Mr. Wada for a Japanese lesson she was tempted to take the next California paper with her. She considered asking him to just skim through it; she wouldn't write it down. But she couldn't, she decided, she'd feel too guilty.

She called Seiji when she got home. "I really want to get back to translating. I've got to have someone read these papers for me."

There was silence.

"Don't you miss me?" she said.

"Very much I am missing you. In summer we will have our own place."

"It's already summer!"

"Meanwhile, there is problem of where to meet."

A little while later he called back to say his aunt would be out the following Saturday, and please to come then.

They met in the tea house and did the first translation of Michi's papers since their trip to the Boso Peninsula. Seiji's reading of the 1950 paper was halting; she wondered if he was worried about coming across something he'd want to censor, like the final section of the 1949 papers. The content was uneventful: the weather at New Year's, the declining health of Michi's father, Ume's slow growth.

"I'm surprised she didn't mention you," Barbara said when he had finished. "Wasn't she visiting you in Fukuyama during that time?"

"I believe so, yes."

"You're sure you didn't accidentally skip over something?"

"No," he said, giving her a sharp glance, "I have not skipped."

They went through the pottery shed into the small room. "Do you think of me when you're in Mashiko?" she said as they lay down on the small cot.

"Very much," he whispered, "especially I think of you in Mashiko."

As they were getting dressed she said, "There must be somewhere else we can go temporarily, until we find a place of our own. How about a hotel?"

"This will be too expensive, I think."

"Well, there's no hurry." She stepped into her shoes. "I'm really busy right now with my classes. And Japanese lessons. My teacher is quite fascinating," she added as he followed her out the door. "He's showed his translations of Noh plays."

"Ah so?" Seiji frowned. "Who is your teacher's name?"

"Mr. . . . ." She felt a stab of fear as she met his eyes. "Wada— or Ueda, I believe."

There was an air of studious quiet on the campus as the girls wrote their final papers and studied for end-of-term exams. The rain seemed appropriate: it made the world serious. Barbara spent hours lying on her futon, reading. After several days of rain the odors of wood were more prominent inside the apartment building. The camphor in the tansu seemed more pungent too, and it was that scent, more than anything else, that made her lay down her book and close her eyes, her desire for Seiji so intense she thought she could not bear it.

The student papers, which came in at the end of the month, showed progress. They were learning, she realized; she was reaching them. The best papers were short stories from the composition class. Junko read hers aloud, a love story about a couple who'd been forced to marry other people. They vowed to meet once a year, July 7, on the Feast of Tanabata, the night when two lovers enshrined in the stars—the Weaving Maiden and the Herd Boy—have their annual meeting. The rest of the year, Junko's heroine was, like the weaving maiden, both glad and sorry because she both loves and suffers and this is better than her former state, when she "neither loved nor suffered." At the end, the class sat silent. Barbara didn't know what to say; the piece seemed strongly autobiographical. Finally Sumi rescued her with "We are too poignant to speak."

Barbara read Rie's story to the class. The title was "The Enemy"; it took place in Vietnam, from the point of view of an American soldier named Smith. Smith found he could not tell who was the enemy. North and South Vietnamese looked alike, and anyone, even an innocent-looking child or woman, might be carrying a land mine or could be a spy. His unit destroyed a village that was thought to be Communist. They killed everyone, including women and children. Smith watched, unable to move, as Jones, his friend, cut off the ear of a Vietnamese man who'd tried to defend his village. Jones ripped the shirt from the body of a pretty young woman "and made some crude comment. Smith hit Jones with his angry fist. Then Jones raised his gun and shot Smith in his face. The captain listed Smith as 'killed by enemy action.' "

At the end there was a wary silence. No one met Barbara's eyes.

"It's an important story," she said. "An act of imagination and sympathy."

Rie shook her head. "It is true story, Sensei, told me by a medical worker, an American I happened to meet in Tokyo."

A couple of days later, Barbara's mother called. "I tell you what," she said in a chipper voice. "Why don't I just fly on over there this summer? I could meet this young man of yours and see Japan again. Wouldn't that be fun?"

"Well, it would, but it looks like I'm going to be really busy this summer."

"You have a vacation—didn't you say something like two months?"

"It turns out not to be that long. I'll be busy catching up with all kinds of things, and people have already asked me to visit. And I promised to help someone with a project."

"I see," her mother said.

"By the way, I'm thinking about the war in a new way," she said.

"What do you mean?"

"I think we're interfering—maybe we shouldn't be there."

"You need to read a little history along with all those novels," her mother snapped. "Hitler nearly took over the world, and the Japanese came damn close."

"What's going on in Vietnam is a civil war."

"If South Vietnam falls, the Communists will be all over Asia, and beyond."

There was a tense silence.

"What was it like, to live here right before the war?" Barbara asked.

"The Japanese were very polite, of course. Up to a point. My camera was confiscated when I took a shot of an innocent street scene in some little town. I knew what we were in for when I saw hundreds of warships in the Inland Sea near Hiroshima. Of course I couldn't write about it. Every night my room was searched."

"You never answered my question about how you got into Hiroshima. Americans weren't allowed there, I thought."

There was another long silence.

"I've gotten to know a couple of people who survived the Hiroshima bombing," Barbara said. "It's been moving, beyond words."

"Don't get sentimental about Hiroshima. That bomb saved thousands of lives—American lives. The Japanese were prepared to fight to the end. Hari-kari, every one of them."

"*Hara-kiri*. Even if that's true, using the atomic bomb changed everything. It still hangs over us—all of us. And the way people died . . ."

Her mother snorted. "Ever heard of the Bataan Death March? The Rape of Nanking? Those weren't exactly glorious deaths."

"You don't understand. You never have bothered to try to understand me."

"Don't be absurd."

Barbara was trembling. "So—could you please answer my question—how did you get into Hiroshima?"

Her mother did not answer.

"Hello? Are you there?"

"I had a friend."

"A Japanese friend?"

"Hardly. No, he was Belgian. A journalist. Or so he claimed."

"And he got you into Hiroshima?"

"Yes."

She could hear her mother lighting a cigarette. "How did you meet him?"

"In the bar of the Imperial Hotel. He knew my name, said he was impressed by my writing."

"And?"

Her mother sighed. "He offered to introduce me to people, to give me leads . . . so I . . . I traveled to several places with him, including Hiroshima."

"You *traveled* with him?"

"He was very handsome." She gave a nervous little laugh. "Clark Gable with a European accent. And charming! Flowers, gifts . . . I was smitten."

"You're kidding," Barbara said. Her mother, with a lover. And all that talk about saving yourself for marriage. "What finally happened with him?"

"He left one day—for Belgium, he said. He said he'd be back. I kept asking around after him; finally a woman from the *Trib* told me he was German."

"German?"

"I'm sure he was a spy. I must have been a great disappointment to him on *that* score—I certainly had no inside information."

"Have you ever— Do you know what happened to him?"

"No. When Pearl Harbor was bombed, I thought: he knew about this."

Barbara remembered that day, her mother staring out the window after she'd heard about Pearl Harbor. She'd been thinking of this man. A spy. "What was his name?"

"He went by Jules André—his nom de guerre, I suppose you could say."

"When you went with him to Hiroshima—did you write anything about it?"

"I actually did, some innocent piece on a place called the Café Brazil. It was the fashionable spot. But Hiroshima was the center of military activity—they were already at war, you know, with China. I'll never forget seeing them unload small white boxes from a boat—ashes of soldiers killed in Manchuria. I believe I may have tried to work in some mention of that. Anyway, my little article never reached the States—my so-called friend probably saw to that."

Back in her apartment, Barbara looked at the fox woman scroll. She'd always pictured a shy, aristocratic young Japanese man running up to her mother, blurting out his compliment— beautiful as a fox woman—as he handed her this gift. But maybe Jules had given it to her. The fox woman seemed to look at her coquettishly, that backward glance more mysterious and alluring than ever.

She rummaged through her desk in the Western-style room for the picture of her mother at Kamakura, standing before the Buddha. Her mother was in her twenties then, just about her age, though she looked older, with her hair pulled up into the tight chignon that her father once described as having been worked out by a slide rule. She hadn't been a mother then, she'd been Janet, Janet Girard. Barbara imagined her turning from the camera, her face softening as she walked toward a man with black hair and a mustache, a smile like Clark Gable's. Then, in a hotel room, unbuttoning her suit, loosening her hair.

The rain had stopped by the end of the term. The last day of classes was warm and brilliantly sunny. The campus was full of people, parents come to pick up their daughters for the summer holiday.

Rie was given a mid-year diploma in a private ceremony in Miss Fujizawa's office, with her father and Barbara in attendance. Afterward, the three of them walked around the campus. Rie's father took pictures of them: beside the Venus de Milo, in front of the lotus pond, in one of the classrooms. Barbara felt desolate. "What will I do without you, Rie?" she said.

Rie and her father exchanged glances. "My father and I wish to invite you to our home in Hiroshima for O-Bon in August. Can you come?"

"Yes—of course. Now we won't have to really say good-bye."

"No," Rie said, "never will we say good-bye."

At Sango-kan, she said her farewells to Junko and Sumi, who would be returning in the fall, and Hiroko, who was leaving to finish a graduate degree in Chicago.

"I will send my impressions of America and capitalism," Hiroko said. "Also I shall study hard to become a teacher like you."

By evening, all the students had gone, and the campus seemed like a painting cleared of all figures, beautiful and calm.

PART THREE

25

Toward the end of June, Seiji came to see Barbara at Sango-kan. Miss Yamaguchi rushed up to tell her. "You have a gentleman calling," she said, then skittered back down the stairs again.

He was in the vestibule, looking out at the misting rain.

"Konnichi wa," she said.

"Ah—konnichi wa." They looked at each other, smiling. "Will you take a walk?" he said. "I have some news for us," he added in a low voice.

She stepped beneath his umbrella and they walked along the little path through the woods. He seemed jittery, nearly burning his fingers as he lit a cigarette. "Shall we go see how the plums are doing?" she said. They went past the lotus pond and the Venus de Milo, glistening white in the rain, then cut across the sodden grass toward the trees.

The wet leaves shone in the pale light. Most of the plums

had already fallen, small and golden, scattered in the grass. Barbara picked one up, remembering what Michi had written about the fruit feeling like a cool egg in her hand. "This is the first year Michi-san isn't here to make wine," she said.

"Yes." He looked away from her.

The rain dripped steadily onto their umbrella.

"What is your news?" she asked.

"I have found a place where we may go, in Asakusa. My friend, Kojima-san, has a florist shop there and once lived above it but does no more now that he has married. He says I may use this upstairs apartment, as he has no need of it."

"So—we can meet there—anytime?"

"As often as we like. On weekends we will have building entirely to ourselves. Already I have moved futon there."

"Oh, that's wonderful," she said.

"We can move the tansu there as well," he said.

"You mean—Michi-san's tansu?"

"Yes, this will be more convenient for us, I think."

"But I could just continue to bring the papers."

"If we have tansu there it will not be such a trouble to you. And we can easily spend long time together, translating at our leisure. Kojima-san may take holiday in August, then we will have apartment in privacy for many days. Will you like this?"

She touched his face. "I will love this." And you, she said silently, with such intensity that she thought he must feel it. "We'll be able to become so much better acquainted."

He looked around, then gave her a lingering kiss.

"When can we move there?" she said.

"I think in July, after students and teachers have left for their holiday."

They returned to Sango-kan in silence. Standing by the front door, she watched as he walked down the gravel path and out of sight. She held the plum to her nose; it had grown warm and fragrant in her hand.

She went upstairs, took off her wet dress, and lay down on the futon. Their own place. She imagined the apartment, tatami rooms, a tokonoma where they would hang a scroll and place Seiji's ceramics. The tansu could go next to the tokonoma.

But in the morning, when she awoke and looked at the tansu, she felt a shock at the thought of its absence.

By the end of the first week in July, many of the teachers who lived on the Kodaira College campus had left for the summer. Barbara had Sango-kan to herself, except for Mrs. Ueda.

Barbara had heard Mrs. Ueda say that she was going to spend a few weeks at the campus ski hut in Nagano. She and Seiji were waiting until after her departure to move the tansu. Days passed, and Mrs. Ueda showed no signs of leaving. Finally Barbara asked her one afternoon in the hall when she was going to Nagano. "Alas," Mrs. Ueda said, "I have many things I must accomplish in Kokubunji, so I have had to delay."

The next morning Barbara noticed that Mrs. Ueda's car was gone. She must have started on her list; with luck she would be away for several hours. Barbara called Seiji to tell him the coast was clear, and packed her overnight bag.

He didn't arrive until noon. With him was a young man whom he introduced as Hiko-chan; Barbara had seen him working in the restaurant kitchen and roaring down the street of Takanodai on his motorcycle. Hiko seemed a little sullen, but maybe he was just shy, Barbara thought, or uncomfortable about his task. She had no idea what explanation Seiji might have given him.

The two men were carrying the tansu down the stairs when Mrs. Ueda appeared in the hall; she had a string bag of groceries in each hand. Seiji and Hiko bowed to Mrs. Ueda as they went past with the tansu; she stared after them.

"Where is he taking Nakamoto-sensei's tansu?" Mrs. Ueda said.

"Just—out for some repairs."

"Is it damaged?"

Barbara turned quickly, pretending not to hear, and walked toward the door.

Mrs. Ueda followed. "You must not allow this."

"It will be all right, he's an excellent craftsman." Barbara stepped off the platform and into her shoes.

"I see you have your bag. Are you spending the night out?"

"I might stay at the International House—in case I'm delayed."

She hurried outside. Seiji and Hiko were wrapping the tansu in heavy cloth; they lifted it into the back of the truck. Hiko hopped into the bed of the truck beside the chest. She and Seiji got into the front seat and they drove through the campus. As the truck turned onto the main road toward Tokyo, she felt shaky with relief.

"Mrs. Ueda is a busybody." When Seiji looked at her quizzically, she said, "A snoop. A spy."

"She does not like for you to leave with me."

"No. She doesn't."

Seiji was frowning, concentrating on the traffic. She put her head against the seat and closed her eyes.

The truck lurched to a halt at a stoplight. "Be careful," Barbara shouted, looking over her shoulder into the bed of the truck. Hiko was gazing out at the sights of Tokyo, one arm draped casually over the chest as though it were there for his convenience. "He's not even holding on to it," she said.

"Hiko is reliable boy," Seiji said. "There is no need for alarm."

The apartment was in the Asakusa section of Tokyo, on Kappabashi Street. "This area is well known for its kitchen-wares," Seiji said as they drove down the street lined with small shops. "Our restaurant buys its equipment here; that is how I came to know Kojima-san."

"What did you tell him about us?"

"I have explained it was necessary to have a quiet place to do some important work of translation. Also, some writing about my tea bowls."

"So he'll think the tansu is full of pottery." She smiled, remembering that had been Miss Fujizawa's speculation.

"Kojima-san will not inquire."

He pulled the truck into an alleyway. Seiji and Hiko carried the tansu into the florist's shop. Seiji called out a greeting to Kojima-san, a man in thick, dark-framed glasses who was behind the counter helping a middle-aged woman decide between two vases. The shop was smaller than Barbara had expected, and the air damp and funereal, heavy with the mixed odors of flowers.

Seiji and Hiko headed up a stairway with the tansu. Barbara was disappointed; she'd imagined a separate entrance.

The apartment was small, just one tatami room, a tiny kitchen, and a bath. Seiji and Hiko put the tansu below the solitary window and, after a curious glance around, Hiko left.

They went out to buy groceries for dinner. When they returned the florist's shop was closed. Seiji opened the outer door with a key. She thought he might have a romantic impulse to take some flowers up to their room, but he headed right up the stairs.

She had decided to stir-fry salmon and snow peas, as Michi

had taught her. There was a skillet in the kitchen and a small, thin pot, in which she cooked the rice. The gas burner was hard to regulate and she was nervous; the rice ended up scorched on the bottom.

"It's terrible," she said.

"No, excellent," he protested, but as they crunched on the rice, both of them began to laugh. "I'd better send you to cooking school," he said.

"What about you?" she said. "Next time you can cook."

"Oh, this would be disaster," he said. "I want to compliment you highly on your cuisine."

They sat smiling at each other, then rose and took out the futon.

The next day was Sunday; the florist's shop was closed. They slept late and spent most of the morning in bed. It was afternoon before they began their work.

They opened the middle drawer of the tansu and took out the 1951 wine, the next one in the sequence they'd been following. It was the year Michi-san had gone to California, one of the papers Mr. Wada had translated.

"The seal is broken," he said, glancing at her in surprise.

"It's not just this one." She could feel her face reddening. "Actually all the seals are broken. I was trying to find Michi-san's fox print."

"You have opened every wrapper?"

"Yes—to look for the print. I did find a few pictures."

"Which pictures?"

"Photographs—there's one of Ume and Michi-san, and one of you. Then there's another of the three of you together—you and Ume and Michi."

"Why have you not spoken of these?"

"I didn't think to—the time never seemed right."

"Where are these pictures?" His face had gone rigid.

"It's nothing to be upset about—they're right inside the papers. There's one here"—she touched the 1951 bottle—"and another one in 1958, I think." She unrolled the 1951 paper and took out the picture of Michi and Ume, holding it in her palm. "They're in California, in San Francisco," she said. "That's the Golden Gate Bridge behind them."

He studied the photograph. "How can you be certain?"

"It's a very famous bridge. I've seen hundreds of pictures of it."

He pulled open the top drawer and took out the 1958 bottle. Inside the wrapping was the photograph of him at the pottery exhibit. He looked at it a moment, then scanned the paper.

"What does it say?" she asked. "I guess she wrote about the exhibit."

"Yes," he said. He put the picture inside the paper and began to roll it back up. "I cannot understand why you have not mentioned."

"As I said, it just didn't occur to me." She tried to keep the exasperation out of her voice. She put her arms around him. "Please, let's not fight. Let's not spoil this lovely day."

He kissed her. For a few moments they held each other, then moved to sit at the table. As he translated the 1951 paper, she wrote it all down diligently as though she'd never heard it before: Michi in Berkeley, enticed there by Ko's letter from California a decade earlier; Ko's children and her poetry; Ume's unhappiness. Barbara wished that she hadn't read the paper. It was so intimate when they made discoveries together.

As soon as he finished reading, she jumped up, went to the tansu, and brought back the 1952 bottle.

He smoothed out the paper and went through it silently.

"Did she find her?"

"You will hear," he said. "She begins, 'January 2, 1952. Even at New Year, California is sunshine state. It is too bright and cheerful, and abundant growth of plant life is strangely oppressive. In garden of apartment house are jumble of rose and wisteria vines, and huge avocado tree with fruit of unnatural size. There is plum tree in next yard, but it is not our Japanese plum. In summer, it makes purple fruit rather than our small yellow one. I am missing Japan very much and long even to see the gray sky, more in keeping with my present mood.' " He paused. " 'At times, melancholy threatens to overcome me.' "

"Was Michi sometimes depressed here too—or was it just being in America?"

"Why do you ask this?"

"I was just wondering about—later—her death."

He shook his head emphatically. "This is just some passing mood. It is difficult to be away from home country."

She looked at him, sitting erect at the table.

"It's painful, though, isn't it, to read about her sadness."

Although he said nothing, she felt an agreement in his silence.

He bent over the paper. "To continue, Nakamoto-sensei says Ume does not like bright sun and squints her eyes against it. 'One day we went to Tilden Park, very pretty place, with lake and such green grass I feel I am walking in a postcard. Together Ume and I rode . . .' " He opened the dictionary, searching for a word, and showed it to her.

"Carousel," she said, "merry-go-round. It's a children's ride."

"I see. She writes, 'Together we went up and down on the painted horse, but Ume cried and must be taken off. After I had quieted her, we took a walk along edge of park to lookout spot called Inspiration Point. There we had a fine panorama view of San Francisco.' "

"It's the picture!" Barbara picked up the photograph of Michi and Ume, San Francisco Bay behind them, Michi directing Ume's gaze toward the camera.

"Inspiration Point," Barbara whispered. She and Seiji leaned together, shoulders touching, to look at it. "I wonder who took this," she said.

"Some passerby, I imagine."

He read on in a quiet voice. " 'I told Ume that somewhere down below us lived her great-grandmother Ko, though of course she cannot understand me.

" 'I worry very much for Ume, as she is not developing normally. She can speak only simplest words and has not yet learned her toilet habits, though she is five years of age. We visited respected doctor in San Francisco who tells me she is quite retarded. I do not like his cold word. He asked me questions about circumstances of her birth, but I cannot talk to American doctor' "—Seiji paused—" 'about his bomb which has harmed her.' "

Barbara touched Seiji's arm. "It's all right," she said. "You can read anything to me."

"You will be very interested in the next part," he said. "Nakamoto-sensei writes, 'In past summer I gathered my courage to seek for Grandmother Ko.' " Barbara put down her pen to listen. " 'One day Ume and I took bus to area of San Francisco called Japantown, and spent several hours in attempt to find Pine Street address written on Ko's envelope. Ume was very patient during our long walk, though several times we must stop to rest. Finally we came to the address, at some distance from Japantown. There is new brick house lived in by family named Smith. At first, I think must be some error.' But Nakamoto-sensei says she has learnt that Japantown, 'changed after the war when Japanese-Americans returning from imprisonment camps found property had been taken in their absence.' "

Barbara asked him to read the part about Ko again. As she transcribed it, she thought of Michi at Kamakura, her wanting to guide Barbara to the sites of her mother. There had been no one to help Michi, no American who would have known what questions to ask.

"Let's read the next one," Barbara said. "I have to know if she found her."

He stretched. "I am rather tired."

"You could skim it." She got the 1953 bottle from the tansu and, kneeling beside him, unwrapped the paper. "Just look at it," she said, holding the page up to his face. "Is she still in California?"

He read for a moment. "Yes," he said, laughing, "she is."

"Why are you laughing?"

"You are not patient."

"Patience is not my virtue."

"What is your virtue?" he said with a smile.

"Passion," she said, embracing him.

"Kirekitsu." He let go of the paper to unbutton her dress, and they lay down on the floor beside the tansu, in the honey-colored light of late afternoon.

26

The following week it was scorchingly hot in Tokyo, and stifling in the Asakusa apartment. Barbara and Seiji went out to buy an electric fan, but it was of little help, merely shifting the turbid air about and languidly riffling the edges of papers on the table.

Barbara took off her dress and sat down to work in her slip. Seiji looked taken aback, even slightly shocked, she thought, but she persuaded him to take off his shirt. She brought damp washcloths from the bath and as they read the next of Michi's writings they wiped the perspiration from their faces and arms.

" 'There is much to record this year,' " the 1953 paper began. " 'A visit from Ota-sensei cheered us in November and we had many heartfelt talks and enjoyed cooking together our Japanese food. She is devoted to Ume, who takes to her as if she were grandmother.' "

Dear Miss Ota. Barbara could see her in her kimono, looking

slightly out of place in an American kitchen as she made chawanmushi custard for Ume.

"Nakamoto-sensei says when she told Ota-sensei of her effort to find Ko, she suggest they telephone to Yokogawas listed in telephone directory." Seiji read ahead silently, running his finger down the page. "She says she has already done this, to no luck. They make some attempts to search records in offices of the city, but are not successful."

"Does she say what records? Some archives?"

Engrossed in the paper, he did not answer. "Next Nakamoto-sensei writes that she and Ota-sensei took Ume for an outing to Japantown in San Francisco, where they had a lunch of soba noodles. Ota-sensei asked restaurant manager as they were leaving has she heard of Ko Yokogawa, a woman famous for haiku and tanka poetry before the war. She does not know her. 'Many look at us curiously,' Nakamoto-sensei writes, 'and I am embarrassed by Ota-sensei's British Japanese voice, although she means very well. Ota-sensei wishes to make further investigation elsewhere in the area but Ume has become cross and I am glad to have that excuse that we must go.

" 'Some weeks after Ota-sensei's departure I have returned to Japantown alone and made discreet inquiries of elderly people whom I met on the streets and in shops. Finally . . .' "

"Yes?"

" '. . . at one shop, Watanabe's dried goods, I am met with some success. Mother to store owner is there that day to arrange kimono. She says she did know Ko Yokogawa who was writer of poems!' "

Barbara gasped. "She found her!"

"Do not be too hasty," he said. "Nakamoto-sensei says she was extremely agitated—like you," he added, smiling at Barbara. "But she calmly says, 'Are you certain?' 'Oh yes, she was very memorable woman, quite beautiful with heavy eyebrows and fine pale face. She worked at a boarding house with her daughter.' "

"Does she give the name of the boarding house?"

He shook his head. "She says Ko was known for her ability to predict the future as well as for her haiku and tanka."

"I guess Michi-san inherited the gift for poetry from Ko," Barbara said.

"Has she read her poems to you?"

Barbara started to speak, then stopped. The only way she knew about the poems was from the paper she'd had translated. "I was thinking she had," she finally said. "We had many discussions about Japanese literature, including haiku." That much was true.

He was watching her closely.

"Isn't it fascinating that Ko had an ability to predict the future? Since Chie herself felt that about Ko, even when she wasn't physically there."

"Eh?"

"Ko predicting that the bomb would fall, and warning Chie to go protect Michi and Ume."

He laughed. "Can you believe this?"

"Well—in a way."

He shook his head, still smiling, and looked back at the page. "Most people in America do not like Ko's fortunes. The woman tells Nakamoto-sensei her predictions were always foreboding, with warnings of betrayal."

"Ko probably felt deeply betrayed herself, by the Takasu family, so she would see betrayals looming everywhere."

"Sometimes I think you are translator of this story," he said with a laugh.

"Don't you speculate about what lies underneath what's written? Reading between the lines, we say in English."

He shrugged. "I only read."

"Well, read then," she said with a laugh. "What comes next?"

"Watanabe tells Nakamoto-sensei that after the incident of Pearl Harbor, Ko and two of her children went to imprisonment camp somewhere in West—Idaho or Wyoming. Her oldest son joined army."

"Which army?"

"American one. He eventually became interpreter for American soldiers in Pacific. This is strange turn, ne?"

"Very ironic. Michi's relative was fighting against her own husband."

He nodded. "Nakamoto-sensei says she is shaken to learn these things and wants to verify, but says 'It seems futile, as Father warned. I think I will never find her. Ko and her children are gone far from here, somewhere in the huge continent of America.' "

"Is that the end?"

"Yes."

"I wish you'd *say* when it's the end. I'm sorry," she said, shaking her head, "I'm just so frustrated."

As Seiji went to return the bottle to the tansu, Barbara sat doodling in her notebook. She began to sketch a fox woman. Michi had to find her grandmother. Ko would be stunned at first; she had probably not even known that Michi existed. Barbara imagined Ko standing in silence—regal, betraying no feeling—then folding Michi in an embrace, the curtain of her hair falling around both of them.

She looked up. Seiji was still beside the tansu. "Is something wrong?" she said.

"There is one we have not seen." He turned to look at her. "Nineteen forty-five."

"Oh. It's something very sad. I meant to show it to you, but ..."

Her voice trailed off as he lifted out the bottle. She went to sit beside him. He laid the wrapped bottle on the tatami, untied the cord, took off the outer papers and the cloth wrapping. The exposed bottle lay between them. The only sound was the whir of the fan and the click as it turned from side to side.

"Again you did not tell me."

"The time never seemed right. It's not as if I was trying to hide it from you."

Seiji put the bottle away and closed the tansu.

"Let us go out for some cooler air," he said.

Outside, the heat shimmered on the pavement, rising into watery-looking mirages in the distance. They were grateful to find an air-conditioned teashop just off Kappabashi Street. Sitting at a table with their knees touching, they drank ceremonial tea and ate some fancy sweet cakes. Seiji lit a cigarette and leaned back in his chair. He seemed relaxed, his equilibrium restored.

"We're going to have a great summer, aren't we?" she said.

"Yes," he said, smiling at her. "I think so."

"After we finish Nakamoto-sensei's papers, let's start work on something else. Maybe I really could write something about your ceramics—I'd love to give it a try." The apartment was awfully small, she thought, but they could find a larger one. Not all the foreign teachers stayed on campus. Mr. McCann had his own place, no one seemed to know quite where. Tokyo was so large, it would be easy to disappear into it.

Walking back in the direction of their apartment, they saw a fortune-teller near the Asakausa temple; she insisted they stop to have their fortunes told. Each of them chose a stick with a number on it; the fortune-teller then gave them a sheet of paper with the corresponding fortune. Seiji's said that he was powerful and would be well known. There was no mention of love in Barbara's fortune, just the familiar Japanese prediction

that she would find some object that had been lost. She threw
it away and bought another fortune that said love would soon
flower.

"You cannot do this," Seiji said. "Only the first one is true."

"No," she said, "I just got the wrong one the first time. I'm
surprised you'd be so superstitious."

"But you are superstitious too—otherwise you would keep
the fortune you do not like."

They went down a street that specialized in butsudan, the
ancestor altars like the one Barbara had seen at Seiji's house.
There were many small shops with butsudans displayed in the
window. As they stopped before one, Barbara thought of the
picture of Michi-san on her butsudan shelf, youthful in her
summer dress.

"Michi-san would be happy for us, don't you think?"

He gave a short laugh and turned away to light a cigarette.
"Always you like to imagine," he said.

They decided to go to a movie, a samurai film she couldn't
understand a word of, but it was pleasant to sit in the cool theatre with him. She took his hand. "An American custom," she
whispered. They sat throughout the movie with their arms and
shoulders pressed together, their fingers interlaced.

After the film, they walked back to the apartment—stopping
on the way for some barbecued chicken at a street vendor's
cart—then went upstairs hand in hand. "I like this American
custom," Seiji said.

It was beginning to grow dark. "It's so peaceful here, isn't it?
No aunts or Uedas to worry about."

She thought he seemed distracted when they made love.
Afterward she lay with her head on his shoulder, drifting
toward sleep.

"We must go now," he said. "It is late."

"Why can't we just stay here? We have to read the 1954 paper in the morning."

"You must be discreet."

"I can tell them at the college I've gone on a trip. Everyone travels in the summer."

"I have my responsibilities at home." He stood and began to pull on his clothes.

She opened the tansu and took out the 1954 bottle. "Let's do it now, then. I have to know if she found Ko."

"I believe Nakamoto-sensei returned to Japan in next year, so I think she has never discovered her. There is no hurry. We can do next time."

She felt a flash of anger. "Why do you get to decide all the time what we're going to read and when?" She took the paper off the bottle, jumped up, and thrust it at him. "Here. If you can't read it, I'll find someone who will." They stood glaring at each other.

"You would not do this," he said.

"I would not want to. But I need to have this translated."

He grabbed the paper and snapped it open.

"Be careful." She reached for the paper, but he held it out of reach. He looked through the page, then said, "As I predicted, she does not find Ko."

"Does she mention her at all?"

"Yes."

"Well, what does she say?"

"She says last months in America very hard." He gave a dismissive wave with one hand. "Very melancholy, cannot attend classes." Another wave of the hand. "She left in disgrace without degree, still thinking of hopeless quest. All is as I said."

"You've already said you said it. Is there something more?"

"There follows something about return to Japan ... we can

read next time. You and Seiji. Watakushi. I." He pointed to himself.

"Yes, you and me. I didn't mean what I said before. It just gets to me sometimes, the way you're always in control, deciding when to leave, what to read."

"I cannot control that I must work. And when I read something you do not like, you become very angry. Boom." He gestured upward with his hands. "You say you will find someone else."

"I didn't mean that, honestly. And I don't really feel angry— just disappointed. But not disappointed with you." She put her arms around him. He was stiff, unmoving. "I'm sorry," she said. "I know I've been difficult. Let's not leave like this. Please, will you forgive me?"

He looked at her solemnly. "Yes, I can forgive."

They were subdued as they drove back through Tokyo to Kodaira. He stopped at the gate of the college. Please don't go, she wanted to say, but it would only make things worse. It took him time to get over being angry; he needed to be alone.

They met at the apartment two days later, on a Friday. She decided to take his favorite lunch, bento boxes of rice and broiled eel. That morning the tailor had called to say her new dress was ready. She stopped by on the way to try it on. It was flowered cotton with a becoming flared skirt. "I'll wear it," she said, and put her other clothes in the suitcase she'd brought with her for the weekend.

When she arrived at the apartment, she was startled to find Seiji already there. He was at the table, poring over one of the papers. He jumped up when she entered. "You have come early," he said.

"So have you." She glanced at the paper on the table. "I've brought lunch."

"Ah, very nice." He made a little bow. "Thank you. I am

reading to become a better translator. This is my surprise for you."

"And here is a surprise for you." Speaking in Japanese about the bento and the warm weather, she set the boxes of food on the table. He applauded, and she went into the kitchen to make tea. When she came back he had put away the paper and cleared the table of everything but their lunches.

She poured tea and raised her cup in a toast. "Here's to a happier day," she said in Japanese.

"Kampai." He took a sip of the tea. "You are very pretty," he said, also in Japanese.

She said the words for new dress, then stood up and twirled around.

He laughed. "Kirei. Beautiful woman."

She knelt beside him. He kissed her, running his hands down her sides, and said something she could not understand.

"You'll have to translate, I'm afraid."

"Even more beautiful without dress," he said.

"I think I'll keep it on for a while," she said, laughing. "It's cooler today, isn't it?"

After they had eaten and cleared the table, Seiji took out the 1954 paper. "I have been too hasty," he said. "There is something here which will interest you."

"About Ko?"

"Indirectly," he said. "More about Nakamoto-sensei. It is very heartfelt."

He read through the part he'd already summarized, so she could write it down, then said, "Here is the part I mentioned. Nakamoto-sensei when still in California says, 'One day when I was in despair, Ume came into my lap. As I stroked her head, it struck me that when I became mother ... I am ... discovered'— it is hard to say correctly—'I find a mother in this way.' "

" 'When I am a mother, I find a mother in myself '?"

"Yes, exactly."

She thought of the night she arrived at Sango-kan, Michi reaching out to take her hand, then running back and forth between apartments, bringing her everything she might possibly need.

"Yet, Nakamoto-sensei scolds herself. She says she has been a selfish woman to put search for Ko ahead of her care for Ume. That is reason why when she first returns to Japan, she goes immediately to Hiroshima, to take Ume to Red Cross hospital. Here is what she writes: 'Doctor explained to me that many babies in mother's stomach at stage of three months' or so development when bomb dropped are born with this form of retardation called microcephaly. He says there is nothing to be done for her but patient caretaking. There is an organization of such parents in Hiroshima called Mushroom Club and he has introduced me to them. At their meeting I was greeted with much warm understanding. I think I should stay in Hiroshima but Ota-sensei has kindly arranged for me to have position at Kodaira, in spite of incomplete degree. Incidentally I discovered that my friends from Fukuyama have moved to Tokyo. . . .' "

"Isn't that you?" Barbara interrupted.

"Yes, my mother, aunt, and myself. My mother has invited Nakamoto-sensei to stay for time being, as there is no room in Ota-sensei's apartment. She says it is like colony of hibakusha in Tokyo, so this is making her more at home." He looked at her. "And that is *the end.*"

They both laughed. He took her hand. "Now I think we should enjoy ourselves, not work so hard."

"Kojima is still here."

"We can be quiet." When she began to laugh, he kissed her. "This way I can keep you silent," he said.

They stayed in the apartment all afternoon, until after Kojima had gone, and took a bath together before going out to walk in the early evening. They had dinner at a nearby restaurant, then walked back to Kappabashi Street, unlocked the door of the florist's, and went upstairs.

"Very pretty dress," he said, reaching behind to unzip it. They took out the futon and lay down.

After they made love, they lay with their arms wrapped around each other.

"It feels so comfortable here now," she said. "I feel at home with you."

"I am the same," he said. "But I hope you can understand me. I must make ceramic to support my family. I cannot desert my work entirely."

"Yes," she said, "I understand."

Her time with Seiji fell into a rhythm; they met at the apartment a couple of times a week, did some translating, went for a walk, and, after Kojima left for the day, took out the futon. They rarely spent the night, but he promised that they would spend a week together soon, on a traveling holiday, "anywhere that Kirekitsu decides."

When she returned to Sango-kan, Barbara lay in the slight indentation in the tatami where Michi's tansu had been, and read over the day's translations.

In 1955 Michi returned to Hiroshima with Ume to see the doctor at the Red Cross hospital. "It is very strange to see modern buildings sprouted up out of ash, yet to know that bones continue to wash onto shores of the rivers." Thinking about the trip at New Year's, Michi wrote, "Tonight as every night I am thinking how I am responsible for having caused Ume harm. If I had not been so foolish as to keep up search for many days in poisoned city and gone instead to Kaidahara with Father, perhaps Ume would not be as she is, a child of four or five, though ten years in age. It seems that more than once I have made error of searching in futility, only at this time the consequences have been of very grave order."

"But she had to search for her family in Hiroshima," Barbara had said.

"Yes," Seiji had said. "She must do this. But I think it is difficult for foreigner to understand guilt of hibakusha, especially hibakusha who has survived without any harm to her own body."

Inside the next paper was the picture of him sitting at a table with Ume and Michi. Michi was watching Ume as she ate her noodles. "Was this at your house?" she had asked.

"At a restaurant, I believe." He had glanced at the picture, then set it aside.

There was no mention of Seiji in that paper, nor in the next one. In both entries Michi wrote of her classes and her efforts to write about Commodore Perry. Visits to Hiroshima with Ume were noted, more briefly than before.

The dignified picture of Seiji in front of his tea bowls was inside the next paper. Michi had written about the event, the fine day, the crowd come to see his work. "There were many who bought tea bowls, and he has also had essay published in two journals of craft and art. In both cases his fine technique and taste has been praised."

"Michi-san must have been so proud," Barbara had said. "Were the essays in Japanese?" He nodded. "Will you read them to me?"

"Perhaps so, someday." He had put the picture inside the paper and began to roll it up.

"Is that all Michi wrote about the exhibit? I think you're too modest."

He had shaken his head, smiling, and did not answer.

*   *   *

It was toward the end of July when Seiji and Barbara read the
1960 page, which Mr. Wada had already translated for her. She
felt uncomfortable as Seiji unwound the paper from the bottle,
composing her face to look surprised and touched, as though
hearing the section about Ume and then the tanka poems for
the first time.

As he translated, Barbara kept her head down, transcribing
once again Michi's description of helping to make the New
Year mochi cakes. " 'I went to my room to rest on futon. Ume
lay down beside me, her face against mine. At moments such as
these I cannot think of her as retarded. Understanding crosses
between us like electrical current.' "

"Very moving," Barbara murmured.

"Yes," he said with a sigh, and, picking up the paper, began
to slide it around the bottle.

"Did you read the whole page?" Barbara asked. She'd reread Mr. Wada's translation of the haiku on the train that
morning.

"Yes," he said.

"Are you sure?"

"Of course. Why do you question this?"

"I don't know; it just seemed so—brief."

He shrugged and turned to replace the bottle in the tansu.

Looking at his back, the muscles beneath his thin cotton
shirt, she thought of the 1949 paper about Hiroshima: Michi
pierced with joy when Ume was born and Seiji helping them.
"In this moment he has become a man." He might have been
leaving out other parts all along.

"I'm really tired today," she said. "I think I'd better go
now."

"Right away?" He looked startled.

"Yes. I forgot I have to stop by Shinjuku for an errand—another dress I'm having made."

"I see," he said, frowning.

"Maybe you won't mind," she said. "You can get to your responsibilities sooner."

He did not reply. They walked downstairs without speaking.

"Good-bye," she said after they went out the door. "I'll take the subway to Shinjuku—it will be easier."

She could feel him watching her as she walked down the street, then she heard the sound of his truck starting, screeching off in the other direction.

She found a seat on the train to Shinjuku and opened her translation book. There was the poem:

> White cloud of feathers
> Captured by the trees . . .
> Suddenly, two birds break free into the air.

She compared the two paragraphs of narrative. They were much the same, except that Mr. Wada's version contained two sentences that Seiji's did not: "I suggested to Kondo-san that we buy mochi from shop and she was very sharp to me in her reply," and, after Michi went to rest in her room on the futon, "I cannot help but cry." They were inconsequential sentences; he must have been translating carelessly. Or maybe there was some strong taboo about revealing any little thing about the family. But he'd left out the poem. It didn't make sense.

Barbara got off the train at Shinjuku and took the subway back to Asakusa. Kojima-san was still in the shop, squatting beside a tub of chrysanthemums. He looked up at her, open-mouthed. "I have forgotten something," she said, and ran upstairs.

In the room, she opened the middle drawer of the tansu and took out the 1960 page. It did look shorter than she remembered. Maybe he had erased part of it. She held the paper up to the light; there were no marks that she could see. Still, she'd have Mr. Wada have a look at it again, along with all the other pages Seiji might have censored.

There were voices downstairs. She held her breath. A man's voice, a woman's. Then Kojima-san's, welcoming them. Customers. She took out the 1962 paper, then all of the other pages Michi had written—1949, the 1950s, the 1960s—and rolled them into one sheaf. She started toward the door, then looked back at the tansu. It was even possible he had decided to edit some of Chie's writing. She sat down beside the chest. It was her tansu; these were her papers. She removed all the remaining papers; then, holding the thick roll on the left side of her body so Kojima-san couldn't see it, she hurried down the stairs and back to the subway station, where she boarded the train for Higashi Koganei.

27

The Wadas were eating dinner when Barbara arrived. Mrs. Wada insisted that she join them, "Just soba noodles, good for the health in our hot weather."

"Thank you, but only a little—I'm not very hungry." Mrs. Wada went to the kitchen and Barbara put the sheaf of Michi's papers on the tatami beside her. "Would you have time to look over some writing with me afterwards?" she asked Mr. Wada.

"I believe so," he said, though he glanced at the large roll of papers with alarm.

"I'm sorry to come so suddenly—but it's an emergency."

"Eeh?" he said, turning to look at the papers again. When his wife returned with soba noodles and sauce for Barbara, he spoke to her in Japanese, gesturing several times toward the papers.

Barbara ate enough noodles to be polite, then laid down her chopsticks. Mrs. Wada tried to hurry her husband along, scolding him in Japanese and making motions for him to eat more quickly, but he continued to consume his noodles at a slow, deliberate pace. Finally he rose, nodded at Barbara, and headed toward the study. Barbara picked up the papers and followed. "Everything okay," Mrs. Wada said, patting Barbara on the arm. "Okay, I hope."

"Yes, okay," Barbara said. "I'm sorry to be troubling you."

Mr. Wada took his place at his low desk and folded his hands before him. Barbara sat across from him and looked through the roll of papers for the 1960 and 1962 pages.

"Could you please read this one for me?" she said, handing him the 1960 paper.

He put on his glasses, smoothed out the paper before him, then glanced up at her over his glasses. "This is urgent, you say?"

"Yes. It's hard to explain, but I would be very grateful if you could help me. Could you please tell me—is there a haiku on this page?"

"The haiku poem?"

"Yes, yes, the haiku poem."

"An emergency involving haiku. Very interesting."

He went through the paper, following the calligraphy with one finger. She had never seen him read so slowly; it was maddening. Finally his fingertip reached the last character. He looked up at her. "No haiku," he said.

"You translated this page for me before—do you remember?"

"I do, yes."

"There was a haiku before."

"Yes. Very strange." He shook his head. "No haiku now," he said.

"Could they have been erased?"

"This would not be possible."

"Will you please read the paper?"

"I have just read. No haiku."

"I mean, please read it aloud. I'd like to hear what is there."

As he read aloud, Barbara followed along in her notebook with the version he had translated before. The two sentences about Mrs. Kondo's anger and Ume's crying were missing. "It's not possible," she said aloud.

He leaned forward to peer at her notebook. "We have some mystery, I think."

She gave him the 1962 page; the poem was also missing from that page, along with Michi's final comment, that she felt like a demon mother.

On the verge of tears, Barbara fumbled through the rice papers until she found the three sheets from 1949. "Please read me the last few lines," she said, flipping through her translation book to Michi's story about Hiroshima.

"Let me see . . . 'I took my meals with the Okadas next door. Mrs. Okada has been unfortunately blinded in bombing and I was able to be of some assistance to her. Mr. Okada was missing, also young daughter Itsuko. Some days Okada's son Seiji and I went through the city together, in search of our lost relatives.' These are final lines."

"There's nothing about the birth of Ume," she said, "or about Sei-san becoming a man?"

"No." He looked up at her, his eyebrows raised. "There has been some mix-up—or perhaps some mischief? Maybe fox at work?"

"Fox—why did you say that?"

"It is our Japanese superstition. We have many sayings and ancient stories about fox, snake, badger, and other mischief animals. There are fox stories I have translated in Noh. Are you familiar with the 'Little Swordsmith' story?"

"No—please, Mr. Wada, this is important for me to figure out right away. Is it possible to tell the difference in Japanese handwriting? To tell if different people have written different pages?"

"Yes, particularly when the writing is made with brush as these are—grass writing, as we call it."

"Then I have a big favor to ask you. Could you look at all the pages and compare the handwriting, and tell me how many writers there are?"

"Examine all these papers? This will take a great deal of time, I am afraid."

"Wouldn't it be possible to just look at a little bit of writing on each page? It's not necessary to read it—just to compare the handwritings. Please—as I said, it's of great importance."

He studied her closely. "You wish me to do this at the present moment?"

"Yes, if you can. Please."

After a long exhalation, he said, "I will try my best."

She slid the papers across the table. He unrolled them, holding down the edges as he stared at the top page. Then he stood, calling to his wife; the papers curled back up again. When Mrs. Wada appeared, he asked her for "O-sake, kudasai"—honorable sake, please. He went to his bookcase and brought back a volume of his Noh plays, which he set before Barbara. "Here you will find one of my translations of play about fox—'Little Swordsmith.' Perhaps it can amuse you while I am completing my task." Shaking his head, he began to thumb through the pages.

Mrs. Wada returned with a tray, on it a ceramic bottle of warm sake, two small cups, and, on a fan-shaped plate, sembei crackers wrapped in seaweed. She poured out sake for each of them and set the plate of crackers in front of Barbara. "Dozo," she said, "please eat," then left the room.

Mr. Wada drank two cups of sake before he started to work. Barbara held the book he'd given her but could not read; she watched as he examined the characters on each paper. She kept his sake cup filled but took only a sip of hers; it made her think of Seiji and the Kamiya restaurant. But she ate all the crackers, one after another without pause, monotonously crunching; when they were gone she wanted more. Mrs. Wada reappeared, took the plate, and refilled it. Mr. Wada continued drinking, and she eating. Finally he began to sort the papers, resting his palm lightly on each one as though making a diagnosis through touch. He divided them into piles and made notes on a small pad of paper.

Looking up at her with a triumphant little smile, he said, "Now I have some conclusion. The solution to your mystery, I believe." He laid the notes before him and began writing on a fresh sheet of paper. Barbara watched, reading upside down as he wrote:

Years 1930–1943, First Hand. This is Takasu Chie.

Year 1949, pages one and two, Second Hand. Nakamoto Michiko.

Year 1949, page three, and Years 1950–1965, Third Hand. Our fox.

He turned the page around before her. "Three writers," he said. "First writer makes some nonsense writing in final pages, but still her hand. Second hand composed only two sheets, first two pages of 1949. This is in very different style from third writer."

She stared down at the spidery handwriting. Her mind labored. "You mean . . ."

"Our fox has made an error, you see. He did not write over pages one and two of the year of 1949, only the last one where he wished to omit some passage."

"Are you saying . . ."

Mr. Wada laid a hand on one pile of papers. "Years 1930 to 1943, old-fashioned writing, very distinct. Year 1949, pages one and two, also distinct." He held them up toward her. "Different writer, you see." He laid the two pages on the table and touched the remaining pile with one finger. "All the rest, third hand."

"You are certain?" She thumbed through them. "These are all Michi-san's writings?"

"Yes, I am afraid so, quite certain."

"Then someone copied—all her pages. Except those two."

"It would seem to be the case," Mr. Wada said.

The room spun; for a moment she thought she would faint.

"I am sorry to have brought you a troubling solution."

"It's all right. Excuse me, I have to go." She started to gather the papers, but he said, "Wait, wait," pushed himself up from the table, and went to a tansu in the corner of the room. She fumbled in her pocketbook for a money envelope, put a large bill inside, and laid it on the table.

He walked across the room. In one hand he had a pair of scissors, in the other two balls of silk twine, one white, one black. "Just a moment, I will arrange for you." He sat down, laid the scissors and twine on the table, and picked up the pile of third-hand papers. She watched him roll the copied papers together and tie them with the white twine; then he took Chie's papers and Michi's two pages from 1949 and bound them with black string. "Now you can easily tell true papers from the false. Black is true, white is false."

She took them and burst into tears.

Mr. Wada hurried out of the room ahead of her; when Barbara came out, he was talking to his wife in a low voice.

Mrs. Wada ran to her side. "Not okay. You sleep here."

"I've got to go home."

"You stay. I am worry for you." She turned to her husband and began talking to him in an angry voice.

"Ah, ah," he said, ducking his head, then turned to Barbara. "I am very sorry I have injured you. Perhaps I am mistaken in my conclusion."

"No, I don't think so. Please don't be upset, Mr. Wada, this isn't your fault." Her tears had stopped abruptly. "I'll be fine, but I really must go."

There was another consultation between the Wadas, then Mrs. Wada went off toward the kitchen. "You must take taxi," Mr. Wada said. "My wife is calling now. Only a few moments. Please sit and rest yourself." He knelt and smoothed a cushion, indicating for her to sit there.

He looked so abject that Barbara sat down next to him. Mrs. Wada returned from the kitchen. "Taxi soon," she said, and lowered herself to the tatami beside Barbara.

They sat in silence, both of the Wadas looking at her. "I am grateful for your help," she said. "Please don't worry—I'm all right, really."

The Wadas began speaking to each other; Mrs. Wada rose, went back to the kitchen, and soon returned with a tied furoshiki. "More o-sembei for later," she said. "Also some fresh bean cake."

The buzzer sounded. "Taxi has arrived," Mr. Wada said in a relieved voice.

The Wadas went downstairs with her. Mr. Wada opened the taxi door and gave the driver lengthy instructions. Barbara heard him say she was a sensei at Kodaira College and not feeling well.

"Hai, hai," the driver said, stealing occasional glances at her.

Then the door closed, Barbara raised her hand in farewell, and the driver pulled away from the curb.

*   *   *

The outside light was on at Sango-kan, but all the windows were dark. Inside, it was pitch-black. Fumbling along the wall, she found the electric switch. Pale yellow light bathed the hall. She walked to the telephone, picked up the receiver, listened to the dull rasp of the dial tone, then put the phone down and went upstairs.

In the three-mat room she stood holding the papers, staring at the space where the tansu had been. The pair of foxes in the corner of the room and the fox woman on the wall gazed back at her. What a fool she'd been. Outfoxed.

He'd deceived her so completely. And elaborately. But why? She knelt on the tatami and unrolled the false pages. The paper looked no different, the same nubby grain, the same texture that she remembered. But he'd have had to make new seals. She looked closely at the bits of wax on the edges of the 1950s and 1960s papers. The wax was new, there was no doubt of it, the bright red color of fresh blood.

The next morning she put all the papers in her black bag and took the subway to Asakusa. She wanted to be there when he arrived, have the evidence spread out waiting for him. But he was already there, kneeling at the table. Behind him, the drawers of the tansu were open.

She put the black bag on the table.

"Where have you taken the papers?" he said in an angry voice.

She opened the bag, took out the roll of false papers, and threw them down in front of him. "These aren't Michi's papers," she said. "You wrote them."

He raised his chin slightly. "All Nakamoto-sensei's papers were written by her."

"Maybe. But they were copied by you—with parts left out."

He said nothing.

"A very good translator has looked at every one of the papers yesterday." She pulled out the other roll and laid them beside the copied papers. "Some parts that were on the page before are strangely missing. For instance," she added in a singsong voice, " 'In this moment, Sei-san has become a man.' " They stared at each other. His nostrils flared out, making him look almost ugly. "Also," she went on, "there are three handwritings." She took Mr. Wada's note from her pocket and gave it to him. "You made a little mistake—you forgot to copy pages one and two of 1949."

He crumpled the paper and threw it to the floor. "You have done this behind me," he said.

"What was I supposed to do, just pretend everything was fine, when you were leaving out parts of Michi-san's writing?"

"Ah—but how did you know of such parts?"

She looked away from him, at the tansu. "From a couple of pages I had translated—1960 and 1962, for instance, with some haiku that are now missing."

"As I thought," he said. "Therefore I could not trust you." He slowly stood up.

"But you had no right ... where are Michi's papers? I want them." He stared silently back at her. "They're mine," she said. "How could you do that?"

"There were some references Nakamoto-sensei made to me personally."

"So what?"

"She has forgotten that she wrote these parts."

"How do you know she forgot? Are you reading her mind—her dead mind?"

He made no answer.

"You admit it, then," she said. "You copied the papers. Forged them."

Silence.

"You don't even have the courage to say it. Okay. Just give the original papers back to me."

"This is not possible."

"What do you mean, not possible?"

"I cannot give you."

"Why not? She left them to me. They're all I have."

"Do not shout, please," he said. "Kojima-san is below."

"Oh, Kojima-san might hear. That's all you care about, what people think. Appearances. *Tatemae,* isn't that the word?"

He stepped around the edge of the table and began walking across the room.

"Where are you going? You have to give me those papers first." She reached out for his arm; he pulled away and headed for the door.

"Seiji, stop. . . ."

But he was going down the stairs. She ran to the window in time to see him get into his truck and roar off down the street.

28

Barbara had seen a large roll of brown wrapping paper in Mr. Kojima's shop. She went downstairs and, through a combination of pantomime and elementary Japanese, asked for thirty sheets of the paper. Mr. Kojima complied quickly, muttering numbers under his breath as he tore off the sheets. "Iie, iie," he said, shaking his head. He would not accept money. He just wanted her out of there, Barbara thought.

Back upstairs, she wrapped all the bottles in the paper so they wouldn't break on the return trip to campus, and went outside to flag down a taxi. During the drive she made a plan: she'd go to Seiji's house right away and—in front of his aunt and mother—demand the original papers.

At Sango-kan she and the driver carried the tansu upstairs. An elderly, gray-haired man, he was surprised by her strength, but she was not; she felt invincible.

She took all the bottles out of the tansu and removed the brown wrappings. Using scissors and notebook paper, she made labels for the 1950–1965 bottles and taped them onto the bare glass, then put the unspoiled papers around Chie's wines and the 1949 bottle. The roll of false pages went into the bottom of her closet. Finally she rearranged the bottles in the chest, reversing the order, with Chie's wines in the top and middle drawers. The others followed chronologically, with the 1965 bottle where the 1930 wine had been.

She replaced Michi's picture and the foxes on the tansu. The fox with the open mouth painted in as a triangle reminded her of a little bird waiting to be fed. The other looked reproachful. Her energy began to ebb. It was midafternoon, as hot and humid as the most miserable summer days in North Carolina. She thought of her room in the house on Stone Street, the fan in the big window by her bed, afternoon naps with the shades drawn. Rest was what she needed. She pulled her futon and pillow from the closet and fell instantly to sleep.

It was morning when she woke, groggy and soaked with perspiration. She forced herself up and into the kitchen, returned with tea. As she made tea she reviewed her plan for confronting Seiji. Perhaps it would go better in private, though still within earshot of his family. She could appeal to his sense of honor. If he was difficult she could raise her voice; he wouldn't want them to hear. She dressed and left her apartment. Downstairs, she stopped at the phone. Maybe she ought to call and make sure he was home.

Mrs. Kondo answered. No, Seiji was not in, she didn't know when he would be returning. Was he out of town? Perhaps so, it was possible, she had not been apprised of his exact whereabouts.

Barbara went outside and walked up and down the drive. There seemed to be no one else on campus; even Miss Fujizawa's car was gone. There was a low, monotonous thrum of cicadas, almost a sinister sound.

She returned to her apartment and slumped onto the futon. She tried to envision another one of his telegrams, or a gift of flowers left downstairs in the entranceway, along with Michi's original papers. He must realize what he had done to her; he wouldn't want it to end this way.

She drank a large glass of wine, then another; she lay back down and fell asleep.

When she awoke in the dark, she sat up and looked at her watch: 3 A.M. She turned off the light and, guiding herself along the walls, went into the Western-style room and sat on the window seat. The protruding L of the building, which contained Michi-san's empty apartment, was a blurry coffin-like shape against the dark sky. She thought of Michi's photograph on the funeral altar, her head cocked to one side. She had to get those papers back.

Moving to her desk, she turned on the lamp and got out some paper and a pen. "Dear Seiji," she wrote, "I am sorry that I lost my temper. Michi was very very important to me, I hope you can understand that, so her papers are most precious to me. I ask that you please return the original papers to me as soon as possible. I will even agree to your painting out the parts you do not wish me to read. Although this would be extremely painful to me, anything is better than not having her papers at all. I do want to understand, however, why you didn't want me to read those parts. If you can tell me this, then maybe I can understand your actions better. We must meet and talk as soon as possible. Sincerely, Barbara."

The next morning Barbara walked to Takanodai with the letter. She rang the bell by the front of the house. When there was no answer, she went into the restaurant. Hiko was inside, sweeping the floor. She asked if Seiji was there; he shook his head, not looking at her. Kimi came out of the kitchen. "Okada Seiji-san?" Barbara said. Kimi also shook her head and, covering her

mouth—Barbara couldn't tell if she was laughing or crying—
ran back into the kitchen.

She went out and walked into the pottery area, peering into
the shed and the studio. On the pottery wheel was a lump of
clay he had begun working. She touched the clay; it had turned
hard. There was a film of dust on the finished tea bowls set out
on the tables. She glanced toward the small room where they
used to go. The door stood partway open; she could see one
rounded corner of the cot, like an elbow. She headed toward
the house, willing herself to go past the gate and across the
courtyard.

The sliding doors at the back of the house were pulled all the
way open; from inside she could smell something cooking.

"Konnichi wa!" she called out.

Mrs. Okada came into the tatami room and began walking toward her, one hand outstretched in her direction, saying
something in a quavering voice.

Barbara said hello and identified herself in Japanese, then
put the letter into Mrs. Okada's hand. "Please give to Seiji-
san," she said.

"Sei-san," Mrs. Okada said, nodding and giving the envelope a little shake. "Hai, hai."

Mrs. Kondo emerged from the depths of the house. Her hair
was sticking up at a wild angle; she looked as if she'd just gotten
out of bed.

"I'm sorry to disturb you," Barbara said. "I gave Mrs. Okada
a letter to give to Seiji. I don't suppose he is here?"

"No. He is not."

"Is he in Mashiko?"

"Perhaps so." Her face was even less friendly than usual.

"Well, please give him the letter when he returns." She hurried through the courtyard and out to the street.

She walked home on the path through the woods. As soon as

she got back to the apartment, she'd call Rie and work out travel plans for next week.

The front door of Sango-kan was open but the building was deserted. It had never seemed so lonely. If Miss Ota were here, she'd knock at her door. She could picture herself at the table with a cup of English tea, Miss Ota's kind, perceptive gaze fixed on her. She took her address book downstairs to the phone; the first person she called was Miss Ota.

A young woman answered at the Yonago number. Oh, yes, her aunt was available, just one moment, if you please.

"Dear child! How delightful that you have called. I hope that you are coming to visit. We are quite ready for you."

"Thank you, Miss Ota." She could feel herself smiling. "I am quite ready to come. How about next week, August seventh? I could come after O-Bon in Hiroshima."

"This will suit us exactly. You must take the train up the Japan Sea coast—it is a splendid view all the way."

Barbara said she would call from Hiroshima with the time of her arrival, then phoned Rie. Rie asked her to come on the fourth or fifth, before O-Bon on the sixth. This was the twentieth anniversary of the bombing, Rie said, so there would be large crowds. "My father has worried that you may not be comfortable. Our apartment is quite modest."

Rie seemed to be suggesting a short visit. They agreed she would arrive on the fifth, then she called the Wadas, "just to say hello." She was grateful when they invited her to dinner the next night.

Two days later, she went into Tokyo to get her tickets. When she returned to Kokubunji, she got off the train, stepped past a man urinating in the gutter, then walked past a row of small shops. She glanced into the pachinko pinball parlor. There was Seiji, playing a machine near the window.

She stood watching him a long time. He did not move except to work the buttons and feed money in. She tapped on the glass. He stared for a moment and came outside. His eyes were red and he smelled of beer.

"Did you get my letter?" she said.

"Hai."

"Why didn't you call me?"

He looked down at the ground, shaking his head. "I have much shame. You can never forgive me."

"Maybe I can—if you give me back my papers."

He made a face and scratched the back of his neck.

"I've got to talk to you," she said.

He looked up at her, swaying slightly. "Babala-san."

"You're drunk."

"I have much shame," he said.

"Let me walk you home." She took his arm and steered him up the main street. Once they were at his house he couldn't refuse her the papers.

They walked in silence. He stumbled once or twice, but she held him upright.

When they came to the wooded area, she led him onto the path toward Takanodai. It was twilight in the woods. There was just room on the path for the two of them to walk side by side.

"Seiji," she said, "you know that Nakamoto-sensei was very important to me."

He stopped to light a cigarette, his hands shaking, then indicated with a nod of his head that he wanted to sit beside the canal.

They sat at the edge of the stream on hummocky grass. She looked down at the water, just perceptibly moving. "About Nakamoto-sensei …"

"Nakamoto-sensei."

"She cared about me. I know she did, like a mother. That's why she gave me her tansu and family papers."

"She had anger with me," he said. "Otherwise she would have given the tansu to me. Okada Seiji." He pointed at himself.

"I'm not going to argue about *that* any more. As I said, if you want to paint out those parts, like they did your history books ... I can stand that ... but I have to have the papers."

He shook his head.

"Let's go get them now," she said, starting to rise.

He threw his cigarette into the water; it made a small hiss. "I do not have."

"Where are they?"

He put his head in his hands.

"What do you mean, you do not have? You didn't—destroy them?"

"It could not be helped," he said in a muffled voice.

"Why?"

He mumbled something in Japanese.

"In English!" She pushed at his shoulder. "Look at me."

He raised his head but did not meet her eyes. "There are personal references. Nakamoto-sensei and I ..." He trailed off.

"Nakamoto-sensei and you what?"

He closed his eyes. " 'White cloud of feathers captured by trees, then two birds break free into the air.' This haiku is describing Nakamoto-sensei and myself."

"That refers to Ume—a visit they made to the rookery."

"No." He shook his head. "Nakamoto-sensei and myself. For a time—we are together in intimate way."

"Intimate?" His features were indistinct in the dusk; it was as if he were fading from view. "What does that mean?" she whispered.

"Like husband and wife—for a time." He dropped his head into his hands again.

She stared at him, then gave a short laugh. "I don't believe it."

He did not move.

"She was so much older."

"Only by nine years."

"Michi-san? You ..." For a moment everything went black, then her head cleared. She jumped up. "You used me. The only reason you wanted to be with me was to get those papers."

"No. We would be together in any case. Babala-san ..." He reached for her, touched her leg.

She kicked away his hand and stepped back. In the distance she could hear the traffic on the road, a steady sound like water. She turned and ran toward it.

In the taxi going back to Sango-kan, Barbara imagined smashing all Seiji's tea bowls and plates, even the haniwa, throwing them against the wall of the pottery shed, hearing them shatter. The precious Hamada bowl she'd save for last.

When she got home, she opened the refrigerator, took out leftover food from the Wadas ... pickles, bean cakes, a cream puff from the bakery below their apartment. She ate standing in the kitchen. Michi and Seiji: it was unbearable. There was peanut butter, almost half a jar. She ate it using one finger as a scoop. She took out a beer, Asahi, but could not find the bottle opener. Frantically she fumbled through the drawer, then dumped everything out in the sink. A coin rolled into the drain and lodged there. She started to cry, let out a ragged sound, then stopped.

She walked into the sitting room and took Seiji's two tea bowls off the tokonoma, stacking them roughly one inside the other, then went outside, to the back of the building. Though it was dark, a moon had risen; she could see the trash dump clearly, and the telephone pole between the dump and the cryptomeria trees. Taking aim at the pole, she threw the first bowl. It hit with a satisfying crash. The other landed with a small thunk on the pile of garbage.

There was a sound behind her. Mrs. Ueda was at her kitchen window, looking out at her; she must have just returned.

Back inside, she tiptoed up the steps to her apartment and paced through her rooms. She snatched the picture of Michi off the tansu and stuffed it beneath some blankets in the chest. The roll of papers Seiji had tried to pass off as Michi's she put in a cupboard in the Western-style room, out of sight.

There was a tap at her door, then another. "Barbara-san?" She went still.

After Mrs. Ueda left, she dragged her futon away from the tansu into the sitting room and went to sleep.

The sound of a blaring horn woke her. She went into the bedroom and looked out the window. Seiji's truck was in the driveway. He was outside the truck, yelling "Babala-san—Jefferson-san." The horn was still blowing; for a moment she thought it was stuck. Then she saw a figure in the truck on the driver's side.

She ran downstairs. Mrs. Ueda was already in the hall.

"There is quite a going-on," she said.

"Yes, I can take care of it," Barbara said, and went outside. The car horn stopped. Barbara recognized Hiko in the truck. Seiji came weaving toward her. "Babala-san."

"What are you doing here?"

"Come to Hiroshima," Seiji said. "In Hiroshima, I can make explanation to you. Then you can understand me."

"I'm not ever going with you anywhere again—can't you understand that?"

"O-Bon is next week. I will take Nakamoto-sensei's ashes . . . we have talked of this."

"That was a long time ago. And I'm already invited to Hiroshima for O-Bon."

"I will find you."

"It's too late—just leave me alone."

Seiji glanced toward the door, at Mrs. Ueda standing there.

"Go, please," Barbara said, and ran back inside. She and Mrs. Ueda locked the door as the truck drove away.

"You were right to warn me about him."

Mrs. Ueda sighed and shook her head. "I am very sorry he has upset you."

"Did Nakamoto-sensei talk to you about him? Were they—in love?"

Their eyes met. "He has caused her much grief," she said.

29

Barbara could not sleep that night, even after several glasses of wine. In the morning she looked into the refrigerator: empty except for a bean cake wrapped in a paper napkin, and one cracked egg. Some of the yolk had dribbled out and crusted on the wire shelf. She didn't have the strength to clean it up.

She sat down at her table with tea and the bean cake. On the bare tokonoma shelf were two small circles in the dust where Seiji's bowls had been. She could not keep her eyes from the empty space. Michi-san's papers were gone. Erased, blank. She had to get away from here.

During the spring holiday she'd spent one night at a Zen Buddhist temple in Kyoto that welcomed foreigners. The priest and his wife spoke excellent English; they'd invited her to return.

She made the call; yes, there was a room, the priest's wife said; she could come that very day. She packed—enough clothes for the two weeks in Hiroshima and Yonago—then called a taxi to take her to the station.

In downtown Tokyo, she changed her tickets. There was a seat on the new bullet train to Kyoto, leaving in thirty minutes; everything was falling into place. The train moved out of the city, sliding past ugly concrete buildings, factories, refineries. Soon they were going through flat green fields. In the distance was a line of dun-colored mountains. Suddenly the clouds above the mountains parted; Mt. Fuji hung in the sky like an illusion. Images of Hakone, the ski lift, Seiji's face close to hers, rose to her mind. She got up, stepped past her seatmate—a young woman crocheting a baby blanket—and went to the refreshment car, where she spent the rest of the trip watching the blur of landscape on the other side of the train.

At the temple she was shown to the same small tatami room where she'd stayed on her previous visit. It was only midafternoon but she got out the futon and lay down with one of the books she'd brought to reread, Faulkner's *Light in August*.

The next morning, before dawn, the gong for zazen meditation roused her. Tomorrow, she told herself, and fell back to sleep. At breakfast in the Zen study room, she met the other guests, two young American men from a commune in California. Both had recently burned their draft cards and were now seeking satori—enlightenment. One of them, bespectacled and with a bad case of acne, consulted his volume of Schopenhauer during lapses in the conversation. The other, who had long hair and a slightly crazed look in his eyes, said he really grooved on this place, the whole scene.

Barbara slept through meditation the next day too, and did not go out sightseeing as she had planned. She stayed at the temple, drinking coffee and reading. Occasionally her mind strayed, touching on Seiji and Michi in sharp, hot flashes: the two of them together in the tea house, in the small room inside the pottery.

In the afternoon she took a walk in the temple gardens. The priest's wife had told her there were nightingales in the large bamboo grove, and sometimes foxes, but she did not see or hear signs of either. There was only the relentless drone of cicadas. If emptiness could be expressed in sound, she thought, it would be this cicada noise. Suddenly there was nothing in any direction but bamboo, green trunks tinged blue and orange. She was lost. She began to run, dodging through the thicket until she saw the temple roof, then fled to her room, to Faulkner: red clay, scrub pine, the landscape of home.

After breakfast the next morning the priest came into the study center for an audience. A sweet-faced man in glasses, he had an air of infinite patience. He talked in a low voice to the young men, who told him they wanted to become disciples, novitiates.

"Why do you desire this?"

"To seek enlightenment," the Schopenhauer reader said.

"And what is enlightenment?" the priest asked.

"Man, if we knew the answer to that," the other one said, "I reckon we wouldn't be here."

"Ah, but perhaps you would," the priest said, with a slight smile.

"What is enlightenment, then, Sensei?" the first man said.

"The Zen master Dogen said that enlightenment is like the moon reflected on the water. The moon does not get wet, nor the water broken. The whole moon and the entire sky are reflected in dewdrops on the grass, or even in one drop of water."

There was silence. The men looked expectant, but when the priest said nothing further, they bowed and quickly left the room.

The priest turned to Barbara. "What do you seek?"

"I just want to forget."

"To forget we must first remember."

"I remember all too well."

He studied her a moment. "You have much pain," he said. She nodded.

"The practice of zazen meditation can help you. Think of the painful thought, then let it flow out in the tide of your breathing." Closing his eyes, he drew in a deep breath and exhaled slowly through his nose. "Very simple idea but difficult in practice," he said, looking at her again. "You must be patient. Even a moment of sitting can begin to free you from painful attachments."

The next morning before dawn Barbara took a place at the end of a row of monks in a cold dark room. After only a few minutes of sitting in the lotus position, her legs and back began to ache. She had a long day ahead, going to Hiroshima. She should have slept instead. One day of this would do no good.

The bell sounded, she drew in a breath. She thought of Seiji on the athletic field, holding out the raku bowl. For you, dozo. How excited she'd been, hurrying along the path by the canal to see him that first time, the smell of spring in the cold air.

They had sat by the canal on that soft grass; he would not look at her. His cigarette hissed in the water. She heard Mrs. Ueda's voice: He has caused her much grief. She thought of Ume, her small head and large body, a thorn in her heart. Michi raised a hand to her face. It was wet; she'd been crying without making a sound.

In the taxi, going to the station, she stared out the window. All these people, each one so vivid—the woman in a white kimono, carrying an orange furoshiki; the businessman consulting his watch—she'd never see them again. On the train she bundled her coat against the window for a pillow. Forgive me, she imagined telling Michi, I should have guessed about Seiji. Now your papers are gone. Please forgive me, please forgive me, over and over, the sound of the words catching in the rhythm of the train until finally she slept.

Rie and her father met Barbara at the station. "Very nice," Mr. Yokohagi said, several times, bowing. "My daughter has been waiting."

"I am glad you have come, Sensei," Rie said.

They took a crowded streetcar to their apartment building in the middle of the city. Standing beside Mr. Yokohagi, Barbara noticed a prominent wen on top of his head. She wondered if it was cancer caused by radiation; Rie said he had not been well. She looked out at the square concrete buildings, the buses, the streets full of people. A different city was here before, replaced with this one. She thought of the photograph of her mother in Hiroshima, she and her guide tiny figures in front of the Kabuki theatre that was now gone. Seiji had known that theatre, and Michi; Michi had probably been there many times. A headache started behind her eyes. They crossed one glistening river, then another. Along the riverbanks were enormous shrubs of oleander in bloom. The streetcar rattled over yet another river.

"So many rivers," she said.

"We have seven rivers in Hiroshima," Rie said, "all branches of Ota, which forms in the mountains." She counted them off on her fingers. "From the east, Enko, Kyobashi, Motoyasu, Honkawa, Tenmagawa, Kawazoegawa, Koi."

Mr. Yokohagi leaned forward and, looking at Barbara, asked a question in Japanese.

"My father wants to know your first impression of our city."

"It's pretty," she said. "But strange."

Rie translated for her father, then said in a quiet voice, "Perhaps you can understand if you think of 'unreal city,' as Mr. Eliot speaks in his *Waste Land*."

The Yokohagis lived at the top of a drab apartment building. There was no elevator, so they climbed the six flights of stairs, Mr. Yokohagi running ahead with both of Barbara's suitcases. They went through a door onto a balcony, where there was a clothesline sagging with underwear and shirts. The Yokohagis' apartment was at the end of the balcony.

"Please welcome our modest home," Mr. Yokohagi said. There was a hall, a bath on the left, a toilet on the right, then a large room that included a kitchen area. At the end of the apartment were two small tatami rooms. Rie put Barbara's bag in the room they'd be sharing, and left her to put her things in the closet and an empty tansu drawer.

Barbara shook out a dress and reached into the closet for a hanger. A face with bulging eyes stared out at her from a shelf. Then she realized it was just a clay head, a sculpture. Except for the eyes, it looked a little like Rie. A frightening thing to keep in a closet, though, and weird; the placement seemed almost deliberate.

Rie had tea ready at the kitchen table. Barbara asked for aspirin; Rie gave her some grayish powder mixed in water. Mr. Yokohagi sat down to join them. There was a discussion of what to have for dinner, then Mr. Yokohagi said something to Rie in Japanese.

"Hai," Rie said. "Okada-san has telephoned for you."

"Okada Seiji?"

Rie nodded.

"But—how did he know I'm here?"

"He is aware we are acquainted. So he thinks perhaps you will visit me, or I will know where you stay."

"What did he say?" Her stomach tightened. "Is he coming here?"

"I believe so, yes." Rie exchanged glances with her father. "I am afraid we have caused you some trouble."

"No, no, you haven't." She made herself smile. "Please don't worry. Everything is fine. Really—fine."

"Shall we visit the Peace Museum?" Rie said. "Tomorrow will be too crowded, with many thousand of people here for the August sixth commemoration."

"Yes—good—let's go right now." If he came she wouldn't be here.

On the way to the museum, Rie pointed out landmarks from the streetcar: the Hondori shopping district with its famous lily of the valley lamps; the Fukuya department store, partly standing after the bombing, now completely rebuilt; the Atomic Bomb Memorial Dome, the ruins of a huge building that had been preserved as a memorial.

They got off the streetcar and walked toward Peace Park, a grassy area full of trees and crisscrossed by walkways. Although most of the people in the park were Japanese, Barbara saw a number of foreign faces too. She kept looking around, expecting Seiji to materialize.

She thought of him in the Peace Museum as she and Rie moved silently through the rooms of exhibits with a long line of people. There was a photograph of a man's back, so deeply scarred it looked like a topographical map; a schoolchild's lunchbox, its contents radiated, blackened into one mass; a watch without hands, but the shadow on the face showed the time: 8:15. She walked out exhausted, blinking, into the scouring light.

They walked along the edge of the Motoyasu River. "Here we have ground zero," Rie said, nodding toward a stone tablet. As Barbara bent down to touch the marker, she felt electricity up her arm. She stood and looked around her at people walking across the bridge, sitting on benches in the park. A little boy with a popsicle ran past, his mother hurrying after him. It was a hot day, August. Twenty years ago it had been hot too, an ordinary August morning, dust rising from the road. Seiji was lying down with a toothache; she imagined a cloth tied around his head. Michi was cooking, thinking of a slice of lemon. "What were you doing that day?" she asked Rie.

"I recall nothing, but Father has told me Mother's experience." They began walking more slowly. "Mother was carrying me on her back as she weeded sweet potatoes in the garden. Then huge flash and such big explosion she fell to the ground. She cannot believe what she sees as she ran down the streets past Hijiyama hill to search for Father. Everywhere people lay dead or moaning. One young girl held eyeball in her hand. Huge cloud with eerie purple lights was rising over city. She think world must be coming to its end. She wants to find Father so we can all die together, but when black water starts to fall from sky she wraps me in her kimono and carries me home. Perhaps this has spared me from radiation disease of which Mother later died."

Rie's stoical expression had not changed. "It must be hard for you not to hate Americans," Barbara said.

Rie shook her head. "I know Japan is aggressor in war. And army was not pure. Here in Hiroshima, for example, Koreans were living almost as slaves at time of bombing. No one has even found their names. But how can atomic germ be cured? Maybe if people know consequence, there can be some hope. This is why I write my father's story."

"You said he was saved by an undignified miracle."

"Yes. He was close to here. Less than ninety meters from ground zero, a soldier on parade ground. I have asked Father— he says he is glad for you to know his story. We can tell you tonight."

In the evening Barbara helped Rie cook tempura while Mr. Yokohagi sat at the kitchen table reading the newspaper and drinking sake. They made awkward conversation during dinner,

Mr. Yokohagi trying out his pidgin English and Barbara her scraps of Japanese. After they finished eating, Rie went to her room and returned with a manuscript. "This is my book I am writing." She put it before Barbara on the table. "One section is my father's life."

Barbara thumbed through the pages; they were written in longhand, in calligraphy.

"You've done so much," she said. "I hope you've made a copy."

Rie shook her head. "I have no worry, I know this story by my heart. Will you hear it now?"

"Yes, thank you." The three of them sat down together on the tatami.

"My father, Yokohagi Shoichi," she began, bowing toward him, "was of humble origin, as I have said. As a private, however, he was a favorite of his commanding officer. On day of the bombing as I told you earlier he was marching his drill with companions on parade ground. It was just a little after eight A.M. that father asked permission to visit the latrine." Barbara glanced at Mr. Yokohagi; his eyes were fixed on his daughter. "The officer granted his request. The privy was a modest hut yet it spared his life. While he was inside the bomb fell with huge flash and sound like thunder from center of the earth. The privy collapsed and the tree beside fell, pinning him inside, yet somehow he was able to get free. He came out to find almost all other soldiers dead or dying, some burnt black like logs. Above is heavy dark cloud. He cannot see. Smoke singes his eyes. How is he still living? It could be nightmare dream. Or maybe he is a ghost. Everywhere are such terrible sights, he thinks this must be Buddhist hell.

"But then he heard a comrade call out, 'O-mizu, kudasai'—water, please. He took him on his back and began running toward a river. Along the way a few of his fellow soldiers were weakly crying out—the last words on soldier's lips were supposed to be praise of emperor but in every case was for water or mother. He did what he could to help, though most died, then ran home to see about Mother and myself.

"Only later did he realize a nail has been riven through his back, and there are burns over all his body. But he went back to center of city and worked without cease for days helping victims and doctors, carrying out cremations, whatever needed to be done.

"So you see he showed his true valor, which rises above any class. Even after Mother died he has kept his pluck and tried to show me how to live."

She said something in Japanese to her father, bowing to him again. He murmured something and bowed back.

"You must be very proud of your father," Barbara said.

"Yes," Rie said.

There was a silence. Barbara and Mr. Yokohagi looked at each other. She was looking into the eyes of a Japanese soldier, she thought. The enemy.

Mr. Yokohagi rose, went to his room, and came back with a huge sword. He stood in the middle of the room and brandished it several times.

"This is special sword he wishes you to see," Rie said. "It was given him for bravery during the war . . . an officer gave it to him afterwards, he says. He kept it secret from occupation army."

At the end of the sword performance, Mr. Yokohagi went back into his room and emerged with a small brocade box, which he set before Barbara. "For you," he said. "Noodle."

"These are from my father's own shop," Rie said.

Barbara opened the box. Inside were several rows of needles, arranged by size. "Oh, thank you, these are wonderful, very useful." She looked at Mr. Yokohagi and Rie, both smiling at her now. She restrained an impulse to hug them. "Thank you most of all for telling me your stories."

"Thank you for your listening, Sensei," Rie said.

"I should call you sensei."

"We are both sensei, ne?" Rie said with a laugh.

Barbara helped Rie lay out two futons in her room. They got into bed and turned out the light. Barbara thought of the head on the shelf, staring into the dark. "Rie, what is that sculpture in your closet?"

"This is my self-portraiture. We are required to make such a thing in mortuary school. Has it shocked you?"

"Well—yes."

"Sometimes I think to take away but where can I throw it? Beneath clay are bones of some other person."

"You mean—a skull?"

"Yes. We must begin with this skull and add clay to reproduce our face. This way we can learn to make new face for dead man."

"I don't see how you have the courage."

"Courage is ordinary thing to people of Hiroshima."

"What about love?" Barbara asked. "Is it hard for hibakusha to feel love—having gone through . . . all that?"

"All hibakusha are not the same." She paused. "Do you have some hope for Okada-san to come tomorrow?"

"I don't know—he's done a cruel thing."

"He has done?"

"Yes, it has to do with some papers that were very important to me."

There was a silence, then Rie said in a soft voice, "I am sorry, Barbara-san."

30

The next morning Rie painted several signs for the Peace March—"No More Hiroshimas" in English and Japanese—and Mr. Yokohagi nailed the placards to flat sticks.

"Will you go with me, Sensei," Rie asked, "or wait for Okada-san?"

Barbara looked out the window, scanning the faces of people on the street. I'm looking for Seiji, she thought. "I'll come with you," she said.

"Your father isn't going to join us?" she asked as they started down the steps.

"He does not like crowds—particularly at this time of year."

On the last flight of steps they met Seiji coming toward them.

Barbara stopped, holding on to the banister.

"We are headed for the Peace March," Rie said.

"I see."

301

The three of them walked down the last steps in silence. Seiji was carrying a white furoshiki in one hand.

At the curb, they hesitated.

"I must talk to you urgently," Seiji said.

"Why didn't you come yesterday, then, if it's so urgent?"

"I hesitated to tire you further after your journey."

Barbara turned to Rie.

"Go with him," Rie whispered. "I think is important. I'll see you this evening." She hurried off to the streetcar stop.

To avoid looking at Seiji, Barbara stared across the street at a tall mesh fence around new construction. "I broke your tea bowls," she said.

"Ah." There was a long silence. "I understand," he said. He gazed at her steadily. "I am going to lay Nakamoto-sensei to rest." He lifted the furoshiki: it was the wrapped box of Michi-san's ashes. "Will you come? I would also like to make my explanation to you."

"Okay." They walked to his truck and got in. He put the furoshiki on the seat between them. She kept glancing at the furoshiki, the shape of the box inside.

When they came to the western part of the city, narrow streets winding up a hill, he said, "This is Koi, where Nakamoto-sensei and I grew up." He pointed out a stone wall. "I ran beside that as a child."

She leaned out the window to see it more clearly. "The bomb didn't destroy it?"

"No, there are many sites still standing in Koi. Nearby was my house and Nakamoto-sensei's—shall we go there?" They got out and walked slowly up the street.

They stopped before a large wooden house with a curved tile roof; around it was a wall. "This is site of Sensei's childhood home."

"Right here—she lived in this house?"

"It has been replaced." He nodded toward a house next to it. "The house beyond was my childhood home, this same building."

She looked at the tiled roof, a round window, tatami visible beyond the open sliding doors. There were morning glories spilling over the gate. "Have you been back inside?"

"No," he said. "I do not care to."

"You and Michi-san lived side by side." She looked up and down the street. An old woman pushing a cart passed by; she bowed and smiled, showing a toothless mouth. "You were both born here."

"I knew her my entire life," he said. "Sometimes she watched out over we younger children as we swam in the river." He pointed down the hill. "We cannot actually see from here—but the river is there, not too far."

"The Koi River?"

"Yes—I liked to jump off the bridge and make a loud splash,"

She could see him. A skinny little kid, arms outstretched, yelling "Banzai!" as he hit the water.

"The tea house has been torn down behind Nakamoto-sensei's house, but the plum trees are still there, I believe."

They rang the bell and he received permission to go into the garden.

There were three gnarled plum trees, all in full leaf. Barbara touched the trunk of the largest one. The bark was pinkish tan and stippled with small nodules. She looked around her: mossy ground, a pond with a slightly askew stone lantern at the edge, some potted bonsai. Ume had been born here. "Where was the tea house?" she said.

"This way." He led her to the far end of the garden, to a place beside a stone wall.

"I wonder where Chie buried those papers," she said.

"Beside the tea house, I believe."

"Why did they tear it down?" she said.

"It was in poor repair. Also, the present owner is not much interested in tea ceremony." He looked close to tears.

"Was it hard—delivering Ume?"

"After bombing, nothing could frighten me."

They walked back through the garden—Barbara stopped to pick a leaf from one of the plum trees and put it in her pocketbook—then got in the truck and drove on up the hill. "Where are we going now?" she said.

"Mitaki Temple. This is where we will lay Nakamoto-sensei to rest."

They rode higher up the mountain. Barbara caught the wrapped box as it slid, and took it in her lap. About a year ago she'd first met Michi, when she stepped up onto the platform at Sango-kan. "How tired you must be," Michi had said, and took her hand, holding it for a moment in her firm grasp. Now, nothing but ash.

The temple grounds were green and deeply shaded by enormous trees. They walked along the paths looking at the gravestones. Seiji stopped before two statues of Jizo, the protector of children. "These Jizo commemorate children who were not found. He pointed to a small Buddha-like figure on the right. "This one is for my sister. Her name is there on the marker, Okada Itsuko." They were silent. "The Jizo next to it is for Haru, sister to Nakamoto-sensei."

"Side by side," she said.

"Yes, just as in life."

Inside the temple they met the priest, a bald, solemn man dressed in white and yellow robes. Seiji introduced Barbara in English. "Nakamoto Michiko-sensei was like Japanese mother to her."

The priest bowed. "I regret your sorrow," he said.

He led them to an altar in a large tatami room. Seiji untied the furoshiki and took out the white brocade box; the priest placed it on the altar and, bowing, chanted a sutra. Then he ceremoniously removed the box from the altar and settled himself on the tatami facing Barbara and Seiji. He placed the brocade box on the tatami, opened it, and lifted out another, smaller box of white wood. Barbara leaned forward as he removed the lid and brought out a pottery urn. It was dark brown, mottled with black and gold. Seiji's work. He was looking down at the urn, his face drawn. The priest set a pair of long chopsticks before Seiji and spread a square white cloth on the tatami. His hand trembling, Seiji lifted the top from the urn. Barbara drew in a sharp breath: there were shards of bone inside, along with the ashes. Using the chopsticks, Seiji delicately removed a small bone and placed it on the white cloth. After saying another short prayer, the priest swaddled the bone in the cloth, and the three of them rose.

The priest carried the wrapped bone, leading the way from the temple, down the steps and toward the graveyard. "What about the urn?" Barbara whispered to Seiji.

"It will remain in a special room of the temple. Only the throat Buddha is placed in the grave."

The gravestones were stone obelisks set on marble platforms. Michi's family gravestone was beneath a huge camphor tree. Seiji said in a soft voice that her parents, her brother Shoichi, and Ume had already been laid to rest there. In the base of the obelisk was an open, empty slot reserved for Michisan. The priest, and then Seiji, said something in Japanese. "Now you say that I Barbara Jefferson am here," Seiji told her.

Barbara announced her presence, then watched as the priest placed the wrapped bone in the stone drawer. Seiji stepped forward, took a white rectangular envelope from the inside pocket of his jacket, and laid it inside the drawer. Maybe a photograph, she thought, or a letter of farewell.

They bowed good-bye, walked to the truck, and got in. Seiji's head was bowed, one hand over his face. She slid closer and put an arm around him. He reached for her hand. He started the truck after a few minutes and they drove away from the temple, heading farther up the mountain. She didn't ask where they were going. They climbed higher and higher, rounding sharp curves. "What is the throat Buddha?" she asked.

"Here." He pointed to his Adam's apple. "Place of speech— the bone protecting vocal strings."

Barbara's eyes filled with tears.

Seiji pulled the truck to the side of the road and turned off the ignition. "This is Mt. Mitaki," he said." You may recall Nakamoto-sensei's writing of this place, coming here with her family to gather chestnuts."

As they walked through the woods, Barbara took in the trees, the carpet of dead leaves, a fallen log covered with ferns. Michi had scampered around on this ground, playing hide-and-seek behind the trees with her brother and sister. Lively like a monkey, her mother had said.

They came to a clearing at the edge of the mountain. Below them, in the valley, lay Hiroshima.

She and Seiji sat on a large rock overlooking the city. Michi had written that Hiroshima meant broad island, but it was more like a series of long peninsulas separated by rivers. All the rivers ran to the Inland Sea, a shimmering expanse of water to their right. Crowded on the fingers of land were houses and, in the central area, taller buildings. The green area near the center must be Peace Park. Ground Zero.

"After the bombing," Seiji said, "all that you see below, with the exception of Koi, was desert. Only five or six buildings remained even in part—all the rest was ash and rubble. That hill, Hijiyama"—he pointed to a small mountain on the far side of the city—"held back the bomb's power, so some houses on other side—in Donbara-cho—were spared. Only areas of city not to be destroyed completely are Donbara-cho and Koi, also some houses near Ujina port."

"I'm glad Koi is still here—at least some of it."

"Why should we have a house when others' houses are gone? Why should we live when others have died? It seems we have bought our life at expense of others.

"This is bond between Nakamoto-sensei and myself. When I say why should my sister be killed working in fire lane and not I, she knows my feeling exactly. She has suffered that she lived by miracle of her mother's rescue, yet her brother and sister have died.

"She and I are not like ordinary lovers. Fate of our experience has brought us together. We are welded together like pieces of glass in explosion." He held his palms tightly together. "Can you understand me?"

She thought of the deformed glass bottle in the tansu. "Yes," she said, "I think so. To the best of my ability."

"I have promised to tell you entire truth, even to my shame." He lit a cigarette, closing his eyes against the smoke for a moment, then took a deep breath and sat up straighter. "After aunt and mother settled in Tokyo and Nakamoto-sensei came to Kodaira, she stayed with us as I have told you. Our mutual trust and dependence on each other deepened. We became like family, all of us, in a sense, because we are united in concern for Ume.

"Aunt became jealous of Nakamoto-sensei when she sensed our closeness. She insisted I marry with a young woman who will not know our past and bear children to continue our family. But I had no wish to pass along contamination of

Hiroshima—maybe radiation will cause deformity in my children. Also, I felt obliged to Michiko-san, and I had come to
think of Ume as child I would care for."

It was the first time she'd ever heard him use her given
name.

"Why didn't you marry her?"

"In truth I must confess I did not love her as I should. I was
weak man, a coward, standing between disapproval of aunt
and mother on one side and Michiko-san's wishes on the
other.

"So we remained in Takanodai for some time. Michiko-san
and aunt were in a sense like daughter-in-law and mother-in-
law. This is difficult in Japan usually, but worse in this case
without marriage, especially as Michiko-san was rather strong-
willed. Also, my aunt resents her to go out to her teaching and
leave care of Ume to others. One day she and aunt had bitter
fight and I did not stand up for her as I should. This was the
tragic matter."

"What happened?"

"It was in middle of summer. Michiko-san was making the
plum wine with Ume's assistance. They had spent long time
cooking fruit and preparing large jars of umeshu to be aged.
Ume insist to help carry jars to large tatami room for storage.
Somehow she tripped and fell down, spilling wine on tatami. I
was in nearby room reading. I heard aunt shout, 'Stupid girl!'
and Michiko-san shout to her, never to speak to her daughter
this way. Ume ran away crying but aunt continued to scold, saying Michiko-san and Ume were nothing but a trouble. 'If not
for you my nephew would be married to a young woman by
now.'

"Michiko-san walked by room where I sat. She stopped at
door. 'Did you hear what your aunt has said?' she asked. Her
eyes pierced me. 'Hai,' I said. I could not speak further, nor

move. She ran down the hall. I should have gone to her then. Instead I went to my pottery." He put his face in his hands. "All night in my pottery. Next day they are gone."

"Moved out?"

"Yes. I tried to find them but for long time could not. To tell the truth I did not try so hard as I might at first. In my selfish pride I reasoned that Michiko-san did not appreciate my care of her and had failed to understand my delicate position in our household. I have much obligation to my aunt for her years of helping my mother and myself, especially in Fukuyama when we were both invalids. And I would not have pottery were it not for her. Later I learned that Michiko-san had met with much hardship, first having to board in a sort of hotel. Eventually she found caretaking home for Ume and she moved to Kodaira campus. Not long after, Ume was found to be ill; the next years were very difficult time. I tried to help, pleading Michiko-san to hear my apology and to return, but she would not. She was alone in her grief. She bore grief of her daughter's illness and death alone.

"Babala ... sometimes you have asked me do you think Nakamoto-sensei has taken her life? I believe so, yes, she has done this, and underlying reason was my cowardice and poor treatment of her." He looked at her. "This is my deepest shame."

"But ..." She touched his arm. "When was this fight with your aunt?"

"In 1961, summertime."

"That was years before—four years before her death."

He shook his head.

She moved closer and put her arm around his shoulders. "I'm sorry you've suffered so much. But maybe she didn't kill herself ... or if she really did, there must have been many complex feelings. Remember what you said, 'It is impossible to know the soul of another'?"

"In her writing, she has revealed her soul. She asks what purpose is there to live, with Ume gone. She says she has leukemia of the spirit, and wonders if she may have physical disease of leukemia as well. But the worst despair is that I have just described to you, to bear her grief alone."

"Did she write about that?"

"Indirectly, yes." He looked at her. "This is why I have destroyed the papers—for my shame."

They drove back down the hill to the city. Barbara stared numbly out the window as they went through Koi, crossed over a bridge, and entered the center of the city.

"If you didn't want me to read the papers, why didn't you just destroy them and be done with it? Why did you go to all that trouble of making copies?"

"I did not wish to lose you."

"Why not?"

He did not answer.

As they crossed another bridge, Seiji said, "This is Motoyasu River, where Chie has brought Michi after bombing."

She stared down at the water glittering in the sun, trying to imagine the river choked with bodies, Chie holding Michi on her back.

"In Hiroshima we celebrate O-Bon festival of the dead on anniversary of bombing. On this day, spirits of the dead are believed to return to their home. In evening we set bright lanterns on river to guide spirits back to land of rest." He paused. "Tonight I will bring lanterns for Michiko-san and others. Will you come?"

"Yes," she said, "I will come."

At dinner, Rie said that she and her father would celebrate O-Bon at the Enko River in Donbara-cho, where they had lived before the bombing. "I'm going to the Motoyasu, with Seiji," Barbara told her.

"You have reconciled then? I am glad for you."

Barbara took her hand.

"We have improved too, ne, Sensei?" Rie said.

Seiji picked Barbara up just before dark. There was a huge crowd along the edges of the Motoyasu River. She helped Seiji take the lantern boats from the back of the truck. They were made of straw; each one had a small paper lantern in the center, and a candle beneath the lantern. Seiji had written the names on the lanterns in black ink. There were sixteen of the boats: for Michi, Ume, Chie, Ko and her other relatives, and several for members of his family. Barbara watched Seiji light the candles beneath the lanterns, and they set the boats afloat along with all the others. Most people shoved theirs out into the stream, using their hands or a stick. Seiji waded out with his until they were taken by the current. Then he and Barbara ran to the first bridge to watch them float past. It was dark now, the river water dark too, reflecting hundreds of yellow and orange lanterns, the spirits of the dead returning to their place of rest.

"Can you see Michiko-san's boat?" he said. "It is burning more brightly than the rest."

She looked at him. "Her papers," she said.

"One of them, yes."

"Nineteen sixty-one?"

He nodded. "The others have already been burned. Some of those ashes were placed in her grave."

"In that envelope!"

"Yes—and other part of paper ashes in the urn."

She watched the lighted boats sliding from under the bridge, bobbing slightly on the current. "You didn't even tell me," she said.

They walked on beside the river, watching the lanterns drift past, hundreds of spirit boats moving toward the sea. On the other side of the river was a line of Bon Odori dancers with a long, brilliantly colored dragon over their heads and shoulders.

"I have one other confession," Seiji said. "At times I have felt much jealous envy. I think Nakamoto-sensei has left tansu to you to revenge me. Giving tansu and stories of our Hiroshima experience and life together to an outsider is a vengeance upon me. Forgive me for saying this, but I believe is truth, no matter that she was fond of you."

She glanced at him, then looked at the water, the reflected lights of the lanterns. There was a silence.

"Do you ever regret ... our meeting?"

"No." He shook his head violently. "Do you remember the festival day, when you came to raku demonstration?"

"Yes, I remember very well."

"On that day, I have known ..."

She waited for him to finish, but he said nothing more.

They went into a bar and sat at a small table. Seiji ordered beer. She drank one, he three, in quick succession. They left the bar and walked on along the river. He stopped in front of a hotel. "Hotel High Up" was on the outside in neon. "This is where I stay," he said.

They craned their necks to look up at the roof.

"It certainly is high up," she said. "Is it nice?"

"Not so nice as ryokan. Would you like to see? We can have a good view of the river."

"Okay," she said. She felt light-headed as the elevator carried them up to his floor.

It was a Western-style room, very plain, a bed, a table, one chair. "Not so nice as a ryokan," he said again with a laugh.

To avoid looking at the bed she walked to the window. He

came to stand beside her. Far below them the lantern boats drifted slowly along with the tide.

"You can never forgive me, I think," Seiji said.

She pressed her forehead against the glass and stared down at the boats, blossoms of light on the dark river. She thought of Ume running awkwardly along the river of iris with flowers in her skirt, and Michi feeling guilty because she'd scolded her. Now they were both spirits, moving toward the open sea. Chie too, and Ko. She thought of her brother, who died before he was given a name, and her mother, her life more than half gone.

"I forgive you, Seiji. I more than forgive you."

"But we will not meet as before?"

She turned and put her arms around him. "Of course we can meet."

"Barbara-san," he said, pronouncing her name carefully. "Once I said I cannot love someone. But if I can, she would be you."

"If I had the terrible fortune to be born here, and to live through the bombing, I couldn't accept my fate. I'd fight against feeling tainted. I'd love whom I pleased."

"This is true," he said, "if you are Barbara." Then after a pause he added, "But you would not be Barbara."

31

Early the next morning Seiji picked Barbara up from the Yokohagis and took her to the station where she was to catch a train to Yonago. Though they said little during the drive, there was an almost palpable closeness between them.

They stood silently in the ticket line as it inched forward.

"I don't want to leave," she said in a low voice.

"I can drive you," he said. "I have been thinking of it."

"All the way to Yonago?"

"We can go to Hagi, beautiful town on the Japan Sea, which is famous for ceramic. You will enjoy very much, I think. If you don't mind to delay your visit to Yonago a day or so."

"I don't mind at all."

"Let me show you." He led her to a map hanging on the wall and traced the route from Hiroshima to Hagi. "Then, after our visit, you can take train to Yonago." His finger moved north along the coastline. "Nice ride of only a few hours."

They stood smiling at each other.

"How long will it take to get to Hagi?" she asked.

"We can reach there this afternoon."

"So we will stay tonight?"

"Many nights," he said.

"I think maybe just two days ... Miss Ota is expecting me."

She was nervous, going to call Miss Ota. As she dialed the number, she tried to think of an excuse, but all she managed to say was "I'm sorry, I've been delayed."

"It is no matter," Miss Ota said. "Arrive anytime at all, my dear, just let us know when you are coming. I imagine you must find the experience of Hiroshima enervating."

Seiji telephoned an inn in Hagi to make a reservation, and they carried her bags back out to the truck.

She noticed his suitcase was already there, in the bed of the truck. "What were your plans?" she said.

"To go to Hagi," he said with a grin.

"You're very sure of yourself."

"No, it is only I have foolish hope."

They drove through the city and into gently rolling farmland. After the past few days, everything seemed miraculous to her—the orange groves, the air fragrant with the smells of earth and growing things, his hand on hers. She sat close to him; the wind blew her hair against his face. She held it back with her other hand, then took out a scarf to tie it back. "No," he said, pulling off the scarf. He caught a handful of her hair and held it against his face.

They began to climb into mountainous terrain, with deep, heavily wooded valleys. At Tsuwano—a famous old castle town, he told her—they got out to stretch their legs, walking along the narrow streets past thatch houses and shops. They went into a small museum devoted to the work of Hokusai. On display was the series *Thirty Six Views of Mt. Fuji*. Seiji pointed

out one of the prints and said, "This is at the Tokaido Pass—
very near to us in Hakone."

Back in the truck, she asked, "Why did you leave so suddenly from Hakone?"

"I was frightened by strong feeling I have not experienced
before."

"Were you ever in love—as a young man?"

"Only schoolboy love. Then came war and my illness, after
that my time with Nakamoto-sensei."

Barbara stared past him out the window, wondering what
Michi would think of their affair. She imagined her shocked
face. But I didn't know, Barbara wanted to tell her, I had no
idea. She looked at Seiji, the profile she'd come to know so
well. Michi would have forgiven him everything, even the
papers, if she could have seen the care he took yesterday, laying
her to rest.

"Thank you for taking me to Mitaki Temple yesterday," she
said, "and for showing me where you and Michi-san grew up.
I'll never forget that."

"I wish I could forget," he said.

They stopped once more, for lunch, then she went to sleep,
her head against his shoulder, not waking until he touched her
arm.

"We are here," he said.

The inn was elegant and quiet. They were shown to a large
room with sliding doors that opened onto a private garden.
Their host—a shy man in glasses—said that dinner would be
ready soon. Would they care to bathe first? He didn't look at
Barbara. She wondered what Seiji had said about them. He
must not have said there would be a Mr. and Mrs. Okada
checking in.

There was no one else in the women's bath. She washed

quickly, put on the hotel's cotton kimono, and went to join Seiji.

Dinner was served in a private tatami room separate from their bedroom. There was a procession of dishes she didn't recognize, most of them fish or plants of the sea, Seiji said. There were two cooked sea urchins; Barbara couldn't imagine eating one but Seiji carefully folded back the spiny skin and delicately ate the flesh with his chopsticks.

"I want to know everything about you," she said. "What were you like as a baby?"

He laughed. "I cannot remember."

"What's your first memory?"

"Some red-striped candy at New Year's. And when I was not very old I remember I got in trouble for taking a schoolmate's lunch." He laughed, then his face grew somber. "Always I was hungry—it seemed there was never enough to eat during those years." After a pause he said, "What do you first remember?"

"One thing is that fox woman scroll hanging on the wall of our living room. I used to stand on my father's lap and look at it. Even before I knew it was associated with Japan, I felt some mystery about it. It seems that I was always drawn to Japan."

"Did you find what you expect?"

"Not at all," she said.

The futon had been laid out in their room. They sat on the tatami by the open door to the garden. There was a small pond shining in the moonlight, and the occasional startling sound of a bullfrog, like the loud plucking of a stringed instrument.

"There is a saying about frog in Japan, that frog says please return to this place."

"We will," she said.

They undressed in the moonlight and lay down on the tatami.

He pushed back her hair to kiss her neck. "Kirekitsu."

"Not Kirekitsu. Barbara."

"Baba-san." He held her face and looked at her.

"Seiji," she said. "I love you."

He buried his face against her chest.

"You love me too," she said. "Don't you?"

"Yes," he said in a muffled, agonized voice.

The next day they went to the beach. With wooded sheltering islands just offshore, the surf was gentle. They took off their shoes and walked along at the edge of the waves. Seiji spread out a blanket he'd brought from the truck.

They sat looking out at the water and islands. Barbara leaned against him and closed her eyes, listening to the sound of waves. "I wish we could stay in this moment forever," she said.

A wave unfurled, spreading across the sand to their feet.

"I wish so too," Seiji said. "But we cannot."

"Why not?"

He laughed. "Always you say, Why not?"

That night in their room she lay listening to the strident bullfrog long after Seiji had gone to sleep. In the middle of the night she woke to find him gone. He was sitting by the open door, smoking. She went to sit beside him. It was dark out now, with no moon, and the frog was silent. "What are you thinking about?" she said.

"Tomorrow you will leave." He kissed her hand and put it inside his yukata, against his chest.

The next morning he drove her farther up the coast to the town of Iwami Masuda to her train, which was already in the station. There were several people on the platform, so she and Seiji awkwardly bowed good-bye.

"Always I will remember Hagi," he said in a low voice.

"We'll return someday."

She got on and he stood outside her window, looking up at her solemnly. When the train began to move he lifted his hand. She kept him in her vision, watching until the train rounded a curve and he was out of sight.

As soon as the train left the small town, they were riding along the ocean, jade green with high waves crashing against jagged rocks. To the right of the train were rice fields, brilliant green, rice stalks blowing in the breeze. How beautiful the earth was, here in this moment. She caught sight of a small red torii in a field right beside the train; probably there were fox statues there too, a personal farm shrine. She thought of the fox woman scroll in her apartment; she'd gone all the way down the fox woman's path, deeper into Japan than her mother had ever been.

She turned back to the ocean and was gradually lulled to sleep. She awoke to the conductor calling out "Izumo, Izumo," holding the *O*, a mournful, mysterious sound. Ko had been from what used to be called Izumo Province, but she hadn't known there was also a town by that name.

They traveled on, the ocean no longer in view, but soon there was a broad expanse of water on the left. She asked the schoolboy sitting in front of her what it was. Lake Shinji, he said. It was the lake Michi's mother Chie had written about; Ko had lived by its shores. She was in their country now. Ko's. Chie's. Michi's. The light seemed different here: brighter, yet more ethereal.

The town of Matsue was just beyond the lake. Ko's home. She felt a ripple of excitement as the train moved slowly past the old houses, a canal lined with ancient pine trees. Except for the cars and telephone lines, it must look much the same as it did a century ago.

Yonago was a half hour beyond Matsue. Miss Ota and her

niece Keiko met her at the station and drove her to a large house hidden from the street by a stone wall. Near the entrance was a Western-style room that looked like a scene from Victorian England: a horsehair sofa, velvet armchairs, old-fashioned glass lamps with fringed shades, and a piano. Then there was a honeycomb of tatami rooms and, at the far end of the house, the small tearoom where Barbara would be staying.

"How lovely." Barbara looked around at the honey-colored tatami floor, the fresh flowers in the tokonoma. The paper doors were open to a shaded garden.

"Tonight we are having special dinner," Keiko said. "My aunt's work is complete. We have been waiting for you to have our celebration."

"Is it *The Figure in the Tatami*?" Barbara asked.

"Yes," Miss Ota said. "I have finished off Mr. James at last."

After her bath, Barbara went back to the main room for the celebratory dinner. Miss Ota's manuscript lay in the middle of the table; beside it was a bottle of decanted plum wine Keiko had made. Keiko's husband, Akihiro, a tall, ascetic-looking man whose face was transformed by a playful smile, toasted Miss Ota's opus, Mr. James, and Barbara, for good fortune in her travels. The children, Eiji, a boy of eleven, and Yuko, six, stared at Barbara throughout much of the dinner, then Yuko put her doll in Barbara's lap.

"I think you are a member of the family now," Keiko laughed.

Keiko went to put the children to bed and Akihiro excused himself to make a telephone call.

Barbara and Miss Ota sipped Keiko's wine and looked out into the garden. It had grown dark; fireflies were blinking here and there in a slow, silent music.

"Miss Ota," Barbara said, "I want to ask you something—about the writing Nakamoto-sensei left to me."

"Yes, certainly."

"She mentioned your visit to California—with great pleasure."

"I am glad," Miss Ota said with a little bow.

"I've been thinking about what you said—how you tried to help her find her relatives."

Miss Ota nodded.

"Do you mind my asking what kind of records you were looking for? You mentioned displacement of Japanese-Americans during the war. Were those records of . . . the camps?"

Miss Ota cleared her throat. "Yes. But we found these closed to us."

"Do you think they would be open now?"

"I am not certain. In any case, it is too late for poor Nakamoto-sensei." She sighed. "I wish I could have been some assistance to her in this regard."

"I'm sure she was just happy to have you with her and Ume in California."

"I have done what little I could. It was a difficult time."

"Did she ever visit you here? I was wondering if she'd ever been to Matsue, to look for Ko's home."

Miss Ota shook her head. "She intended to do so, but unfortunately the opportunity kept slipping past us." She looked at Barbara. "You are quite familiar with the particulars of Nakamoto-sensei's history, I believe. This is all in the writing to which you have alluded?"

"Yes."

Miss Ota was looking at her expectantly.

"Do you remember the tansu Michi-san left to me? It was filled with plum wine."

"Ah yes, I recall Miss Fujizawa's distress," she said, with a little smile.

"The writings that Nakamoto-sensei left to me were wrapped around those bottles of wine. They were New Year's writings—Michi's and her mother's."

Miss Ota studied her a moment. "This is a rare legacy to you."

"It's the most important thing that ever happened to me," she said, with a catch in her throat. "One of the most," she added, thinking of Seiji.

"By the way"—Miss Ota raised her cup—"this wine is made from Nakamoto-sensei's recipe. During her years in California, she asked if my niece Keiko could make the wine for her. She did not like to miss a year."

Barbara looked down at her wine. "Did you know that the recipe was originally Ko's? It was handed down to Michi-san by her mother, but Ko brought it from Matsue as a bride. And here we are, drinking it."

"It seems quite fitting," Miss Ota said.

They drank a toast to Ko.

"I think we had better visit Matsue tomorrow," Miss Ota said. "You can go there in Nakamoto-sensei's place."

The next day Miss Ota, Barbara, and Keiko set out for Matsue in Keiko's car. Miss Ota suggested they visit an ancient Inari shrine. "You will be particularly interested, I think, Barbara-san, with your curiosity about our Japanese fox." As they walked along a canal lined with pine trees, Barbara thought of Ko walking here; this was the place where Michi's story began. She paused, looking down at the reflection of pine branches and her face in the water. Michi would be glad she'd come. A legacy. She felt the words settle into her.

At the entrance to the shrine were several pairs of large foxes, then a long hill of steps up to the shrine. Both sides of the steps were lined with small fox figures made of dark weathered stone, tier upon tier of them. "Many years ago this was a most popular shrine," Miss Ota said. "Each fox has been donated by a patron with some particular supplication."

"You know that pair of antique foxes I showed you?" Barbara said.

Miss Ota nodded.

"They were in the tansu. I think they might have come from here."

"Ah *so* desu ka?" Barbara had never heard Miss Ota sound so thoroughly Japanese. She began to talk in Japanese to Keiko as the two of them went up the steps ahead of her.

There seemed to be thousands of the foxes. So much prayer and longing in one space. Barbara studied the small stone carvings as she slowly climbed the steps. Some of them were comic or wild-looking, almost all were weathered and dirty. Quite a few were broken, with missing ears, snouts, or heads. Any one of them might have been put here by Ko. She imagined a young woman in a red flowered summer kimono, her long black hair shining in the sunlight. Ko could never have guessed what would befall her in Hiroshima, or that she'd end up so far away, in America.

As Barbara went on up the steps, she reviewed in her mind the efforts Michi had made, looking for her relatives. The telephone books, the camp records. Maybe they were no longer sealed. One of Ko's sons had been in the army. There couldn't have been many Japanese—certainly not many Yokogawas—in the U.S. Army. There might have been magazine or newspaper articles about Japanese soldiers, the irony of their situation, the difficulties. And the army would have records in Washington, only five hours' drive from North Carolina. She could ask one of the investigative reporters at the Raleigh newspaper how to begin. Her mother might be able to suggest someone.

At the top of the steps she joined Miss Ota and Keiko. Keiko pointed out the hole in back of the shrine, where real and spirit foxes were said to nest. When Barbara leaned down to look inside the hole, Keiko pulled her back. "Do not have your nose bitten!" she said.

Miss Ota and Keiko started down the steps. Barbara lingered, stopping to look at the foxes along the way. There were little dishes of fried tofu in front of several of them; surprising, since the shrine didn't seem to be much visited or well tended. She bent to pick up a fox that had fallen over in a puddle of water: a speckled gray fox, covered with slime.

As she set the figure upright, she heard a sound, a slight scuffling in the leaves. Something ran out of the bushes—a small animal, a mahogany-colored blur—brushed against her leg and darted back into the shrubbery. She parted the branches with both hands, peering into the darkness. It had been a fox. A baby fox, a real one. Seiji would say she was superstitious, but it seemed like an acknowledgment, or a blessing.

They had lunch at a small restaurant near the shrine, then drove away from Matsue along the coast, where they were to stay the night at a hot-spring inn on the beach. Barbara rolled down her window and breathed in the salt air. She thought about Seiji at the Boso Peninsula, wearing his mask, and at Hagi, sitting beside her on the beach. Without him she would have missed so much. Everything. Even this moment.

At the ryokan she and Miss Ota and Keiko were shown to a large tatami room they would be sharing. They stood looking at the ocean below them and enjoying the air that blew in through the windows.

A maid brought them cotton kimonos and they went outdoors to bathe. It was an open-air bath in an area sheltered by large rocks and bamboo. Near the door of the ryokan were faucets, buckets, soap. They took turns washing one another's back. Miss Ota had parchment-colored skin with prominent blue veins. She and her niece Keiko were so natural together. She'd never take a bath with her aunt or mother.

They got into the pool and sank to their chins in the hot water. Barbara could hear the faint rhythm of the surf below them. It was sunset. The sky was streaked with salmon-colored clouds and the moon had risen, a pale disk above them. "I think this must be paradise," Miss Ota said.

Barbara closed her eyes. There was nothing but the sensation of her body in the hot water, the sound of the ocean, and her awareness of the quiet presences of Keiko and Miss Ota.

32

When Barbara returned to Tokyo, there was a postcard from Seiji saying he was in Mashiko. He did not know when he would return, he said; there was much work to be done for Hamada. There was no mention of their time together, no hint of affection. It was his pattern, she reminded herself. After a week she called his house. There was no answer. A few days later she called again, then walked to Takanodai. His truck was gone and the pottery was closed. When she went to the front gate and rang the bell, no one came. She felt a shiver of dread.

A week passed, then two. She rarely left the apartment building, waiting for him to appear.

Finally, in mid-September, soon after classes began, there was a call from him. His voice was formal, saying hello, asking how she was.

"I'm fine," she said. "When did you get back?"

"A few days ago." There was a pause. "My mother has been ill."

"I wish you'd called. I've been worried."

"Please meet me at Kamiya tomorrow night," he said in a low voice. "I can explain."

He was already at the restaurant when she came, sitting at the table beneath the Sharaku print. Apparently he'd been there awhile, drinking sake. They ordered food; he did not touch his.

"What's the matter?" she said.

"I cannot be with you," he said. "My fate is sealed." He looked so melodramatic she almost laughed.

"What do you mean, 'your fate is sealed'?"

"I have behaved too badly in this life."

"But everything that happened was understandable. Think about the circumstances—the war, your aunt. And you couldn't help it that you didn't feel more passionately about Michi-san. Feelings can't be forced."

"I should have stood by her."

"Maybe that day Ume spilled the wine—but you would have parted anyway, don't you think?"

He poured another cup of sake and drank it down. "In 1961 paper written after our parting, there is a haiku: 'Night after night / this solitary body digs a trench / in the futon.' This is proof I caused her death."

"It doesn't sound like proof to me. She was in a state of grief, but she lived on—four more years."

"Only for Ume. Then she can no longer live."

"You've got to get rid of your guilt." She reached for his hand. "Please. Let me help you."

He shook his head. "It is not possible. You can never understand."

"I want to be with you."

He said nothing, staring down at the table.

"You won't even look at me."

She jumped up and hurried out of the restaurant. It was raining, a sudden downpour. The street looked desolate, grimy concrete buildings, trash washing by in the gutter. She ran toward the bus stop, the rain plastering her hair against her face, soaking her clothes. There was the light of a taxi in the distance; she stepped into the street and frantically waved her arms.

At Sango-kan, she changed clothes and went downstairs to knock on Mrs. Ueda's door. "May I please talk to you?" she said. "It's urgent."

Mrs. Ueda led the way down the hall and they sat down at her table.

"I'd like to ask you a frank question," Barbara said. "Do you think Nakamoto-sensei took her own life? Sumi mentioned finding a pill bottle."

Mrs. Ueda looked out the window, into the darkness. The rain had stopped, but Barbara could hear it dripping from the eaves. "I would call her death a hastening of the inevitable. She felt that she was ill with leukemia."

"Did she have tests?"

"I believe so, yes. What I recall her saying is that she had exact symptoms of her daughter Ume, extreme fatigue, for instance. She spoke of the many hibakusha who have died of this disease. Therefore I was not surprised when she was found to be—no longer living." She paused. "I think she feared to be a burden without family to take care of her. Though of course . . ." Mrs. Ueda turned away, coughed into her hand. "We women of Sango-kan would have cared for her."

"So—again, please forgive my bluntness—do you think this had anything to do with Seiji Okada?"

"Maybe he would like to feel himself this important. But her death was in an ultimate sense the result of illness caused by radiation."

The next weekend Barbara went to Seiji's house. In her furoshiki was a book on Chinese porcelain he'd lent her, the excuse for her visit.

It was a brisk day, with the first touch of real cold in the air. The sky was deep blue and the leaves in the woods were beginning to show color, tinges of scarlet and gold. She passed a mother holding onto her son's jacket as he threw sticks and handfuls of grass into the Tamagawa Canal. She lingered, watching the little boy's boats move along the sluggish current, then crossed the road that led to Kokubunji and walked quickly through the darker part of the woods.

At Takanodai, she walked slowly down the street and looked in the restaurant, which was open but empty of customers.

When she walked into the studio, Seiji was working his pottery wheel with one foot and shaping a blur of clay between his hands. At first he did not see her. Then he looked up and abruptly took his foot off the wheel. There was the sound of the wheel going around and around until he put one hand out to stop it. The clay had slumped to one side.

"I'm sorry," she said, "I've ruined your piece."

"It is no matter." He stood. "I am surprised to see you. But very glad," he added.

"I've brought your book," she said, holding it out to him.

"Thank you." He looked down at it. "Shall we have tea?"

They walked to the tea house by the back path, just as they used to do.

"I apologize the room is not fresh," he said. He took the cushions outside to dust them off, then put them back in place. The table they'd used for translating was no longer there. The charcoal in the brazier was not lit, as he hadn't been expecting to make tea, he said. "I will prepare in kitchen instead."

She sat on the cushion listening to him move about in the kitchen, the clink of utensils, the sound of running water. It was chilly without the warm brazier, and she had on only a light jacket. She thought of the jacket he'd given her to wear the first time she came, its warmth and the softness against her neck.

He brought out the tea already made, one bowl for her, another for himself, no shared bowl as in earlier days. "I am sorry not to have cakes or other refreshment," he said.

He sat opposite her. She turned her tea bowl in her hands, admiring it in the way he'd taught her. They drank the tea silently. She noticed that although he'd washed his hands there was still clay caked beneath the fingernails.

"Seiji," she said, putting down her bowl, "I've learned something important about Michi-san's death. She did have leukemia—Mrs. Ueda told me. Mrs. Ueda said she had only hastened her death—and only for that reason."

He looked down at his tea bowl, running one finger around the rim. His mouth was twisted in a curious expression, something between a grimace and a smile.

"So what I'm saying is—she didn't die from some other grief."

He said nothing.

"It wasn't your fault," she added.

"Had I stood by her, she wouldn't hasten death."

She looked around the room—the tokonoma with its scroll and arrangement of stones, the low door, the pine tree framed there—then back at him. He hadn't moved, still sitting with his head bowed, his jaw clenched. He wanted his version of the story; he'd never give it up.

She stood. "I guess I'd better go now."

They went out the low door of the tea house and stepped off the platform into their shoes.

"Good-bye, Seiji." She took his hand. "This is"—she could hardly speak—"very sad."

"May I see you, now and then?"

"I'd like to, but—I don't think so, this way." She turned and walked quickly away before she could change her mind.

The next few days, she could hardly get through her lectures: Hawthorne again, and original sin. In conversation class, the students wanted to talk about Vietnam, now that the fighting had intensified. To keep up with them, Barbara forced herself to the library each day to read whatever she could find about the war. At night, she drank herself to sleep with plum wine.

Rie sent her a story she had published in a Japanese literary journal, along with a translation. It was based on her father's life, a fictionalized version of what she'd told Barbara last summer. Barbara called to congratulate her and asked her to come visit.

"Is something the matter, Sensei? You do not sound well."

"Seiji," she said in a low voice. "It's over."

Rie came the next day, and stayed for a week. She went to classes with her; in the afternoons, they rode bikes, read, and went grocery shopping. They went to Kamakura, walking the hilly streets, visiting temples Barbara hadn't seen before. They stood before the huge bronze Buddha, then Barbara showed her the view Michi had liked best, where they could see his shoulders "humbly bearing all our troubles."

On the train going back to Tokyo, Rie said, "Maybe you and Okada-san will make it up as before?"

Barbara shook her head. "He's caught in the past."

"But this must not be the case for you, Sensei."

After Rie left, Barbara returned to a Zen temple in Kamakura where Rie had introduced her to the priest; he invited her to join in zazen meditation. She began going there on weekends, spending two nights, getting up before dawn each morning for the meditation. Sitting in the dark, silent hall with other people brought her some moments of peace.

In early November she went with Junko and Sumi to an antiwar demonstration at a temple in downtown Tokyo. There were speeches, singing, and at the end a long dance in a snake-like line. A Japanese man announced over a bullhorn that "there is an American GI here, showing his support of us." Barbara spotted the American, a man about her age. After the ceremony she ran up to him and introduced herself. He wasn't a GI, he told her, but a conscientious objector, working with wounded and orphaned children in Vietnam.

She asked him what conditions were like there. At first he didn't answer.

"I understand if you don't want to talk about it, but I would sincerely like to know," she said.

He looked at her, his eyes dark and intense. "Do you have any idea what napalm can do to human flesh? Right before I left there was a kid with his chin melted to his chest by napalm. He died in my arms."

The encounter haunted her for days. One evening she sat at her desk in the Western-style room, trying to grade papers. As she looked out at the trees receding into the dusk, she imagined Seiji holding the child with melted flesh. She put her head down on her desk and sobbed.

At Thanksgiving, she went with Junko to stay with her family in Kyoto. Junko's large, old-fashioned house made her think of Miss Ota's, and how happy she'd been there. Her room opened onto a garden. In the mornings she sat on the tatami looking out at the shimmering, wine-colored maples, and tried to meditate.

Barbara and Junko played with her young sister Chiyo, throwing a bright string ball with her in the garden. Chiyo sat in Barbara's lap and read to her from her first English book. It was a comfort to hold the little girl, the solid warmth of her, the hair and skin that held the fresh scent of outdoor air. Chiyo cried and clung to Barbara when Junko said they'd be leaving tomorrow. Barbara promised that she'd write to her; they could be pen pals, even after she went back to America.

"Dear Michi," Barbara wrote in her journal the next day. "I dreamed we were in the ocean, lying on a raft I'd made of sea-weed string. It was a deep mat like tatami but it was also edible. I'd used up all your recipes on it, but I could tell you didn't mind."

When the holiday was over, time seemed to speed up. In December Barbara worked on the final exams, made travel arrangements, and bought gifts. She spent days combing the department stores for presents to take home and to give here. In one store she saw an exhibit of contemporary tea bowls. Seiji's name was not on the list of exhibitors, but it should have been, she thought; his work was as fine as anything on display. She resisted the temptation to call him.

Mr. Doi had a farewell party for her three days before her departure. The whole faculty and many students were there. The surprise guests were Rie and Mr. Yokohagi. "We have come from Hiroshima to bid farewell," Mr. Yokohagi said in his carefully rehearsed toast, "but we would have traveled even further miles than this."

Miss Yamaguchi had made a card, which she read aloud. "At first we think you are a little kooky"—on the front of the card was a colored drawing of a small star-shaped cookie—"but now we think you are *Far Out!*" On the inside of the card was a drawing of a star shining in the sky. Everyone laughed, though no one as much as Miss Yamaguchi.

Mr. Doi offered a rendition of the ending lines from *A Midsummer Night's Dream,* which had been cut off prematurely in their production last February: "If we these shadows have offended / Think but this, and all is mended / That you have but slumbered here / While these visions do appear. / Gentle Jefferson, please not reprehend / If you pardon, we will mend." He bowed, red-faced, to the applause. Barbara looked around at the room full of people; it was going to be wrenching to leave them—Rie and Miss Ota, especially, and Mrs. Ueda, Junko, and Sumi, but everyone, even Mr. Doi.

After they had returned from the party to Sango-kan, Junko followed Barbara up to her apartment. "I have something for you in private," she said. "First, Sensei, I must tell you a sadness. My parents insist I must agree to arranged marriage after graduation. But last night I have spent together with my boyfriend. We have made our pledge to meet once a year, on July seventh, the Feast of Tanabata, like Weaving Maiden and Herd Boy."

"It's like the story you wrote."

"Yes—I am recalling what you said, that I must obey my heart. Now here is my gift, a calligraphy I made this morning. It is my interpretation of a haiku by Issa, which says, 'What solace, the River of Heaven, seen through a tear in the paper door.' "

"There's no chance your parents will change their minds?"

"I've always known they would choose this for me. But one night a year, I can have joy. Remember me as happy, Sensei, for I have both loved and wept."

The afternoon before Barbara was to leave, the workmen Sato and Murai were in her apartment, packing her things for shipment. Her trunk and the crated tansu would be sent to North

Carolina, but she was going to stop in San Francisco to retrace Michi's steps. It was even possible that Michi had missed some lead in the phone directories, or in Japantown. In her carry-on suitcase were a few bottles of plum wine to take to Michi's relatives, wherever she should find them, and the roll of Chie's and Michi's papers, with her translations. Ko, or Ko's children, would want to hear it all.

Mrs. Ueda knocked on the door. "Okada is here," she said.

Barbara hadn't bought him a gift. But there was a haiku she'd composed for him last summer and written in calligraphy on rice paper; she'd found it in her desk today, rolled up and tied with a ribbon. She picked it up and ran downstairs.

Seiji was waiting in the drive, a wooden box in each hand. He looked pale and did not meet her eyes. "Will you take a walk?" he said.

They went first to the plum orchard. The trees were in bud; she was going to miss the blooming. She looked at Seiji standing silently beside her. She would never see him again.

They walked to the athletic field and sat on a bench at the edge of the grass.

He handed her one of the boxes. She untied the ribbon and lifted the lid: inside was one of his tea bowls. She held it in her hands turning it side to side. It was black with splashes of brown and gold, shining in the winter light.

"It's gorgeous—I love it."

"Will you break it?" he said with a smile.

"Never."

She opened the other box: a tea bowl from Hagi, the delicate pink of a shell. She looked at it silently.

"Please remember us in Hagi," he said.

"Oh, Seiji, I wish I could stay."

"In some other world."

"Why can't it be that world?"

"It can't"—he stopped himself, made a wry face—"be helped."

She put the little scroll of paper in his hands. "For you," she said.

He untied the ribbon, unrolled the paper, and sat looking at it for several minutes.

"It's my attempt at haiku. Can you read it?"

"Not entirely," he said with a little laugh.

"Let me translate." She took it back and read aloud, "From your lips / I came to understand / The language of plum wine."

She gave the paper back to him. His fingers trembled as he held it. "This will be my treasure," he said. She watched as he rolled up the paper and carefully retied the ribbon.

They stood and walked along the edge of the field.

"I believe you will be happy," he said. "I am hoping this for you."

She touched his arm. "What about you?"

"I have my pottery. Always, there is ceramic."

"I think you'll be successful. I envy you—I wish I had some artistic gift."

"You have a vigor for life," he said. "A passion that is rare, I think."

"But you also have passion."

He looked away, into the distance.

"I wonder if someday, when your memories are further behind you, you might find someone...."

"A woman?"

"Yes."

"Maybe someone ... now and then."

"Ah."

"But no one like you. Never." He turned from her, then took off running, his head down, across the field.

ABOUT THE AUTHOR

Angela Davis-Gardner is the author of the internationally acclaimed novels *Felice, Forms of Shelter,* and *Plum Wine,* which was inspired by the time she spent teaching at Tsuda College in Tokyo, Japan. An Alumni Distinguished Professor at North Carolina State University, Angela has won nearly thirty awards for writing and teaching. She lives in Raleigh, North Carolina, where she is at work on her next novel. Visit her website at www.angela davisgardner.com.

Also by Angela Davis-Gardner

Forms of Shelter

Perched among the leaves of the Osage orange tree in her step-father's backyard, Beryl Fonteyn observes the life around her—Mama's desperate attempts to keep Jack's attention by writing her novel, which he mercilessly critiques; her brother Stevie's retreat into religion; and Jack's obsession with his bees. As Beryl's adolescent turmoil collides with her growing distrust of her step-father, the shelter that her family has found will be torn apart forever.

"Davis-Gardner skillfully renders the fine lines that connect sympathy, intimacy and menace.... A wise novel."
— *The Washington Post*

"What a strong voice Angela Davis-Gardener has, and what a listening heart. *Forms of Shelter* shows the transcendent power of childhood to heal itself when the adult world cannot or will not." —Anne Rivers Siddons

Felice

In a remote convent school in Nova Scotia, an aging nun has a miraculous vision; a mute, injured man washes up on the nearby shore; and a group of girls is busily creating a reckless drama of excitements real and imagined. Here, amid the vows and rituals of Lent, a young girl named Felice has been sent following the death of her parents, poised somewhere between childhood, womanhood, and sainthood. A tragedy, a shocking revelation, and a baffling disappearance will set Felice on a staggering passage to self-discovery—armed with miracles that are uniquely her own.

"A triumph." —Mary Gordon, *New York Times Book Review*

"In order to love *Felice,* all you need is a memory of what it was to be a child.... *Felice* is filled with surprises.... Beautiful, sophisticated, sensual and rare." —*Los Angeles Times Book Review*

Available in trade paperback in Fall 2007 from
The Dial Press